D1018600

BLOOD TRINITY

"Kenyon and Love have masterfully constructed a fascinating world where the bizarre is totally believable and the uniquely interesting characters are appealingly captivating."

—*Single Titles*

"A fantastic start to a new urban fantasy series. The world built by Kenyon and Love [is] intriguing, but the characters populating that world are irresistible."

—*Fresh Fiction*

"Meticulous plotting and thorough world-building add up to a whole lot of interesting characters."

—*RT Book Reviews*

SHERRILYN KENYON

AND

DIANNA LOVE

RISE

OF THE

GRYPHON

BOOK 4 IN THE BELADOR SERIES

POCKET BOOKS

NEW YORK   LONDON   TORONTO   SYDNEY   NEW DELHI

Pocket Books
A Division of Simon & Schuster, Inc.
1230 Avenue of the Americas
n ew York, n Y 10020

This book is a work of fiction. Any references to historical events, real people, or real places are used fictitiously. o ther names, characters, places, and events are products of the author's imagination, and any resemblance to actual events or places or persons, living or dead, is entirely coincidental.

First Pocket Books paperback edition August 2013

Po CKEt and colophon are registered trademarks of Simon & Schuster, Inc.

For information about special discounts for bulk purchases, please contact Simon & Schuster Special Sales at 1-866-506-1949 or business@simonandschuster.com.

The Simon & Schuster Speakers Bureau can bring authors to your live event. For more information or to book an event, contact the Simon & Schuster Speakers Bureau at 1-866-248-3049 or visit our website at www.simonspeakers.com.

Manufactured in the United States of America

10 9 8 7 6 5 4 3

ISBn 978-1-4516-7199-5
ISBn 978-1-4516-7201-5 (ebook)

We dedicate this book to the Kenyon Menyons,
who show their support in a million ways. Thank you for
being there for us at every stop when we tour and for sending
your love through emails and letters.

ACKNOWLEDGMENTS

FROM SHERRILYN AND DIANNA

Thank you to our family, friends and fans. We love you all and couldn't do this without you! A special shout-out to our amazing husbands, Ken (Sherri's) and Karl (Dianna's), who make it possible for us to write a bazillion hours a week.

No book happens without the early beta reading and feedback from Cassondra Murray, Dianna's assistant, who is always ready to do whatever is needed. Jerry Brandon, former mayor of St. Marys, Georgia, and proprietor of Riverview Hotel, was very helpful when Dianna visited to research St. Marys and Cumberland Island. Dianna has Donna Browning to thank for introducing her to Cumberland, which is steeped in history and home to wild horses. Thank you also to Steve Doyle and Joyce Ann McLaughlin for being early readers whose insights were invaluable and deeply appreciated. We want to give a shout-out to Barbara Vey, a *Publishers Weekly* blogger who supports readers and authors everywhere. Thanks also to Sara Reyes and her *Fresh Fiction* team, who do an outstanding job of getting the word out to readers every time we have a new book release and who organize so many events for readers and authors throughout the year.

We appreciate Louise Burke, our dynamic publisher whose enthusiasm is only surpassed by her genius, and no book reaches its full potential without the review and terrific editing of the talented Lauren McKenna. Lauren's commitment to publishing the best story possible makes working with her a pleasure. We would be remiss if we didn't send another high-five to the Pocket Art Department, which has once again rocked on an incredible cover, and the Pocket staff who keep all the gears moving smoothly. We appreciate Robert Gottlieb's dedication to managing this series and seeing that it continues to reach our audience.

And saving the best for last, we want to thank our readers, who come out to see us in every city, send encouraging messages that touch our hearts and read our stories so that we may continue doing what we love. You mean the world to us.

We look forward to hearing from you anytime at authors@beladors.com, or stop by www.SherrilynKenyon.com and www.AuthorDiannaLove.com, and make sure to visit the "Reader Lounge" at Dianna Love's Fan Page on Facebook, where you'll find free Belador items and scavenger hunts.

ONE

Dependable intel made the difference between walking away from a dangerous situation alive . . . or not.

Evalle Kincaid stared down the rocky slope in the North Georgia Mountains at bad intel.

She'd dug up one slim lead in forty-eight hours of racing to find Tristan. He was an Alterant like her. Similar powers and the same glowing green eyes, except he hadn't been gifted with her natural night vision, an ability she'd needed to hike up this mountain in the middle of the night.

Disgusted, she muttered, "That's no coven meeting."

"No," Storm agreed. He squatted next to her, his breath puffing white clouds against the chilly October air. "Looks more like a midnight festival for all things strange and dangerous." Coal-black hair grazed his shoulders and blended into his black leather jacket. Soft hair Evalle loved caressing. The coppery skin and sharp angles of Storm's cheekbones had been handed down through a mix of Ashaninka and Navajo genes, as had his Skinwalker ability to shift into a deadly black jaguar. That meant he *also* had preternatural night vision and saw just fine in the dark.

Evalle leaned forward where they hunkered down behind an outcropping of boulders, and searched the area a hundred yards away where moonlight cascaded across a valley. At least twenty people—mostly nonhumans— had gathered, and more were coming. "You see any female in that bunch that *might* be a witch?"

Storm shook his head. "Only male human forms so far. Not even sure what some of those things are that have both animal and human parts."

One creature with an eight-foot-tall orange lizard body, two sets of human arms and a vulture's head skulked through the crowd that parted like the Red Sea in front of him. Most of the beings meandered around the edge of a thirty-foot-wide circle created by torches stuck in the ground.

A ceremonial circle?

Whatever it was, Evalle wanted the show to get rolling soon.

As if sensing her concern, Storm asked, "Think the goddess'll extend your deadline?"

"Again? Not a chance. I was amazed when Macha gave me four more days." That had been two days ago, and Evalle had been given that reprieve from losing her freedom *only* because she'd defeated a demonic Svart troll before it killed everything in its path.

Opportunities like that didn't come along every day.

Good thing, too, or she'd stay in perpetual traction.

But gaining two extra days of freedom from Macha had balanced out getting beaten to a pulp by the Svart. Macha was goddess over all the Beladors, a race of powerful Celtic warriors who protected humans. She'd offered sanctuary in her pantheon to all Alterants who swore fealty to her.

With a catch.

Evalle first had to deliver the origin of Alterants, who were part Belador and part unknown. Since Alterants changed from human form into beasts that could kill even very powerful beings, Macha wanted that *unknown* part cleared up before giving carte blanche freedom to Alterants.

And Tristan had that information.

Unfortunately, while helping Evalle escape a deadly enemy last week, Tristan had been captured. Evalle didn't want to think about the hideous ways he might be suffering. Freeing him was her first priority.

All she had to do was find a witch called Imogenia, who was rumored to have information on Alterants, Tristan in particular, and the location of TÅµr Medb, home of the Medb Coven of deadly Noirre majik practitioners . . . and the place where Tristan was being held captive.

Imogenia was supposed to be attending this event in the valley tonight.

A sick ball of regret rolled around in Evalle's stomach every minute the witch didn't show. Evalle had left Atlanta two hours ago with Storm to hike up the side of Oakey Mountain. She wouldn't have gambled the time spent coming here if she hadn't trusted her Nightstalker source. Generally, Grady was a dependable ghoul.

"Damned ghouls," Storm grumbled, his deep voice ending in a growl.

"Are you sure you aren't reading my thoughts?" she asked, still unsure of everything Storm could do.

"I'm not telepathic."

But he was a powerful empath who picked up on her anxiety, which probably explained his comment. "Don't blame Grady," she said. "He can only repeat what he hears." Evalle shifted on the cold ground to find a comfortable position. She knew Grady's limitations as a Nightstalker, a homeless person who'd died years ago on the streets of Atlanta.

These days he was her best source of intel. Usually.

A muscle played in Storm's jaw, the only sign of his frustration. "When we do find Tristan, I want ten minutes *alone* with him before you hand him over to Macha."

"I need him *alive*," she reminded Storm, though she knew he didn't mean to kill Tristan, but those two couldn't stand in the same zip code without the threat of blood being shed. "I need *every* Alterant I can find. As it is, Macha's insulted that none have come forward to accept her offer. I have no idea where I'm going to come up with another Alterant besides Tristan and, hopefully, his sister." She released a long breath, aggravated. She'd been so sure this would be the break she needed.

"Grady said *this* was the place?"

"Yes. Said he heard that Imogenia had a meeting in the valley north of Oakey Mountain when the clock strikes between Friday and Saturday."

"How specific was he on this information she supposedly has about the Medb?"

"That's where Grady got vague. He said while he was eavesdropping, he started losing his corporeal form, which caused him to miss parts of her conversation. He did get that she mentioned something about Alterants and was going to deliver *it* to the Medb, plus she mentioned Tristan's name specifically."

"It. Hmm. Maybe she's here looking for *more* information she can sell to the Medb."

Evalle considered that possibility. "I just hope she shows up and, if she does know anything about other Alterants, that I can convince her to trade with me instead of the Medb."

"Think you have enough to outbid them?"

"I don't know. Somebody in Imogenia's Carretta Coven wants to take over by using Imogenia as a blood sacrifice. A dark witch like her *should* be willing to sell her mother's soul to get that name." She checked the valley again. Something about the gathering sent bony fingers of anxiety clawing up her spine. What was going on? Evalle opened and closed her fisted hands, grumbling, "When we first showed up, I knew this location didn't look like somewhere witches would meet, not in an area this exposed."

"True, but I had hopes."

"You're really wanting that ten minutes with Tristan, huh?" Evalle teased.

He shifted around, using a finger to turn her chin to him. "You've been running on no sleep, little food and pure frustration for the past two days straight trying to find *one* lead on Tristan. This is *it*, and digging up this tip was tough. I want to get that witch's information *to-night* and find Tristan as much as you do."

"Really? But—" She caught herself. *Why are you questioning him?* Storm couldn't lie without enduring pain, a downside of the gift he possessed that allowed him to discern immediately if someone *else* lied.

He chuckled darkly. "Don't misunderstand me. I still don't give a rat's ass about Tristan. He can rot in hell for all the times he's let you down, but if there's a chance Imogenia has *any* information on Alterants, we can't leave until we know for sure she's not here."

"Agreed." Between the frigid air and being immobile, Evalle was losing feeling in her legs and butt. "Being still would be easier if it wasn't so freakin' cold up here."

"This isn't cold. You'd like it if you were doing something fun like camping or hiking."

"No way." She grumbled, "Anyone who'd hike up a mountain in the winter for fun would go to hell for a picnic."

"It's not even winter yet." He tugged her around onto her knees and snaked an arm inside her jacket, pulling her to him.

She snuggled up close, welcoming the heat that surged off of his powerful body. The man was a natural furnace and smelled like the outdoors and . . . male. Very male. He cupped her face and kissed her as if he had every right to do so.

As far as she was concerned, he did.

His lips played with hers, teasing, inviting her to do things her body wanted to go all in on. Her heart kept yammering at her to take that leap with Storm. Make a decision.

But her mind had not climbed on board with her heart yet.

He had more patience than a man should need. And to be honest, she was sick of letting her past rule her future. But she had good reason to hesitate even though she knew Storm would be an amazing lover. Her worry stemmed from fear of losing control, which might end with her killing him.

A very realistic fear for an Alterant like her.

His fingers curled around her neck, softly massaging her tight muscles as he kissed her ear and chin. "Stop stressing over the small stuff, sweetheart."

His endearment spawned a silky swirl of heat in her stomach, as if he'd planted it there with his kiss.

When he pulled away, he dropped his forehead against hers, his deep voice rumbling against her skin. "I miss having you wrapped against me in front of my fireplace. I want you back, and rested. I'm getting damned tired of sharing you to help a renegade Alterant, but I'll do this to get Macha off your back. And when we find Tristan *this* time, he *is* coming in to meet with Macha if I have to drag his miserable carcass all the way there."

That sounded more like the Storm who'd clashed with Tristan since their first encounter. To be fair, Storm only told the truth . . . *if* you looked at Tristan's past actions in strictly black-and-white terms.

But her job often required dealing with the gray areas in between.

Such as right now, when everything about this situation had taken an unexpected turn. From the looks of that group below, this had trouble written all over it in bloody ink. She'd asked Storm to come with her only to use his exceptional tracking skills to follow Imogenia once the coven meeting ended, not to put his life at risk to help someone he barely tolerated.

How was it right for her to always accept the comfort and support he offered when she couldn't even meet this man halfway to the bedroom?

A place *any* woman would rush to for someone as considerate, attractive and sensual as Storm. Raw masculinity that women ogled everywhere he went.

Like she was doing right now. *Mind back on business.*

There'd be time for exploring that next step when they got back in front of his fireplace. After she'd met Macha's demands.

She broke the contact, twisting around to scan the growing crowd in the valley. He did, too, and stroked his fingers lightly across her shoulder.

Storm tensed, leaning forward. "*That's* got to be her."

Evalle searched the odd mix of figures milling around for someone who matched the description and zeroed in on the new arrival. Torchlight reflected off a gold mask that adorned the face of a woman of medium height, with white hair. Not silver, not blond, but white curls that fell past her shoulders. "At least the description I was given appears to be sound. But what has she got chained that's standing next to her?"

"I'm thinking demon with its head covered and the

metal collar, but I don't understand why a witch would need to chain something if she has it under her control."

Evalle fingered the top of her boot where she kept her dagger, the one with a spell on the blade she'd used more than once to kill demons. "Does seem odd, since he, it, whatever, looks puny. He can't be six feet tall and a skinny sucker, the way his clothes hang off his body. Think he's a sacrifice?"

"No." Storm rocked back on his heels, the movement shielded from the gathering below by the rocks they hid behind. "I need to stretch." In one fluid move, he was on his feet, offering her a hand that she took. He walked backward, drawing her into dark shadows created by a stand of pine trees. "This changes the plan from observe and track."

"Why? We can still wait for her to leave and follow her."

"That was when we thought this was a group of witches getting together. Imogenia has been impossible to find up to this point, and"—he paused, nodding toward the bright pocket of torchlight and the strange group below them—"that's not a meeting of her coven, people she'd trust. With that many dangerous beings in one place, she probably has a way to disappear once she leaves so that no one can track her. Maybe not even me."

That was saying something. Storm had tracked Evalle to South America when no one else could find her. With the exception of hunting someone who'd teleported, Storm could follow a majik trail anywhere across the globe.

Evalle assessed the scene again. "And you don't think this is some sort of sacrificial ceremony?"

"No."

"Then what's your guess?"

"Don't need to guess. I *know* what's going on." Storm leaned forward against a tree, stretching his calves.

"You do?" She would have been glad to hear his decisive answer if not for her own budding empathic sense picking up on a sudden shift in Storm's calm demeanor to one of tense anticipation, as if he expected trouble. "Why didn't you say so earlier?"

"Because I didn't figure it out until just now. Take a look."

She flicked another quick glance down the slope and did a double take.

Two males with humanlike bodies had entered the circle of torches. One had skin a putrid shade of green. He wore nothing but a sheath of gray material wrapped as a groin cover, and he sported a tail that dragged on the ground. His shorter opponent's camo-green vest and brown pants were pulled tight over a squat bodybuilder physique bulging with muscles. He was the most human looking of the two, with his scraggly brown hair, except for the two short horns sticking out of the top of his head.

Well, that and red glowing eyes she could see even from this distance.

"Demons," Storm said without any question, and she agreed.

The two demons circled each other, bodies hunched forward and arms raised, ready for attack.

She shoved her hands in the pockets of her jacket. "What're they doing?"

"Fighting."

"Why?"

"It's a Beast Club."

Her face must have shown her confusion when she looked at Storm to see if he was serious.

He explained, "Think illegal fight club, but with non-humans."

Now it all started to fit. People were crowded around the ring, already shouting like she'd seen on television when humans wrestled or boxed. "I've never heard of a Beast Club. How do you know what it is?"

"They had these in South America. The only way you found out was by being a sponsor . . . or a fighter."

She wanted to ask more about when he'd lived there, but there wasn't time for that now.

The hurling scream of something in mortal pain echoed across the mountains.

Evalle snapped around in time to see the green-skinned demon rip the head off the one in camo, silencing his opponent. She hadn't expected the beefy guy to lose—at least not so quickly.

Rubbing her neck muscles, she struggled to come up with a new plan. "I have to inform VIPER."

"You contact them and they're going to order you to sit tight and wait for them to raid this. If by some small chance that valley is owned by a person with diplomatic immunity from VIPER operations, the owner is technically within his or her rights to host the fight. By the time VIPER finishes busting up the party, your witch will be gone."

As an agent with VIPER, a coalition of powerful beings who protected the world from supernatural predators, Evalle would be in trouble if this did turn out to be an illegal operation and VIPER found out that she knew about it but failed to report it.

Caught between her responsibilities to VIPER, her promise to bring Tristan in to Macha and her commitment to the Beladors, Evalle's duty to the Beladors and Macha came first, which meant saving her own hide came last, as usual.

But that still didn't solve her problem of talking to the witch if they couldn't track her. "Crap. What's the possibility of getting to Imogenia now?"

"Pretty good, actually. If she's got a fighter entered, she can't leave until her demon, or whatever it is, fights."

"Then we need to get to her soon, but how?"

"That part's easy. We just walk in."

Evalle didn't like the I-already-have-a-plan-in-mind sound of that. "They aren't going to notice a couple of uninvited people?"

"You don't need a formal invitation to a beast fight like that one. All you have to do is"——he paused, locking his hands behind his head and twisting, stretching his shoulders and chest——"show up as a fighter or with a fighter and you're in."

Grace be to Macha. Evalle figured out what he was proposing. "No. I watched you almost die once. I'm not going through that again."

He dropped his arms and stepped close, pulling her against his chest and whispering into her ear. "I don't know why there's a Beast Club in North America, but now that I do and that witch is involved, I know better than to risk leaving here and you hunting for her later without me. I'm going down there to find Imogenia *now*. You can be my sponsor, or you can wait up here."

TWO

Storm kept his face calm and his movements easy-paced for Evalle's benefit. Nothing frightened the hellion, but if he told her that he'd come close to decapitation the last time he'd been in a Beast Club fight, she'd call in VIPER just to protect him.

She'd make the call, knowing she'd lose her best shot at meeting with Imogenia.

Evalle's determined steps followed him down the mountainside. She grumbled, "I wish you wouldn't do this."

Not as much as I wish you weren't going with me. "I can use the workout."

"Thought you said you were a hundred percent again."

He'd spent weeks in a coma with his body a mass of broken bones after interfering when Evalle was being taken into custody. He'd do it again. "I am a hundred percent and feeling good, but it won't hurt to test my reflexes before I go back to active duty."

"So you *are* coming back to VIPER?" she asked casually.

"Maybe. VIPER still needs a tracker in this region." And Evalle needed a partner who'd watch her back and not stab it.

"Well, I hope you *are* in shape, because if you're going to be stupid, you gotta be tough."

He chuckled, ignoring the caustic edge she used to shield her real feelings. Evalle's natural reaction to worry was anger. He reached over and brushed his knuckles against her cheek, drawing her to a stop. "I'm tough to kill."

"Says the man who spent three weeks in a coma after Sen tried to kill him," Evalle pointed out in a frosty tone.

Sen had taken a shot at Storm once as payback when Storm had interfered in Evalle's arrest. As liaison between agents and the VIPER coalition, Sen had authority over the agents and an unnatural hatred for Evalle, Alterants or both. Sen had set his sights on Storm when Storm refused to use his lie-detector ability against Evalle.

Storm was more concerned about keeping *her* safe than anything, but telling her that would only raise her hackles. He let his finger trail across her smooth cheek. "I'll be ready for Sen if he tries to kill me again."

She growled something and caught Storm's hand in hers. "How're you going to be ready for someone who can teleport and has powers that are godlike? I might even believe he *was* a god or demigod, except he's clearly being forced to act as liaison for VIPER. By a more powerful someone. The next time he slams you up against a brick wall, he might have enough time to make sure you're dead and hide the body before he leaves."

"Just like last time, my spirit guide will show someone where to find the body."

"Comforting."

"That's tomorrow's worry. Tonight we have a different fight." Giving her a gentle shove, he kept them moving down the hill toward a smorgasbord of deadly beings.

He hadn't really thought she'd wait up on the ridge, but just once he wished she wouldn't go racing into danger. If not for knowing that Evalle would go searching for Imogenia on her own and end up somewhere like this without backup, he'd pack her up and take her to Atlanta right now.

With her badass fighting skills, she could handle herself in a fight with most supernatural beings, but he'd feel better if she would tap *all* her powers, not just energy force and telekinetics.

But demons would turn into choirboys before she did that.

Evalle would never break her vow to the Beladors and shift into her more powerful Alterant beast state, even if her life was at stake.

Storm had the benefit of majik and his jaguar form, but using majik in a Beast Club promised a nasty fight. Like the bloody battles he'd been forced to endure when he'd belonged to a sponsor back in South America.

Before he'd escaped that sponsor . . . the witch doctor.

With the terrain already leveling out as he and Evalle drew closer to the firelight in the valley, Storm had little time left for conversation. "When we get there, I want you to follow my instructions *exactly*."

Evalle's quick bristle of irritation pricked his skin.

He didn't need his empathic gift to know he'd poked

at the badger. "You aren't catching my drift. This isn't about me being in charge. *You're* the sponsor. I'm the fighter. As far as they're concerned, I *belong* to you."

"Belong? You mean I *own* you?" She turned a sour face toward him.

"Yes. These are like cockfights, but the fighters here are usually demons or some other subservient being." He could feel her thinking, trying to figure out what that meant about him fighting in South America. A dark time he didn't want to discuss right now, when it would involve bringing up that bitch witch doctor who had killed his father.

He never risked thinking the witch doctor's name, couldn't as long as she held his soul, or she'd ride that connection like a superhighway to find him.

Bitch fit her just fine as a name.

Dead Bitch would fit even better.

But when he was ready to make that happen, he wanted to find *her* first rather than call her to him and have her show up unexpectedly. Based on Storm's visions, the witch doctor had an interest in Evalle.

If Storm thought, as he first had, that Evalle was at risk, he'd tell her about the witch doctor, but knowing Evalle, she'd go hunting the witch doctor on her own. Not happening. The evil bitch had been in the Atlanta area for the past week, according to Nightstalkers. That meant she'd probably learned enough about Evalle to avoid confronting an Alterant with capabilities that few knew of or understood.

After discussing it with his guardian spirit, Kai, Storm

now felt he was still the witch doctor's ultimate goal. He'd be ready for her when she showed her face.

But one thing tapped at his skull. How much did the witch doctor know of Storm's interest in Evalle?

The bitch fed off of pain.

She was almost certainly lying in wait with a plan to dole out as much misery as possible, because he'd humiliated her when he'd escaped.

His bet? The witch doctor would not come for him until she had a plan in place for payback, something Storm hadn't been concerned over until meeting Evalle. His gut muscles twisted into a pretzel at the thought of anything happening to Evalle. Blood would run knee deep first.

"Do you get to choose who you fight?" Evalle asked, thankfully pushing the subject away from his past and back to the Beast Club.

"No."

"Can you turn down a fight?"

"Doesn't work like that in these smaller venues. First we have to find out what's at stake, and the rules, then the sponsors start negotiating fight positions. Your fighter's first match has to be in his designated category. Fighting one match fulfills the Beast Club requirements. After that, your fighter is welcome to take on any and all opponents as long as the sponsors can agree on terms."

"You mean like side bets."

"Right."

She was quiet for a moment, then asked, "So we can find an easy fight?"

Doubtful with his being able to shift into another form, which brought out deadly creatures, but he didn't want her worrying, so he said, "Maybe."

"What do the sponsors get if their fighter wins?"

He'd really like to be able to lie at a time like this, but he couldn't afford to weaken his body with the pain lying brought on. "Nothing for the early rounds and, so you know, they sometimes call one round of fighting, or each battle, a *mash* at a venue this size. The winners keep fighting until they're either killed or they forfeit. Once you win, the only way to *not* continue fighting is to forfeit a win, which rarely happens."

"Then what?"

"The winner in a category receives anything from money to something a nonhuman would value. Whatever you do, don't ask what the final prize is in my category or you'll throw up a red flag. Anyone who knows about this fight should know the stakes."

Her footsteps stilled for a moment, then moved forward again.

Before Evalle could press for more answers he didn't want to speculate on, Storm turned the conversation back to preparing her before they reached the fight circle. "Let's focus on what you have to do. I'm your fighter. You're the only one who can accept or decline a fight offer, but like I said, you have to accept at least one fight once we're there."

Disgust rolled through her voice when she asked, "What are you? My slave?"

"Pretty much." Then to take the edge off her stress, he

tried to lighten her mood with, "I wouldn't mind being a *love* slave."

She rolled her eyes and huffed, all an act to hide the brush of awareness that sparked from her. "In your dreams."

"Always."

"You're impossible." But a smile tugged at her lips and happiness swirled from her.

Seeing her smile gave his heart a punch. From what he'd gathered, she hadn't had a lot of reasons to laugh before he met her. He didn't know why it mattered so much to see her happy, but it did.

This night couldn't end soon enough so they could get back to his house. He wanted to give her another reason to smile.

Eyes locked on the valley they were approaching, Evalle asked, "Who came up with this demeaning event?"

"Greedy people." He forced his mind back to preparing her. "This is all about posturing, so you need to walk in there like you own the place. No one touches a sponsor." Which was why she should be safe. "But some people get mouthy. Don't get physical with anyone, but don't let them shove you around verbally either." *Or I'll have to hurt them.*

"Got it." Evalle raised both hands, smoothing loose hairs off her face, then she tightened the elastic band holding her long black ponytail. A simple, yet adorable, look. At five-ten she was a lot of woman, all packed in one fine carry case. Snug jeans covered long legs capable of drop-kicking a demon. She wore a steel-gray Gore-

Tex motorcycle jacket, and her black leather boots concealed fighting blades.

Lethal and hot. She was damn hot.

And if he kept thinking how much better she'd look out of those clothes, he'd be limping soon. But, son of a bitch, he wanted her. Had since the first time they'd met. But she'd been hurt by someone, and he would not rush her.

She was a jewel worthy of the wait, whatever time it took for her to feel comfortable with being touched and loved, but it might not be too much longer. She'd been making encouraging noises lately, a sign that she wanted more.

The minute she was ready, he'd give her everything and then some.

Evalle stared off into the distance, muttering, "I wish I'd known about these Beast Clubs. I'd have studied up."

"You'll be fine." He gauged how far they had left to go and took in the stand of trees they were passing. "Stop for a minute and let me have your dagger."

She pulled the blade out of her boot, whispered something to it and passed the dagger to him.

He felt a buzz of energy coming off the spelled weapon. Pushing aside one side of his knee-length leather jacket, he used the blade tip to pop a yellow diamond the size of a half marble from where it had been inserted as one of the jaguar eyes carved in his silver belt buckle.

He handed the stone to Evalle. "This is your buy-in stake."

She studied the gem through dark sunglasses she

wore even at night, which would seem strange to anyone who didn't know her. The sunglasses hid her glowing green Alterant eyes that were uber sensitive to any light and offered night vision similar to his.

Except that he had no problem with daylight, or the sun that would kill her as well as blind her.

He unbuckled his belt and pulled it through the loops. "I don't want to wear anything of value around this crowd. Do me a favor and use your kinetics to toss this up in that tree to your right."

Closing the jewel in her fist, she asked suspiciously, "What's this worth?"

A rare canary-yellow diamond? Lot of zeroes for the matched set. "Enough to get us into this event."

She pointed her finger at the belt he held in an open palm and flicked her hand up toward an old oak tree that had lost its leaves. The belt flew up and double wrapped a branch.

He nodded. "We'll get it on the way out. Ready?"

She hesitated, saying nothing, but worry rushed off her and raced across his senses. If he tried to console her, she'd just get pissed off. "Make sure you stay close to me without my asking you or they'll suspect we're not sponsor and fighter."

She started walking again. "What would happen then?"

"They'd assume we're not here to fight, which would be interpreted as a threat. Wouldn't take much for the organizers to make the leap to us being VIPER agents and the entire place would turn on us."

"Lovely." She grumbled something under her breath.

"Tristan better appreciate this. If you don't walk out under your own power tonight, *I'll* be the one dragging him to Macha by his family jewels."

That might be worth getting bloody.

Hiding his smile, Storm turned back toward the raucous crowd surrounded by bright lights and kept coaching her as they moved toward the battles. "Think superior attitude, because in this circle sponsors are power brokers. I'll enter ahead of you as if I'm doubling as your bodyguard. When we find the Domjon, just say you're requesting a fight."

"What's a Domjon?"

"The ringmaster, man in charge who pockets the buy-in stakes. His word is final on anything that happens in a Beast Club, even an altercation between sponsors. Once he takes your stake, we move around and check out the competition. The minute we locate Imogenia, we'll scope out her demon for a challenge. That'll give you a chance to cut your deal with the witch."

"Sounds too easy."

And anything that sounded easy was usually far from it, but Storm wasn't through giving her instructions. "The Domjon will throw out anyone who abuses power in his arena, but even so, remember not to let the witch touch you, and tell her nothing personal about yourself."

"My friend Nicole has warned me about dealing with witches."

"Nicole isn't a dark witch."

"No, but she's not your *average* witch either." Evalle shoved her hands in the pockets of her jacket and fell silent. "Don't take this wrong, but what's the best way to gain an easy match?"

He could use the concern playing through her words to motivate her for pulling off this role. "Do what I told you. Bring plenty of attitude. The more arrogant you are, the better shot you'll have at getting your choice of who I fight."

That brought her chin up with a bold jut. "No problem."

Had he said she was hot? Smoking body, exotic eyes and legs that went on forever, but he found her confidence sexy as hell. It also kept him constantly worried for her safety.

She whispered out the side of her mouth, "Anything else before we're too close to talk?"

"I'll get us to the Domjon. Once a deal is made, you take the lead when we walk around looking for a fight. That's a clear statement that I'm your muscle and you call the shots." Storm slowed when they reached the perimeter of the fighting zone and he noticed flashes of green and blue lights flickering in a halo that circled the valley. "There's a ward protecting the event."

"We can't get in?"

"I'll know in a minute." When Storm reached the outer mist circling the area, he pushed his hand into the halo. Light sparked across his dark skin, and tiny fireworks of white and blue burst away from him until an arch formed above his head wide enough for two people to pass through.

Just to keep humans out and probably prevent them from seeing any of the fight or attendees as well.

He nodded at Evalle, then stepped in ahead of her, holding his hand up to keep the arch open.

The thud of fists and legs hitting bodies had been evident as they'd drawn near, but inside the warding the sounds were painful and rocked the air between shouts from the jeering crowd. Some*thing* in the ring released a high-pitched squealing sound. Bodies pressed close, blocking their view of the fight.

Striding a step ahead of Evalle, Storm recognized the familiar smell of sweat, alcohol, incense and unusual nicotine odors as he entered the fight camp.

Some days he wished his olfactory senses weren't so sharp and his memory so close to the surface.

He slapped a look of threat back at the curious gazes, warning them he was just as deadly as he looked, and off the leash.

Evalle strolled close enough behind him he could scent her. Good. The less he checked on her, the more convincing a team they would be, since this crowd would assume he had some ability to keep track of her without requiring her to be in sight, or better yet . . . that she might be just as deadly as he was.

As he scouted the jumble of faces for the Domjon, Storm caught a whiff of something that could be smoke and licorice. A smell that belonged to some who practiced witchcraft on demons, like the witch doctor from South America.

Storm followed the scent, angling through the crowd until he found the origin of the smell.

An old woman wrapped in a blanket covered with

Asian symbols sat on the ground with several incense burners in front of her that pumped out the sharp smell. She waved a red-tipped incense stick in the air. "Pure Fenghuang at special Beast Club price."

An opiate. Now he understood the licorice smell.

Rolling his eyes, Storm muttered, "Vendors," and led Evalle back toward the area of congestion, where he should find the Domjon. He spotted the Beast Club host standing an easy head taller than the crowd. Upon closer inspection, Storm realized the little round man wearing a red wool sport coat with yellow collar and cuffs was perched on the back of a massive tortoise. Curly brown hair fringed beneath a black bowler hat. Nickel-sized earrings with laughing skull carvings stretched and distorted each earlobe. Piles of necklaces of rare metals adorned with flashy jewels hung around his neck.

The Domjon called out in an auctioneer's voice, "Demons two, quads one, unknown are playing the edge, step up, step up, step up and take a mad chance, no challenge too small, no death too fast, but we love ya when you make it last."

Storm stopped in front of the squawker. He spread his feet apart and crossed his arms, waiting for Evalle to sidle up beside him. When she did, she sniffed and wrinkled her nose in distaste.

Nice touch.

The Domjon noticed her with the speed of a rattle-snake picking up the heat of a prey. His beady eyes lit with interest that had nothing to do with money.

Storm thought about shoving the yellow diamond

down the Domjon's throat—with his fist attached. But he had a role to play, too.

"Okay, okay, okay, fresh meat," the Domjon chortled, grinning at Evalle. "Whadda ya want, little lady?"

Evalle smiled right back at him and expelled a sound of sinister amusement. "Your throat if you call me little lady again."

That took a notch off the Domjon's leering. "No insult, none a'tall, gotta go with the flow, have a sense of humor, don't be gettin' mean 'lessen you're inside the ring. Whadda ya have?"

"I request a fight."

"Buy-in's high, but lower than the sky. Show your flash for a chance at a mash."

Withdrawing her fingers from her coat pocket, Evalle flipped the sparkling yellow stone to the Domjon as if it was no more than a coin she'd found.

He snagged the jewel from the air. Holding the rock up to his moon-shaped face, one eye ran out on a stem and studied the gem all over before sucking back into his eye socket.

The crowd had quieted to a low rumble. Some turned from the fight going on to find out what new meat had entered the fray.

Storm had a momentary concern the Domjon might try to pull a fast one and declare the gem not worth enough for an entry spot, but the mouthy little turd told Evalle, "He's in."

"Rules." Evalle gave that one word as an order.

"Fight to the death, no draws allowed, unless your

opponent's sponsor accepts a trade. A deal's a deal, without a will." The Domjon swung his beady eyes to Storm. "Declare yourself."

Decision time.

Declaring himself as anything other than Skinwalker, which meant in his case that he could shift *and* had majik in his arsenal, was reason for disqualification if caught. Fighting as a shifter allowed for no majik in the ring, but he shouldn't need it to win against most were-animals. Bring majik into the picture and the odds of winning went up significantly in favor of those who wielded far more majik than he did.

Besides, he only needed one fight to give Evalle time to talk to the witch. Getting disqualified or forfeiting after that would work in their favor to offer a quick exit.

He took the gamble and said, "Dual form. Animal."

"Shifter?" the Domjon asked.

"Yes." Storm's chest tightened with a quick twist of pain he barely kept from betraying with his expression. A mild reaction to lying, since he was technically correct about shifting into animal form and the Domjon had not specifically asked, "*Are you a shifter?*"

An "ah" floated through the crowd.

The Domjon snapped his fingers three times. "All right, all right, all right, go find yourself a fight."

He flipped a silver disc that Storm caught in the air and lifted into view. A skull with two horns had been carved into the center, and a clip dangled from a hole at the top. Storm clipped the coin on one of his belt loops, declaring himself a contender.

Tension sparked off Evalle, but when he took in her face she released a sigh born of boredom for those watching her.

As if everyone wasted her time.

He was proud of her, but he enjoyed a moment of ego satisfaction that she had eyes only for him.

When she swung around to walk away, Storm followed, sweeping his gaze over everyone they passed and sending a silent message that the safest place was as far away from her as they could get.

The area had a dogfight atmosphere with sponsors either cutting deals or sizing up fighters for a mash. One woman had a two-headed Keelter demon that hissed in stereo.

Evalle had been strolling along calmly until Storm noticed a hesitation in her next step.

He swept the crowd, searching until he found a man up ahead whose gaze had locked on her. He had maybe two inches on Storm, which would put the guy at six feet four inches. A thick mat of inch-long, lemon-yellow hair carpeted his head, and he had a face the color of saffron, with a hooked beak nose center stage. Nothing remarkable that would cause Storm concern, until he took in the predator-black eyes, empty as two holes in a skull.

Having tightened down his empathic senses to pick up only Evalle's emotions, Storm opened them wider now to reach out to the man. Anger simmered beneath the blank face, and power coiled around his slender body.

Witch. Maybe a wizard or a mage.

Evalle paused as though considering a mash.

With one look at Storm, the wizard ignored her interest. In a moment, Evalle would notice the shiny red disc hanging from a black cord around the neck of the woman standing next to the wizard, her head shoulder high to him. This fighter would have to wait for a majik mash. She was bald except for a chin-length strip of violet hair hanging off one side of her head, heavy kohl-black eyes, thick lashes, purple lipstick and body cut with muscle. She posed, moving slowly so the soft-looking leather that crisscrossed over her breasts and shorts of the same material showed off cinnamon-colored skin that shone. She didn't look the least bit cold in this chilly temperature.

Must have plenty of majik if she wasted it to keep herself warm.

When the punk-haired wizard ignored Evalle, she dismissed him right back and walked on. They'd covered several yards when a loud snarl erupted from Storm's left.

Evalle slowed her step at the sound, taking in the creature making that noise at the same time Storm did.

That thing stood eight feet if an inch, and had a head covered in spiked horns and a jaw wide enough to snap a man's leg in half. Dull skin the color of dried mud and dotted with pink warts the size of Storm's thumb sagged on its body. Thick legs ended at feet with opposing joints, similar to a monkey's. But Storm had never seen a monkey or ape with curved claws like that or fangs as long as his fingers.

Or the batlike wings that just flapped into view.

Two arms hung past the creature's waist. It lunged against some invisible leash, long arms stretched out with the razor-sharp claws. All it had to do was get something in its grasp to slice off the head and win a match.

His master was an average-height man who had the unassuming look of a bland office worker, with his thinning hair and a beer gut stuffed inside a pale gray business suit.

But he controlled the thing without an obvious show of power. Another mage or wizard? Was that thing on the invisible leash some type of golem? The master waved a silver disc in his hand and called to Evalle in a surprisingly deep voice, "You have dual form. I have dual form. Only three here so far. We should talk. I'm Zymon."

Unease fingered along Storm's neck.

What the hell did that thing shift into? Storm had yet to fight something he couldn't kill if he didn't face majik more powerful than his. If this thing had the benefit of a mage or wizard's majik, Storm might lose. Zymon would be disqualified if he was found out, but if that thing on the leash *was* a golem, Zymon would just make a new one.

And Storm would be dead, leaving Evalle's back unprotected.

In direct conflict with the couldn't-give-a-shit mask she'd dropped into place, anxiety shot off Evalle like lightning bolts that Storm gritted his teeth against. She had to be thinking along the same lines as he was, but she stressed over his possibly dying.

Zymon prodded harder, his strange accent coming

through. "Come, come. We must deal or Domjon will choose a match. Hard to find fight and I need win to-night."

Evalle put a finger to her cheek, studying. "I'll need plenty of incentive to waste getting mine dirty killing yours."

That's my girl.

Stepping out of the shadows, Zymon studied her with a glimmer of appreciation in his flat gray eyes. "Confident, eh? Tell you what. I will sweeten pot. You win, I will throw in a demon."

Ah, hell. If Evalle turned her nose up at a bonus wager, she'd look suspicious. Storm began assessing Zymon's beast more closely, preparing to fight the thing.

Evalle laughed, clearly buying time to figure a way out of their situation. "A demon? That's your best offer?"

A woman called out, "Don't be so hasty when you haven't seen all the dual form competition."

Storm and Evalle turned in unison to find Imogenia standing twenty feet away with her chained fighter.

To Evalle's credit, she didn't show the relief that Storm felt coming from her. She gave Imogenia a look of disbelief. "What does it turn into? A badger? Mongoose?"

"Nothing quite so attractive, but he's a strong fighter."

Now there was a stroke of luck.

He'd take Imogenia's skinny bastard over Zymon's creature that very likely harbored majik or poisons in its claws.

Evalle cocked her head with the arrogance he'd told her to exude and studied the witch's fighter. She gave a dismissive snort. "I won't insult mine by expecting him to fight . . . *that*."

What? Now would be a great time to have the telepathic ability Evalle shared with her Belador friends.

Storm's fault. He should have coached her better, because he had no way to tell her to accept this fight without blowing their covers. If Zymon was right, Evalle had only two options, and she had just shot down Storm's best chance at a win if Imogenia walked away.

THREE

Watch Storm get ripped to pieces by one beast or stomp a puny one into the ground?

Either way, Evalle couldn't see this evening ending well. If Storm fought the witch's guy and Storm held back, he'd raise suspicions. If he fought too hard, he'd maim or kill the guy.

But she didn't want him fighting Zymon's beast either.

Imogenia's lips curled, tightened, then with some effort softened back into a taunting smile, as if the witch struggled to hold back her reaction. Short-fuse temper?

Evalle had blown off the witch's offer in order to buy time to figure out a move and because accepting too quickly might not look good. Right? But irritation had wicked off Storm, meaning Evalle had probably just screwed up by refusing the witch.

Could she change her mind?

Imogenia shook off the anger that had appeared to grip her and cocked her head at Evalle with a smile. Light from the torches ignited a glow on the golden mask hiding her forehead, cheeks and nose. She nodded toward Zymon's howling beast. "If your pet wins our fight, you'll be able to raise the ante with Zymon for a match."

Pretty determined to have Storm fight her guy. Did she really think Storm would lose?

If he did, the witch's demon would still face Zymon's . . . *thing*.

Zymon's monster roared.

Evalle gave him one more glance in time to see blood drool from his lips. Sold.

She shrugged at Zymon. "I'll entertain your offer while I let my fighter warm up on hers." Then she swung what she hoped was a haughty look at Imogenia. "I accept."

Imogenia's teeth sparkled when she smiled. Too confident.

Evalle scrutinized the witch's fighter more closely. His hand trembled.

Was she missing something about those two?

With the mash set, Evalle walked over to stand outside the circle of torches marking off the fight ring. Storm stepped up on her left, jaw as rigid as his body, eyes focused on the fight starting between a nine-foot-tall troll and the orange lizard-body guy.

Imogenia stepped up on the other side of Storm and tugged the chain hooked to her fighter, pulling him to stand behind her. She leaned forward, speaking across Storm to Evalle. "How many do you own?"

"One." Evalle snapped that out too quickly, but she detested the idea of owning anyone.

"One?" Imogenia chuckled derisively and murmured, "Amateur."

Was the witch putting up a good front or trying to

psyche her out? Evalle figured Imogenia had pressed for the fight with Storm rather than risk her little guy getting eaten by the crazed beast that belonged to Zymon.

She looked down her nose at the witch, who was a good five inches shorter, and considered several scathing replies until she caught herself. *The better I play my part, the safer for Storm.* Plus, she had to figure some way to talk to Imogenia, which wouldn't go well if Storm killed her fighter.

Staying in character, Evalle lifted a finger, which she stroked along Storm's cheek in a proprietary way as she loaded her voice with what she hoped sounded seductive for Imogenia's benefit. "If you had one like him at your beck and call, you'd understand why one is all I need."

Storm cut his gaze over to Evalle, and the heat that flared in those dark eyes turned her stomach into a circus act of backflips. He gave her a wink that promised he'd remind her of the suggestive comment later. Evalle gave him a "behave" look, and he just smiled until he returned to watching the fight again, stone mask still in place.

"Oh, really?" Imogenia asked with catty sarcasm. Her fingers curled halfway with a slight tremble as if she fought to keep from fisting them. She drew a long breath and that phony smile popped up on her face again. "In that case, *if* I can keep mine from *killing* yours, I may use this one"—she paused, stroking a slow glance over Storm—"to stud if we can reach an agreement."

It took all Evalle's will not to lunge across Storm and choke Imogenia for daring to think she'd *ever* own him. Or touch him.

Too bad the sponsors couldn't have a go in the ring.

Storm was doing his part, not showing a flicker of interest over Imogenia's comment, so Evalle arched an eyebrow at the witch. "Enjoy your fantasy for the few minutes it lasts."

At the sound of a guttural growl, she turned her attention to the current fight. The troll circled orange lizard guy, whose two sets of arms dangled. Lizard guy snapped wide jaws at the troll, who jumped back and forth, dodging until the wide lizard jaws spewed a dark cloud of air that stank like a sulfuric gas.

Evalle covered her mouth and nose with her hand when the smell drifted outside the ring.

While the troll coughed and flayed his arms to break up the nasty cloud, lizard guy swatted his tail, knocking the troll's feet out from under him. He landed facedown. The lizard guy used his four arms to fold the troll in half—backward—with a loud *crack* that had to be the troll's backbone.

The Domjon called out, "Trolls out by a backward fart, demons still winnin' and lookin' sharp. Duals up next to give it a go. Let's hope they shift and make it show."

Evalle met Storm's gaze and saw nothing but ruthless determination in his eyes as he started shedding clothes. His leather jacket landed on the ground first, then he yanked off his shirt, boots and socks.

She'd never seen him shift with clothes on, but she had no doubt he could rip out of his jeans.

Imogenia hovered too close for Evalle to say anything to Storm besides, "Don't disappoint me."

Understanding lit his eyes. He caught her meaning that he'd better walk out of there alive. Giving her a curt nod, he stepped into the circle, then crossed to the other side and turned, waiting on his opponent.

Evalle watched with everyone else as Imogenia unclipped the collar around her fighter's neck.

Fear shanked off the little guy so strongly Evalle could practically smell it. She felt sick over what was going to happen and glanced at Storm, who had his arms crossed, face empty of any emotion.

When Evalle turned back, Imogenia pulled her fighter around to face her and the crowd, his back to Evalle and the fight ring. "Ready for a new challenge, beaniepole?"

"No." The word whispered through the black cloth that trembled.

"Don't be shy. We both know what you're capable of." Imogenia lifted off his hood.

Gasps ricocheted through the air.

From where Evalle stood, all she could see was a partial side view of his scruffy red beard. He had short curly hair the same color, but without seeing any more she'd guess he was no older than twenty-three or four. Close to her age.

Just a young man. Could this get any worse?

Imogenia told him, "Showtime, beaniepole. Where's your spirit?"

"My name's Bernie." His fingers curled into fists, but tremors still wracked his body.

"Beaniepole fits you so well," Imogenia whispered softly as she leaned in, but Evalle heard her. "Get into that ring and don't kill him until I tell you to, or I'll have to visit your girlfriend. Tonight."

"No. Stay away from her." Bernie's hoarse words shook with anger and fear.

"Then get moving. I've stayed here longer than I planned already."

When he turned to enter the ring, Evalle finally got a good look at his face.

Glowing green eyes.

An Alterant.

She whipped around to face Storm, whose eyes took in Bernie, then narrowed. Storm's gaze shifted to her long enough to send a warning glare she understood. *Don't interfere.*

Storm had fought demon trolls, warlocks and probably many other things she couldn't name, but he'd never gone up against an Alterant. At least not that she knew of, since she was the first one he'd ever met. Based on what little information she'd gathered on other Alterants besides her, they tended to have a power or unique ability of their own.

What about Bernie?

Evalle suffered a deadly reaction to the sun, but she hadn't met another Alterant with *that* same issue. Did Bernie even *have* a weakness?

Imogenia cackled with delight. The bitch had disguised the Alterant. Evalle doubted she even needed the chain and collar, not with the threat of the boy's girl-friend hanging over him.

Storm unfolded his arms and stepped forward, body ready for attack. Muscles rippled up his arms and across his shoulders when he fisted his hands and arched his back, growling.

Bernie just stood on this side of the ring, shaking.

Imogenia unbuttoned his shirt and pulled it off, re-vealing a bony body. When snorts and chuckles erupted from the crowd, Imogenia rose up on her toes and hissed, "Need I remind you what happened in Tennessee?"

The young man's body went taut as a bowstring.

He jerked his head to the side, looking over his shoulder at her with murder in his eyes, then roared and turned back to Storm.

Bernie's jaws widened, teeth lengthening into fangs as his jaws expanded and his head grew larger. Cartilage popped and bones snapped in his arms and legs that ex-tended and thickened. His feet grew as long as Evalle's forearm, with four toes each. Bright red hair on his arms and legs lengthened. Clothes shredded and fell away as his body grew ten feet tall with black veins popping along his back and chest.

He raised four-fingered hands, fisted them and bel-lowed again.

Would Zymon's monster have been a better choice?

Storm slid his jeans off and tossed them to the side, not the least bit insecure about being naked.

Evalle ignored the female murmurs of appreciation.

Hard to blame them. She'd ogle him, too, if not for being more concerned over his keeping that amazing body in one piece.

Storm's human form immediately shimmered as he shifted into a massive jaguar much larger than a natural one, all in a matter of seconds. Gleaming black fur blanketed the two-hundred-and-fifty-pound predator. His head lifted as high as Evalle's shoulder. He roared at the Alterant Bernie, the sound echoing through the valley.

Bright jaguar-yellow eyes glared death at Bernie, who could rip Storm in half.

Evalle had to stop this, but to do so would pit her and Storm against this crowd. Calling in VIPER would put Storm at just as great a risk with Sen gunning for him.

But she would not let him die in that ring.

The giant mass of hair, muscle and fangs that Bernie had shifted into plodded forward and made a swipe at Storm's animal form, but Storm had the reflexes of a preternatural cat. He raced around the Alterant, slashing a claw across the back of the giant's thigh, drawing first blood.

Evalle cheered silently in her head, forcing herself to maintain a composed demeanor. She cut her eyes at Imogenia, who watched, transfixed by the scene.

Just as Evalle looked back, the Alterant stomped back and forth, causing the ground to vibrate beneath her feet.

Storm stalked one way then the other, taking a swipe here and there, not cutting Bernie deeply enough to do real harm, but blood flowed freely. The big jaguar raced around and around Bernie, causing the Alterant to turn in circles.

Evalle realized Storm was trying to wear Bernie down, catch him off balance and maybe tackle him.

Bernie's frustration erupted in a screaming howl. His arms twisted in their sockets. They were . . . *double-jointed*? Bernie slashed across Storm's back as he came around Bernie.

Blood streamed down the jaguar's hindquarters.

Evalle felt the blow to her center.

Storm's jaguar swung around, facing the Alterant. He roared a vicious sound that would bring the dead back to life.

Imogenia yelled, "*Acath-amee*," at Bernie.

What could that mean? Evalle hadn't felt any power or majik cast with the word. Imogenia had said it the way a dog trainer used a foreign word to train an attack dog. A term the animal wouldn't normally hear from someone else.

Bernie stopped moving around and extended one arm, hand turned up. He made a scooping motion.

As if snatched off the ground, Storm's jaguar form flipped up in the air and rolled backward, landing hard from the kinetic hit.

Now Evalle understood. Bernie's weakness was lack of aggression. The witch was using the commands to force him to fight.

Swinging his big head around to look at Imogenia, who smiled and gave Bernie thumbs-up, the Alterant went back to work on Storm. Bernie pointed a finger at the inert jaguar body and used kinetics again to toss Storm fifteen feet in the air for another backflip before dropping him to the ground.

The third time Bernie used the same tactic, Storm rolled in the air to land on all four paws, but took a sideways step and shook his head, dazed.

Evalle's heart hammered.

Her Alterant beast wanted out to fight. Muscles rippled along her arms, threatening to expand and strengthen. She shoved her hands in her jeans pockets to keep from throwing a kinetic blast at the Alterant to knock him on his ass, then focused her attention on not shifting. Unlike Bernie, she couldn't shift into beast form without consent from Macha or Brina. And if she used kinetics to interfere, everyone in this place would know she and Storm were not really sponsor and fighter.

Bernie pounded his feet back and forth, like a kid waiting to play tag football.

Storm wobbled left then right and stood very still, his head hanging low to the ground as if he'd forgotten where he was. Bernie took one step then another, creeping over to Storm with his head angled in a thoughtful way.

Evalle knew of only one other Alterant besides herself who could control his beast state. Tristan. Bernie acted based on fear and anger. Now he studied Storm with curiosity. Did he retain enough humanity that he regretted slamming Storm around like a rag doll?

Imogenia said to Evalle, "Give me your fighter and I'll spare him."

Storm had warned her deals were binding here, but even if they weren't, this witch was crazy if she thought she could have Storm. "Want to make me the same offer?"

Imogenia hissed in reply. "Fool."

Everyone around the ring quieted, leaning in, watching to see what Bernie would do.

Imogenia didn't appear bothered by Bernie's passivity. Why? Then it hit Evalle.

Because Bernie wasn't really passive. Not in his beast state. He just needed prompting.

When he shifted into an Alterant, Evalle figured out too late that this was all part of Bernie's act.

Imogenia bared her teeth and shouted, "*Now!*"

FOUR

Bernie lunged at Storm. A towering mass of beast that could crush a jaguar.

Evalle only saw a dark blur, Storm moved so fast.

Where his jaguar had been standing still as death, he leaped away just before Bernie the Alterant slammed to the ground facedown with the force of a building being knocked over.

The jaguar snarled a roar and pounced on Bernie's back. Huge jaws clamped around the Alterant's neck. Bernie jerked twice, then didn't move.

Cheers went up in the crowd.

Imogenia screeched, "*Noooo!*"

Evalle locked her legs to prevent her knees from buckling with relief. Storm had intentionally lured the Alterant in, using Bernie's size and clumsy movements against him.

The Domjon howled with happiness. "Dual on the mountain for a prime-time show. Shifter one, Alterant *zeeeroooooo*. That's a guaranteed pass to the big night."

Evalle wanted to ask the Domjon what "big night" he referred to, but that would throw up one of those red flags of suspicion Storm had warned her about. She'd learned enough about Beast Clubs for one night and just wanted to get Storm out of here before he had to fight Zymon's behemoth creature.

But she still had to deal with Imogenia.

The witch lashed out at Evalle. "You killed my Alterant, you bitch. You'll pay for this."

Talk about screwing up a mission to gain intel.

Nothing to lose now by tossing the witch's words back at her. Evalle said, "Shouldn't have brought your second string. Oh, that's right. You don't have a first string."

Imogenia vibrated with fury. She wrapped her arms around herself as if trying to keep from going for Evalle's throat.

Bring it, witch.

"Ladies, ladies, ladies," the Domjon cooed in their direction. "No loss yet. The shifter waits for his sponsor to call thumbs-up or thumbs-down. Either way, it ends the round."

Imogenia snapped back to face the ring. "He's alive?"

The crowd started chanting, "*Death, death, death!*"

Was this what it had been like back during the days of lions in a coliseum?

Had Storm used his majik to put the Alterant into a semi-comatose state? Was that allowed? From where he stood with his jaws on Bernie's neck, all Storm would have to do was rip apart the Alterant's neck muscles and the head would fall loose.

But an alive Bernie just changed the game with Imogenia.

Evalle asked the witch, "You willing to deal to keep your fighter?"

Imogenia focused on Evalle, finally giving her the respect she should have from the start. The witch visibly fought to pull her emotions under control. What, exactly, had Imogenia so jumpy and on edge?

Imogenia stepped close to Evalle, even though the crowd noise covered their conversation. "What do you want?"

"Information."

That drew a hard line across Imogenia's pert lips. "Too vague."

Time to gamble. "I'll make this more than fair. I'll give you back your Alterant if you answer all my questions *truthfully* about TÅµr Medb, the Medb Coven and Tristan. If not, I leave with both fighters."

Imogenia's eyes narrowed behind the mask. "What makes you think I know anything about those?"

"I don't *think*. I know you do."

Comprehension flooded Imogenia's angry gaze. "That's why you came tonight."

Not a question, but Evalle answered, "Part of the reason. Make a decision. I have another commitment tonight."

"Deal."

Evalle waited as Imogenia told the Domjon she'd reached an agreement to spare her fighter. The Domjon reminded Imogenia she would not be free to leave the fight zone until Evalle gave him thumbs-up that the deal was satisfied.

Evalle called over to Storm. "Let the Alterant live."

The crowd booed, but from the looks of this crowd there'd be more blood spilled before long.

All was moving along nicely until Storm turned demon-yellow eyes to Evalle. She had a disconcerting moment as he hesitated to step off Bernie. Was Storm caught up in a moment of bloodlust? Would she have to walk out there to stop him?

Did a sponsor do that?

He finally jumped off the Alterant and walked over to his jeans, where he shifted back into human form on all fours.

Evalle's lungs relaxed. Storm had just been putting on a show for the crowd.

Imogenia called out to Bernie, but she spoke in a language Evalle couldn't identify. After several moments of sluggish movements, the Alterant shifted back into his body, panting by the time he was done. He pushed to his feet, but with no clothes to put on he huddled into himself as he crossed the open ground to Imogenia.

She tilted her head at a spot behind her near the outer perimeter of the event area and ordered Bernie, "Wait for me by that tree."

Once Storm had his jeans on, he swaggered back across the ring to Evalle.

He deserved to swagger after that win.

When he stepped out of the ring and turned to lift his shirt, Evalle gritted her teeth at the blood leaking from slashed skin on his back. Storm had some majik and preternatural ability that allowed him to heal faster than a human, but she hated seeing him hurt.

Imogenia watched Evalle's every move, so Evalle made a show of passing a clinical assessment over his body before she gave a dismissive shrug and turned her attention back to Imogenia. "Let's find a secure place to talk."

Leading the way, Imogenia picked a spot beneath several towering pine trees and gave Storm a pointed look when she asked, "What about your fighter?"

Dressed again, Storm took up his place next to Evalle and crossed his arms, a silent sentry. Evalle said, "He stays."

"Very well." Imogenia lifted her arms, whispering as she turned in a circle. When she stopped, she said, "I've used a spell to guard the others from observing us or hearing our words."

Evalle turned to the witch. "What do you know about Tristan?"

"He's an Alterant working for the Medb."

So the Medb were feeding that lie into the rumor mills, huh? Evalle shook her head and scoffed. "Tell me something I don't know."

Imogenia toyed with a silvery-white strand of hair. "He's building an Alterant team of fighters."

Could that be true? "Alterants are harder to find than a trustworthy deity."

"Tell me about it. Why are you looking for Tristan?"

Evalle could have shut down the witch by refusing to answer, but it was better to give her the information Evalle wanted repeated instead of leaving her to speculate. "I'm going to be generous and answer your question in spite of owning *both* fighters right now."

Tension stiffened Imogenia's posture, but she kept her tongue still, waiting on Evalle's answer.

"Tristan left in a hurry the last time I saw him, slipped away before he paid a debt I intend to collect." Evalle cast a look over Bernie's dejected form. "Where'd you find your Alterant?"

"Not far from here, but I don't have to tell you where, since that wasn't part of the *deal*."

"In that case, let's get back to what I want. Is there a way into TÅµr Medb undetected?"

Imogenia snickered. "I can't tell you that."

"Looks like we're done then."

"I didn't say I *wouldn't*, I said I couldn't."

Evalle turned to Storm. "Is she telling the truth?"

He gave it a second, then nodded.

Imogenia leaned forward, staring at Storm. "You want me to believe he can detect a lie?"

"Believe what you want, but lie to me one time and I'm walking away with your Alterant." Evalle regretted having to leave Bernie with Imogenia, but Storm had taken this risk to get information she needed. She wouldn't waste it. She'd search for Bernie later, once she got Tristan back.

At this rate, she'd need business cards soon for Evalle's Alterant Rescue.

She continued her interrogation. "I heard you planned to trade your Alterant to the Medb."

Inside the eye slits of her mask, Imogenia's gaze narrowed with menace. "Who told you about that?"

That had been a guess. "Let's revisit the fact that *I'm* not the one answering questions. How'd you intend to meet with the Medb if you don't know where TÅµr Medb is?"

"Same way as everyone else looking to cut a deal," Imogenia said with a wave of her hands, indicating this was common knowledge. "At the ABC."

Evalle debated admitting she didn't know what Imogenia referenced, but the minute Evalle left this venue she lost her best shot at intel. Go strong or go home. She raked a hand over her head. "ABC?"

"You don't know?" Imogenia enjoyed a smug moment. "The Achilles Beast Championship."

"Championship fights. Where? When?"

Time slid by as Imogenia debated something. "Tomorrow night. Cumberland Island."

Three hundred plus miles away, just off the southeast corner of Georgia, but Evalle would gain more information by sounding unfamiliar with the area. "Where's that? We've just arrived from Brazil a couple days ago."

Imogenia nodded and seemed to relax. "I was wondering why I hadn't heard about you . . . or *him* around the beast fights. Can't be too careful these days." She explained about accessing Cumberland Island by ferry from a town called St. Marys at the farthest southeast corner of Georgia on the Atlantic coast.

Evalle cast a look over at Storm but spoke to Imogenia.

"Is that what the Domjon meant by the big game?"

"Yes."

"What's the buy-in for the ABC?"

"They want strong competition. Sponsors of dual forms and Alterants need a Volonte as buy-in, but any Alterant *without* a sponsor gets in for free. All others negotiate at the door."

"What's a Volonte?"

"I didn't agree to be your private tutor on all things powerful."

Evalle let silence fill in the next moment until Imogenia made a noise in her throat that sounded like rocks being ground. "Volonte are bones from the grave of the sorcier Guillory."

"And," Evalle prompted before she strangled the witch for feeding out information in tiny pieces, "who was this sorcerer?"

Imogenia made a dramatic show of "whatever" with her hands. "Guillory died in France in the tenth century. When his followers stole his body and reburied him, many thought it nothing more than grave robbers who were after the spell-casting rings he wore on his hands. That was until just over a year ago, when an archaeological dig uncovered his grave and identified him by the rings bearing the Guillory crest. Then his body disappeared again several weeks back. Those of us who *are* informed know his body was stolen for the bones."

Those of us meant dark witches. Evalle turned to Storm, who drew in a slow breath, then nodded. "She's telling the truth." But he clearly didn't trust her. "What makes these bones valuable?"

Imogenia looked to Evalle, who shoved the look right back at her. "Answer his question."

No doubt surprised at being addressed by someone the witch considered nothing more than a glorified slave, Imogenia shrugged it off. "Any of his bones have power, but the ones from Guillory's hands still carry *his* power. In the hands of a skilled owner, a Volonte provides power over spirits and demons. For example, if I wanted to speak to the dead, the bones of his index finger would give me the power of necromancy. Guillory delivered kingdoms to kings . . . until he slept with a ruler's favorite mistress."

Imogenia sliced a finger across her neck. "Heads roll when that sort of thing happens. Guillory's body was found headless."

Evalle didn't care about a sorcerer who couldn't keep his pants zipped, tied or whatever they did back then. "How many of those bones could be floating around?"

"Not many, since they're illegal to trade."

"Then they can't be expecting a high turnout at the ABC."

"Oh, but they are." Imogenia preened at being the one in the know. "With the Medb making a show and cutting deals prior to the matches, they expect a very high turnout."

If not for the excitement buzzing in Imogenia's voice, that would be great news about finally locating a concentrated group of Alterants.

"What's the payoff for an Alterant sponsor?"

"Plenty if my Alterant makes it to the final round."

This was going to take all night. "The more specific you are and the quicker you answer my questions, the better chance you'll have of leaving with Bernie."

Behind Imogenia's mask, her eyes flared with anger, and her fingers curled again, as if she had claws, which she didn't. She stretched her neck and gave her shoulders a little shake, then lifted her fingers to toy with the sparkling fire-opal pendant caught in the valley between her breasts. After taking a breath, she finally started rattling off specifics.

"Stakes are highest for the Alterant matches. If your Alterant dies, you're out of the competition, but the last five to survive the finale Elite rounds earn the sponsor a chance to negotiate a trade with the Medb."

Imogenia didn't have to spell it out any better.

Every dark witch on the planet salivated at the idea of gaining Noirre majik knowledge from the Medb. Handing over Noirre spells to five black witches powerful enough to have acquired Alterants would be like trading the plans for a nuclear bomb to the top five terrorists in the human world, *and* supplying the uranium.

Right before the Medb captured Tristan, he told Evalle the Medb were hunting Alterants to use in a plan against the Beladors. What a brilliant way to capture the Alterants. Let everyone else do their work by holding a competition with high stakes.

Rescuing Tristan and his group, which included his sister, Petrina, and two friends, had just gotten more complicated. Now Evalle had to also figure a way of preventing the Medb from taking possession of those Alterant fighters entered in the Achilles Beast Championship.

But Imogenia could have lost her Alterant tonight.

Evalle asked, "Why risk your fighter here?"

"I don't have to answer—"

Storm cut in. "To train him."

Imogenia sliced a mean look at Storm and muttered, "*I* wouldn't tolerate insolence."

Evalle ignored her. "What about the Alterants without sponsors? What are they fighting for?"

"Oh, all five of the top Alterants are also offered a chance to escape persecution and become immortal warriors."

If Evalle hadn't been clenching her teeth up to this point, her jaw would have dropped. The chance for immortality should bring in any loner Alterants.

Was that why Tristan had signed on with the Medb? *If* he had?

Evalle asked, "Do you have more than one Alterant?"

"No."

No reaction from Storm, so that had to be the truth. Now what? Use the intel tip Evalle had been hoarding to trade with? She cast a thoughtful glance over at Bernie. "I doubt I'll run across any sacred bones before the ABC, and I do plan to enter, so I may have to take your Alterant after all."

"No. I answered your questions." Energy sizzled around Imogenia. Her hair lifted away from her shoulders and body and her shoulders shook, but Evalle couldn't pin down if the reaction was from fear or anger.

Her senses picked up paranoia . . . and worry. How often would any witch have a chance to get Noirre majik from the Medb without risk to her person? Evalle said, "No, you haven't answered all my questions. You don't even know how to access TÅµr Medb. I'm not feeling satisfied."

But Imogenia had to be planning to show up with a Volonte bone to get her Alterant in. If Evalle could get her hands on that, she'd have a way for herself and another VIPER member to enter the championship undercover. As an Alterant, Evalle could enter for free *if* she entered as a fighter. But she couldn't do that unless she wanted to die, since she was forbidden from fully shifting. A Volonte would guarantee her access if she had someone else with her.

Someone other than Storm.

No more death fights for him. Evalle would not allow him to put his life at risk for her again, and definitely not for VIPER. Sen could choose who went in undercover as a fighter.

Imogenia worried the chain holding her pendant. "What else do you want to know?"

Evalle crossed her arms, tapping a thumb against her bicep. "To be honest, I'd rather enter my shifter in the ABC than your Alterant, so here's the deal—I keep your Alterant until you bring me a Volonte bone, then you get Bernie back. Simple as a pawn deal."

Imogenia released her necklace and fisted her hands.

When she spoke, it was in a voice meant to raise the hair on any living creature. "He's *my* Alterant."

The witch must be drinking her own cauldron brews. She was jumpy as a crack house junkie.

Imogenia took a ragged breath and, on the exhale, calmed down but still threatened, "If I go to the Domjon and he believes you're dealing in bad faith, he'll rule in my favor. If that happens, I walk away with both fighters."

Ah, crap. *If I back off now, she'll know she has me and turn the tables.* In spite of that threat freezing the blood in her veins, Evalle forced a confident expression and responded as if nothing mattered. "Maybe, but what if he doesn't? You'll lose your Alterant for sure, because I *won't* continue to negotiate at that point."

Imogenia became very still.

Evalle pressed her slight advantage. "Seems like you'd know where to get a bone if you were all set on entering Bernie. If you can't tell me how to get into TÅμr Medb and you don't have a bone, we're at a stalemate for a satisfied deal."

Imogenia spent the next few seconds stewing until her mask lit up, a bright, blinding white. When her mask settled down to a soft glow, she released a stream of air from between clenched teeth and said, "I *have* a Volonte."

"Where?"

"Here."

No way. This was too good. "Show it to me."

Imogenia raised her forearm that sported an armband woven of gold and bronze threads. It smelled old and strangely alluring.

Evalle and Storm leaned forward at the same time. A small bone that could be from the tip of a man's pinky finger had been caught inside a web of crisscrossed bronze threads.

Sounding more like a witch in control, Imogenia said, "Make me a *worthy* trade and I'll give you the bone *if* you'll declare this deal satisfied."

"What do you want?"

"A strand of hair."

Storm's jaw flexed against the "*No*" Evalle knew he wanted to shout. She laughed at Imogenia, making it clear she thought the suggestion stupid. "As if I'd give you something you can use against me?"

"I use hair for many things. It's not always about the donor."

"Tell you what. I'll give you something better."

"Such as?"

"The name of a witch in your coven who wants to take over and intends to use you for a blood sacrifice to do it."

The witch's mouth dropped open in shock. "You're lying."

"No, I'm not, *Imogenia*," Evalle emphasized. "I'll prove it. In your last Carretta Coven meeting, one of your witches sacrificed the wrong animal. A wolf you had other plans for."

"How could you—"

"Let's not waste time asking who told me that or

how I know your name. I needed something to trade for information that I heard you had on Tristan and the Medb. Do you have anything else to tell me about those two?"

"No."

Evalle checked Storm, who lifted his chin, confirming the witch wasn't jerking Evalle around. She turned back to Imogenia. "I'll make a final offer. You hand over the bone. I give you the witch's name. We call it even. Bernie leaves with you."

"Agreed."

Storm asked, "How will you get your Alterant into the ABC?"

Imogenia smiled. "I have a source. Now, I want that traitor's name." Fury seething in Imogenia's eyes this time was clearly for the traitor.

"The bone first."

"This armband must be given and accepted. You have to want the Volonte. Do you want it, and do you accept possession once I take it off?"

Storm growled in aggravation, but Evalle rolled her eyes and said, "Yes. Can we get on with this?"

"Your arm must be free of tattoos, piercings, jewelry, anything from the elbow to your fingers." When Evalle shoved her sleeve back, showing that she had nothing but bare arm, Imogenia lifted her arm and whispered, "I am gifting you to another. Release." The armband unclasped, dropping into the witch's waiting hand.

Evalle held out her palm to accept the jewelry.

Imogenia slapped the armband on Evalle's forearm, and the clasp clicked shut.

Storm moved as fast as a thrown dagger, grabbing the witch by her throat. He lifted her off the ground. "Get it off of her *now!*"

Everything around Evalle blurred at the edges.

Imogenia flailed her arms, eyes bulging. She squeezed out, "She . . . she . . ."

Evalle stared at the band locked on her arm and had the strangest relaxed sensation, as if nothing was an issue. She didn't feel any tingling or power sensation, just a sense that all channels were open and flowing in her body.

A gurgling noise drew her attention from the armband to Imogenia's mouth, which was pulsing like that of a fish out of water gasping for air.

Evalle shook her head and everything came back into focus. She didn't know the rules of a Beast Club, but she doubted she and Storm would walk out of here alive if he killed a sponsor. She touched his arm. "Put her down. The armband isn't doing anything to me."

He reluctantly lowered Imogenia until the woman's kicking feet hit dirt, but he kept his fingers around her throat and demanded, "Why do you smell of licorice?"

"What?" Imogenia's eyes were still bulging. "Incense. Bought it."

He growled at Imogenia, "Take off the armband and *hand* her the finger bone."

Imogenia coughed and sputtered.

Evalle said, "Let her breathe, Storm."

When he released the witch reluctantly, Evalle told Imogenia, "Now take it off."

Imogenia rubbed her neck, then held up shaky fingers. "Give me a chance to explain. The bone was already woven into the armband when it was gifted to me and can't be removed. The gold and bronze is five centuries old and protects the Volonte powers." Nodding at Evalle, Imogenia continued, "She'll have to free the armband the same way when she hands it over to the next owner or the bone will attack her. It resents being stolen. Every time it moves from one person to the next, it must be passed as a gift or it attacks both the new owner and the previous one. And—" Imogenia's eyes smirked at Storm. "If you give it to a shifter, they can't shift."

A pet bone with emotional issues. Just what Evalle needed. "Can I take it off to shower or go to bed?"

"No. The Volonte will retaliate if you try to remove it for any reason other than gifting the armband to a person who accepts it."

"Retaliate how?"

"You'll be blinded." Imogenia looked at Storm, whose chest moved up and down with angry breaths. "I'm telling the truth."

"What else do I need to know about this thing?" Evalle asked, eyeing the creepy armband.

Imogenia must not have answered quickly enough to suit Storm. He growled at her and the witch started issuing instructions. "Before you give it away, you have to take full possession by telling the bone it belongs to you."

Evalle felt heat around her wrist. "When?"

"Sooner than later. It will get hot when it's angry to the point of a burn scar if you wait too long. Then the bone will burn through your arm. Once that starts, your body begins to die. Is it warm yet?"

"Yes," Evalle hissed.

"Then talk to it."

"I can't believe I have to—" The skin on her arm felt as though she held it in a flame. "Okay." Evalle lifted the bone into view. "You belong to me." She'd read her horoscope in the paper this morning.

There hadn't been one word about owning slave fighters or sentient cadaver bones.

Imogenia continued her directives. "When you're ready to hand off the Volonte, do the same thing I did. Just tell the bone that you're giving it as a gift, then order it to release *and* put the armband on the arm of the new owner."

Storm stared at Evalle's arm, then warned Imogenia in a low voice, "If that bone harms her, expect to see me again."

"If she does what I told her, she'll be fine."

He wasn't sold. "Did you give her that armband to harm her in any way?"

"No."

"How will it affect her?"

"Unless she uses it in the dark arts, this bone's power will only enhance her desire for whatever she wants." Imogenia shoved her attention back to Evalle. "Now, you owe me a name."

How could enhancing be harmful? Other than that

one moment, Evalle still didn't feel anything playing around with her Belador powers, so she told Imogenia, "The traitor is Daniella."

"That evil, backstabbing bitch." Imogenia waved her hands and muttered a string of words, then turned to Evalle. "I've cleared the shielding spell. We're done."

When the witch took a step to leave, Evalle said, "One more thing."

"*What?*" Imogenia snarled, hair whipping around when she spun to face Evalle and Storm.

VIPER needed the name of the person who'd be offering the trade at the games, the person who would spend eternity locked away for dealing Noirre majik. "Who's negotiating on behalf of the Medb for the five Alterants at the end of the ABC?"

"Tristan. He's in charge of all Alterants for the Medb."

Tristan? "You held that back."

"I did not. Thought you knew that. It's common knowledge."

"How will anyone believe him?"

Imogenia muttered something to herself. "Do I look like your tour guide?"

Evalle took a menacing step toward her and said, "Do I look like someone with patience?"

Imogenia didn't cower, but she did back down in a silent standoff.

"I didn't agree not to warn Daniella that you're coming for her," Evalle pointed out. "You tell me why anyone would accept the Medb's word and how I find the ABC location, Daniella's all yours."

That got through to Imogenia. "The Medb are sponsoring this championship and have given a blood oath to back their offer. Plus, the Medb are sending a woman with Tristan and she'll be ordered to state the agreement the Medb have made under a truth test. If she fails the test, she'll die on the spot, but the host is not saying any more than that so there's no way to prepare for the truth test."

"And access to Cumberland?"

Imogenia muttered to herself about dragging this out. "The host will arrange for boats that carry nonhumans, and those boats will know where to go. I don't know the pickup point yet, but the source who told me about this Beast Club is finding out for me, so ask *your* source."

Evalle didn't have a source except Grady. If he'd known any more, he'd have told her.

Not waiting for another comment from Evalle, Imogenia waved at the Domjon to get his attention.

When his gaze shot to Evalle, she lifted her thumb up, signaling they'd reached an agreement. How was she going to find out the pickup point?

The witch strode off in a huff.

Evalle turned to Storm. "Tristan wouldn't work for the Medb."

Storm's attention stayed on the witch, who slowed long enough to drag poor, naked Bernie to his feet, then exited the fight camp. "She *was* telling the truth, but even I'm surprised at Tristan helping the Medb. Maybe he's suffering from Stockholm syndrome."

"Or Tristan may be compelled, but without any way

of proving it, he'll be as guilty as the Medb once he does this."

She had the sudden urge to hunt down Kizira, the Medb priestess who'd captured Tristan, and choke her until she released him. What had Quinn ever seen in Kizira? As Quinn's best friend, Evalle tried to be open-minded about Quinn's mysterious history with the Medb priestess, but he was a Belador who deserved a woman worthy of him. He shouldn't be friends with the enemy, and Evalle would tell him the next time she saw him.

The Medb were a bunch of murdering witches and warlocks who deserved to die slowly. Fury blazed through her, demanding justice. Now.

"Evalle?" Storm asked softly. "What's wrong?"

At the sound of his voice, she blinked, surprised she'd forgotten he was standing there, or where she was for that matter. She never lost touch, especially in a danger-ous environment. It grated on her that she had this time, which came through her voice when she answered with a sharp, "Nothing's wrong."

Storm studied her with concern. "Did you forget that you can't lie to me?"

Well, yes.

She pinched the bridge of her nose, confused at the burst of anger. Storm was right earlier when he said she needed sleep. "Sorry. Just worried about Tristan. And his sister. And his two friends captured with him." She looked around. "Can we leave now that you've fought someone?"

Storm studied her an extra second, then said, "We're done once we tell the Domjon we'll forfeit so Zymon's beast can win my category."

"Let's get out of here. I need to figure out some things." Like how she was going to convince anyone to help Tristan now.

VIPER, Macha and the Beladors would expect her to hunt Tristan and any other Alterant aligned with the Medb. Evalle had to get inside the beast championship— without Storm involved—and convince Tristan to leave with her.

She might as well bet on world peace as long as she was going for long shots.

FIVE

Hiking a mile up one side of a mountain then back down the other side at three in the morning in the face of a chilly breeze should have taken the edge off of Storm's frustration.

But, no, he still wanted to rip something to pieces.

Evalle's emotions had been flying around from anger to worry to irritation to anxiety to fury to something that felt very much like desire.

That last one might bring on the "Hallelujah Chorus" if not for his concern over her unusual roller-coaster emotions.

Evalle looked over at him, gaze dropping to the belt he now wore again. "You never told me what that stone from your belt buckle was worth."

Not going to either. "It's replaceable." But she wasn't, and that bone put her at risk. He groused, "That armband is coming off tonight."

"No, it's not," Evalle argued. "You heard Imogenia. I can only give it to someone who wants it."

"I'll take it."

"You don't want this thing. You couldn't shift into your jaguar form with this locked on your arm."

"You can't shift either," he pointed out.

"I'm not supposed to unless I want to face a Tribunal

hearing or get torched by Macha, so there's no harm in it being on my arm." She stalked along beside him. "It's fine, Storm. *I'm* fine."

"No, you're *not*. You lost contact with me *and* your surroundings back there. I could feel the aggression rolling off of you." He had his own aggression he'd like to release and nowhere to point it. "You're wearing an armband with an artifact that can control spirits. We have no idea if that bone can do anything to the host owner."

Evalle grumbled back, her voice as weary as her movements. "I'm tired and irritated, that's all. I just found out that Tristan's in a worse jam than I thought, and I'm not sure how to help him now."

"That worthless Alterant is going to get you killed." If that happened, Tristan would need the entire Medb Coven at his side when Storm went after him. "I know what you're thinking."

"Oh, really? You're telepathic *now*?"

She hadn't been this antagonistic since they first met, but he ignored the bite in her voice that a few hours of sleep *might* help. "You're planning on going into that beast championship, which is the last place you should be. The Medb are actively looking for Alterants, and you already know they're after you and don't need to see your neon green eyes to recognize you on sight." He shook his head.

"My choice."

He would not snap at her. She didn't mean to sound so cold and distant. It was the Volonte bone and exhaustion. "What if Tristan signed on voluntarily with the dark side?"

"I have to give him the benefit of the doubt, a chance to walk away."

"And what if he hands you over to them?"

She walked along silently for another minute, then said, "He won't do that."

Her sense of loyalty was both admirable and damned irritating, because she gave it to someone who didn't deserve the sacrifice she would make. "If you're determined to go into the games, I'll be your fighter."

"No. You're not risking your life again for this. It's not your problem."

Storm stopped.

When she did, too, and turned to him, he cupped her chin and cheek with his hand. "That's *my* choice. You need a way to get inside the ABC and unload that armband. If you're going in, then I'm going with you."

"I have an idea of what to do."

"Take that armband to VIPER?"

Wind whistled through the trees and swirled loose hairs around Evalle's face. She swiped them out of her eyes. "Not exactly. I can't just walk into VIPER and say I happened upon a Beast Club fighting ring and forgot to call it in, then entered my own fighter in the battles. Oh, and I ended up with a stolen Volonte bone to boot."

"So what is your plan?"

"First I have to tell Macha what I've learned."

Storm groaned. "Those conversations always end up with you bloody, owing her more, or both."

Her voice was calm as she explained, "Not this time. I've found where Alterants will be congregating. Macha wants the Alterants found and Tristan to tell us what he knows about Alterant origins. I'll point out to her that I had to go into the Beast Club tonight to see Imogenia because of my obligation to her. She's got pull with VIPER. If she informs them about the Beast Club, they won't question how she knows."

Good point, *if* he trusted that goddess. *Not a bit.* "What about the armband?"

"She can tell VIPER she's sending it into headquarters on my arm, which would be true, and that someone needs to take the armband to keep the Volonte safe. That should get this thing off my arm immediately, since Sen wouldn't trust me with a magical paper clip."

Storm had to admit that Evalle had thought this through and hoped that meant she was gaining control of the bone.

She finished, "Once VIPER knows what's going on, they can use the armband to send in a covert team."

Call him cynical, but that still sounded too easy.

Storm started walking toward his truck again. It should be in sight any time now. "Sen may bar you from being on the covert team that goes into the ABC." One could only hope.

Evalle fell into step with him again. "Not if Macha demands that I'm on the team, and you know she will, so that I can get to Tristan and maybe some of the other Alterants."

"I'm still going with you."

"You're no longer with VIPER, and Sen may not take you back."

True and true, but Evalle needed someone else to watch her back besides Tzader and Quinn. Those two Beladors cared for her as if she were a little sister, but they couldn't watch only her on an op. Storm could and would.

He offered, "We'll cross that bridge when we get to it."

She made a gritty noise that might be an agreement. "How's your back?"

He let her change the subject. "Fine."

"I'll want to see it."

"You know I'll heal by the time—"

"I *said* I want to see it," she said with determination, which probably came from worry.

Okay, Miss Cranky. "Fine. When we get to the truck." She picked up the pace down the rolling elevation to the foot of the mountain, where pine trees swayed in the breeze.

Evalle reached the sport-utility vehicle and turned to him with a stubborn look burning in her eyes. She knew he could draw on his jaguar powers to heal and had already started the process, but she had that single-minded look, and he wanted her calm for the drive back so she might sleep. She'd had no real rest in over three days.

Reaching his SUV, Storm opened the door to the back seat on the driver's side, shrugged out of his jacket, then tossed it in. No interior lights came on.

He'd disconnected those for situations just like this one.

It would have been simpler to wait until he got home

to remove his shirt and use a healing chant to aid his powers in sealing the cuts, but the smell of his blood might be bothering her, reminding her of the fight, so he yanked off his shirt, ripping open the scab that had already formed.

She walked around to the passenger side and pulled out a bottle of water from the console. When she returned to his side, she snagged the shirt from his hand and ordered, "Turn around."

Any other time, he'd find her bossiness sexy, but there'd been nothing playful in her tone. Worry poured off of her in angry waves.

The things a man did for a woman.

He complied, closing the door, then putting his crossed arms against the top of the car and leaning on them.

She grumbled under her breath about how letting him fight was stupid. Just as he'd thought, she was stressing over his fight with the Alterant.

Water sloshed behind him, then the wet rag brushed gently across his back. He still flinched from the cold contact. Good thing he kept an extra change of clothes in his truck. While he let her clean off the blood, he tried to be at ease with her attention, but just having her hands so close to him raised an interest he'd be hard-pressed to hide soon. He hadn't been injured enough to warrant this much concern. The cuts were more nuisance than serious for him and she knew that.

Evalle didn't nurture, but like everything else she did when she cared about someone, it was all or none. That meant she'd dive into battle with any creature if it meant protecting the ones who mattered to her.

But she was no Florence Nightingale.

Not that he was complaining.

Especially when her fingers grazed his skin.

Heat blazed a trail from his back to his groin from just that slight touch.

No longer grouching at him, she moved the rag over his skin slowly in what she probably thought was a soothing way, but having her touch him was killing him. He stayed in perpetual arousal around her as it was.

Shutting his eyes, he tried to focus on the cold mountain air, the soft breeze, anything but how much he wanted her hands everywhere on his skin. This was neither the time nor the place. *Tell your body that.*

The rag disappeared.

Her hands slid up his back, slowly, inching her way to his shoulders.

Really?

He froze, straining not to flex muscles that urged him to push against her hands. Her warm touch crawled up his neck, fingers gliding through his hair, then moving back over his shoulders and along his arms. She paused, then placed her hands on each side of his waist.

His lungs tightened, holding his next breath while he waited to see what she'd do.

In the past few weeks, she'd become more trusting of his advances, more open to the first stages of passion, but her instigating this much touching was unexpected.

Her fingers slid around front to where she ran her hands over his stomach.

That brought her chest to his back.

Her breasts nudged him.

Blood surged in his groin.

His heart beat out of control. He'd known this moment when she'd be ready for intimacy was coming, but damn, he hadn't wanted it out here in the woods.

What had brought out her amorous side tonight? Seeing Storm so close to being killed? He'd envisioned her naked in front of a roaring fire or spread across his bed or under a rush of water in his shower.

She hugged him.

Her fingers inched up to hook his shoulders.

Sweat beaded on his forehead. He had to be careful with his next move. Someone had hurt her physically in the past, to the point that she avoided intimacy. She was afraid of losing control of her beast and killing him. He'd intended to spend hours when the time was right, taking it slow, halting the minute she showed any sign of panic.

But not here.

With natural and unnatural creatures roaming this mountain, this was the last place he would lower his guard to put all his attention on her.

On the other hand, if he stopped her now, she'd feel rejected.

She kissed his back and moved her fingers down to toy with his nipples. Erotic chills skittered across his skin. He shook with the effort of holding back, caught in indecision. His heart thudded each beat, a fist pounding his chest. If he got any harder he'd burst out of his jeans.

Easing away from the truck, he lifted his arms and turned slowly until he had her wrapped up against him.

She laughed and the sound floated around him, warming his heart when she hugged him back.

This was the woman he wanted with all his being.

When she lifted her head, her eyes were hidden behind the dark sunglasses. She could take those off with so little moonlight filtering down through the trees above them. But he didn't need to see her eyes to know she was happy. Pleasure flowed from her, wafting across his empathic senses.

Then her desire rushed around him, flooding his senses as if released from a gate.

Hell, yes, he wanted this. Wanted her.

She licked his chest and he shuddered.

Protecting the hellion came first, but that didn't mean they couldn't indulge in a few minutes of play. He'd scent anyone long before they got close.

Slowly, carefully as always, he lowered his head and kissed her. His lips melded with hers. His kisses had been the one pleasure she'd taken to enthusiastically from the start, even when they'd first met as adversaries. Holding her head, he turned her gently for better access, deepening the kiss little by little.

Energy surged through his veins. His jaguar growled for more. To mark her as his.

To mate.

But Evalle's skin was hot, so hot it felt combustible, and that had *him* thinking about combusting.

Evalle's passion ignited suddenly.

She grabbed his hair, yanking him closer and kissing him as though fire roared through her blood. She ground her hips against him, rubbing the rigid erection already aching inside his pants.

He clenched his jaw and groaned at the throbbing.

That was his Evalle, never halfway in on anything. She finally trusted him enough to let go and explore what had sizzled between them for weeks. Felt like eons.

He loved her mouth, gorged himself on her.

Don't rush her.

Just one more step forward for now. Holding her head with one hand, he moved his other to tug the bottom of her T-shirt free and slide his hand up silky skin. She shivered as he caressed his way up to . . . her sweet breast. No bra. Mercy.

His thumb brushed across the beaded tip and she sucked in a harsh breath. "Oh, yesss."

Damn right. He kissed her with raw passion, no holding back. A kiss that told her everything he wanted to do to her, and more. Her tongue danced with his in a sensual tangle. His fingers played with one breast then the other until she was shaking with need.

Hell, *he* was shaking with need.

An earthy moan escaped her. Another sound like that and he'd drop to his knees and give her everything she wanted. She hissed and arched her hips forward, and every muscle in his body clenched when she brushed his erection with bold intention. She bit his lip gently, then licked it, soothing any pain. Heat built low and pooled in his balls.

She was so potent that touching her was killing brain cells by the second.

He had to slow down or he'd rip her clothes off right here and now. Just as he lifted his head to catch a breath and suggest they make plans to go horizontal in a comfortable spot at home, she unsnapped his jeans and shoved her hand inside to grasp him.

"Holy shit!" He couldn't breathe.

Wicked intentions bubbled in her laugh.

She stroked up and down.

He shuddered, fighting against the climax threatening to explode through him, and grabbed her wrist. *Hold it, Houston. We've got a problem.*

Pulling her hand up, he understood the meaning of agony when her fingers released him.

Lust clouded his mind.

He had to think. Hard to do when not a drop of blood stayed in his brain with a party going on in his crotch.

"What's wrong?" she demanded.

At least she hadn't sounded hurt, like he expected. He grabbed her by the shoulders and gently, but firmly, pushed her arm's length away. "Hold on a minute."

"I *had* a good grip. You're the one who made me let go." She reached toward his still unzipped pants again, a smug smile curling her lips.

He tightened his grip and shook her. "Whoa."

Damn, he couldn't believe he was stopping her, but Evalle wouldn't be this aggressive.

Not the first time.

She shoved away from him. "Make up your mind if you want it or not. I don't have all night."

Who was this woman, and how did she get inside Evalle's body? That damned bone had to be influencing her. He'd know whether or not he was talking to *his* Evalle if he could see her eyes. "Take your glasses off."

"What kind of bullshit is that? You wanting to screw a beast? I'll have to shift for the full effect."

Warning signals blared in his head. There were so many things wrong with that statement that he didn't know where to start counting.

First, Evalle had cursed. She never cursed. Brina, the Belador warrior queen, forbade it. More than that, she'd described exactly how this felt, as if this was just screwing. More than that, to even suggest she'd shift into her beast form was insane.

He repeated slowly, "Please take your glasses off."

She snatched off her glasses. Green eyes glowed in her face, standard for an Alterant, but a fog dimmed her glowing eyes, as if she had glazed vision.

Just as he'd thought. That bone. He had to figure out . . .

She slapped the glasses against her leg. "Now, you want to get back to it, or do I have to go find someone more willing?"

The streak of jealousy that shot through him drove a feral growl from the depths of his chest.

Evalle blinked, face rigid with anger, then she stepped back and stomped her boots, releasing hidden blades.

Oh, boy. Here came the warrior.

He had to get himself under control first, which was no small effort with his body begging for release and her standing there offering him what he'd dreamed about every night he *had* slept recently. He held up a hand, asking her silently to give him a minute, then scrubbed his hands over his face. *Think.*

That wasn't Evalle talking.

In *his* fantasy she wanted sex any time of day.

She kept slapping her sunglasses impatiently against her thigh, drawing his eyes down her arm.

How was he going to get that damned bone off her arm? He didn't know, but in the meantime he had to help her gain control. Taking another breath to bring a calm he didn't feel to his words, he told her, "The armband is influencing you, Evalle."

She glared at him and huffed out a chesty breath of aggravation. "If you don't want me, just say so. Don't give me lame excuses."

As if. "Oh, I want you, sweetheart, but not like this."

Seeing a glimmer of the woman he knew, whose eyes softened when he called her sweetheart, gave him a boost of encouragement, but this wasn't settled yet. "I want you so much I ache, but I want you when *you're* the only one making the decisions."

Her eyes turned stony with threat. "I *am* making the decisions. If we're done here, I'm heading out to find someone who'll satisfy me. Stay out of my way or I'll hurt you."

Definitely not Evalle talking.

Storm kept a lid on his rage this time, but she *would*

act on her words—over his dead body—if he didn't get her out of this situation for now.

He could end up bloody trying to get her to listen, but he had to help her get a rein on her emotions. "You don't have to look for someone else." He used his most accommodating voice, then added in a husky tone, "I'll take care of you."

She grinned at him as if he'd just agreed to be her full-time man toy.

Talk about missed opportunities.

Could he temporarily block the bone's influence long enough to get through to the real Evalle? Maybe, *if* she gave him the time he needed for the spell to work. But if she figured out what he was doing too soon, she might go from being aroused to furious. That could end with her shifting into her beast and killing him, because he would cut his arms off before he harmed her.

Smiling to keep up the charade, he said, "Ready for something special?"

Her eyes glowed brighter, almost as bright as the dazzling smile she gave him. "Absolutely. Bring it."

"Then close your eyes and cover your ears with your hands."

That earned him a confused frown. "Why?"

"Closing off your senses heightens your sensitivity to touch." True, but he was playing on her sexual naïveté. She might be able to kill a demon six different ways, but she'd had very little experience with men.

"Oh. Okay." Hooking her glasses in the opening of

her shirt, she slapped her hands over her ears and closed her eyes.

As if the real Evalle would go along with anything that easily?

Keeping his voice soft, he immediately started chanting words he'd learned among the Ashaninka tribe where he'd grown up, and moved in a slow circle around her.

By the time he reached her front again, her smile had deteriorated into a flat line of discontent. A crease formed at the bridge of her nose with her concentration.

His words were getting past her hands. She was hearing him.

Her eyes flew open, glaring with promise of retaliation. She dropped her hands and balled them into fists. "You lied to me."

He kept chanting, his voice growing stronger.

It wasn't working.

Storm could feel the bone's power fighting him, trying to push him away. Moving back a step out of her reach, he shouted native words in his chant, telling the bone, "You can't have her. She's *mine*."

She took a step toward him, fists cocked. "Stop it. I told you to *never* use your majik on me."

True. He'd just broken his word, but he'd do far worse to guard her from harm. His chants were loud now, harsh, biting sounds he forced power into, rushing the spell.

"Damn you!" She dove at him, hands stretched out toward his neck.

Just as he raised his arms to deflect her hands, Evalle's face changed in midflight from fury to confusion. He caught her when she fell against him, limp from the sudden loss of the unknown power. Chugging in deep breaths, he lifted her up and hugged her close, whispering words to soothe her.

She panted and trembled as if she'd run to the top of Mount Everest.

Their hearts beat in a staccato, so fast he couldn't tell his from hers. She got her footing and tightened her grip on his arms, then pushed up to bear her own weight. He let her ease back, but he held on, watching a mix of emotions flash through her eyes until one came through clearly. Humiliation.

Damn that witch to an eternal hell.

He couldn't let go of Evalle yet, not with her looking at him as though she'd degraded herself.

She drew in a deep breath and said, "That was—"

"Not you, sweetheart. It's that freakin' bone. It started to influence you as soon as it wrapped around your arm back at the Beast Club."

Evalle looked down at her wrist then back at him. "What's it doing?"

"Imogenia said unless you intended to use it for dark arts it *only* enhances your desire. I'm guessing it amplifies or boosts your intention to get what you want. I think when you want something, the bone drives more power into that want until it overrides everything else, demanding you fulfill the urge or desire above all."

Nodding her head, she looked away, eyes glancing

here and there. "I can't tell when anything changes. I need to figure out when the Volonte's power is taking over."

He thought on that and recalled how her skin had turned to fire as he held her. "Try to notice when your skin heats up. I could feel it getting hotter as that armband influenced you."

She lifted her gaze back to his with a wry smile tilting her lips. "Sure that wasn't *your* influence?"

Glad to hear the amusement in her voice after what she'd just gone through, he leaned close, inhaling her delicious scent. "You'll know when it's me, and I'll make you hot in a far better way."

She shivered, and he knew damn well she wasn't cold.

"Careful," she warned. "Or we'll be right back where we started." But she'd said that in a breathless voice that was so damned sexy it rode along his senses, stroking him even harder.

Evalle whispered, "What'd you do to . . . uhm, stop me from attacking you a minute ago?"

That broke the tension threatening to snap his body in half. He sucked in a deep breath and straightened away from her, anything to keep from pulling her up against him. "I used a spell to wrap you and dilute the power, but it's probably only temporary. I doubt it will hold long. We need to get that thing off your arm."

She wiped a hand over her face. "In the meantime, I'll be . . . dangerous to be around."

He could see where this was going. "I'm not letting you out of my sight. I'm not concerned."

"You should be. I'm not Bernie. I *can* kill you."

He had more faith in her than she had in herself. "I'll take my chances."

She got that stubborn look on her face, but she didn't argue with him. "That armband had to be why Imogenia was acting erratic when we first met her. I thought she was on some cooked-up drugs. Think she was using a spell to block her reactions?"

"Possibly, and one much stronger than mine."

"She could have told me about *this*. She might have told us the truth, but she was twisting the words. Probably pissed that I got the upper hand on her." Evalle pounded her fist into her palm and started pacing. "I'm going to find that bitch and break her—"

"E-*valle*."

She snapped her head around to him and snarled, "What?"

Ah, hell. "You're letting the bone influence you again."

Her mouth opened and closed. She started to say something, then just growled. "Crap. I have to talk to Macha and VIPER. If I go around Sen with this thing, it'll end in a bloodbath."

Of her blood. "You're taking it off."

"I have to *gift* it to someone. Remember? Who am I going to give it to?"

"Me."

"We already had that discussion. No. Besides, I wouldn't give this to my worst enemy." She rubbed her arm. "I'm tired, Storm. I need to go home and get some sleep."

Telling Evalle he wanted her close to keep her safe would probably set her off again, but he couldn't leave her alone with her wearing the powerful artifact. "You're staying at my place."

"No."

Didn't she realize this was not up for debate? She wasn't safe being out alone, when anyone could trigger a reaction from her. "Why not?"

"I don't want a replay of Sex in the Country."

"You know I won't do anything."

"I'm worried about what I might do to *you*, Storm, plus I need to talk to Macha before she hears about these games another way and thinks I'm holding back information."

Had she lost her mind? "Talk to *Macha* while you're wearing an ancient bone that shoves your pissed-off level into hyper speed? She's dynamite and you're a hot fuse. She raises your hackles when she's in a good mood, and right now she's at the end of her patience with Alterants. Snarl at her once and she'll destroy you with a flip of her finger. You can't do this."

Evalle leaned forward, her mouth rigid as she gritted her teeth against unleashed anger. "I *am* doing this, so let's hope your spell helps channel my inner passive child."

Yeah, right. She didn't have a passive bone in her body and there wasn't a spell on this earth that would turn her into a docile woman.

SIX

Storm drove through downtown Atlanta with one hand on the steering wheel and his other toying with a strand of Evalle's dark hair while she slept in the passenger seat. This woman had breathed life back into his heart. Had made him care about living again.

How was he going to keep the hardheaded Alterant safe?

If his visions and his spirit guide were right about the witch doctor from South America being close, he had to figure a way to keep that bitch away from Evalle, especially with Evalle's control compromised.

Turning off Marietta Street, he drove down to an area below the main street levels. His truck tires bumped over the rails of an old train track that gave history to the iconic Underground Atlanta entertainment mall.

Jostled mildly, Evalle slept like the dead, just as she had for the whole trip back from the mountains. He didn't want to wake her, but she had less than fifteen minutes to get inside her apartment before light leaking over the eastern horizon turned into full-blown daylight.

He didn't want to leave her either, but he'd finally relented when she'd argued she wouldn't rest if she spent the whole time worrying about what she might do to him.

Also, with her safe in her underground apartment he'd have time to do some tracking.

Driving across the last section of the cracked concrete lot where knee-high weeds sprouted, he parked in front of a crumbling brick building that shielded Evalle's basement home.

And sat there for several seconds, indulging in a stolen moment. Just the two of them. No one to save. No one to kill. What he wouldn't give to make this time stretch into infinity.

He leaned over the console and kissed her softly.

She woke with a start, alert. Her bright green eyes met his. He'd taken her sunglasses off when she'd fallen asleep. They were parked in the dark shadow of the building, where no light would harm her eyes.

Evalle breathed deeply and smiled.

Sunshine came in many forms. The ball of fire that burst into the sky daily had nothing on one of her smiles. She leaned forward and kissed him back, fingers gliding into his hair, then curving around the back of his head to pull him closer.

And just like that, he had the erection from hell.

He held her face, tasting slowly, when he practically shook with wanting her. When he traced his fingers down to her shoulder, he slipped his hand around her neck.

Her skin started to heat, but he was ready this time and broke the kiss. Or tried to.

She wrenched him closer, kissing with more urgency.

"Evalle . . . honey," he murmured when he could get a word out. "Have to stop."

"No."

He didn't grab her this time. No sudden moves unless he wanted to go airborne. Instead, he said, "The armband."

She paused, kissed him again, then paused once more, hesitating with indecision, but this time she pulled away and released a sigh weighted with frustration.

He could sympathize. Frustration had become a natural state for him, but it appeared that some of his spell was still holding. "Are you sure you'll be okay?"

"Yes." She snagged her glasses off the dash and shoved them onto her face before opening the door to get out. He met her at the front of the truck.

Light glowed in the eastern sky, but she had eleven minutes left until the first rays of the sun broke the horizon. He wanted eight of those but wouldn't push her for more than she could handle right now, so he stood a few steps away, hands loose at his sides.

Had to be ready for anything.

She crossed the few steps separating them and lifted her fingers to his chin, then her lips to his, kissing him gently. Pinning his hands at his sides to keep from touching her took all the control he had left.

A man could only resist so much.

When she moved back, she kept her fingers on his face. "I'm ready for . . . more. For us."

Words he'd dreamed about hearing. "You have no idea how much I'd like that to be the case but—"

"But nothing." She lifted her glasses long enough for him to see her clear gaze before she dropped them back into place. "This is *me*, Storm. Not the bone. You said to trust you. When I get this thing off my arm, I want to try . . . with you."

Those words hadn't come easily.

Her pride had prevented her from taking the plunge before now and either making a fool of herself or harming him. But that same pride forced her to face her fears. To meet him on equal footing. With Evalle's deep sense of honor, she'd follow through no matter how much the idea might terrify her.

Humbling to be given a trust so precious.

He'd never let her get to the point of feeling terrified, and he believed she had plenty of control over shifting when she was fully in charge of her actions.

No woman could stack up next to this one.

Wrapping his fingers around her hand, he turned her palm to kiss the soft pads. "I'll be here when you're ready, but not until you really *are* ready. Right now, I just want that thing off your arm before you try to kill Sen or Macha."

She laughed. "Let's hope I have more control around those two than I seem to have around you."

He'd like to be near when she saw those two. "Where're you meeting Macha?"

"Upstairs here in the building, on the roof."

Evalle would be in her apartment until dark, which would give him time he needed. "Come to my place before you go to VIPER."

"I don't want you signing on with VIPER again. Not for this Alterant issue."

"I'll be looking for you."

She rolled her eyes and grumbled something acerbic under her breath. "This is my fight. Even if you sign on with VIPER again, only two people can get into the beast championship with this armband. I'll probably have to argue hard to get on that VIPER team, but Macha's opinion should sway Sen. I'm telling you right now that I'm not going to vote for you to go, so you have no reason to come back to VIPER."

"With my background, I'm the best piece of intel on these beast fights, and I plan to dig up more on the ABC." That made Storm the prime candidate to be entered as a fighter. Something Tzader would agree with. The only other choice would be entering Evalle, but she couldn't shift into her Alterant beast state, so she couldn't possibly fight another Alterant and win.

Didn't matter. Storm was going with her regardless.

She said, "Then share what you find out with me and I'll give the information to VIPER."

"We'll talk."

"It's a good thing I've got my inner beast under control, because I have the urge to beat some sense into you."

He gave her a quick kiss. "You're out of time. Get inside and don't forget to stop by after you talk to Macha."

Shaking her head, she lifted her hand, fingers pointed toward the metal door that covered her elevator. The door slid open and an oversized elevator appeared. All directed by her kinetic power. When she stepped inside, she turned around. "Where're you going?"

"Home." He hadn't lied. He was going to his house first to grab a shower before he headed back to the area where the Beast Club had been held in the mountains.

Then he'd shift into his jaguar so he could track the slightest scent.

He'd find Imogenia and persuade her to tell him everything about that bone that she hadn't shared the first time.

SEVEN

Imogenia dragged Bernie along on his spelled chain leash that clanked every time he caught up to her. She should make him shift and carry her, but he'd whine about that.

Worthless excuse for an Alterant.

Couldn't even kill a jaguar.

Thorns on a bush caught her dress and snagged a hole.

Next time I make a deal, it won't include traipsing all over a mountain in the middle of the night.

With the sun finally ready to appear, Imogenia picked her way along the base of Oakey Mountain, relieved this miserable morning would come to an end. How was she going to gain Noirre majik with this wretched beast?

Why couldn't she have captured an Alterant with some backbone?

A man like that jaguar shifter who'd kicked Bernie's butt.

She passed through a copse of trees that shivered in the wind and entered a clearing she'd visited before midnight on her way to the Beast Club.

Rattling erupted all around her, as if hundreds of rattlesnakes circled where she stood.

Bernie whimpered.

Sorry excuse for a man. She yanked the leash. "Shut up."

A woman emerged from the shadows cast by a stand of trees clustered on the shadow side of the mountain. When she came into focus, Imogenia could see that she wore an ankle-length hooded cape the color of a violent sea. Two red boot tips peeked out. She lifted her head enough for the light to catch her face, and thick lashes outlined exotic brown eyes.

Everything about that face was too perfect.

Imogenia never trusted perfection in anything. "Nadina."

"You left plenty of trail, yes?"

"I zigzagged all over the place for the past four hours." Imogenia had no idea why that had been part of the negotiation. She shouldn't have been so anxious to deal, but the chance to get Noirre majik didn't come along often.

Like never.

"When you leave, walk back the way you came until you can circle around this clearing, then go to your car."

"I will do that." Imogenia didn't know why she had to make a wide arc around this clearing, but in the interest of getting along, she would.

"You were successful at the Beast Club?"

"Of course." Imogenia flipped her chin up. "Not like I would have missed finding the target. Talk about diva attitude. She was the only woman wearing sunglasses at night. It turned out better than I expected."

"*Bueno*."

"Except for one thing."

"What?"

One word shouldn't raise the hairs along Imogenia's arms, but Nadina had loaded that one with plenty of threat. "Did you know Daniella was a traitor in my coven?"

"Of course. Do not look so put-upon. Evalle needed something to trade with you."

You better hope I never see a chance for payback. So Evalle was the name of that mouthy bitch with the jaguar. "Well, I have no strand of hair from her because she had Daniella to bargain with."

Nadina studied on that for a moment. "What of the armband? It is now on her arm, yes?"

"Ye-sss," Imogenia stressed impatiently. *Nadina must normally deal with morons to keep asking me stupid questions.* "I told you I was successful."

Waving a hand tipped with long red nails, Nadina said, "Then the strand of hair is of no importance."

Would have been nice to have had *all* the information before walking into that Beast Club. Imogenia should never have dealt with this unknown witch, but she needed more power than she held. She'd suspected a traitor in her coven for a while. Nadina had shown up with Volonte bones Imogenia would never have located. Even for one who practiced dark majik, Nadina had some serious connections. The Noirre spell Nadina agreed to give her in exchange for getting the armband locked on Evalle had seemed like a small favor until the woman's jaguar almost killed Bernie. "Back to Daniella."

"You should be thankful. Now you know about Daniella. Consider it a bonus."

"How did *you* find out?"

"I have my ways, just as you do. Had I not gotten that information to Evalle, she would have had no reason to come looking for you. *Comprendo?*"

Imogenia had enough survival sense to be careful around an unknown dark witch, but no witch played her and got away with it. "Who else knows about Daniella?"

"A ghoul in Atlanta."

"Nightstalkers? They'll talk to anyone with power who shakes their hand."

Nadina had that cat-sly look on her face. "No, they won't. I've taken care of that."

"How?"

"Come to me, my Langau," Nadina said in response.

Imogenia started to ask what this certifiable witch was talking about when a dark figure moved into the clearing. The figure coalesced from a smoky image to a solid person, an attractive twenty-ish woman with brown hair cut in a chic style that fluffed around her face and disarming hazel eyes. She wore navy slacks and a mauve sweater with a plaid scarf of both colors.

And smelled graveyard dead.

Necromancy.

That was award-worthy conjuring, but on the intimidation scale this spirit ranked below zero. Imogenia asked, "And you think *she's* going to keep Nightstalkers from running off at the mouth?"

Nadina was amused. "Not impressed with my Langau?"

Imogenia sensed she was heading into dangerous water by amusing the witch doctor, so she shrugged. "First impressions and all that."

"Do you think a Nightstalker would hesitate to shake with this one?"

This one never showed any hint of acknowledging the conversation. Her eyes had a blank expression. Should have a *Vacancy* sign painted on her forehead. Imogenia replied, "No. I think any ghoul would shake hands with her."

"That is exactly why I have five of these in Atlanta right now, searching for Nightstalkers and shaking hands, which infects the ghoul with a highly contagious virus. The infection is then passed by handshake to preternaturals, where it attacks their abilities. Kinetics become faulty and weak. The virus passes through telepathy, too, then attacks the host. Word is already getting around to avoid shaking with a Nightstalker."

Imogenia nodded with admiration. "That is impressive."

"But she"—Nadina waved a hand at her Langau—"is not?"

"For a preternatural viral carrier, she's scary, but beyond that not so much." Imogenia barely got the words out when the Langau's vision sharpened and her gaze snapped to Imogenia.

Hazel eyes turned into two pools of fire.

The Langau opened her mouth to reveal needlelike teeth.

Fingers shifted into long digits that curved with razor

claws. A muscle twitched above the Langau's left eye. She twisted her neck and opened her mouth, her forked tongue slipping out on a hiss.

Imogenia sucked in a breath.

Nadina chuckled. "Did I fail to mention her bite and claws can also infect? More impressive now, yes?"

Bernie started panting and backed up until the leash went tight.

Imogenia yanked on it, but the chain slipped in her damp palms. She hurried to agree with Nadina. "Yes, very much so."

Nadina lifted a hand and the Langau began vanishing. She told Imogenia, "As you see, there are no worries about Nightstalkers talking. Besides, you plan to go home and deal with Daniella, yes?"

"Bet on it." But Imogenia couldn't get to Daniella for another two days, not until after the championship fights. "And my Noirre spell?"

"What of it?"

"Are we still in agreement on the terms?" *Since you clearly change the rules as you see fit.*

"*Sí.* You will receive the spell the minute the Achilles Beast Championship is over. Thanks to me, you will have a chance to gain two Noirre spells that night." Her gaze swept over to Bernie, who stood half behind Imogenia. "That is, *if* your Alterant does not die by the final round."

Bernie whined softly.

The mirth clinging to Nadina's comment had Imogenia grinding her back teeth. "Bernie might be a sniveling human, but he's an impressive Alterant. At least, he *was* until I had to put him against that jaguar."

"Better to know his ability now than tomorrow. You got what you wanted. I got what I wanted."

"Not exactly. I don't want my Alterant to face that jaguar again."

Nadina moved around, gazing up at the branches that swayed lightly with the breeze. She looked at Imogenia. "That is simple. Take your beast to the games and accept the Medb's offer to negotiate for a trade before entering him in any battle. They clearly want many Alterants, or they would not make that offer for those who expect to lose their fighter in early rounds."

"I can't do that."

"Why not?"

"Because the Medb won't offer Noirre majik for anything less than the top five Alterants who win the final Elite matches. They won't give me squat for an unproven beast."

"You become tedious, Imogenia. You would not have this dilemma if I had not found this Alterant for you. Now you complain about the product. There is no pleasing you. This is clearly a win-win, no?"

No, it wasn't, but saying so could bring back that needle-tooth bitch. What drove all this with Nadina? "What's your interest in Evalle?"

Nadina surprised her by actually answering. "I want her jaguar."

"Good luck with that. I doubt even a dark witch can take that beast from her," Imogenia quipped.

Nadina's lips curved up, but not with humor. Her eyes glowed a deep yellow-orange. The sheer energy of Nadina's stare forced Imogenia to take a step back.

Hadn't Nadina already proven Imogenia was not in Nadina's league? Yes, much as Imogenia hated to admit it. Next time, she'd be more careful with her words.

Nadina warned, "I am no simple dark witch."

"Then what are you?"

"Far more dangerous." Nadina floated back a few steps and paused. "But I will grant your wish. Bernie will not face the jaguar in the ABC."

At one time, Imogenia would feel relief over that offer of help. Not now. She regretted putting herself in the position of being any more in this witch's debt than she already was. "Why would you do that?"

"Why must you question good fortune?"

"Because nothing in our world is free. I want to know what you want in return first."

Nadina gave her a look one used on a mentally challenged pet. "I have not decided, but I will let you know when I do."

No, no, no. And Imogenia had no desire to be at this woman's beck and call. "I'll be out of touch until the championship match, so you'll have to tell me how to find you. Unless *you* plan to attend," Imogenia added, fishing.

Nadina didn't answer her, so Imogenia pressed cautiously, "If you don't attend, how can you be sure that the jaguar does not face my Alterant?"

"I come from a long line of Ashaninka witch doctors

with powers you could only fantasize about. Follow my instructions and you will be fine. I'll let you know when I want something."

Imogenia muttered to no one in particular, "Just said I wouldn't be available without notice."

"Oh, but you will." Nadina laughed, immensely entertained. She lifted her hand, palm up, and whispered soft words Imogenia could not hear. Nadina crooked a finger in a sign of *come here*.

Imogenia felt a sharp spike dig into her chest as if something had hooked her. The pain cut deep.

She took a reluctant step forward, then another toward Nadina.

Fighting the pull only made her chest ache more. She walked with spastic motions all the way until Nadina held up a finger and said, "Stop."

Imogenia obeyed, panic-stricken. She'd never given Nadina anything a dark witch could use against her. "What did you do to me?"

"I bound you to me through the Volonte bone, just as I have bound another to me who has worn that armband. Why do you think I wore it first?" She caught herself and cocked her head in thought. "To be honest, I did need it to create my Langaus with necromancy, but now I can find you or Evalle whenever I want."

Sweat trickled down the side of Imogenia's face. This was worse than a traitor in her coven. Imogenia could make Daniella disappear in a painful way, but she had no idea how to break this connection with a witch doctor.

Nadina's eyes sparkled with happiness. "Speak a word of my existence to anyone or share anything about the Volonte bone after this point and I'll first dismantle you slowly and the person you tell next. Then I'll feed you to your Alterant one limb at a time and use your blood for something . . . special."

Imogenia's skin crawled at the idea of being a blood sacrifice for this witch. "I won't say a word."

"*Bueno*. As for my jaguar, he will not be able to fight against your Alterant . . . or any other one at the games."

Nadina turned and vanished into the darkness.

EIGHT

Storm shook off the urge to climb a tree to find a safe place to sleep in his jaguar form.

After spending all day covering a vast amount of Oakey Mountain, he was whipped.

And empty-handed.

He'd taken his time tracking Imogenia's scent trail, moving slowly, sometimes backtracking, because he thought he'd missed something due to the erratic way she and Bernie had crisscrossed down the mountain. Going from point to point, then sometimes turning around and covering the same ground again or crossing over an earlier trail.

She had trudged around and her Alterant had dragged his feet most of the time. Not the footsteps of someone comfortable in the woods. Had all that hiking cost Imogenia a bit of majik?

He hoped so. And maybe some golf-ball-size blisters.

Her trail had ended near tire tracks where she'd parked a vehicle. Small car with narrow wheels.

Had she made so many stops and direction changes along the way to confuse someone who might try to follow her? Afraid someone would try to steal her Alterant?

Or had there been another reason?

Storm was past the point of being able to think. He had to get some sleep.

He'd been tracking since eleven this morning.

Rubbing a paw over his face, he yawned, then loped off, heading back to his truck. If he went home now, he could grab a few hours' sleep before dark, when Evalle would leave her apartment.

He wanted to get on top of her building to be there in case things didn't go well with Macha.

When he reached the spot where Imogenia's trail had curved in an arc, he remembered having been curious as to why she'd done that when the simpler, and most direct path, was through a clearing.

Had she gotten lost?

Blinking away sleepiness, Storm took in the woods that thinned ahead of him to an open area sixty feet across.

Imogenia's route had paralleled the shape of that clearing.

Had something frightened her?

Storm didn't sense any animal or threat in the area now. He stalked ahead, intending to enter the clearing, until he had an overpowering desire to avoid the area.

Pausing, he sniffed. No smells came from there.

Everything in the forest had a scent.

Moving forward, one slow step at a time, the closer he got the more hair roughed up along his neck and shoulders. His instincts were screaming at him to back up, but the warning came from something unnatural. He pushed ahead, determined to find the source.

Was this why Imogenia had avoided the area?

His nose bumped against an invisible force that felt thick and cold.

He considered stepping back. These woods had been full of preternaturals last night, and some might have lingered. But this didn't feel like a warding. A yawn overtook him, stretching his jaws. He shook his head, trying to stay alert.

Just go and get some sleep. Storm turned away and had made it two steps when he sniffed the faint scent of licorice.

Could be residual from incense if someone had burned it out here, but there were no signs of any camp having been made nearby.

He took a deeper breath and still picked up only that subtle scent.

Turning around, he walked back to where he'd butted up against the cold barrier. Calling forth his majik, he pushed a paw through dense air. It took more effort than normal. He put his head down to force his way into the clearing. The invisible shield dragged along his fur as he struggled through the resistance and into the open space.

He sucked in the staggering stench of licorice.

Not the nice smell of candy but the smoky odor that came from dealing in the dark arts. Deadly dark arts.

He gagged and coughed, also smelling something dead that should be buried far away and deep.

That was the moment he realized he was not alone.

"*Buenos días,* Storm," whispered around him.

The witch doctor.

He spun in a circle, searching for her. That was her voice. And this was her spelled area. He'd walked right into her trap. This wasn't the way he'd planned to face her, exhausted and in her territory, but his enemies had never played fair.

Neither would he.

He roared, challenging the witch doctor to show her face.

Laughter bubbled all around him, echoing as if he stood inside a canyon instead of a grassy patch surrounded by a circle of trees. "Not yet, my black demon. I am not quite ready to risk standing so close to you. Soon, very soon."

Should he be glad he'd have a second chance to be better physically prepared or concerned about why she would delay this meeting?

She made a *tsk*-ing sound. "You have cost me much time. You foolishly think you can outplay me, but in the end I will win." Her words whipped past his ears, sliding away then zinging back at him. "You wish for blood. That is not the way for us to be. We are much alike, you and me."

I'd cut my own throat to protect the world if I was anything like you.

"You are not ready to come to me voluntarily today."

Hold your breath and wait for that to happen. Should he shift so he could talk to her? Or was she hoping for that? He was strong in his human state, but far more powerful in his jaguar form.

"I must leave you, Storm. I have much to do, and

we will see each other again, but I cannot allow you to interfere with my Langaus now that you have the scent. Why do you make my life so difficult?"

Langau? He searched his mind for what she could have brought to this country . . . or created since coming here.

"I will allow you to live because you have much to do for me. You force me to make you regret coming in here *unless* you are ready to give your word and come to me on your own."

He snarled, showing his fangs.

"So stubborn. It is a shame that you do not accept your destiny. Perhaps a lesson in humility will show you who holds the most power between us. *Adiós*, Storm." In the next moment, he saw the witch doctor outside the clearing, walking away.

Still beautiful and hadn't aged a day. Had gotten younger looking if anything.

Or was that a spell?

If so, did she have to renew it often? Something to keep in mind when he did face her later.

She looked back once, smiled, and continued on, disappearing in the trees.

Storm tensed for whatever threat she'd conjured up, sure he could not simply walk out of here the way the witch doctor had. And neither could he turn his back on an unknown threat.

A form wavered into view.

As it took shape, Storm moved toward the invisible perimeter around this clearing. He kept an eye on the image of a brunette woman as she solidified into a human form. She had a college-girl face with deep golden skin and layered hair that stopped short of the black-and-pink scarf draped over a pink sweater. An unnatural breeze swirled through the clearing, lifting strands of her hair and ruffling her black pants.

Pretty hazel eyes without a flicker of life to them.

Now he understood what the witch doctor had done. Her Langau was an *alma condenada,* or a condemned soul. Very likely a soul the witch doctor had stolen, then used to create demons.

Just like she wanted to do with Storm, since she owned *his* soul.

That meant this Langau was deadly, but the witch doctor had indicated she would see him again.

That meant she wanted him left alive, but she'd said nothing about what condition he'd be in.

The brunette took a tentative step toward him.

He'd never harmed a woman, but he reminded himself this was nothing more than a creature the witch doctor created from dead parts and blood sacrifices. Fighting it was not an issue, but the witch doctor wanted to punish him.

To slow him down from hunting her Langaus. Plural.

Where had she released them?

What made the witch doctor think he couldn't kill this thing? She had to know better, which meant she might have given the Langau a poison to inject in some way. A poison from South America she'd know would cripple him.

Avoiding this Langau was the smartest move.

The creature sauntered closer with a feminine sway.

He snarled, a low, throaty sound that stopped her and warned another step could be her last.

Her slender hands twisted and lengthened into razor-sharp nails with enough curve to cause maximum pain. Or death. Her face lost its youthful appeal, skin wavering and sliding until rotted flesh showed through in spots and the eyes sank in.

Her mouth widened and lips narrowed, much like a mouth on a large snake, but this one was filled with spiked teeth.

That's how she'd inject the poison.

She lunged at him, but adrenaline had kicked in and Storm leaped to the side, leaving her to stumble through air. He bumped into the barrier and mentally marked the spot for when he had an opportunity to get out. He couldn't now, with this threat at his back.

Swinging around, she came at him, claws in the air.

He dodged to the side again, but she did, too, this time. There was nothing for it but to attack. Ramming her with all his power, he knocked her backward and she went down.

But not before raking her claws across his shoulder, cutting three deep gouges. Storm ripped her throat out. Her head rolled to one side and her body jerked back and forth.

Fast and final, but his shoulder burned as if acid had been poured in the wound.

He took a couple of steps toward the center of the

clearing, then turned around and dove headfirst through the invisible barrier. Going back through was painful and a battle, but he made it. When he landed on the other side, he looked around and saw only trees, bushes and grass.

The Langau was gone.

Storm's shoulder ached, telling him to get moving. He took off at a quick pace, in a hurry to reach his truck two miles away. By the time he got to it, his mouth was dry as cotton, and an ache had settled into all his muscles, much like a bad case of the flu.

Shifting into his human form took longer than normal. He was panting by the time he finished. He guzzled a bottle of water, then put on his jeans and shirt over his clammy body. When he climbed into the truck, the clock on the dash showed the day closing in on three in the afternoon.

That would give him time to get home and drop into a deep, healing sleep to push the poison or whatever that Langau had injected him with out of his system. He could do that and still get to Evalle by sundown at half past seven.

Black clouds joined ranks overhead, and thunder pounded.

On top of fighting off whatever was in his system, he'd have to drive through rain to get home. He groaned over the effort it took to lean forward and crank the engine, then he eased back for the half-mile ride to the highway.

His vision doubled. He squinted and realized he

might not make it home. Sleeping out here was a bad idea.

Storm chanted, tapping his majik to flood him with energy.

That should keep him awake long enough to make it home if this was only poison. He read road signs and . . .

Time disappeared between thoughts.

One minute he was driving through the forest, and the next he was on the interstate heading south into Atlanta.

Cold seeped inside his hot skin.

He'd never encountered a poison like this one. Chanting to keep himself awake and more alert, he finally pulled into his driveway just over an hour later, never so glad to see his house. His mind blanked and the next thing he knew he was at his front door, checking the warding before he entered.

Another lost blink and he was stretched over his bed, panting. Why the gaps between his thoughts?

He called up his jaguar to start the healing process now that he didn't have to remain conscious.

His jaguar barely stirred.

What?

Storm drew on his healing powers again, and his muscles quivered with the effort. What was wrong with his jaguar? Poison had never stayed long in his body or debilitated him this badly.

Why hadn't the witch doctor stuck around? She could have taken advantage of his weakened state.

But she'd tried that once before and it hadn't gone well for her.

She feared him, which she should, considering they shared blood. He hated her more every time he thought about how she'd tricked his father into breeding her a Skinwalker she could turn into a future demon.

Storm's eyes drifted closed.

All he wanted to do was sleep, but he had to wake up in time. Reaching over to his clock, his hand flopped on the nightstand, knocking the small digital unit to the floor. He had no control over his arms.

Poison had never made his limbs rubbery.

His body started shaking with tremors hard enough to rock the bed.

Not a poison . . . an infection.

He fought the sleep dragging him under. And lost.

NINE

That bloody woman is going to wish she'd never crossed me.

Vladimir Quinn shoved the hotel security card into the slot to activate the elevator that would take him to the penthouse floor of his hotel in downtown Atlanta.

Alone, thankfully.

He wasn't ready to go down to the suite he was actually staying in and deal with his teenage cousin Lanna, yet another problem he had to handle. Dark was coming on soon. Perhaps she'd be asleep if he gave it a couple of hours.

Self-loathing should be done in private.

He was a trusted Belador in a high-level position, and for him to give a Medb priestess, sworn enemy of the Beladors, access to any Belador information deserved brutal punishment.

Especially for bloody classified information.

And that's exactly what he'd done.

The fact that he'd done so unintentionally didn't matter. The information had been his to protect. But now Kizira would find out what it meant to double-cross a Belador as powerful as he was.

Quinn would willingly accept his due from Macha for opening his arms to Kizira.

But he hadn't just opened his arms to her. He'd made love to the woman four days ago, and only hours later she'd launched an attack on Treoir Island, putting their warrior queen's life in danger and threatening the seat of Belador power.

He'd done the kind of damage expected of the traitor everyone was hunting.

All because he'd believed Kizira when she'd claimed she wanted to end the conflict between the Beladors and the Medb so they could be together. That she cared for him.

So damned convincing. What else was he supposed to think when she'd given him permission to breach the barriers to her mind and withdraw what he could find about the Medb plans?

She took a hell of a risk to come to you. That was what his heart had said four days ago. But his heart would no longer call the shots where Kizira was concerned.

She'd made it clear that being compelled by the Medb queen prevented her from giving him anything voluntarily, but she'd given permission for him to retrieve whatever he could on his own. Hell, she'd practically begged him to try even though she'd doubted he could actually get past her shields.

He'd jumped at the chance.

And when he'd broken through, he discovered the Medb had sent Svart trolls, deadly black ops mercenaries, to quietly invade Atlanta.

On the surface, that had appeared to be a win-win, since he wouldn't deny that he enjoyed having Kizira back in his arms, but he'd been a fool to think he'd been the only one fishing for intel.

Love did that to a man.

Turned a highly respected warrior into an idiot.

Couldn't even blame his actions on thinking with the wrong head. No, his heart had convinced him that Kizira had told the truth, and he'd trusted the traitorous organ.

Not again.

The intel he'd gained that day had saved many human lives, he'd give Kizira that.

But she'd teleported away with a far greater treasure, withdrawing vital classified information from his mind on how to locate Treoir. Only a handful of chosen Beladors had known the location of the island hidden in a mystical fog above the Irish Sea.

Now Kizira knew. A powerful Medb priestess.

While he'd worried over her fate if the Medb figured out she'd clued the Beladors to the Svart troll invasion, she'd been sending another army of Svarts to kill Brina.

That his people had managed to shut down both groups of Svarts didn't matter. Beladors had been lost in the battle to protect Treoir. And the Medb now possessed the route for teleporting to an island that had been successfully hidden for two thousand years.

Kizira hadn't made a peep since then. Not a single attempt to contact Quinn telepathically, and he'd been too busy to deal with her. Until now.

Time to turn the tables and make the witch pay.

When Quinn reached the suite he'd booked just for

meeting with Kizira, he wanted to slam the door after entering, but he closed it quietly. Why should anyone else suffer just because his chest felt caved in where his heart used to be?

Jerking off his wool overcoat still damp from the drizzle he'd walked through on his way to the hotel, he tossed it on the sofa and stalked to the bar to pour Boodles and water over ice.

A stiff one. Just what he needed for this showdown.

He settled on the sofa and dropped his head back, eyes closed, preparing to reach out to Kizira. He called to her silently. *Kizira?*

No answer. Did she think she could hide from him? That bloody connection went both ways.

Quinn put force behind his next telepathic shout. *Kizira!*

A soft cry fluttered through his mind, sounding like the scattered pieces of an eggshell voice that had been shattered. Then one word squeezed through in a plea. *Quinn.*

What was she up to this time? Did she think he'd be so easy to trick again? He bit down on the urge to unleash his foul temper and kept his telepathic voice calm. *I'm in no mood for games. Come and see me. I have something for you.*

He fished a slender weave of braided hair from his pants pocket. No thicker than a strip of chewing gum and just long enough to fit around Kizira's narrow wrist. She'd recently given him the thirteen-year-old keepsake made from his hair as an apology.

One he'd accepted, but he knew better this time. *What's going on, Kizira? I'm tired and I haven't got a lot of time.*

Cold fingers clawed into his brain. Sharp as talons with a fierce grip, they jerked him from his relaxed state. He slapped the drink down on the glass table at his side and grabbed his head. *What the hell?*

Quiinnn? quivered through his mind in a pitiful cry.

Stop it, he shouted back at her.

Trying to . . . talk to you . . . but I need help.

Lies. Always lies. Why wasn't she teleporting in? Did she suspect retaliation for what she did? *I know you're compelled to do things. Come see me. This may be the last time I can talk to you.*

Let her think something was going to happen to him.

No . . . wait . . . trying.

Her fear clutched at him, scratching for a hold. Blood trickled from his nose. He clenched his jaw, debating on using power, but he had to prevent a Medb from taking control of his mind. He shoved a blast of energy back through the connection.

The pressure stopped immediately.

What was going on?

For the slimmest moment, he considered her fear. Was it genuine? What could stop her from teleporting to him?

Nothing. Just another Medb trick.

He had to get her close enough to him physically for any chance of taking her captive.

This time, when he took her into his arms—and he

would—Quinn would use his mind lock to prevent her from teleporting away. He swallowed against what he had to do. *I thought you cared about me.*

A rock of guilt balled in his throat and sank to his gut. He'd been a fool, still caring about the woman he'd met thirteen years ago. When he hadn't known she was Medb.

Don't think of her any other way and this will work.

Chilly energy swirled near him, brushing the skin on his face. Quinn opened his eyes to find an image trying to take shape between him and the window, where night still ruled. Kizira's form normally coalesced quickly when she teleported, but the figure coming into focus now was nothing more than a wispy shape, blurry from the neck down.

Her eyes were red-rimmed, not glowing like they'd always been before. Beautiful, sad eyes stared at him, damp and pained, as though she'd been crying. Her lips moved.

No sound came through.

She tried talking again. Her face erupted with panic, then she squeezed her eyes shut. Veins on her forehead stuck out as if she was concentrating all her energy on one thing.

He sat forward, studying the strange vision, and spoke out loud. "What are you doing?"

Slowly, her neck and shoulders came into focus. She opened her eyes and took a couple of panting breaths. "Trying . . . to communicate."

"Why aren't you teleporting in?"

"I . . . can't."

"Why?" he asked with a load of suspicion.

"Locked . . . in dungeon."

Truth or trick? He suffered a moment of ambivalence over the misery pulsing from her. Was she projecting her body from inside TÅµr Medb and really in a dungeon? "Who locked you up?"

"Flaevynn."

The Medb queen. But could he believe her? "For how long?"

"Don't . . . know." Her words came out in spurts, and sweat streamed down her face. The bulk of her body still hadn't taken shape. "Sorry about trolls. Don't . . . hate me."

There was one way to determine if she was jerking him around or not. Reaching out to her mind, he lowered his control until he could enter hers without giving her warning, something he never did unless the safety of others was at stake. Right now, the safety of all Beladors was on the line.

The minute he entered her mind, sharp stabs shot back through the connection. He could feel the ward preventing her physical body from teleporting. She shivered in a cold room of stone. He hissed at the blades of pain streaking through her. "What . . ."

Her eyes widened. She shouted, "Stop!"

He snapped his control back in place, shutting down to the minimum access he'd allow to stay in contact with her. He'd planned for anything but this. Kizira really was locked away somewhere, and logic said the one person powerful enough to bind a Medb priestess would be the Medb queen.

His heart thumped with worry. What were they doing to her? Who other than Quinn would go up against Flaevynn to help Kizira?

What the bloody hell are you thinking?

He couldn't cross that line again with her, could he?

Evidently so, because he asked, "How can I help you?"

"You. Can't."

She'd very likely ended up in this situation by allowing him to access her memory and pilfer intel on the Medb, but Flaevynn still controlled Kizira, and Quinn still needed information. He swallowed a lump of regret, forcing himself to stick to his duty. His vow to the Beladors came first, so he'd retrieve what he needed for the Beladors, then he *would* find some way to free her.

But would she answer his questions?

She must have seen the dilemma in his face. "Ask. I'll answer . . . if I can. Little time."

She probably couldn't hold this out-of-body projection for long. He shoved aside his conscience, which would only get in the way of his interrogation. "How did Svart trolls find their way to Treoir?"

"Teleported."

"By whom?"

Her face fell. "Me."

The truth crashed hard between them. "You used me."

"No. Flaevynn . . ." Her neck muscles clenched and she struggled to breathe. Then she said, ". . . compelled me."

He knew that, but it didn't alleviate how deep the betrayal had cut. The last time he'd seen Kizira she'd warned him, "I can't promise that we won't meet on a battlefield or that I won't be compelled to do something that will make you hate me, but I don't want to do it, and I don't want to be your enemy."

Was he just supposed to overlook the invasion at Treoir? Dismiss the deaths of the warriors and the threat to the Belador race? He clamped his hand on the arm of the sofa, fighting against the frustration building in his chest. "Did Flaevynn compel you to steal the location of Treoir from my mind?"

"Not . . . intentional." Kizira's shoulders moved with the battle she fought to maintain her image.

Every time that happened, Quinn forced his hands not to reach out to drag her away from whatever was holding her prisoner. *Stay in the game.* "You may not have intentionally skimmed the information from my mind, but you intentionally used it."

"Yes. No choice."

Always the same answer. He surged to his feet. "How am I supposed to believe you when your catchall answer is 'I was compelled'?"

Tears pooled in her eyes, but not one broke loose. "Came to help. Can't hold long. Ask. Now."

She wanted to give him information in spite of being locked away? If he believed her, believed that she was imprisoned, then he had to let go of what had happened. Accept that some things were out of her control. "Okay, what *can* you tell me?"

That got him a cranky eye roll and one-word command. "Think."

He nodded. "Let's try this. You want to stop Flaevynn."

"You understand."

It took a moment for him to realize that she couldn't say yes or no to that because it had been too close to a question. How could he find out what Flaevynn was after? He asked, "What would be a good gift for Flaevynn?"

Kizira's eyes sparked with relief. "Alterants."

Plural. How many was Flaevynn looking for and why? While he tried to figure out another question, Kizira added, "Evalle."

"You can't have her."

"Number. One."

Did Kizira mean Evalle was the most important one to Flaevynn? *Why?* Just to be clear, Quinn added, "Would Flaevynn be unhappy if someone harmed Evalle?"

"Maybe."

"If Flaevynn tries to take Evalle, Tzader and I will come for her."

"No. You lose."

What did that mean? Quinn paced away, then back and said, "I don't give a damn who loses."

"I. Do."

How could two words twist their way inside his heart? Was he really going to buy this act? He didn't know, but his gut said to keep pushing. Back to the clever questions that sounded stupid to him. "Would Flaevynn be happy to receive a group of Alterants?"

"Very much."

"What would a group of Alterants be called?"

"Army."

"What would an army of Alterants be capable of accomplishing?"

She shook her head. "Beladors . . . dead."

He stared at her in disbelief and argued, "Flaevynn can't kill *all* the Beladors without facing massive retaliation from VIPER across the world. There are millions of us, many who work among humans in everyday jobs. Even if Flaevynn could destroy all the Beladors currently with VIPER, she'd face an army of our own that would step forward to take the places of those who fell."

"Not. Necessarily." Kizira whimpered and her image flickered.

Quinn moved toward her as if he could do something, then clenched his fists. Kizira would lash out before she'd cry. He thought he'd closed his heart against her, but no matter how much he fought it, he wanted to protect her. Wanted to believe she was just a pawn being tossed from one side of the Medb chessboard to the other, sacrificed for their queen.

That was the problem with love.

It constantly wanted to overrule logic.

Weary from an internal battle that showed no end, he finally asked, "How can I trust you?"

"Because . . ." Her form shuddered. She worked for her next breath and on the exhale said, "I. Love. You. Always have . . . always will."

Quinn had offered to turn himself in to Macha when

he'd realized his mind had been breached by Kizira. To do so would have meant Quinn's death, a sanction he would accept for his failure, but Tzader was convinced that the Beladors needed Quinn's powerful mind to protect Brina and to defend Treoir. Once Quinn had accomplished all he could to help Tzader ensure the future of the Beladors, he would leave. Go far away where he couldn't be the weak link, because he'd never stopped loving this woman either.

But he'd broken enough vows today. He wouldn't add admitting to that love when there was no way for them to be together. "What can I do for you, Kizira?"

She stared at him, the love in her eyes fading. "Nothing."

The words gutted him. He ran his hand through his hair, pacing to and fro, but never more than two steps from her image. He stopped in front of her, torn between doing his job and caring for her. "What do you want me to do then?"

Her face altered into fierce determination, but her shoulders trembled, starting to lose shape. "Leave North America. Now."

That wouldn't bloody happen. "Why?"

Sweating, she implored him with her eyes. "Think, Quinn."

Right. He'd asked a direct question. How was he supposed to know what to ask? He searched his mind, going back over Kizira's last statement to leave this country. "Does Flaevynn value North America?"

"Sometimes."

"Would she value it over Treoir?"

The weary arch of her eyebrow said that was a stupid question. Her form wavered again, jamming Quinn's pulse into overdrive.

Her next words seeped out weary and strained. "Too slow."

He'd heard about a game once where one person had a hidden word and tried to get another team player to guess the word by giving suggestions. "I've got an idea. I'll say something and you say the first thing that comes to mind. Okay?"

"Yes."

"Beladors."

"Enemy."

He had to fine-tune this better or they'd need two days to share information. "Treoir."

Her eyes stared off for a moment as she thought, then her gaze returned to him. "Immortality."

Now he was getting somewhere. Flaevynn must be after immortality, which would make sense. But what made her think she could gain it by capturing Treoir? He thought she couldn't leave TÅµr Medb. He wouldn't get the answer he needed this way, but Tzader might know, so Quinn moved to specifics. When would Flaevynn make her next move? "Deadline."

"Three days."

"For what?" he snapped.

She just sighed.

"Sorry," he muttered and concentrated. So she was talking about . . . "Tuesday?"

"Funeral."

Who was going to die? He countered with, "Funeral."

"Flaevynn."

The Medb queen would die in three days for some reason? Now all the attacks made sense. She had a deadline for gaining immortality and couldn't afford to lose.

What happened if Flaevynn lost? "Missed deadline."

"Retribution."

What type of vengeance would the crazy queen seek? He tossed back, "Retribution."

"Annihilation."

"Location."

"North America."

How would a dead queen accomplish that? She'd need an army, which meant . . . "Warriors."

"Alterants."

He had the next word before the question fully formed in his mind. "Leader."

"Evalle."

Quinn couldn't accept that. The Medb queen really thought she could send Evalle and other Alterants to destroy North America if she died? Impossible.

Kizira gasped. "More."

He couldn't watch this any longer. "Tell me how I can bloody get to you, Kizira."

She wrenched her neck, struggling as if she was being dragged backward. "Should have told you . . ." Gasping, she said, "Save . . ."

"Who?"

Kizira vanished, a whip of smoky image sucked out of the room.

Dropping his shield, he reached out to touch her mind.

And slammed into a wall. Had Kizira thrown up a barrier powerful enough to keep him out? Or had someone else entered her mind and caught her talking to him?

His hands shook. What should she have told him?

Who had she been telling him to save?

Kizira, Evalle . . . or someone else?

TEN

Don't attack Macha. Evalle kept repeating that in her head, hoping she'd survive this meeting with the goddess.

Storm had good reason to question whether she could do this.

She'd lost patience while brushing her hair. A tangle had caught in the bristles.

She'd yanked.

The tangle hadn't loosened.

Note to self: buy new brush.

Showered and dressed, she rode the elevator from her underground apartment back up to ground level the minute sundown was official. Food and sleep had gone a long way toward rejuvenating her. She'd even had an hour to play with Feenix, her pet gargoyle.

Glancing at the freaky armband on her wrist, she muttered, "Mess with me while I'm meeting with Macha and we'll both end up in the spare parts yard."

Great. Now she was talking to inanimate objects.

Most anyone who witnessed that would call her mentally unstable.

Anyone, that is, except Storm. He'd understand. He always understood. The man had more patience than any other human being or preternatural she'd ever met.

Last night she'd tried to peel his clothes off and swallow his tongue, then she'd attacked him.

Foreplay with an Alterant.

And the ultimate humiliation for her.

But even now she wanted him. Wanted to feel the taut muscles flex across his chest like they had when she'd reached inside his jeans and grabbed him.

Heat washed across her face, but in spite of how embarrassing that had been, she'd thought about nothing else since then except being with him. Her breasts ached, missing the way he'd brushed his fingers across her nipples and—

Whoa! Were those *her* thoughts or the blasted armband's influence?

Panting as if she'd been in a dead heat race, she sucked in a couple of calming breaths when her elevator reached the top floor. Then she took the stairs up to the ten-foot-square structure that jutted above the roof.

Wind carried a drizzling rain across the roof in gusts. Very little light from the streets below reached over the thigh-high parapet wall that enclosed this rooftop, but neither she nor Macha needed light to see up here.

Macha generally popped in to see Evalle whenever the mood struck, but she'd told Evalle how to call her if necessary.

That meant, don't call her for anything less than the apocalypse.

In Evalle's opinion, if the Medb took control of Alterants and turned some of them into immortal warriors, they'd have the ability to cause an apocalyptic event.

Leaning out a little but staying under the protection of the short overhang, Evalle called out, "I request Macha, goddess over the Beladors, to please grant me a visit. Your humble servant, Evalle."

She actually managed to get all of that out without gagging. That proved she had *some* control over her mouth.

A cloud of glittering light pooled ten feet away, in front of where she stood. It swirled, reminding Evalle of iridescent ice cream. When the glitter suddenly burst away, a woman not quite as tall as Evalle glowed into form.

Rain stopped falling on the roof.

The last time Evalle had seen Macha, the goddess had auburn hair flowing to her waist. Today she'd gone with blond curls falling around her stunning face and the rest of it piled into some kind of deity 'do.

Must be nice to be a goddess.

No demolished hairbrushes.

Thankfully, Macha normally shielded her luminous image from humans. Even if someone happened to look down at this rooftop from a higher building, they'd be hard-pressed to figure out that Evalle was speaking to anyone, and would likely not even see her or the goddess in this light. "Hello, Macha."

Disgust molded Macha's hazel-green gaze and Hollywood-gorgeous face into a dazzling picture of threat. "You're working under the false impression that these are social visits."

In other words, get to the point. "I've located Alterants."

Interest lit Macha's eyes, shoving the disgust away for now. "Where are they?"

"That's why I asked to meet. The Medb are offering them a deal—"

"They dare to take that over my offer?"

The building shook with the force of an earthquake. Thunder pounding all around had nothing on Macha in a snit.

"No, that's not the case," Evalle hurried to assure the female A-bomb before she leveled the building. If not for Quinn's guarantee that the renovated basement she leased from him could withstand anything, she'd be worried about having left Feenix down there. "I need a minute to explain."

"Your seconds are ticking."

Muscles constricted in Evalle's chest. *Don't snap at her. No attacking the goddess.* She took another stab, starting out by explaining about the Beast Club. Evalle finished with, "If I'd gone to VIPER before entering to meet Imogenia, I wouldn't have found out about the Achilles Beast Championship. The Medb are clearly using this to bring the Alterants together in one spot."

"Clever. Surprising, considering the source." Macha floated inches above the roof as if afraid she'd touch something mortal and not be able to get the grime off later. She shot a pointed look at Evalle. "Why didn't *you* think of that?"

Grinding her back teeth, Evalle counted to five, since Macha would never wait for a ten count. "To begin with, the games are illegal. Number two, I doubt you want to offer Alterants immortality."

"That's a phony offer. The Medb have not had an immortal queen since Maeve was killed. Even if they did, they can't just offer immortality to anyone. It's not like being knighted."

Evalle guided the conversation back to her goal—getting Macha's help in delivering this Volonte bone to VIPER without having to admit to them how she came to wear it. "Supposedly, the person hosting this ultimate event has a way of vetting out a lie. Word is the Medb's sponsorship is backed by a blood debt and they'll send a female Medb to face a truth test in front of everyone the night of the games. If this Medb representative lies, she'll die on the spot."

Macha moved around, floating just above the ripped-up roofing material, and circled around to face Evalle again. "What's your plan?"

The goddess very likely had a plan of her own, but gods and goddesses were a sneaky bunch. Why make a decision if someone else could carry the responsibility for anything that went wrong?

But Evalle had dealt with Macha several times already and came prepared. "I can't walk into VIPER and tell them how I got this Volonte without causing a lot of problems, like them asking me why I had to go meet with Imogenia." Insinuating she'd been there for Macha was much safer than pointing it out specifically. "I was thinking you could send me to VIPER with a message that this armband is a gift from you that VIPER can use as buy-in to the beast championship for an undercover op. No one would question how this came into your possession."

Use some of that goddess mojo.

When Macha didn't comment, Evalle continued. "Everyone expects the Medb to trade Noirre majik for the final five Alterants. We could bust the Medb and take custody of all the Alterants. I think they'll come with us voluntarily once the Medb on site are neutralized and if the Alterants are offered amnesty for surrendering without a fight."

Macha lifted her finger to her neck, tapping a lengthy gold fingernail—very likely solid gold—against her cheek. "Is the land owned by someone with immunity?"

"We don't know yet, but it's possible."

"More than possible," she snapped. "Highly probable, since no one would dare hold illegal beast fights in VIPER's jurisdiction. If the landowner has immunity, VIPER has no say over that."

"What if Noirre majik is being traded?"

"Do you have proof?"

Evalle bit down to keep from shouting that she'd just explained all that. "No, but with Imogenia and other witches—"

Macha dismissed it with a flick of her shiny nails. "There's nothing illegal about offering a chance to negotiate a trade."

"But we know dark witch sponsors won't trade for anything less than a Noirre spell and the Medb are hosting this event for the Alterants. The trade seems obvious."

"VIPER will not move on an assumption of illegal activity if the property has immunity. To do so would set a precedent that would undermine the coalition agreement that prevents misuse of power." Macha's hair spun with the energy she stirred up. All at once, the blond strands settled back into a happy pile of flowing curls. "*But* now that we know where all the Alterants are going to be, you need a plan for bringing them in."

Me? "You just said VIPER can't do anything."

"True, but this isn't really a VIPER issue. *You're* the one who has to deliver Alterants to me in two days. Which reminds me, will Tristan be there?"

She *would* ask about him. "I heard he would be."

"I've waited long enough for Alterants. If the Medb want five, then so do I. Bring me Tristan and three more."

Was the goddess paying attention to anything Evalle said? "You expect me to get *four* Alterants, *and* myself, out of that place without anyone noticing and no help from VIPER?"

"I expect you to fulfill your part of our agreement. Have you changed your mind?"

"No, but I could use some help on this."

In a rare show of drawing a line on her smooth face, Macha scowled. "Must I do everything?"

The rage bubbling up through Evalle's chest would explode if she took that bait. She had a simple choice. Open mouth and die or stay quiet.

But her temper pushed at her control. Sweat drizzled down her back. She was heating up, just like the last time the armband pushed at her to do what she wanted.

Macha didn't seem to notice the internal war Evalle fought. She asked, "Tristan teleports, right?"

"Yes." Evalle squeezed that out between tight jaws.

"You've constantly asserted that he is imprisoned by the Medb, that he can control his beast, and that he has the origins of Alterants. You have the buy-in for this event. Get inside, find him and convince Tristan that it's in his best interest to come with you. He can use his teleporting to get out. If he doesn't come out with you, I will mark him as a declared rogue and have the Tribunal order VIPER to hunt him down."

How had this gone from Plan A to rid herself of the armband and gain VIPER's help to rescue Tristan and other Alterants to Plan B, where any hope for Tristan's freedom was destroyed if this didn't go well?

Oh, and Evalle would enter a beast championship illegally without VIPER knowing.

Stellar negotiation skills, Kincaid.

In her supreme *goddess* voice, Macha ordered, "Get to those Alterants, but I do not want Beladors involved in this."

"None? Tzader should be informed."

"Absolutely not. Tzader and our warriors have enough to do with reinforcing the wards around Treoir now that the Medb know the location. I can't afford for him or any of the others to be involved in these beast battles. If something happened to him in particular, I would be most displeased." She paused, pinning Evalle with the sharp point of her gaze. "You don't want to face my displeasure. I'm not as merciful as the Tribunal."

Evalle would never use *merciful* in the same sentence with *Tribunal*, three entities who performed the duty of judge and jury over agents in conflict with VIPER.

Been there. Done that. Got the scars.

Evalle still needed Macha's help with VIPER. "If I could show up with this armband as a buy-in, VIPER might go along with sending in a covert team of just two of us who could scout for Noirre. If a trade went down, I could call out for more teams that would be close by, and I'd still have a chance to bring back the Alterants."

"You want me to implicate myself in the theft of a rare artifact with unknown powers?"

Why did it sound so wrong when she put it that way? So much for goddess mojo. "That wasn't what I meant."

"That's exactly how it sounds. Once again, you bring me problems with no plan. I'm beginning to wonder what I saw in you."

Evalle wanted to strike out with kinetics and knock the smug goddess on her ass.

And she could. Just like when she'd told Storm she'd kick his ass.

Heat wrapped her arm, forcing her to look down.

The bone. She had to get a grip and calm down. Taking a deep breath, she said, "I still think my best chance is with VIPER support. If not, I'll go in on my own."

There had to be a way out of this mess. Tzader would

understand her predicament, especially if Macha supported her and . . .

Macha snapped her fingers. "For someone with your training, I'd expect better survival skills than to daydream while in a meeting with me." Before Evalle could comment, the goddess asked, "What is your plan for explaining to VIPER if you're discovered in this event?"

She keeps asking that as if I have a notebook full of plans. "I figured you'd explain that I went in for you."

Macha laughed cynically. "For me? *You're* the one who believes Alterants deserve to be recognized as a viable race."

"True." Evalle would not stop believing that, no matter the cost.

"I'm the only one offering Alterants the chance to belong to a pantheon. *Our* agreement did not involve the entire Belador tribe or VIPER, only the two of us. You're the one who claimed you could deliver Tristan, who supposedly knows the origins of Alterants. I have yet to see him or any other Alterant, even though I've already offered amnesty if they prove control of their beasts and swear fealty to me."

"I know, and I'm working on—"

"I am *still* holding up my end of the bargain, *and* in a show of appreciation for what you did in the battle with the trolls at Treoir, I've extended your deadline, which will *not* happen again in this millennium. I suggest you come up with an adequate plan that does not involve everyone else, and do it soon."

Evalle had only thought she understood. She couldn't

walk away without losing her freedom along with Tristan's and that of all other Alterants. But neither would she insert into the ABC with her hands tied. Shoving a determined look back at Macha, Evalle nodded. "Fine. I'll get inside those games on one agreement."

A puzzled look came over Macha's face. "What?"

"I understand that you will disavow any knowledge of my actions with VIPER or the Tribunal. I'll bring back Tristan and *any other* Alterants I can convince to return with me, but I want autonomy over *all* my decisions without threat of penalty." She had no idea what she might have to do, but she was done with playing these games on Macha's rules alone.

Macha took her time answering. "You are free to act as you see fit without threat of repercussion from me as long as you do not place my pantheon in conflict with VIPER and you put the best interest of the Beladors first above all."

Which would be based on Macha's subjective opinion.

In other words, fail and face the brunt of Macha's anger. The chances of improving on this agreement were nil, and the harder Evalle pushed this, the more she risked getting tangled even deeper in one of Macha's sly, one-sided deals. "Understood."

Surprisingly, Macha appeared content. "I'll make this simple for you."

Evalle deserved credit for not rolling her eyes as she held quiet to hear Macha out.

"Stop the Medb from creating an army of immortal

Alterant warriors, return with Tristan and three others, and I'll clear you of any complications with VIPER, plus I'll decree *every* Alterant protected under my pantheon. Do that and you may have all the time you need to determine the origins."

Now that was an offer. "You're on."

Raising her arms, Macha turned into a swirl of glittering lights again and disappeared.

Rain!

Evalle dove for the stairwell, wet, but not as bad as it could have been. She made the trek back downstairs, dialing Storm on the way. His voice mail picked up, so she left him a message to call her. She'd just reached the elevator to her apartment when she got a group text from Tzader, which seemed odd, when he could just call out telepathically to his warriors.

She punched up the message that read, All Belador agents receiving this come to headquarters immediately. Do not use telepathy for ANY reason in the meantime.

What in the world had happened?

ELEVEN

On his way through TÂµr Medb, Cathbad whistled a sad Irish tune older than the original Cathbad the Druid, his namesake. TÂµr Medb held all the pleasures one person could want in a hidden realm, but after six hundred years here, a prison was a prison no matter how grand the architecture and the trimmings.

In three days, he'd be free of this place forever.

And free of Queen Flaevynn if things went his way.

But the time had come to save his child.

He silently ordered the tall gold-and-silver doors carved with images of sexual acts to swing open ahead of him before he entered Flaevynn's chamber.

Inside, two virile males dressed only with belts of gold medallions draped around their waists lounged on thick white fur rugs that floated near the arms of her throne. A dragon-shaped throne that curved around her protectively. Positioned right above her, green eyes in the dragon's head stirred with menace when it stared at Cathbad.

He ignored the throne and her boy toys.

After six hundred years of Flaevynn's antics, Cathbad couldn't muster the energy to care what his wife did to amuse herself, but with mere days left to fulfill the prophecy, it was time she got down to business. "Get rid of them, Flaevynn."

She stroked her long nails over the back of one male and sighed. "They're soothing me. Don't be a bore, Cathbad."

"Take your time. All three days of it."

With a look of loathing, she snapped her fingers and both men disappeared. Midnight-black, waist-length hair coiled around her shoulders, slithering like asps searching for a victim. No siren of the deep had ever drawn a man the way Flaevynn's beauty had sucked in hundreds of foolish men.

Maybe a thousand, considering how often she indulged.

All within these walls.

Cathbad had been cured of her seductive draw a long time ago. He was plenty attractive to gain all the women he wanted. "We agreed upon releasin' Kizira."

"We *discussed* that."

"'Tis no the time ta let your anger rule ya, woman."

"She betrayed me."

He sighed. "I'll no spend my time arguin'. We either work together or lose this battle." If he could take control of TÅµr Medb from her, he would not need this witch, but any attempt to overpower her would result in a deadly battle that she might just win.

After all, she'd trapped *him* in the dungeon until recently.

Flaevynn's lips twisted with a pout. "How can I trust her when she tried to invade Treoir without my knowledge last time?"

Pointing out that Kizira was also Flaevynn's daughter

would not work in Kizira's favor. "I told ya she had your best interest at heart. If ya do no live, Kizira does no either." Unless his cunning daughter had figured out how to reach the river beneath Treoir Castle and knew the spell needed to draw immortality from it.

Flaevynn should have passed that spell along to her daughter with the words that allowed Kizira to take the throne upon Flaevynn's death. But the queen bitch, er, witch refused to allow anyone to live unless she did. She cared not if all of TÅµr Medb crashed down with her demise.

Fortunately for the rest of the Medb, Cathbad had unlocked much about the prophecy, or the curse, as Flaevynn called it, and quite possibly the spell that would ensure that he live forever once he swam in Treoir's hidden river.

Oh, yes, he would do that. If all went as he planned, he would teleport away before Flaevynn realized she was free of TÅµr Medb.

But he had not told her any of this. She still believed neither one of them could leave TÅµr Medb physically until the curse was broken.

Cathbad was sure he had found a loophole, no thanks to the original Medb queen, known as Maeve, and the original Cathbad the Druid. That pair had put the entire Medb race in this situation over two thousand years ago. Every queen after Maeve lived six hundred and sixty-six years. A druid of Cathbad descent was chosen as the mate for each subsequent queen and was the only person privy to that queen's actual birth date. He'd received

Flaevynn's during a dream the night of his eighteenth birthday.

The idea had been to prevent anyone from altering the destiny of the curse.

But each new queen had proven far more powerful than the one before, just as each Cathbad grew in power. Unfortunately, men would always be men when it came to women.

Flaevynn had manipulated him in the throes of passion, learning her real birth date, which was in three days.

That would be the date of her death as well if she did not gain immortality from the water beneath Treoir Castle, a place currently ruled by the Beladors.

Cathbad was not sure what would come of altering the prophecy, er . . . curse . . . time line, but he had an investment, too, since his death would follow shortly after Flaevynn's if he did not become immortal.

Flaevynn levitated from her throne and floated over to a two-story wall of red candles, where she descended to stand in front of her scrying wall. The tower of red candles burst to life, sending a shower of light across her gown that shimmered pale blue and yellow. The dress managed to appear ethereal and electrical at the same time.

Power fed her words. "We don't need Kizira's help now that we have a brilliant plan for capturing the Alterants."

We? That would be the queen's "we," since he had come up with the idea of the Achilles Beast Championship. A plan to fix another mess Flaevynn created. His voice rumbled with anger. "Had you no sent word out ta witches ta capture Alterants, we could ha' waited for the Alterants ta find Evalle, then captured the whole lot of them at one time. Did I no tell ya the beasts would be drawn ta her?"

"Yes, but did you consider what would happen if those beasts just started showing up in an area protected by VIPER? The coalition agents would kill any they thought were a threat to humans. Then where would we be?" Flaevynn lifted her smug chin at him. "You can thank me now."

Do no lose your temper. The witches had already captured many of the Alterants. "You can no stir this pot anymore, Flaevynn. Interfere with the beast championship and you'll be dealin' with Kol D'Alimonte. He's no one to cross and far worse than his brother."

"I have no intention of crossing him."

"'Tis why Kizira must be freed. Ya need her ta be your representative at the beast championship ta deal with D'Alimonte and ta convince the Alterants they want what we offer."

"I have taken control of Tristan and can compel him to act on our behalf."

"Trust someone who is no a Medb? No." Cathbad kept his arms at his sides, where he would not start a battle by trying to choke the crazy woman. "Besides, 'tis you who should be wantin' Kizira ta compel the five Alterants we hunt for."

"Why?"

"They carry powerful majik that we must harness, but if there's a problem the majik may backlash through the connection. We can no risk somethin' happenin' ta ya."

Flaevynn spun around, eyes thinned with suspicion. "Then *she* would suffer the backlash."

He had to answer with plenty of arrogance and make this believable. "Aye."

"Why would you risk that with your darling child?" She sneered the word *child*.

"For one thing, I believe either of ya can handle the backlash." Then he chuckled in a cunning way to sell his next comment. "But let's be honest. This is about survival. If we do no fulfill the prophecy—"

"Curse," she corrected.

Semantics. "If we do no fulfill the curse, you vanish first, Kizira dies next, then I disappear a day later. If it comes down ta you or her, who do ya think I'll be choosin'?"

He waited as his logic pecked at Flaevynn's resistance, but he had given an argument she could not dispute. There had been many times over the centuries that he sided with Flaevynn against Kizira, all for this moment when he had to convince the shrew they were partners in this.

She lifted her hands in the air, her eyes glowing as if on fire. Sure signs she'd capitulated.

Flaevynn held out her hand and pointed at a spot between the two of them.

In the next moment, Kizira materialized on her knees, looking as if she'd been dragged through a field of jagged glass—a beautiful girl with raven hair and soft green eyes who would make a powerful queen if Flaevynn had not denied her the right to succession. Clothes torn, skin flayed open in places with blood seeping out and face haggard from the ordeal.

Cathbad bit down on the urge to snarl at Flaevynn, who had clearly done this to Kizira to strike back at him, and called her forth in this condition to see if he really would sacrifice his daughter.

Kizira held her head up, a proud and defiant gaze turned to Flaevynn.

Ah, child, do no be makin' this more difficult. To keep her from speaking up and setting Flaevynn off, Cathbad asked Kizira, "Ha' you learned your lesson, child?"

She twisted to him, eyes shocked for a moment until what light had been there dimmed. He'd suffer her disappointment for any hope of saving her.

Looking to Flaevynn, he asked, "Did ya take away her tongue?"

"No, she did not," Kizira answered. "What do you two want now?" She pushed to her feet, wobbly but proud, and swung back to Flaevynn. "Because you wouldn't call me back unless you needed me for something."

Flaevynn's face brightened, a sure indication of a cruel thought. "Cathbad claims you're bright, although going against me undermines that claim."

Kizira didn't respond, which only encouraged Flaevynn to fill the void. "We've come up with a way to locate Alterants quickly, something far more efficient and foolproof than your ideas. Cathbad can fill you in on the details. He pointed out a risk to me I hadn't considered. A witch must link to the Alterants we're capturing and take control of the beasts in order to compel them. Five will be extremely powerful, the kind of power that could rival ours, which means there's a chance they could drive that energy back through the link to their master."

Kizira perked up. "Afraid of your new toys?"

"Fear has nothing to do with it," Flaevynn answered with chilling softness. "This is about winning. I will compel you, then you will form a link with the Alterants and compel them. As Cathbad pointed out, of the three of us I am the most valuable and you are the most expendable."

Turning slowly, Kizira faced Cathbad.

He had expected hurt and accusation of betrayal to line her gaze, but a cold wash of anger swept aside any other emotion. That worked best for now. He would explain to Kizira later.

"But be forewarned, Kizira," Flaevynn said, drawing everyone's attention back to her. "If I so much as suspect you trying to usurp me in any way, you will die slowly and painfully. Your value to me has run its course. Your choice. Do you return to the dungeon to finish out what time you have left, or will you perform your duty as a Medb priestess?"

"Tough choice. I may have to phone a friend."

Tiny blue-and-yellow lightning bolts flashed with energy, snapping around Flaevynn. "Do you think I'm joking?"

Cathbad shook his head. Spare him from sharp-tongued women in his next lifetime. "Stop it, you two. Ya want the same thing we do, Kizira. Freedom from this." He hoped his last comment broke through his daughter's haze of anger to remind her of their last conversation.

Kizira's condescension disappeared. Her shoulders softened. She nodded. "You're right. I want to be free of this tower forever." Directing her words at Flaevynn, she said, "For that, I'm willing to do anything you want."

"We shall see." Flaevynn floated inches above the shining marble floor for several seconds. "This time, I will not be so careless in how I compel you."

What was the witch up to now?

Cathbad frowned but didn't question her on it. He was more interested in getting Kizira alone, and the quickest way to do that was by reminding Flaevynn she was the girl's ma. "Now that we're all together for once, let's share a meal ta catch up and talk business later, shall we?"

Disgust brought out the evil in Flaevynn's eyes. "Indulge your revolting paternal needs on your own time. Had I known who you were the first time I lay with you, I would have been able to prevent the pregnancy."

And if he had not cast a spell of destiny on her during their mating, the witch would have aborted Kizira. "Ya ought ta be thankin' me for makin' sure ya continued ta fulfill the prophecy."

"Curse." She huffed at him. Her hair started twisting and whipping around her, a sign of her rising impatience. "You can explain what we're doing to *your* daughter. I need to finish what you interrupted. Don't bother me unless it's important." With that, Flaevynn waved her hand in front of her and disappeared.

Kizira rounded on Cathbad with threat in her voice. "So I'm expendable, am I?"

"Keep your voice down." He stepped toward her.

She lifted a hand, finger opening to point at him.

"Do no do that if ya want my help."

Her hand shook as she clearly battled to decide if she should strike at him or not.

She had power, but not so much as his. "Ah, child. You're no match for me."

"Don't start acting like you care now." Her finger shook with the indecision warring in her gaze. "And my powers might not equal yours, but I can do serious damage."

This was not going as well as he'd hoped.

TWELVE

Kizira didn't want to die.

Not yet.

But frustration and anger balled in her gut, demanding an outlet, and Cathbad presented an easy target. A deserving target.

Just not an easy kill.

Her attractive father had changed not at all since reaching thirty-five. Same wavy black hair and firm physical build that didn't quite reach six feet. Same powerful presence Kizira had benefited by on occasion. Same piercing green eyes that reflected more knowledge than anyone else in this tower.

Including Flaevynn.

Truth was Kizira couldn't bring herself to strike Cathbad down even after all the things he'd done to her.

Even if she'd held that much power.

He'd been her only true parent at times, and he *had* granted the request she'd made at the age of nineteen for one year to herself before she had to accept her role as priestess. A year spent . . .

Never think about that while inside this place.

Pathetic for a Medb priestess to hunger for a parent's love, but there it was in cold reality. Her whole body shook, as much from her painful time in the dungeon as from fury. Every part of her body hurt.

Cathbad implored her, "Put your hand down, child, and let me heal ya."

She lowered her arm, neither accepting his offer nor refusing him. Just standing there took all the effort she could expend.

He raised a hand over her head, fingers spread wide, and chanted, "Blood of my blood, I share my strength, to heal . . ." He continued in a soothing voice, one that also drew out her bitterness along with her pain while healing her injuries.

Did he think she'd give up her resentment and overlook her time in the dungeon just because he'd quieted her inner turmoil for the moment?

She wouldn't thank him.

He'd paved part of Kizira's hard road himself.

"May Flaevynn burn someday for how she treats her own child," he said as he lowered his hand.

Kizira's body glowed with renewed health.

He smiled at her. "I hope those are the clothes you were wantin'."

She took in her attire. He'd outfitted her in her favorite mortal wear of jeans and a pullover sweater, aqua blue. His favorite color. So he'd been thoughtful in his choice.

That didn't mean she'd trust him. To do so would be foolish.

A platter of fresh fruit, her favorite yogurt and granola appeared, plus a polished wood table and two comfortable chairs.

Now he made her feel like a shrew in the face of this consideration and his healing.

He sat down and opened his hands out like *What are ya waitin' for?*

That brought on a wave of guilt no one else in this place seemed afflicted with, but she ended up muttering, "Thanks."

"My pleasure. Eat while we talk."

Now with their father-daughter moment out of the way, she took a seat and demanded, "What did Flaevynn want you to fill me in on?"

"The Medb are financin' a special event where Alterants will battle."

Her eyebrows drew tight. "Why would we do that?"

While she ate a banana and stirred granola into her yogurt, he explained a plan for something called the Achilles Beast Championship and how it would function, adding that the Medb had offered trades for all Alterants entered to battle and their sponsors. Rubbing his hands together, Cathbad got to the key point. "But the most important element will be gainin' the five Alterants that win the final Elite matches."

"What of the ones who don't win their last match?"

He shrugged. "The matches are ta the death unless someone is allowed to beg for relief and granted such, which means many will likely no survive. The curse calls for the five most powerful Alterants."

"Thought it was a prophecy." Flaevynn refused to call it anything but a curse, which was all the more reason for Kizira to use *prophecy*.

He lowered his voice. "'Tis not the time ta be aggravatin' the queen." It was his raised eyebrows that gave his comment a conspiratorial flare.

Kizira nodded to let him know she understood that she should be careful what she said in this tower whether Flaevynn was present or not.

Accepting her nod, Cathbad went on. "As I was sayin', we will also offer trades prior ta the first match for those sponsors who doubt their beasts will survive. We have uses for the lesser Alterants, but our goal is ta gain those final most powerful five."

She pondered on what he said. "Alterants are hard to find and capturing one would take pretty powerful majik. Why would *anyone* risk losing their Alterant in a death match?"

"Because we are offering a trade to the sponsors of the final five for their Alterants. We anticipate having to trade Noirre majik for the beasts."

The most powerful non-Medb witches would kill to obtain Noirre majik. Kizira put down a strawberry and interrupted. "That will bring VIPER down on our heads. Even our forces can't hold if two or more pantheons attack us."

"VIPER would first ha' ta convince two or more coalition pantheons to start a war. Be that as it may, with death starin' Flaevynn in the face, she does no care. The way she sees it, she'll either be immortal or dead very soon. Either way, she will ha the final say in all this."

Selfish bitch had always had the final say. Kizira was counting the minutes until Flaevynn's death. "What motivation do Alterants have for fighting in this event?"

"The Medb will offer the five who survived the Elite matches a chance to become warriors who can conquer death."

"And how does Flaevynn intend to make good on an offer of *immortality*?"

"We have no called it immortality." Cathbad lifted a hand again. "Once ya see what the Alterants can do, you will understand this offer. I can no tell ya more yet."

He and Flaevynn really believed this would work? "Why would anyone believe the Medb? That's a bold offer."

"A Medb representative will be required ta satisfy a truth test at the beast championship."

She put down the linen napkin that had appeared with the food and leaned forward, arms crossed, mouth set hard. "Let me get this straight. The Medb are making an offer that will bring out every powerful being imaginable, all of whom will expect the offer to be proven bona fide in public, which means *I'll* be the one sent to do that truth test. The only test that group would accept was one of death as a penalty. You let Flaevynn put me in the dungeon and torture me, then expect me to trust you on *this*?"

He moved toward her, and Kizira backed up until her shoulders hit the chair. "Give me a chance ta explain, child."

"Why?"

Cathbad's gaze slid sideways to Flaevynn's throne. When Kizira followed the direction of his gaze, she noticed the dragon's eyes watching them, so she whispered, "Should we leave?"

"No necessary." Cathbad raised his hands, then chanted terse words. A purple fog curled around their feet, then smoked out to wind around and around the two of them.

When it stopped, she and Cathbad were in a cocoon that resembled the lavender cotton candy she'd once seen at a festival in the mortal world.

When Cathbad finished the spell, he said, "That should protect our words so we'll no both end up in the dungeon."

"Won't she notice?"

"The dragon sees us still talking at the table, discussing what you will need in order ta do Flaevynn's bidding. She may be powerful, but she ha never known all that I can do." He grinned, reminding Kizira of the man who used to dote on her as a child when Flaevynn was not around. "Now I'll explain why ya must trust me. We ha less than three days ta break the curse, and now that you are free we must be busy."

"What makes you think I care about that curse anymore?" Kizira challenged, tired of being used in a game that was no-win for her. "If Flaevynn is successful and takes control of Treoir, she'll probably also figure out how to get the water brought to her and become immortal, at which time she'll kill me, and *you*, too."

"True, but—"

"If she *doesn't* take the castle, Flaevynn will die and so will I, since she refuses to pass on any legacy to another queen. Every scenario ends with me dead. Can't say I'm feeling the love."

Cathbad clucked his tongue. "If ya would settle down and listen ta me, you would know what's goin' ta happen. Ya must have more faith."

Was he serious? "Faith is in short supply for me right now."

"Give me one chance ta convince ya."

She muttered to herself until she lifted her eyes to his. "Don't waste it."

"I would no help Flaevynn if I thought you and I would no both survive. All you ha ta do is follow her instructions and I will make sure she never gets out of my sight and does no get there ahead of me."

"As if I have a choice in doing her bidding when I'm compelled?" She'd snapped the words at him but kept her voice hushed.

"Ya ha outmaneuvered Flaevynn's compulsion spell more than once."

Kizira grudgingly admitted, "Yes, but I've never been able to disregard a direct order." Some secrets had to be shielded at all costs. Kizira refused to even think about what was dear to her while inside this place.

"Using that sly phrasin' and your clever mind is all ya need ta do what you must. You may be angry with the way I did no stand up for ya earlier, but it ha taken me all this time ta get you released. That would no ha happened if I ha no convinced Flaevynn I was more interested in savin' *her* than anyone."

Distrust moved through Kizira's chest, but she couldn't argue that she *was* free, so she didn't berate him again. "Okay, I'm here. Now what?"

"For us ta succeed and Flaevynn ta fail, you must do two things."

"I'm listening."

"Ya must show Flaevynn that ya are following her orders exactly while capturing the Alterants, and no interfere with their trainin'."

"Why would I interfere?"

"Because we both know ya are protectin' someone."

The blush of warmth that had returned with her healing rushed out of her face when she was reminded that Cathbad knew a secret Kizira would shield from Flaevynn at all costs.

Cathbad must have taken her silence as denial. He sighed. "Ah, child, we've already been through this. No need to be remindin' you how I know of the soft spot in your heart for one particular Belador. The beasts we capture will be compelled to kill all they encounter." His gaze filled with something she'd almost call regret, but Cathbad was not a man to suffer such a feeling when immortality was on the line.

Kizira shut her mind to keep from thinking about Quinn, or about anything else that mattered to her. This might be a trick to uncover all her secrets. Speaking with an icy calm she didn't feel, she asked, "What are you getting at?"

Cathbad's smile came from a sad thought. He sighed and shook his head slightly. "I will no let you be duped into thinkin' anyone is safe in this game. Once Flaevynn compels you, then you will compel the Alterants we capture at the beast battle. When you do, they will have ta execute your orders. Even Evalle will no be able ta disobey. Give Flaevynn any reason ta doubt your commitment ta this plan by protecting one Belador, and all is lost."

No, all would never be lost.

Cathbad was a fool if he thought she'd just stand by and let Flaevynn destroy everything that Kizira held dear.

Kizira would do Flaevynn's bidding for one reason.

To be the first one inside Treoir Castle and swim in that river so that she would become powerful enough to kill a Medb queen.

THIRTEEN

At nine on the dot, Evalle rode her gold Suzuki GSX-R through an opening in the face of the mountain that housed VIPER headquarters in North Georgia. She slowed her bike and parked near where Tzader Burke stood inside with a group of agents.

By the time she peeled out of her riding gear, most of the Beladors had dispersed, probably headed to the meeting room.

She strode across the stone floor, her boot heels tapping a straight line to Tzader. Just over six feet tall and cut with muscle from head to toe, he was one of her two best friends. He exuded power, leadership and confidence. Beautiful coffee-brown skin covered all that muscle hidden inside a navy-blue collared shirt, jeans and a black leather jacket. The honed cut of his nose and cheeks shaped his face with lethal perfection, but you couldn't call him pretty.

Or maybe you could. But it would only happen once.

Maistir over the North American Beladors, Tzader commanded attention just by entering a room, and he took in everything at once with the eyes of a hawk.

She trusted this man more than she would've trusted a brother if she'd ever had a sibling. "What's up with no telepathy?"

"An infection. One of our Beladors was brought in with severe disorientation and erratic behavior. By the time a Belador healer got a look at him, he couldn't communicate, so the healer tried reaching him telepathically to find out what was going on."

"It had to be bad for the healer to do that." Because Sen allowed no telepathy inside the mountain and no majik beyond what he wielded.

"Yes, but that's how the healer caught the infection."

Now the telepathic silence made sense. "Where'd it come from?"

"Before the healer lost his ability to talk, he shouted *Nightstalker.*" A grave look crossed Tzader's face. "We think the ghouls are passing it somehow in the handshake. This shuts down our best line of intel."

Evalle couldn't help that her first thought was for her favorite Nightstalker, Grady, a grouchy old ghoul she considered a friend. Nightstalkers traded intel for a brief handshake with a powerful being, thus gaining ten minutes of corporeal form. Most spent that ten minutes chugging any liquor they could find.

Grady was in danger. She should go back and check on him. She should . . . *stop panicking*. The bone. She had to keep a grip on the stupid bone. Forcing calm into her tone, she asked, "How many Beladors are infected?"

"We have five here, and I've sent a team to hunt down a couple who've gone MIA who probably thought it was the flu, then lost consciousness, or might be walking around exposed to dangerous elements. That's why I told everyone no telepathic contact until we can quarantine this infection."

Trey McCree walked up, his thick body stuffed in a gray T-shirt, brown corduroy jacket and jeans that might be his favorite pair, based on the worn knees and pockets. He said hello to Evalle, then started reporting on all his people. As Trey was one of the most powerful Belador telepaths, they couldn't afford for him to get infected.

Evalle hated to put one more thing on Tzader's shoulders, but as soon as Trey finished, she had to tell Tzader what was going on. She'd kept her activities with Macha secret long enough, and Macha made it clear Evalle was flying solo now.

Macha might be her goddess, but Tzader and Quinn were the closest Evalle had ever come to having family. If she didn't make it out of the ABC, she wanted Tzader to know the truth behind why she'd entered. Because Sen would convince everyone she'd gone inside to gain immortality.

When Trey finished his report and walked away, Tzader made a move to follow him.

"You got a minute, Z?" Evalle asked.

He stopped and looked over his shoulder. "Is it important? I need to get these agents back out on the street."

Would I ask if it wasn't? Her temper jumped at his sharp tone and her skin started baking. She clamped her jaws to keep from saying something she'd regret. Tzader was doing his job. Breathing through her teeth, she waved a hand to move him on. "Yes, it's important, but I can wait."

With a quick nod, he was off again.

Pulling on the long sleeves of her vintage Army BDU—Battle Dress Uniform—shirt to keep the armband hidden, she followed Tzader.

"Where're you going, Z? The conference room's in the other direction."

"The amphitheater."

"How many agents are in?"

"Thirty-eight. We've alerted the other divisions electronically."

Did that mean there was more to this meeting than discussing an outbreak of infection? Inside the cavernous amphitheater lit by torches, Tzader took the steps down to the stage two at a time.

Why the medieval look, when Sen could conjure up anything with a snap?

Evalle scoped out the crowd, finally locating Trey and a few others she'd teamed up with in the past. The room was curved, with tiered seating of carved stone steps going down to a stage that glowed around the edges. Picking her way across legs that pulled aside for her, she plopped down next to Trey, who sat one row in front of Lucien, Casper and Adrianna.

Evalle nodded at Reece "Casper" Jordan, who was every inch a Texas cowboy, except on rare occasions. He got the nickname "Casper" because he shared his body with a thirteenth-century ghost. Every now and then the ghost would show up for a battle.

A grin lit up his rough and rugged face when he noticed her. "Things sure have been calm since you got over your EMS attack."

She would not rise to the bait. Another agent had accused her of suffering from EMS—Evalle Missing Storm—while Storm had been MIA for three weeks. She'd put a couple of vicious gang members in the hospital on her crankier days. They'd deserved it for raping and killing a young girl. "Surprised to see you here, Casper."

"Why?"

"So many sheep, so little time."

He just grinned that much harder. "But I'll always make time for the black sheep in your Belador tribe."

The hole's deep enough. Stop shoveling now.

Evalle ignored him and spoke to Lucien Solis, who dipped his chin to acknowledge her in his usual mysterious way. The dark Castilian seeped sex from his pores, but none of the women she knew of had made any headway with him. Evalle had heard rumors about Lucien and Trey's sister-in-law, a witch.

But not a dark witch like the one who sat next to Lucien.

Adrianna LaFontaine. Rather than appear a jerk in front of the team, Evalle gave Adrianna a murmured hello. She embodied what Evalle would label "sex kitten," with blond hair falling past her shoulders, full red lips, perfect skin and blue eyes that assessed everyone with cool reserve. Nice to see her in a cinnamon-red sweater and gray slacks instead of what she usually wore—something that showed off her legs.

The Sterling witch cocked an eyebrow in answer. Worked for Evalle.

She still hadn't gotten over the fact that Adrianna had been the one to care for Storm during the three weeks he'd disappeared after Sen had crushed his jaguar body.

Of course, she was thankful Adrianna had hidden Storm's battered body when Evalle was in VIPER prison, but she still wanted to use her foot to wipe the smug expression off Adrianna's face every time they met. Like now.

No. Not now. Not here.

Evalle tucked her fisted hands under her crossed arms, facing the stage and thinking calm thoughts. Storm had said there was nothing between him and the witch, and he would have been hit with pain if he'd lied.

The new part for Evalle was that even without that consequence, she would believe Storm.

He'd earned her trust.

When Sen called the room to order, Evalle sat up straighter. Tzader stood a few feet away from Sen. The way this room was created, no one needed a microphone.

Sen stood a head taller than Tzader, but she'd seen Sen even taller and broader. His body could change as easily as the length of his mahogany-brown hair. It was cut short today. Rarely did he appear in anything other than black jeans and a T-shirt. Today he wore a long-sleeved black tee. Many had speculated about his godlike powers, but no deity would be forced to act as liaison between VIPER agents and the Tribunal.

His origins were anyone's guess.

Much like the unknown origins of Alterants, but many clearly saw Sen's as a valuable pedigree, whereas she was considered mongrel.

When Sen spoke, his voice rolled up the stair-step seating. "By now you know we have a contagious infection being transmitted by Nightstalkers. We have to find the origin of this infection, and we believe someone or something is passing this along when they shake hands with Nightstalkers. Healers are working on our agents to slow the infection, but without more information the diagnosis is grim, because the infected ghouls are deteriorating until their spirits are trapped inside half-visible bodies."

Evalle had to get back to Grady and make sure he stayed away from everyone. He wouldn't like giving up his ten minutes of human form for a handshake with a powerful being, but he wouldn't want to end up with his spirit trapped in a half-dead shell.

VIPER would order those bodies destroyed, but what did that mean for their spirits?

Continuing, Sen said, "We have incidents of the infection being passed through telepathy." Murmuring broke out through the room until the torches on the stage flamed high and bright—Sen letting everyone know to shut up. When the room quieted, he said, "The agents affected are comatose, and it doesn't look promising. We need to find out where this came from and if someone has unleashed this intentionally in the city. Our guess at this point is that someone might be trying to wipe out our intelligence network."

An agent halfway down stood up, taking the floor for a question. "Any suspects at all?"

"No." Sen crossed his arms and took everyone in with one sweep. "Unless you have a case that I've cleared as taking precedence, then every one of you is assigned to this problem until you hand me the person or group behind the infections. Tzader will hand out orders as soon as we finish here."

Another agent rose to his feet, asking about what to do if they found an infected agent, human or other.

"We have a hotline monitored twenty-four-seven. Do not touch anyone or any*thing* you suspect of infection." When no one else posed a question, Sen looked over at Tzader before stepping a few feet away.

Tzader moved to center stage. "We have another issue brought to my attention today. We want to make sure everyone is clear on VIPER laws. One of our Beladors learned of an Achilles Beast Championship event scheduled tomorrow night in the southeast corner of Georgia."

Warning crashed through Evalle's chest. She clutched the edge of her seat.

She should have talked to Tzader before this.

Heat streaked up her arm.

FOURTEEN

T his is *not* a VIPER issue as long as our laws are
not broken," Sen added from the side of the stage
where he addressed agents filling the amphitheater, since
Tzader technically still had the floor.

Evalle was gripping the edge of her stone seat. It
sucked as a stress reliever. Her heart rate had gone into
Mach speed. Where was Storm when she needed a calm-
me-down spell?

Trey glanced over at her. "Problem?"

Yes, I want to shout at Tzader that we need to talk now!
Instead, she whispered back in a strained voice. "Indi-
gestion."

He nodded and returned to listening.

She just had to figure out how to spin this ABC event
to *be* a VIPER issue.

Casper stood behind her. "Whoa now. When I was
in the Texas division, Beast Clubs were illegal. What's
changed?"

Thank you, Casper.

"Nothing." Tzader's gaze swept the crowd. "Beast
Clubs are still illegal and within VIPER jurisdiction for
sanctioning *if* the battles are held on any land that is not
under diplomatic protection. In fact, one of our people

spotted a Beast Club in progress in the area of Oakey Mountain last night. By the time agents arrived there was nothing left but torches staked around a circle." He continued sharing the report, details Evalle knew firsthand.

Cold raced along her skin at how close she and Storm had come to being caught. But they hadn't. She focused on keeping calm. *Don't react here.* She leaned toward Trey, hoping he knew more. "That was some get. Who called in the Beast Club alert?"

"Horace Keefer," Trey said softly. "He heard about it from a Nightstalker, but that must have been before the infection broke out. Old guy comes up with surprising intel sometimes."

"No kidding. Poor old guy needs a hobby."

"I think working with VIPER is the only thing keeping him going after losing his wife and son years ago."

She nodded, listening as Tzader moved on to VIPER's response to the report.

"We've sent out several trackers who are following scents, but no leads as yet. These *illegal* Beast Clubs have sprung up overnight, primarily here in the southeastern region, but we don't expect them to continue once the Achilles Beast Championship is over."

Evalle made a mental note to tell Storm about Horace having reported the Beast Club to VIPER, but she wouldn't reach him by cell phone until she got out of this mountain. If Horace had seen her or Storm, he'd have reported to Tzader, so she might be worrying for no reason.

Down in front, Horace swung his head around, eyeing the crowd, then his gaze paused on her. He gave her his grandfatherly smile, and she returned one as warm to him.

Trey shoved to his feet. "What about this beast championship? What makes that legal?"

What about sitting down and shutting the f—

Evalle sucked in a breath at even thinking a curse like that. Trey was only asking what she'd ask any other time when she didn't have to talk to Tzader about the ABC first. Her emotions were erupting willy-nilly, landing on the closest target for no particular reason. *Please get me out of here soon.*

Tzader turned to Sen, who stepped forward to answer. "I informed the Tribunal, who indicated they knew of the event and the host. According to them, the host is holding the games on his land, and he has diplomatic immunity as long as there's no illegal activity."

How about telling us who the host is? Evalle couldn't ask, because she didn't need to show any interest in the championship, not in front of Sen. Engaging him directly while she was wearing the Volonte armband would be asking for trouble, but you'd think someone *else* would want to know.

A female agent on the far left gained the floor. "You mean like tradin' fairy dust?"

"Exactly."

Evalle had to lock her knees around the edge of the bench to keep from jumping up and asking if Horace had found out that the buy-in was stolen Volonte bones, or that the Medb were offering Alterants immortality. She clutched the stone seating harder, feeling pieces crumble under her fingers.

Saying a word about the ABC right now would burst a dam on questions that would drown her the minute she tried to explain.

Trey sat back down, but his gaze traveled over to where she dug finger grooves into her seat. He leaned over. "I'll explain to Tzader if you need to leave."

Relaxing her fingers, she shook her head and squeezed out, "No. I'm good."

Sen's booming voice drew all attention back to the stage when he explained, "If anything illegal does occur during the event, we won't find out until after it happens. By that time, the event will be over."

The female agent pressed, "Don't you want to send in a couple of agents just to monitor the event?"

Yes! Thank you, whoever you are.

"No. The Tribunal indicated the buy-in is too high to send in a covert team."

Evalle's head throbbed with the need to use telepathy and tell Tzader she had the buy-in.

Tzader asked Sen, "What's the buy-in for these ultimate games?"

"Volonte bone."

"Thought those were stolen."

Evalle wanted to cheer Tzader, to tell him to keep going.

Shaking his head, Sen said, "It's rumored that the bones were stolen after the archaeological discovery, but the humans haven't reported a theft, so we can't charge anyone with theft."

That had to be good and bad news for Evalle, but she wouldn't celebrate until this armband was off. Until then, she was channeling Storm's soothing voice through her mind to hold on to her control.

"And," Sen continued, "those bones are so rare the event host will be lucky if they see two or three." He paused, his tone heavy with warning. "There is another way for someone to get inside the games without a buy-in. An Alterant can enter for free."

Tzader's eyes flicked at Evalle for only a second, but in that moment she could see that he understood the nature of what she'd wanted to discuss.

Evalle pretended that every set of eyes in the room hadn't just locked on her. *Stay calm. Don't smile. Don't frown.*

Didn't take long for someone to ask, "Why would *they* get in free?"

Sen's voice warmed to the subject. "They're the main attraction in this freak show. The marquee battles are a non-Alterant against an Alterant. The last Elite matches are five beast-against-beast battles, with the winners offered immortality by the Medb."

Silence overpowered the room.

Emotions burst forth and raked across Evalle's senses so quickly that she clenched against the onslaught. She shut down her empathic side, but not before shock, fear and anger sang through the energy around her.

She didn't have to hear their thoughts to know many

of them would be quick to believe that she'd enter the championship for a chance at immortality. Sen had to be loving this.

I hate you, you miserable piece of . . . She'd lifted her hand to toss a kinetic blast, but she caught Trey's hard stare. She forced a smile at him, hoping she didn't look like a rabid dog baring its teeth. "Hand cramp."

Nodding, Trey turned back to face the stage.

She was going to snap if this didn't end soon.

Sen had paused, anticipation building during the silence until his voice boomed through the room. "Make no mistake on this, people. *No* member of VIPER is allowed to enter these games as a fighter or observer. The coalition bylaws are clear about any agent fighting for personal gain. It will not be tolerated. To do so is to bring down the full force of our laws on your head. The last time a VIPER agent was caught in a Beast Club, the agent was terminated and his direct supervisor sent out of this country."

Terminated, as in destroyed.

Heavy thumps pounded in Evalle's chest, each beat echoing through her with the finality of a death knell. She crossed her arms again to keep her hands out of trouble and to hide the rage trembling through her. Sen expected her to go rogue.

Someone far down near the front asked, "What about Alterants? They don't have a pantheon. What's their status?"

Another round of stares swept up at Evalle. She kept her gaze locked on the stage.

Sen answered, "*Any* rogue Alterant found after this

event will be considered dangerous and a threat due to the possibility of their becoming immortal." Snickers of disbelief erupted. "Regardless," Sen said, quieting the room. "Once the ABC is over, these beasts are to be apprehended or terminated. Agents have autonomy to make that call."

That bastard. No thought of trying to rescue any Alterants being forced to fight against their will, like poor Bernie.

Sen's motto ran along the lines of the only good Alterant is a disintegrated one.

When rumbling percolated through the room, Tzader took a step forward on the stage, and every Belador in the audience snapped to attention. That quieted the rest. He said, "Finding whoever is behind this infection problem is our priority. I will contact you immediately by text if there is any breakthrough or change in this situation. Until then, telepathic communication risks a pandemic problem. Everyone is dismissed."

Evalle stood on wobbly legs, then made her way downstairs against the throng of agents heading upstairs to exit. She managed not to lash out at suspicious glances and whispers, pushing past the last group, when she came face-to-face with Sen.

Without any preamble, he handed out a dictate. "Tell Storm he either comes back now to help, or he's persona non grata with VIPER."

Did he think he could just dump that on her as if she controlled what Storm did or did not do? She snapped, "What makes you think I'll see him?"

Sen's eyes turned to cold steel but he didn't lash out, which worried her more than his usual temper. He said, "Tell him or don't. Either way, he's got until Monday to come in and declare his status with VIPER. His leave is over."

Of all the people she'd been concerned about attacking in this place, Sen had topped her list. Why the sudden lack of aggression? She should be glad, but all she felt was suspicion.

Evalle looked over at Tzader, who was talking to Horace. Tzader's gaze drifted to Evalle. When he noticed she was standing with Sen, Tzader ended his conversation with Horace.

Walking up to Evalle and Sen, Tzader asked, "What's up?"

"It would be in everyone's best interest to put the Alterant in protective custody."

What? "I'm not a threat."

Tzader gave a resounding, "No. And you know her name. Use it."

As usual, Sen ignored anything to do with showing Evalle respect. He tried to put the yoke on her conscience. "You should do the right thing and offer to stay here. If you're captured and forced to fight in the ABC, you'll either be killed or end up being hunted if the Medb take you into their coven. And once you do that, you can't return to the Beladors without putting them in conflict with VIPER."

Evalle had to hand it to Sen. When he cornered his prey, he made sure the only way out of hot water led into the fire. But she would not plead any defense to him.

Tzader lifted his hand. "Evalle's not fighting in the beast championship, so this is a moot point. Neither is she going into protective custody. Beladors can protect their own."

Sen shrugged as if he really didn't care. "Don't say I didn't offer." He strolled off.

He'd given up too easily. Evalle had a hinky feeling that he'd just set another part of a trap in place. Or was she running on high-test paranoia today?

After that conversation, she couldn't tell Tzader about the ABC.

Once Sen and everyone else had vacated the hall, Tzader spoke softly. "Before you say a word, I'm bound to give the Tribunal any report of Alterants around the beast championship. Even if Macha is behind some plan to capture Alterants."

Evalle's last ember of hope died with his words.

She just stared at him. Her stomach dropped to her feet.

Tzader cursed and turned away, cupping his hand over his eyes. "She can't do this."

"She isn't."

He lowered his hand and turned to her. "Neither can you."

"I hear you."

"Evalle."

She held up her hand to stop him. Tzader would step over the line and put himself at risk for her or Quinn, but she wouldn't let him. "The less said the better."

"I know you won't fight in the ABC, but she better back whatever she has you doing."

No, Macha was not backing her, but telling Tzader that would only add to the worry feeding that bleak look in his brown eyes. He'd been her only hope for unloading this Volonté. The emotional toll the artifact had taken during the meeting left her feeling wrung dry of energy. But she was stuck with it for now.

All her options had just vaporized. Instead of admitting she was rolling solo on this one, Evalle changed the subject. "I do need something."

"What?"

"An SUV warded against the sun so I don't lose daylight hours. You need everyone hunting for whoever brought in the infection." She hated implying that was why she needed the vehicle when in fact she needed something big enough to carry several Alterants if she managed to get some out of the ABC.

"I'll have Sen ward an Expedition. Where's Storm?"

She hadn't expected that question from Tzader. "At his house."

"We could use him."

"I'll tell him, but I'm not encouraging him to sign on with VIPER again." Evalle looked around, making sure they were still alone even though Tzader could see behind her. "Whether anyone believes it or not, I'm sure Sen tried to kill Storm a month ago."

"You can't be saying that around here without evidence."

"I'm not. I'm telling you, because Storm will probably come in to help you and the other agents. Just keep an eye on his back if he does, okay?"

Tzader took his time answering, those dark brown eyes concentrating a little too much on what she'd just said. "I'd think *you'd* be watching his back."

Crap. She shoved her hands in the back pockets of her jeans to keep from giving away her jumpy nerves. She should be helping Tzader. She should be watching Storm's back. She should be able to do a better job of watching over the people she cared about. "I will, but we probably won't be working together the whole time due to how little time I can be in the sun." Especially once she headed out for the ABC without him.

A long, tired sigh wheezed out of Tzader. "Take him with you to do whatever you're doing."

No way. "If I need him, I will, but he'll be more help as a tracker right now."

"Fine. I need you to do something for me, too."

"Name it." Being able to do anything for Tzader gave Evalle a happy moment she needed after hours of stress.

Tzader reached inside his jacket and withdrew a thick legal-size envelope. "Take this to Quinn tonight. I got a text saying that he received the warning about the infection and that he's back in the city. Said he'd be at his hotel all night. Tell him to call me after he gets this. I need to send him back to Treoir to oversee security there until we get this infection figured out."

She took the envelope and followed Tzader up the forty steps it took to reach the hallway that led back to her motorcycle. With every step, guilt dragged at her over leaving Tzader and Quinn to deal with the infection when she should be here helping out.

But she didn't have a lot of time to go see Quinn, check on Grady and talk to Storm before she had to leave for Cumberland Island.

When they reached her motorcycle, Evalle gathered what she needed, while Tzader arranged for the big black sport-utility vehicle that screamed Secret Service.

Tzader put his hand on her shoulder before she stepped into the imposing black ride. "I've never known Macha to intentionally send someone into danger, but I've got a bad feeling about whatever you're doing."

She pulled together all the muscles she could create a believable smile. "Nothing worse than her usual crap."

"Call me if you need me. Even if you can't use a phone."

"I will." *Not.* She climbed into the truck and flipped on the headlights that speared the dark hanging outside the mountain. When she drove out, the entrance formed back into a rock, blending into the surroundings.

She couldn't tell Tzader. And though she needed her friends to know, she hesitated to share any of this with Quinn. Guilt kicked her in the gut every time she thought about him, but much as she didn't want it to be true, her trust in Quinn had a severe crack.

Back before Tristan was captured, Kizira had claimed Quinn had told her where to find Evalle. That knowledge had almost brought about the deaths of Evalle, Tristan and his friends in an underground maze. When Evalle had questioned Quinn, he'd lied about helping the Medb priestess find Evalle. And Evalle knew that to be a fact only because Storm had unintentionally overheard her questioning Quinn.

Even if she could tell Tzader, now was not the time to divide his focus, when his first responsibility was to the Belador tribe. Evalle's should be, too, but she also served Macha now, and Macha topped everyone in the Belador food chain.

That meant Evalle would have to insert into the ABC alone, with no backup, because she would not pit Storm against an Alterant again.

And he couldn't get in without her.

She hadn't gotten the armband off, but she also hadn't tried to kill Sen. That counted for something.

Sen had been too accommodating with this vehicle, and he'd backed off *way* too quickly when Tzader had refused protective custody.

Definitely too easy.

Sen hadn't demanded anything in return for the warded SUV.

Deep in the pit of Evalle's stomach, she had a sick feeling that Sen knew something. About her and Storm being at the Beast Club? But Horace would have told Tzader, who would have told Evalle.

Or was Sen anticipating that she'd make a run for the immortality offer by the Medb and he'd capture her there? If he caught her, he wouldn't hand her over to be judged by the Tribunal.

Not this time. He'd deal out justice himself.

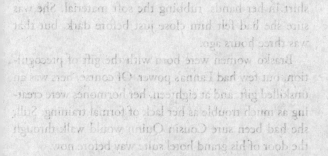

FIFTEEN

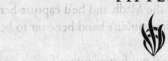

Cousin Quinn should have returned by now. He was near.

Lanna knew this because she held his wrinkled dress shirt in her hands, rubbing the soft material. She was sure she had felt him close just before dark, but that was three hours ago.

Brasko women were born with the gift of precognition, but few had Lanna's power. Of course, hers was an unskilled gift, and at eighteen, her hormones were creating as much trouble as her lack of formal training. Still, she had been sure Cousin Quinn would walk through the door of his grand hotel suite way before now.

She went to the giant window, where rain slapped the glass and blurred lights of downtown Atlanta at night. Her cousin had much money and liked to be high above Peachtree Street. So many umbrellas opened against the drizzling rain, she could not see who was down there. Dark and gloomy skies. Much like her mood.

Where was her cousin?

Suddenly her head throbbed. She dropped Quinn's shirt and grabbed her head, but nothing stopped the pain that came and went.

It meant Grendal, the wizard, was here in this country. Not close, but not far either. She could not let him capture her again. Last time, she had been his prisoner in Transylvania, and he'd forced her to drink a potion her powers had not liked. She'd escaped, but Grendal had found her again. She could feel it.

Her fault that he'd found her, but no choice. Innocent nonhumans would have died if she had not drawn on elements to save them.

Grendal was in Atlanta.

What if he had found Cousin Quinn and harmed him?

She rubbed at the sharp pain in her head. Was not logical. If the wizard knew she hid in her cousin's hotel, he would be here now.

The *snick* of a keycard sounded from outside the hallway door, then her cousin entered.

She released the nervous breath she'd been holding.

Cousin Quinn walked in with his wool jacket in hand. He wore the same light blue shirt she'd seen on him last night. His clothes had suffered. Quinn's eyes were tired. He had suffered, too.

She might have a paranoid imagination, but she had good reason. Her cousin was a powerful Belador expected to fight dangerous supernaturals.

"Hello, Lanna." He moved slowly. Not just tired, but an unhappy slow.

Who had caused this pain in his eyes? Too weary for a man in his midthirties. "You are exhausted, Cousin."

"Everyone is. Another long day in Treoir." His gaze

immediately assessed the room, where magazines were piled on the sofa and the remote sat next to her leg. "Did you stay in?"

"Yes."

"All day?"

"I am eighteen. We are lazy at this age. Enjoy movies and boys." She hoped that sounded like a careless teenager, something she'd never had the luxury to be.

Quinn dropped onto the sofa, pushing aside her things.

He needed fun in his life. What could she do for him? She offered, "Would you like drink?"

"Not yet." He pointed at a chair across from him. "Have a seat. We need to talk."

She sat heavily. Here came round three of "Lanna must go home." She had to think of a new way to delay. Hard to do when her head wanted to explode. Going back to Transylvania was not possible. Grendal would have someone there watching for her return.

Scrubbing a hand over his face, her cousin leaned back, his arms outstretched over the back of the sofa, one finger tapping quietly. "I tried to fix it for you to visit for a while, but I haven't heard anything, which I take to mean the time extension VIPER gave you for remaining in this country is up at daylight."

"I see."

"Don't be hurt, Lanna. VIPER appreciates your help with the Svart trolls, but VIPER still has to follow protocol for visitors with powers. If they let you stay without going through the proper channels, someone will use that as a precedent later on. I'm glad to see you, but it's time to go home."

She would leave soon and find somewhere else to hide in this country.

"Lanna."

"Yes."

"I can feel your brain spinning, but you aren't staying in North America. I have to provide proof of your leaving, which means a second VIPER agent has to be on site with me when you depart to confirm your transportation. Don't get any ideas about slipping out before tomorrow, because I won't leave you alone until this is handled."

She should have left today. Now she was trapped.

Grendal would capture her again. He would . . .

Her head throbbed. She clutched each side. Her body trembled.

"Lanna, stop! You're shaking the building."

She looked up and took in the room. Curtains waved. Dishes in the glass cabinet rattled. Furniture vibrated.

Quinn stood and leaned forward, reaching toward her, then pulled his hands back. Probably remembering last time he grabbed her. His voice was full of concern. "Calm down. Take a breath and relax."

"Yes. Sorry," she mumbled, propping her elbows on her knees and dropping her head into her hands.

When her cousin spoke again, he kept his voice low and soothing. "Time to tell me the truth."

"About what?"

"Whatever is scaring the bloody hell out of you."

When she lifted her gaze to him, he sat down again and propped his elbows on his knees, fingers steepled beneath his chin. "I will help you. You know that, but you have to tell me what's going on."

"I . . ."

"No more lies. We're family. I won't let anything or anyone harm you."

Sincerity in his voice broke through her determination to handle Grendal on her own. Either that or she could not think with so much pain. She wanted to tell someone, needed to know she did not have to fight Grendal alone, but she could not allow that wizard to hurt Cousin Quinn.

He waited patiently.

She finally gave up. "I have trouble at home." She peeked at him, but his face showed no reaction. "That is why I come here. Mama said you would help me, but . . . ."

"But what? Have I ever not come to help when our family needed me?"

"No, and that is problem."

"I don't understand."

"If I tell you what happened, you would go to Transylvania."

Quinn sat up, hands on his knees, fingers tensed. "Did someone hurt you, Lanna?"

"Yes, but not how you think." She took a breath. "I have not been hurt by a boy. I was captured by wizard who wants to use my powers."

Quinn shot to his feet again, raking his hands through his hair. "I'll kill the bastard."

"See? That is problem."

He turned his fierce warrior gaze on her, the one she'd seen make big men tremble, but her cousin did not frighten her even when he demanded, "Who is it, Lanna?"

"I will tell you his name if *you* calm down."

"You will tell me his name. Period. And where I can find him."

"This is why I have not told you. This wizard is dangerous. He has many in his castle. You cannot fight him without army of warriors like you."

"I can call up an army of Beladors."

"Not now, with threat on Treoir and your warrior queen."

Quinn paced to the dining room area. He stopped at the end of the table and turned, arms crossed, gaze demanding. "Tell me everything."

Now was the time for all truth. "His name is Grendal."

"Tell me about him. Who is he? What did he do?"

"Grendal struts much like peacock. Has hook-shaped nose that belongs on vulture." She snorted. "*If* bird was born with ugly yellow skin. Bright yellow hair that is short." *And empty eyes that promise death to anyone who refuses Grendal.* "He is terrible person, Cousin. He poured potion down my throat to make me do what he says, but my majik did not like it. I . . . blow up one end of castle. That is how I escape. Also, that is why my majik has problems. Sometimes it does as I wish and sometimes not. My power grows and weakens."

Quinn stood quiet as a statue, thinking. "Does he know you're here?"

"He does now."

"What does that mean?"

She admitted, "I was careful to only use majik in small ways, not enough for Grendal to notice, but when I called on elements to stop Svart trolls from killing everyone in warehouse last week I showed Grendal where I was. He was watching for me to make mistake."

"Good God," Quinn muttered, then his eyes brightened with understanding. "That's why you concealed yourself and held on to Evalle when our group was teleported to Treoir from the warehouse."

"Yes. I was afraid."

Warmth and admiration shone in Quinn's eyes when he said softly, "Afraid, but you still saved all those captives knowing this wizard would find you."

She shrugged. "No choice. People would die if I did not." Her new friends, the twin boys Kardos and Kellman, would have died.

A double knock at the door made her jump. A second double knock followed, as in some secret code.

Quinn lifted his hand for her to wait, then he walked to the door. "I got a text on the way here, so I know who it is."

When Quinn checked the peephole and then opened the door, Evalle strutted into the living room. Lanna wished to be Evalle in her next life, with long legs to look badass wearing jeans and black boots with hidden blades. She liked Evalle's vintage shirt.

Hard to be thought badass when short. Lanna sighed, resigned to a life as nothing but sexy Brasko female.

Evalle smiled at her. "Hey, Lanna Banana. Like that red sweater and the black jeans. You planning a night out in Atlanta?"

"No. I am prisoner." Lanna sent her cousin a prim look of challenge.

Cousin Quinn rolled his eyes. He did that often around her.

Evalle pretended not to notice. "How are you, Lanna?"

"Good. Happy to see you."

"Same here." Then Evalle reached around and pulled a fat white envelope from her back pocket and handed it to Quinn. "Tzader said to give this to you and for you to call him after you get it. Probably about Treoir. He mentioned needing you back there to oversee security so he can be here to deal with the infection."

"What infection?" Lanna asked.

Quinn murmured to Evalle, "You tell her while I read this."

Evalle explained about a strange infection being passed by Nightstalkers. Until the sickness was stopped from spreading, no telepathy was allowed between any Beladors or agents.

This was bad news. Even more reason for her cousin to send her home.

Folding the papers, Quinn looked at Lanna. "You can stay for a while."

Her heart jumped around in her chest, happy. "Truly, Cousin?"

"Yes."

"How can this be when you said they would not let me?"

Evalle's gaze bounced between the two. "Yeah, how'd you pull that off? I'm thrilled for Lanna, but amazed VIPER cut anyone slack."

Lifting the papers in one hand, Quinn explained, "This is temporary guardianship for Lanna I asked Sen to have expedited, but with him—"

"You had no idea if he deep-sixed it," Evalle finished.

"Precisely." Quinn gave Lanna a pointed look. "I told VIPER you were *seventeen*, not eighteen. Don't forget that if you're asked."

Lanna couldn't believe her cousin had gained her time. She spoke from her heart. "Thank you, Cousin."

"That's the best I can do for now, but I have to leave again—tonight—for Treoir."

Relief poured through Lanna in spite of the dull throb in her head. "Do not worry. I will stay inside."

Evalle said, "Load up on movies. Quinn might be gone for days or weeks at a time."

"It is not problem."

Quinn spoke up. "Yes, it is. You can't stay here alone."

Now what? "I have been good. No running around."

"You have," he admitted. "But now that I know a dangerous wizard is hunting you—"

"Stop there," Evalle interrupted. "A wizard is after her?"

"Yes." Quinn explained to Evalle, then swung his unbending tone back at Lanna. "As I was saying, I will not leave you here with that lunatic in the area."

Evalle gave Lanna a sympathetic look. "He's right. Way too dangerous to be without backup. Even if you could call Quinn, which you won't be able to do with him in Treoir, he can't even contact a Belador telepathically to get someone to you quickly."

Living in this country was much difficult. Lanna waited for her cousin to ruin the last of her good mood. Did not take him long.

"The safest place is in VIPER headquarters."

Evalle ground out a sound of disgust. "That place sucks, Quinn. She won't know any of the agents coming and going."

"But that mountain is safer than a vault."

Lanna would be trapped inside a mountain. What if the wizard had spies there?

Quinn asked Lanna to pack her suitcase. She nodded and trudged to her bedroom, fighting off a new panic. For all her relief over telling her cousin about Grendal, she was now terrified of being somewhere she could not escape if she needed to run.

She glanced out the door, checking to see where Quinn and Evalle were. They stood across the room, having a low, but terse, conversation.

Stepping out of sight, Lanna paused and concentrated on using very little majik. This would be easier if she felt better. She whispered a spell and watched her hands for several seconds until they finally became translucent. Her body disappeared in half a minute.

Practice on one new skill was paying off.

She could now cloak herself fully. But for how long?

Uncloaking, she gathered clothes and stuffed them half-heartedly into her worn-out suitcase that did not belong in this fancy hotel.

Quinn appeared in the doorway. "Are you packed?"

"Yes." She would have to find a way to escape her cousin before they got to the mountain, where she would have no transportation back. She had tried teleporting twice but had not moved more than ten feet. She had been sick afterward.

Evalle stepped into view. "You're going with me."

The elation must have danced in Lanna's face, because Evalle added, "Let's be clear. I'll be gone a lot and Feenix will enjoy the company, but his vocabulary still consists of about twenty words, ten of which are numbers. Sure you wouldn't rather go to VIPER headquarters?"

Definitely not there. "I am sure. Thank you."

Quinn offered, "I'll have my car brought around."

"Don't need it," Evalle told him. "I'm not on my bike. I've got an Expedition from headquarters warded against anyone either trying to bypass the security or drive it."

"Why did you take a truck?"

Evalle hesitated to answer and did not look at Quinn when she shrugged. "Figured I could at least scout around town during the day to keep an eye out for anything that looks suspicious. Might not help Tzader with this infection, but you never know."

Quinn gave Lanna one last order. "Do not use your cloaking ability to slip away from Evalle or I *will* take you to VIPER headquarters." He leaned down, adding, "I want your word."

Lanna's heart dropped. She could not give her word, then break it. She nodded. "I give my word."

Snapping her fingers and sounding more on edge than usual, Evalle said, "Let's go, and don't blame me when you get bored."

"I will be fine." Lanna would not stay with Evalle long enough to become bored.

With Grendal in the city, she could not afford to be locked inside *anywhere*, not even with Evalle. But now that she had given her word that she would not cloak herself to escape Evalle, Lanna would have to use teleporting . . . and hope she landed safely.

Not inside a solid concrete wall.

SIXTEEN

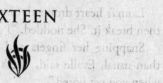

What kind of idiot got cornered into babysitting a teenage girl with the power to call up a thunderstorm?

Inside a building.

Me, obviously.

Evalle cut across the luxurious lobby of Quinn's five-star hotel with Lanna close on her heels. At least, Lanna had *better* be.

A quick over-the-shoulder glance confirmed Lanna kept pace, dragging her beat-up suitcase. Head bent down, Lanna's black-tipped blond curls drooped as much as her slumped shoulders.

Now Evalle felt bad about being perturbed that she'd gotten stuck with Lanna. It wasn't that she didn't like the girl. She did, but timing couldn't be worse with the Achilles Beast Championship coming up in twenty-four hours.

And that was only if she managed to convince Storm to help Tzader hunt down the source of the infection so Evalle could slide out of Atlanta without Storm noticing.

"How was Storm?" Lanna asked.

Was? Evalle slowed to let her catch up. "He *is* fine. I think he's healed completely."

"That is not question. How was date with Storm?"

Oh. Lanna had helped Evalle dress to see Storm after they'd returned from the battle where Storm had witnessed Evalle in all her beast glory. Not one of her more feminine moments. That had happened only because Evalle had been given permission to shift into her Alterant beast state to protect Brina and Treoir Castle from Svart trolls.

Lanna had come home with her and pushed Evalle to go face Storm even though Evalle had been sure he'd been disgusted by seeing her hideous beast form. She'd walked up to Storm's front door wearing makeup and a sparkly sweater for the first time in her life—all Lanna's doing. He'd welcomed her with open arms.

And chided her for doubting him.

Then kissed her and . . .

"Evalle?"

"What?"

Lanna's shorter legs moved quickly to keep up. "I asked how date was."

Slow down and stop being so irritated. Lanna was just a kid. Evalle breathed deep and searched for the calm that seemed just out of reach this evening. "The date was not really a date, but it was okay."

"That is all?"

"It was nice." That night with Storm had been like stepping out of her life and into one that belonged to a normal woman.

He'd made her feel alive. Cared for. Special.

"'Okay' and 'nice' not good." Lanna frowned at her. "Dull. What went wrong?"

Being with Storm was anything but dull. Evalle shot a glare at the nosy teenager. "Nothing went wrong. We enjoyed our evening. That's all you need to know."

"Ah. You spent night with Storm?" A speculative gleam brightened Lanna's eyes.

Evalle had thought Lanna's Russian-ish accent charming until the little busybody had decided to tamper with Evalle's love life from the first moment they'd met. Now the teenage terror rubbed salt into Evalle's wounded ego, reminding her she'd been a coward for backing away from intimacy with Storm.

She didn't need the reminder, blast it.

She was ready for him. Any time he wanted it.

Now!

Who was Lanna to question anything she did, anyhow?

Before they reached the doorman holding the glass door open for them, Evalle dropped her tone to a level meant to end all discussion. "What Storm and I did that night is *none* of your business. Got it?"

Lanna looked over at her, openmouthed.

Guilt stabbed Evalle from head to toe. *Why?* The teenager needed to learn when to talk and when to be quiet.

Outside, the drizzle had turned into a steady downpour. But Evalle was sweating. It was so blasted hot. How could Lanna wear a sweater in this?

Lanna dragged the suitcase along, wheels clacking faster to catch up. Her shoulders drooped teenage disappointment.

Evalle slowed her pace once more and pointed at the covered parking deck ahead. "We're going there."

Big mistake. Lanna took that as a sign that they were chatting again and started yammering, oblivious of poking at a beast. "I do not understand why you did not stay. How can you not want man like Storm? If Adrianna had Storm—"

"*Don't*—" Fury rocked through Evalle so sharply that she couldn't get another word out. Her body burned with the urge to strike out. Just hearing Adrianna's and Storm's names in the same breath spiked her anger off the charts. Gorgeous Adrianna would never turn down what Storm offered.

Muscles rippled beneath Evalle's shirtsleeves and along the sides of her jeans. She shuddered and slowed her pace, clenched her hands together. Imogenia had said the person wearing the bone could not shift. Had she meant it was not physically possible, or had she just been warning not to attempt it? Evalle assumed Imogenia had meant her body wouldn't try to shift on its own, but that's what she was fighting at the moment.

Lanna had continued on several steps and entered the covered parking deck, then paused, turning slowly to look back at Evalle.

Her face lost a shade of color at something she saw in Evalle.

People hurried through the garage entrance, ignoring Lanna, who stood there still as death.

Evalle struggled between embracing her anger and

wanting to tell the girl she was sorry for hurting her feelings.

When Evalle reached her, Lanna spoke quietly. "Your face changing. Are you having trouble with *other* part?"

She meant Evalle's Alterant beast.

Her muscles had swollen with the impending change. The armband was cutting off her circulation. Her skin was on fire.

The Volonte.

Evalle swallowed the snarl clawing up her throat and took a breath, then one more and said, "Don't. Say. Another. Word."

Lanna nodded silently, hurt bleeding into her worried face as if Evalle had just squashed a kitten.

That's all I need. Evalle drew in one more calming breath and leaned close to Lanna. "I can't . . . explain right now, but I'm not myself. Sorry. I don't mean to yell at you. Not your fault. I'm having . . . issues. Our truck's on the fourth level. Big black Expedition. I need . . . peace and quiet. Okay? Please."

She got another nod from Lanna before the girl turned around and headed on, but this time without the misery that had been in her face a moment ago.

Smart young woman.

Gripping her forehead, Evalle fought to calm herself and lower her skin temperature.

Thinking of Storm seemed to push her emotions closer to the surface than anything else. She had to come up with something to tell him about her plans for the next twenty-four hours that wouldn't light up his lie detector. She hated lying, especially to him.

But she'd do whatever she had to do in order to keep him safe.

The elevator stopped with a jolt, and Lanna exited first. She took one look around and started toward the only black Expedition parked there.

Evalle pulled out the key fob and pressed the unlock button for the rear gate. It popped open by the time they got to the truck. "Sorry again about before, Lanna."

"No problem."

"Yes, it is a problem, but I can't explain right now, and it's also a problem because it was wrong to be rude to you."

Lanna smiled at her and Evalle felt forgiven. The girl had given her time to calm down and regroup. She deserved a reward. Evalle offered, "How about some dinner?"

Lanna shoved the suitcase into the back and closed the hatch, smiling big-time. "This sound wonderful."

"I've got a great place—"

The words died in her throat when Storm stepped out from behind the SUV. Arms crossed, eyes like flint and mouth rigid.

Evalle relaxed her fingers, determined to stay calm, or she had no chance at outmaneuvering him.

"*Storm!*" Lanna bubbled, full of happy again.

"Hi, Lanna. Going somewhere?" He gave one of his devastating smiles to the young girl, and Lanna sighed so loudly that Evalle worried the girl might pass out from hormone overload.

Lanna pulled herself together and answered, "I go to stay with Evalle."

"Oh?" Storm's gaze swung back to Evalle.

Evalle jumped in before Lanna could say too much. Handing the keys to Lanna, Evalle said, "I need a couple minutes, okay?"

With a quick look at Evalle and Storm, Lanna walked to the passenger side, climbed into the truck and closed the door.

Evalle walked away, stopping at a spot in a shadowed corner that allowed her privacy while still being able to see the SUV.

Storm followed her. "Where's your bike?"

This was where it got tricky.

Snorting at his question, Evalle asked, "Do you think Quinn would let me put Lanna on a crotch rocket? At least we don't have to ride around in a limo this time." She hoped he'd accept her insinuation that Quinn was behind the SUV. Storm knew her underground apartment was a quick ten-minute walk from the hotel.

He admitted, "No. Can't see him allowing Lanna on a bike, but she'd probably go for it. Why have you got Lanna?"

Relieved to get away with that, Evalle filled him in on Grendal.

His gaze swept over her and stalled at her arm. "Did you get rid of the armband?"

"No, and I haven't been able to tell Tzader about the

ABC yet. There's a lot going on at VIPER that I need to tell you about."

Storm didn't rush to fill in the pause that followed.

She'd told the truth, even if it was misleading. She hadn't been able to tell Tzader because of the warning he'd given her before she'd left headquarters, but Storm's silence was getting to her. "What?"

"You still have that Volonte, and now you've got to watch out for a crazy wizard."

"Lanna thinks he's in the city, but Grendal hasn't actually located her yet. My apartment is underground *and* warded. He won't find her there."

Appeased for the moment, Storm asked, "Why didn't you come by my house?"

The truth would work best right now. "I was afraid."

He made a sound of disbelief.

"Wait." Hoping to smooth out the bristling tension between them, she put a hand up. "You know I'm not afraid of *you*. But I haven't got the best control right now and I . . . don't want to humiliate myself again." If he could change the subject, so could she. "Where were you when I called?"

"I went back to the Beast Club site this afternoon to track Imogenia."

"Why?"

He scratched the back of his neck. "Something wasn't right about Imogenia. The more I thought about it, the more it bothered me that she'd stuck that armband on your arm, as if she knew what the bone would do to you."

"But that would mean she knew who I was and expected to see me at the Beast Club," Evalle pointed out, feeling her body cool off with the change in topic. "I'm the one who went looking for her."

"I know." Storm turned his head, gazing out to where night surrounded the parking deck. "But . . . I don't know, something's off about all of this."

"Did you find out anything else?"

"Maybe." He faced her again. "You recall smelling a smoky scent of licorice around the Beast Club last night?"

"You mean that old vendor's incense?"

"Yes. I tracked Imogenia and her Alterant to where she left the area in a car. Her trail diverted around a clearing in the woods. I went to check it out and found that smoky scent."

Evalle realized where he was going with this. "That scent means something to you. What?"

His jaw flexed while he decided his next words. "Remember the witch doctor I told you about?"

She rolled her eyes and answered with self-recrimination. "You mean the one you came here to find that I promised to help hunt for when we got back from South America, and haven't yet?" She shook her head at herself. Total loser not to do that for him.

"I don't need you to hunt her right now."

Of course not, because Storm always put what Evalle needed first. That was changing after this if she came back from the ABC alive. "We *will* get on it as soon as we get a break, okay?"

He lifted his hand. "That's not why I mentioned her. Her majik has that same licorice scent."

Evalle thought back. "So you think *she* was at the Beast Club last night?"

"No. Maybe." He stared off for a moment. "I'm not sure. I should have sensed her being close, or I could at one time. I didn't. But that smell bothers me."

"Wouldn't she have shown her face at some point? Like when we were alone walking back through the woods?"

"I don't know." He blew out a breath and raked his fingers over his hair, disturbing the straight black locks only for a moment before they fell back in place. "I want you to tell me if you smell that again, no matter where you are."

"I will." Why did she have the feeling that Storm wasn't telling her something? "What else happened in the woods today?"

He studied her, taking his time to answer. "I ran into the witch doctor."

Evalle had a moment of worry until she realized Storm stood in front of her, safe and alive. "Is *she* still alive?"

"Very much so, unfortunately. She disappeared before I could get my hands on her. That's why I want you on your guard and to watch for that scent. Now tell me why you didn't talk to Tzader."

Evalle nodded, still feeling there was more but letting it go for the moment. "Sen and Tzader held a big meeting at VIPER about a couple things. Everyone's forbidden from using telepathy, which means *all* the Beladors, because there's an infection being transmitted through touch and telepathy. They think some powerful being is moving around the city shaking hands with Nightstalkers to intentionally release the infection, but no one knows who or what."

His cheek muscles flexed with angry pulses. "Those are Langaus."

"Plural?"

"Yes, but I don't know how many."

"But you *do* know about this infection. How?"

Storm hesitated, but he would have a tough time getting around a question that direct. "I ran into one up around Oakey Mountain when I met up with the witch doctor. She created the Langaus."

Evalle swiped a fast look over his face and eyes. "Did you get infected?"

"Yes."

"You have to go to the healers."

"I'm good. Now."

"How?"

"That's why I didn't answer your call. I can draw on my jaguar's ability to heal, but to get an infection or poison out of my system I have to completely shut down into a deep sleep. My guardian spirit woke me when the fever broke, or I'd still be sleeping."

When Evalle felt her skin getting toasty, she forced herself to ratchet down the urge to dismember the witch doctor. No time right now, but soon. "Why did she do this?"

"Don't know."

"Is there anything you can tell the healers that will help the Beladors and other agents?"

He nodded. "They have to treat this like a poison instead of an infection, because of the way it was created. I'll talk to Tzader and the healers, but they need a live Langau to make an antidote."

Evalle reached up to feel his forehead. "At least you're not hot now."

"Not there." His lips twitched.

Now *she* was hot again and doubted the Volonte was solely to blame. "Thought you weren't going to encourage me." She gave him a wry smile.

He gave her a smoldering look. "Doing the best I can, considering, but it's a struggle."

She had a feeling if she looked down she'd know just how much he was struggling. *Stop thinking about touching him.*

But how was she supposed to do that?

By talking about something that didn't make her want to reach under his shirt and run her hands over his body.

Nothing came to mind.

Touching him would send her up in flames again.

A dark look passed through Storm's gaze, then he shook his head at some inner thought and helped her out by talking business. "How many VIPER agents are infected?"

The infection. She could work with that. "I don't know. There were a handful of cases by the time I left headquarters, but we've got agents who are MIA that might be infected and unable to call for help. Speaking of help, they need your ability to track."

"I can do that."

"That's great, but I have a message for you from Sen."

"Oh?"

Lots of disdain in that one word. Evalle laid it all out for him. "He said you have until Monday to come back to VIPER, or he's marking you as an enemy of the coalition. I don't want you going back, but neither do I want to see the coalition turned against you." Because if that happened, she'd be expected to hunt Storm and bring him in.

Wouldn't do it.

Now that she thought about it, that might have been the reason Sen had been so happy. He'd figured out a way to force her into conflict with the Beladors and VIPER.

She'd write that on her worry list for later.

Speaking of worry, she still had to get Lanna settled, check on Grady, who she hoped was not infected, and ask if the old ghoul had any intel on the beast championship.

Storm shrugged over Sen's ultimatum. "I'll deal with Sen Monday."

Evalle didn't want to leave, but she had to convince Storm that all was fine, then get moving. "Thanks for helping them track those Langaus, especially now that I have my hands full with Lanna."

He tossed a glance over his shoulder at the truck before his gaze returned to her with a challenge. "Is there something *you're* not telling me?"

What kind of question was that?

One she couldn't answer truthfully without giving away her plan. When all else failed, fake it.

Evalle dropped the don't-screw-with-me face into place that she used when kicking demon butt and snapped, "What do you mean, is there something I'm not telling you?"

Please tell me Storm bought that.

Storm took a step back and raised both hands in a sign of surrender. "Easy. That came out wrong."

Sold. She kept her jaw clenched to avoid grimacing over tricking him and just nodded her okay.

"You're not trying to leave town without me, right?"

He was not part of her plan to enter the beast championship, but what could she say and not get caught in a lie?

"You want the truth, Storm? I *don't* want you to go."

When he looked surprised at her blatant admission, she drove on, hoping to sell this, too. "Bernie might have been a pushover for an Alterant, but others won't be. I know you're capable of killing pretty much anything you fight. The problem is that Alterants are an unknown entity. We come with a mixed bag of tricks and powers."

"I have my own mixed bag of powers."

Thickheaded man. She wanted to beat some sense into him. "I know. I saw you rip the head off a demonic troll, but you *knew* what you were up against. At the Achilles Beast Championship, you would face Alterants with no learning curve in your favor, because I doubt any two of them will be exactly the same. One bad injury and you'll be at the mercy of the next fighter. An Alterant has tremendous recovery ability in beast state." She put her hands up to each side of his face. "Please don't make me watch you get bloodied."

A growl started deep inside Storm, rumbling up through his chest. His shoulders tensed with unleashed frustration. "I won't be the one getting bloody." He huffed out a sigh that blew fine hairs around her face. "Stop thinking I'm going to die."

"So now you're immortal?" What was it about men, especially alphas, that made them believe they were indestructible?

"Of course not, but you know I'm the best choice and I'll survive."

That burrowed under her skin and started irritating her with a burning need to have the last word. She crossed her arms and should probably leave this alone, but the harder he pushed her on this, the more she was determined to win. "If you're not immortal, then technically you can't say you won't die, or you'd be lying. Right?"

He crossed his arms, too, and leaned down, shoving his dark gaze at her to make his point. "You don't have an argument. Bottom line? You aren't going inside that place without me."

"Since when did you get it in your head that you're calling all the shots?"

"Since you came back with that damned bone on your arm and no backup from VIPER."

"That's *my* problem, not yours," she shouted, shoving up in his face. She needed this stupid bone for any hope of getting into the the beast battles as an observer and not revealing her Alterant status. Did he really think she'd give it up? "Bottom line? I'm not taking it off."

"The hell you aren't," he blasted right back at her. He raised his hands in a sign of frustration and muttered, "You're making me insane."

She opened her mouth to give him another dose of her anger and he grabbed her shoulders, crushing his mouth to hers. A demanding kiss, so unlike Storm. One filled with both hunger and caring. After a moment, he moved his hands to cup her face, holding her in place, easing the kiss until he took her on a ride through heaven with his mouth.

Slowly, her anger simmered down, muscles relaxing under the onslaught of new nerves bursting to life. When his fingers smoothed over her face and down her arms, she dropped her forehead on his shoulder, content to just *be* for a moment in her life.

She let out an earthy sigh.

He growled near her ear, gripping her shoulders again. He eased her away from him, cursing softly. "We can't . . . do this."

"Why?" She blinked, trying to focus. "You're blurry."

Taking a couple of ragged breaths, he told her, "It's the damn bone influencing you. I don't want to increase the spell I wove around you, so work on calming your thoughts."

She did, and once her breathing evened out, she could see him clearly, right down to the vexation on his face. "Sorry about blasting you just now."

"No, this time the short fuse was my fault as much as the bone's."

Lifting her eyebrows at that, she asked, "Is the Volonte affecting you, too?"

Storm gave a harsh chuckle. "No, sweetheart. *You're* affecting me."

"If you don't want to get your head bitten off, then just stay away from me."

"That isn't going to happen." He reached over and touched her chin with his fingers. Warmth flooded his eyes. "You piss me off more than anyone else is capable of—"

"Careful or I'll get all tingly," she muttered.

"—but that's not what has my animal on the edge of ripping out of my body every time I'm around you." His eyes took on an unholy gleam of hunger. He leaned in close. "I'm out of my mind, wanting you so much it hurts, and my jaguar wants to be uncaged to release what I keep holding inside."

"Oh." What could she say to that?

He sighed and took another breath. "I'm not going to touch you until that armband is gone, but that doesn't stop me from wanting to feel your skin under my hands and to bury myself so deep inside you we turn into one. I want to taste every inch of you."

Her breasts puckered again in total agreement with everything he was saying.

She grasped his hand, pulling it to her lips, then she kissed his palm and looked up to find a firestorm building in his eyes. She whispered, "I told you, the minute this bone is gone, it's on. We're on."

He kissed her forehead. "Damn right."

Smiling, she stepped back. "Tzader needs help now with this infection problem, and I hear you on the beast championship. Just give me some time to figure out what I need to do, okay?"

"I'll have my SUV warded against the sun. You have to leave no later than four tomorrow to reach Cumberland Island in time for *me* to register to fight. Until then, I'll get in contact with Tzader and help him find as many Langaus as I can before *we* leave."

To avoid getting into *that* conversation with him again, she shifted the topic a little. "I have yet to find out exactly how to get from St. Marys to Cumberland Island."

"Like Imogenia said, private boats. The host will have one specific dock where boats owned by locals capable of ferrying our kind over there will port in. Those captains will know where the drop point is for sponsors and fighters, and they'll have instructions on how to reach the championship site. That keeps unwanted *guests*, like VIPER, from showing up."

"Where'd you find out all that?"

Storm just smiled. "This is not my first beast rodeo."

"You're not going to tell me where to find the boat dock, are you?"

"I don't have that yet, but worst case I'll be able to locate it by tracking the others. So just remember that you *do* need me all the way on this." Then he asked, "Where will you be until I pick you up?"

Another question that could trip her up.

Evalle hoped he wouldn't press for more when she tossed her head at the SUV and said, "My life as a baby-sitter. The things I do for friends. I need to go feed her and check on Feenix."

"What are you going to do about her for tomorrow?"

"I'm working on that. Thanks for helping Tzader."

"You're welcome." He pulled her to him and kissed her one more time with enough heat to make her want to chew her arm off to get rid of the armband. When Storm lifted his head, intense dark eyes pinned her. "I'll see you at four. Be. There."

"I liked you better when you weren't so arrogant and demanding."

Storm's lips curved up on one side. "No, you didn't."

He kissed her once more and strolled away, disappearing into the stairwell.

She'd be halfway to St. Marys by the time the clock struck four tomorrow afternoon and inside the Achilles Beast Championship before Storm could catch up to her on Cumberland Island.

Would that kiss be their last?

SEVENTEEN

W here was Grady? Evalle made another hike around Grady Hospital in downtown Atlanta, searching in every direction for the old ghoul, who could normally be found here at midnight. She refused to believe he'd shaken hands with a Langau.

It wasn't as though he would die. He was already dead. But she didn't want him caught in some torturous half state. She slowed along the quiet back street that separated the hospital from the interstate humming with light traffic.

"When'd you start playin' Secret Service agent and drivin' big black SUVs?" The deep voice boomed so close behind her that she flinched, then whipped around. Cool air brushing her skin dropped another ten degrees with the presence of her favorite pain-in-the-butt Nightstalker.

Grady's translucent form almost took shape, faded, then came back as a thin old man with skin the color of brewed coffee. A week's growth of whiskers stubbled his bony jaw that generally had a stubborn kick to it. He wore his usual red-and-black plaid shirt, short sleeves regardless of the season, and loose pants that might have been his Sunday best at one time.

Ghouls didn't suffer wardrobe dilemmas.

She cocked her head at him. "Where've you been hiding, you old goat?"

"Where's my bag?" His eyebrows waggled over warm eyes full of teasing.

She'd normally have a McHappy sack of hamburger, fries and water to drink, but Grady could be a tough negotiator when it came to dealing intel. *His* idea of a happy sack included a fifth of Old Forester. "I brought your favorite."

At that, his keen eyes focused on the bag she gripped, and he wiped his mouth with his hand, alcoholic hunger glazing his eyes. "What do you want?"

Any other time she'd indulge him and negotiate, but she couldn't shake with Grady, even if he swore he hadn't touched a Langau. She'd broken rules for the old ghoul once and shaken longer than allowed so that he could see his granddaughter get married. That had resulted in his being able to take corporeal form on his own sometimes, and for extended periods.

Seeing him translucent now stirred her pot of worry. "Can you take solid form?"

"Nah. Did it too much yesterday and ain't been able to turn solid since. Just zoned out."

Maybe that meant he hadn't been infected. "So you haven't shaken hands with anyone?"

"No, siree. I'm what you'd call primed and ready. I'll give you a deal." He stuck out his hand. "Shake and you git three questions. Kind of like a genie but you have the bottle." He grinned at his pun.

"Can't, Grady."

His face fell. "Why not?"

"There's an infection going around. Nightstalkers have been catching it and passing it along. VIPER has ordered no contact with Nightstalkers until they get it contained."

"Are you kiddin' me?" He scowled and stomped around. Silent stomping.

"I'm sorry. I'll leave the bottle hidden for you, but I need information."

"Nuh-uh. Not givin' up a word without a handshake."

He could be ornerier than a junkyard dog. "This is important, Grady."

"So is gittin' my handshake. It's the only thing important in *my* world. Why you stink?"

"Insulting me will cost you this bottle." She waved the brown bag and bottle.

He jutted out his chin with his meanest look. "You tryin' to make me mad?"

"No. I'm trying to get some help."

"How come you got a dead smell about you?"

Now she understood. Evalle slid her sleeve up. "It's probably this bone."

Grady backed away, looking at her like she'd shown him a two-headed demon. "You got a *Volonte* attached to your body? Are you crazy? Get rid of that nasty thing."

"I'd like to, but it's locked on my arm. That's why I need your help."

He grumbled and floated a little farther away.

"Get over *here* and stop floating around."

"Don't be yellin' at me," he snapped, but he did move close again.

She grabbed her head. "Sorry. I can't help it. This stupid bone takes whatever I'm feeling and amplifies that emotion or desire."

"Then you better stay away from that Injun. I seen the way you been lookin' at him."

She locked her jaw to keep from telling Grady, again, not to call Storm an Injun or remind him that her relationships were none of his nosy business. When she could talk without shouting, she asked, "Do you know anything about the Achilles Beast Championship?"

His eyes went to the bracelet around her arm. "Nah."

This was a waste of time. "Guess you can't help with the infection either."

"*That* I can help with."

"Really? How?"

The old coot just stared at her. Evalle waved the bottle in front of him.

He scowled. "Saw a Nightstalker fadin' in and out. She was jerkin' back and forth."

A sick ghoul. "Where is she? Did you see anything else that was suspicious? Storm says the host that's infecting the Nightstalkers is something called a Langau."

"If a *lawn*-gal is a demon livin' in a dead body, then I know where *she* is."

Tzader was going to love this. He'd texted Evalle with a message that Storm had contacted him and Tzader had assigned Beladors to support Storm. All info had to be reported to Storm.

"'Bout two blocks over that way." Grady pointed his thumb over his shoulder toward the south. "Brunette walkin' around all sexy lookin' in a red dress and heels. You ain't gonna miss her. She's moseyin' around, callin' out for Nightstalkers."

That was close by. How soon could Tzader get someone down here?

Grady wasn't done. "Saw someone else sneakin' around the same area."

"Who?"

"Your Rambo buddy."

Isak Nyght. She and Isak had an odd relationship. After she'd missed several commitments with Isak, his black ops team had kidnapped her to bring her to a cozy dinner with their boss. He'd kissed her a couple times, too. Once in view of Storm.

That hadn't gone well at all.

Isak was the rare human who knew nonhumans existed, and he built weapons that killed nonhumans. He would blast the Langau into a million pieces with his demon blaster, and VIPER needed that antidote.

Evalle walked over to the wall along the right-of-way for the interstate and stuffed the bottle into a cubbyhole, telling Grady, "It should be safe until you can get to it."

He grunted, clearly unhappy, but when he looked at her, his eyes filled with concern. "I don't know what that Achilles Beast Championship is. You takin' that Injun with you?"

No, but Grady was not a lie detector. "That's the plan."

"Good. He ain't much, but he's better than nothin', I guess."

She smiled. "Thanks for the intel. If I can't come see you myself, I'll ask Tzader to get word to you as soon as the infection threat is gone." If she couldn't get to Grady, it would be because she was dead—or in VIPER prison. Either was a distinct possibility, given the corner she was in. "In the meantime, don't shake with anybody, okay?"

"I'll be careful."

On her way to hunt down the mystery woman in red, Evalle lifted her phone, then paused.

Text Tzader or not? The last time she'd seen Isak, he'd actually helped when VIPER had to battle Svart trolls, but Isak still hunted nonhumans, and there was no way for him to know the difference between VIPER agents and a nonhuman threat.

Isak might not understand VIPER trying to save a Langau. But he wouldn't hurt Evalle.

She'd check it out first, then contact Tzader. Covering the two blocks quickly, she slipped through alleys, keeping her senses open for anything not human. When she came upon a flickering image of a Nightstalker hovering in the back of a closed-in alley, she saw what Grady had been talking about. Parts of a female ghoul—one shoulder, a leg and half of her head—floated into view and faded. She'd had frizzy brown hair and freckles at one time.

The ghoul moaned over and over.

Poor thing.

A noise at the entrance to the alley pinged Evalle into defense mode. She swung around and backed up to a brick wall, hoping whatever gushy stuff she'd just stepped in would come off her boots, because the smell would force her to burn them.

"Want a deal, Nightstalker?" a female voice called softly, heading into the alley.

Evalle eased forward to peek. The owner of that voice was an attractive young woman, a brunette who wore a red dress. The Langau Grady had seen? Probably. The infected Nightstalker started moaning louder and floating toward the Langau, which meant the ghoul was getting close to Evalle. Could the sick ghoul infect her?

Screw it. Time to text Tzader and call in reinforcements, because Isak wasn't . . . .

Boom!

Light exploded all around the Langau as it jerked from being hit. Eyes sank into her head and her fingers sprouted three-inch claws that curled. Her body sucked into itself and vaporized.

The female Nightstalker floated back and up, disappearing into a broken window.

Evalle leaned back against the wall, anger bolting up her backbone. That had to be Isak. She wanted to rip his head off. Literally. Grab that thick skull and use it for a basketball.

True friends are hard to find and should be appreciated, a woman's voice whispered through Evalle's mind. Not telepathy. This voice had been popping in at all hours, day or night and at the most inconvenient times. Evalle would like to know who the voice belonged to and why she shared her sometimes unwelcome nuggets of wisdom.

Just build a fence around my life and call it a supernatural wildlife preserve. Evalle heard Isak's last two steps before his weapon came into view. "It's me. Evalle."

He stepped in front of her and lowered his mega demon blaster, letting it swing from a nylon cord attached to his vest. Black cargo pants and long-sleeved black shirt beneath a loaded Molle vest. "Hey, sugar. Why were you hiding in here? You might have gotten hit by flying demon parts." His blue eyes danced with mirth. He was big all over. Reminded her of a Mack truck dressed up to be a sexy man.

Evalle pushed off the wall. She flexed her hands, working to hold on to her control. "I wasn't hiding. Did you have to do that? I needed those demon parts."

"Why? Saw that thing shake hands with a ghoul, then the ghoul freaked out."

"That *thing* in the red dress was a Langau. We don't know how many are in the city, but they're spreading an infection."

"Then you should thank me, not complain."

"I would, but VIPER needed that one. We have sick agents and need to capture at least one for the healers so they can create an antidote."

"Oops. My bad." He didn't sound the least bit repentant, because he'd only recently decided to allow *some* nonhumans to live. There was a time when Isak hadn't known VIPER existed and thought all nonhumans were a threat to humans.

He *had* pointed a weapon at her once with intent, but they'd gotten past that. She just wasn't sure where they stood now because of that last kiss he'd given her.

Which reminded her . . . "Meant to get your demon blaster back to you."

"No rush." He smiled during the pause. "Bring it when you come to dinner." He stepped up close and ran his knuckle over her cheek. His sandalwood cologne blended nicely with his natural male scent, especially when he was warmed up. Heat rushed into her cheeks and down her neck, into her body. Energy sizzled between them even though he was all human.

All male. But he wasn't Storm, who would go all alpha right now if he saw how close Isak was to her. In fact, Storm had agreed not to harm Isak as long as Isak kept his hands off her, which he wasn't doing.

She opened her mouth to ask him to stop and Isak's finger touched her lips, stalling the words. Evalle, queen of avoidance. She wasn't sure what to say, but she could not let him think they were going anywhere with this strange chemistry between them.

He leaned down to kiss her.

She jumped back, bumping into the wall.

He propped his hands on his weapon in a casual pose. "Something you want to tell me?"

Yes, but you aren't going to like it. "I'm involved . . . with someone."

Isak said nothing for a moment. "How involved?"

She lived on edge every minute right now, waiting to meet Storm in the bedroom. Too much information. "Very."

"What about our dinner?"

She'd given her word to his mom for dinner, which had morphed into a commitment to Isak when he'd helped out with fighting the Svart trolls and hadn't killed any of her nonhuman friends. Plus Evalle owed Isak's mother, Kit, for keeping Kardos and Kellman after they'd been saved from the Svarts. Kit had offered to care for them until Evalle could pick up the twins, so the boys didn't have to live on the streets.

Evalle's debt just kept climbing. "I'll come to dinner, but I need a little time. I'm . . . busy."

Isak was giving her the silent treatment.

"Look, Isak, I appreciate everything you and Kit have done to help with the weapon and the twins. I do, but I would not be honest with you if I kissed you right now." He nodded and she felt relief flood her muscles. "If you find another Langau, will you please call Tzader?"

She got another nod. This was going better than she'd have thought a moment ago.

Then Isak stepped close to her and sent her blood pressure soaring when he lowered his lips next to her ear. He whispered with total confidence, "I'm not afraid of competition. I'll see you for dinner, and I'll be around in the meantime."

Then he sauntered out of the alley.

And she had to report this incident to Storm.

EIGHTEEN

I compel you to . . ."

Kizira's stomach muscles clenched as she antici-
pated Flaevynn's next words. Why was she dragging this
out? *Just say it.* Then Kizira could start working on a way
around the compulsion spell.

Cathbad had been right about one thing.

Kizira couldn't protect anyone while sitting in a dungeon, but he was a fool to think she'd put her life on the
line for him or Flaevynn. If Kizira led the Alterants, then
she would be the first to reach the river of immortality
flowing beneath Treoir.

Perched on her throne, Queen Flaevynn tapped
a long, black-lacquered nail studded with diamonds
against her cheek. Amusement danced in her kohl-
outlined eyes. Thick tendrils of black hair shifted and
curled slowly around her neck and bare shoulders, falling to the strapless gown of liquid silk that reminded
Kizira of a burgundy wine.

Knowing Flaevynn, the dress had been created from
a rare vintage.

"Kneel," Flaevynn ordered, sending Kizira to her
knees with no notice.

She went down so hard that her bones fractured,
shooting pain through her kneecaps. She bit down on

her back teeth, refusing to even wince at the sharp throbbing. Her body started healing the injury. Not as quickly as Cathbad could do it, but it wouldn't take long.

Flaevynn chuckled.

Glad I could entertain you. Kizira stared straight ahead, having learned years ago that the less she said, the sooner she would be released.

"You said you'd do *anything* to get out of TÅµr Medb?" Flaevynn said, reminding Kizira of her words earlier.

Kizira realized she may have spoken too boldly, but she had to be careful how she handled this. "Yes. I like the mortal world, but I can't spend as much time there when you and Cathbad are stuck here. If you gain your freedom, I gain mine."

"We shall see." Pointing one of her black fingernails at Kizira, Flaevynn murmured words too soft to hear, then said out loud, "Kizira, Medb priestess of my blood, I compel you to do as I order you over the next three days. If at any time you do not repeat my compelling orders to the Alterants *exactly* as you receive them, you are to take the life of the person you love the most."

Kizira's jaw dropped. If she took a risk and miscalculated how she circumvented the compulsion spell, it would be a deadly mistake.

Flaevynn had finally actually surprised her with unexpected cunning.

Smiling with satisfaction, Flaevynn said, "Now I don't have to worry about you working behind my back."

The ache in Kizira's knees had dropped from a ten to a

two. She forced her mask of indifference back into place. How could she risk trying to get around the queen's orders now?

"I should give you the enchanted phrase that would allow you to live and be the next queen," Flaevynn mused out loud.

Kizira's pulse tripped over itself picking up speed. If Flaevynn passed those words along, Kizira would outlive Flaevynn and Cathbad. She'd never be able to leave TÅµr Medb again, but she could . . .

Flaevynn finished her thought, saying, "Then you'd know what it's like to be trapped in this realm for hundreds of years, stuck depending on those who are inferior. But not even the idea of your suffering the way I have is enough for me to allow another queen to survive if I don't."

Of course not.

Pointing a deadly finger at Kizira, Flaevynn began her next compulsion spell, and purple energy swarmed Kizira, "Kizira, Medb priestess of my blood, I compel you to attend the Achilles Beast Championship in the mortal world during tonight's full moon. You will bring to me every Alterant that is offered to the Medb prior to the battles or those gained through trade upon winning the final Elite matches."

Not much wiggle room in that order. Kizira said, "I will."

Flaevynn continued, "Once you return from the beast championship, you will link mentally with all the Alterants so that you have sole control over them, including Tristan and any others in my possession . . . even after they evolve."

"Evolve? What do you mean?"

"Cathbad didn't tell you?"

"No."

Genuine happiness rushed across Flaevynn's face as she whispered, but loud enough for Kizira to hear, "I wasn't sure he could be compelled, not at this point in his life, but we now know who is the more powerful between us." Returning her attention to her spell, Flaevynn swirled her pointed finger.

Dark purple energy suffocated Kizira until she had to squeeze out each breath. *Get on with it, bitch.*

"You will ensure that the Alterants follow your every order, just as you are to follow mine, Kizira. You will be bound to my life for the next three days and will die immediately if I do. However, I will not be bound to you if you should die. Once you return from the beast battle with the Alterants, you will be in charge of their evolution and compel them to execute my orders. If any one of them fails to do what I require, you will pay the penalty."

And Cathbad thinks I can outmaneuver this spell?

Kizira held still, begging silently for this to end. Her knees were almost to the point that she could stand without crying out.

"The minute the Alterants invade Treoir and kill Brina, you will bring me water from the river beneath Treoir without touching or drinking that water. Once I gain immortality, I will unleash my Alterant army on the mortal world, along with my entire coven of Medb witches and warlocks. Macha will no longer have her powerful Belador warriors once I control Treoir, because the surviving Beladors will answer to me."

Kizira's blood turned to ice.

Had she and Cathbad underestimated Flaevynn? But the queen had overlooked something. "Macha will not just stand by while Treoir is attacked."

"You think I've underestimated her? Think again. I've been prepared to deal with her all along."

What could Flaevynn possibly have in mind to prevent Macha from interfering? Or was Flaevynn so insane she actually believed she would win no matter what?

Kizira had a sick feeling that Flaevynn had one trick up her sleeve that even Cathbad knew nothing about.

NINETEEN

Evalle parked in the underground level of Nicole's apartment building in Avondale Estates on the east side of Atlanta. Nicole had been her only girlfriend since Evalle first came to Atlanta. She trusted Nicole as much as she trusted Tzader and Quinn.

And Storm.

Lanna climbed out of the passenger side. She'd been happy with the late dinner and chatty at the apartment, playing with Feenix for hours. But she wasn't chatty or happy now.

She wouldn't look at Evalle either.

Evalle opened the rear passenger door with her kinetics and Feenix leaped out, floating to the ground. Seeing a couple walking over to the access elevator, she cut her eyes back and forth. Keeping her voice down, she warned Feenix, "No flying until we get inside, okay?"

He sighed and turned big orange eyes on her. "Thorry."

She smiled. "It's okay, baby."

His gap-toothed grin with a two-fang overbite tickled her heart. She loved her sweet gargoyle. He stood two feet tall and wore his favorite T-shirt that read EVL TOO right above his potbelly. Thankfully, with people either sleeping in or already gone to early morning activities like church, there was little traffic in the private parking space beneath Nicole's building, a remodeled warehouse.

Lanna retrieved her suitcase from the rear of the SUV, and Evalle snagged a tote bag loaded with lug nuts. She grabbed Feenix's pudgy three-fingered hand and gave it a gentle squeeze. "Don't forget to play robot if anyone sees you."

"I know." Feenix sounded exasperated over being reminded, but he did tend to have a short memory on some things.

One look at Lanna, and Evalle suffered a new wave of guilt. "You're going to love Nicole, and it won't be for more than a couple of days tops."

Lanna gave her a weak smile. "I understand."

No, she didn't, but Evalle couldn't tell anyone what she was going to do when she left. No one at VIPER could know, and Lanna talked too much, plus she had a bad habit of sticking her nose where it didn't belong.

Better to keep her out of the loop on this one.

"Leth go." Feenix tugged Evalle's hand, then turned his smile on Lanna. "Like Nicole."

No one could resist Feenix, not even Lanna, who finally gave up and grinned at him. "I am sure I will."

Evalle managed to hustle her group into the elevator and up to Nicole's floor without incident.

Sometimes the world turned in her favor.

When Nicole's door opened, she rolled her wheelchair back out of the way to allow everyone to enter. With exotic brown eyes, slender nose, sculpted cheeks and smooth mocha skin, she could smoke most models with her beauty, and she didn't have a vain bone in her body. Whoever she got those eyes from probably also gave her the straight, light brown hair that normally fell to her shoulders, but she'd twisted the locks up on her head today.

Evalle introduced Lanna, who stepped aside shyly, which seemed so unlike the outgoing girl. Lanna was going to kill Evalle with guilt.

Nicole offered her hand and Lanna took it. "Nice to meet you. I'm looking forward to having company. My partner is out of town this week."

"Thank you for invitation." Lanna gave Nicole a polite smile, released her hand and backed away.

Evalle said a silent thank-you that Red, Nicole's life partner, was a transportation engineer who traveled for work on occasion, which took her out of the picture right now. Standing just as tall as Evalle and the alpha female in this pair, Red would not be happy about Evalle bringing her gargoyle and Lanna to stay with Nicole, even though Nicole was a powerful witch.

Feenix bounced back and forth from one fat foot to the other. Nicole opened her arms for him. "Come on, sweetie."

Batlike wings flapping, he made happy chortling noises all the way to her lap. She hugged him and petted his leathery greenish skin. "I think you've gotten an inch bigger."

Feenix looked over at Evalle with shock. "What ith inch?"

Evalle held her index finger and thumb apart to show him. "A lot."

Nicole patted his head between his little horns. "If you'll play for a bit so I can talk to Evalle, we'll watch television later."

Feenix clapped his hands, wings flapping to lift him off her lap. "Nathcar! Nathcar! Danica!"

"I'm sure I can find a race tonight." Nicole turned to Lanna. "I've got a couple whirligig type toys he'll chase around once I cast a spell for them to fly. Would you get them out of that chest against the wall?"

Lanna retrieved a spiral piece of plastic that fit in the palm of her hand. *She* whispered something and the toy came alive, spinning up in the air, changing colors as it flew.

Feenix took off after the toy as Lanna sent three more airborne.

Nicole nodded in admiration. "Nicely done. Thank you."

Turning around, Lanna said, "Watch this." Then she disappeared.

Nicole shot a look of concern at Evalle, who waved a hand. "Don't worry. She explained to me that she's learning how to cloak herself."

When Lanna came back into view, Nicole asked, "How long can you stay cloaked?"

"Twenty, maybe thirty minutes." Lanna rubbed her head. "Sometimes hurts. Or I'm tired."

Pointing across the room, Nicole said, "Go ahead and get settled in the guest bedroom. Lie down if you want."

"Thank you." Lanna gave Evalle a look. "Do not feel bad about this. I understand, and someday I will ask you to understand for me."

"Fair enough." Evalle thought about giving her a hug, but she'd never been one to hug much. "Either I'll be in touch in a few days or Quinn will, and if not, you and Nicole both have Tzader's number to call."

The minute Lanna stepped into the guest room, Evalle sat down on the end of the sofa that had an open space next to it where Nicole could park her wheelchair. Evalle always felt at home here and was never quite sure if it was due to the comforting autumn colors in the room or some spell Nicole cast to infuse tranquility.

"Lanna is powerful," Nicole stated. "More than a witch."

"She's Quinn's cousin, and he doesn't know *what* she is. Says she doesn't either. Long story, but basically her mother disappeared nineteen years ago for I don't know, like a month, and showed up again with no idea where she'd been or how she'd gotten pregnant."

"I'm fine with it, but I'm concerned that she'll get past my wards on the apartment."

Evalle shook her head. "I don't think so. She's never trained with anyone. I've gotten used to her disappearing around the apartment and in the truck today. I think she enjoys having that control. Thanks for doing this."

"I'm happy to help, but *why* am I doing this?"

Keeping her voice down, Evalle told her, "Quinn asked me to take Lanna while he's gone to help the Beladors with a problem. A wizard is after Lanna, but I drove around with her and Feenix for a while to see if there was any chance we were being followed. I've got an SUV that's warded against sunlight and unauthorized access, and I'm sure I had no tail today. Your place is warded, but if Lanna starts getting bad headaches, call Tzader or one of these Belador numbers and have her taken to headquarters."

Evalle handed over a slip of paper, adding, "I would never bring danger to your doorstep."

"I know that."

"But don't answer the door to anyone you don't personally know or anyone besides Tzader or Quinn who says they're here to see me or Lanna." Evalle leaned forward, gripping the plush sofa arm. "If I'm not back in two days, please call Tzader and tell him you have Lanna. I don't want you keeping her longer than that no matter what."

Nicole reached over and put her hand on Evalle's forearm. "Your gold aura is dark, almost a tarnished color. What's going on?" Before Evalle could answer, Nicole's grip tightened, then she lifted Evalle's arm and used her other hand to slide the sleeve back, exposing the armband. "What is *that*?"

"*That* is a Volonte and part of the problem." Evalle gave Nicole a brief rundown on what had happened since she'd entered the Beast Club in the mountains last night. "That's why I need your help. I have to leave soon so that I can reach St. Marys tonight ahead of Storm. It's six and a half hours down there. If I leave by noon, I'll arrive just before dark so I can scout out all the docks to find the one taking fighters to Cumberland Island." That would give her a four-hour head start on Storm.

Nicole asked, "Is that what you need the potion for?"

"Yes. You have it, right?"

Nicole released her and leaned back, worry ringing her eyes. "Yes, but you need Storm at this event."

"No, I don't. I can actually get in for free as an Alterant."

"But they'll expect you to fight."

Evalle pointed at the armband. "I'm hoping I can make a trade with this to just watch the battles if I keep my Alterant status secret. Once I get in, I'll find a way to get to Tristan and convince him to drink the potion. It's not a great plan, but it's one I think will work."

Nicole handed Evalle a silver flask small enough to hide in her fisted hand. It had a sun and bird engraved on the side. "Thank you, Nicole."

Nicole closed her eyes and leaned back. Her lips barely moved with silent words.

In the past, Evalle had seen Nicole use her skill at foretelling, and she waited for her friend to share what she saw. Finally, Nicole opened her eyes. "I can't see what happens inside this event, but I feel that you can't go in there alone."

Evalle stood up. "Thanks for the warning, but I can't tell VIPER, and I'm not risking Storm's life."

"You should discuss it with him."

"There is no discussing anything with him when it comes to me. He's becoming as overprotective as Tzader and Quinn, maybe worse."

A knowing smile lifted Nicole's lips. "So it's like that between the two of you?"

"Yes and no." Evalle crossed her arms to keep from fidgeting. "He's been so patient with me, I may have missed my window of opportunity with him, so to speak."

Because she might not make it back alive.

"Did you tell him . . . about your past?"

Evalle had never told anyone about that night, not even Nicole, Tzader or Quinn, but trying to keep something like that from Nicole was futile. "No, but he's empathic, so, like you, he has a pretty good idea that I'm screwed up when it comes to a relationship."

"I haven't spent much time with Storm, but that one time I was around him I sensed the heart of a good man."

Shaking her head, Evalle swallowed her regret. "The sad thing is that I'm ready to try for more with him, but I may not get a chance. If I don't make it back, I'm hoping he'll come to you to find out where I am. If he does, don't show him where I am. Don't show anyone."

"You can't do this alone, Evalle."

"I have to." She pinched her eyes and struggled to get a grip on her control. Evalle had to prevent her emotions from rocketing out of control for just a little longer. She couldn't wait to hand this bone over to someone at the beast fights.

But right now, the pain of lying to Storm, even by omission, and possibly never seeing him again, was stomping her heart.

She flexed her hand, took a breath and said, "If he

does come looking for me after tomorrow, please give him a message. Tell him that he was the one, the *only* one I've ever wanted, and I'm sorry I missed my chance with him. But that he should not come after me."

Nicole held a finger against her lips, looking as if she'd been asked to write Evalle's eulogy.

Evalle really didn't do touching, but Storm had influenced her too much with his touch. She couldn't *not* bend down and hug Nicole to thank her. It was brief, but when she stood up, Evalle was glad for the contact. Nicole had become more than a friend over the time they'd known each other. She was a sister of the heart. Or what Evalle would envision a sister to be.

"Please come back to us," Nicole said as if issuing an enchanted wish.

"Going to do my best." Walking over to the foyer, Evalle lifted the tote of lug nuts from where she'd dropped the bag.

Nicole took the tote. "Are you going to say good-bye to Feenix?"

Throat thick, Evalle said, "No. I already told him this was a sleepover. If I talk to him now, he'll know something's wrong. I want him happy as long as possible. I'm sorry to impose on you, but if I don't come back . . ."

"I will always care for Feenix," Nicole said quickly, then added in a quiet tone, "But you have to take Storm in the games with you. I . . . I need to tell you what I saw."

Leaving the door open, Evalle stepped back over to her friend's chair and leaned down. "What?"

"If you don't take Storm, you won't leave those beast games alive."

Giving Nicole's hand a squeeze, Evalle nodded and walked out, closing the door softly. She hadn't needed Nicole's special ability to know she was going to die. She'd felt it in her heart all day.

TWENTY

Someone was following her.

Evalle had felt a presence all the way to this sleepy
coastal town in southeast Georgia.

Lifting halfway up from a squat, she made a slow vi-
sual sweep of the dark woods behind her that hid her
and her SUV. It was an hour after sunset, and nothing
moved in the black void. Every breath of salt air invigo-
rated her after six and a half hours of driving.

Bending her knees, she resumed her position behind
a thick pine tree to watch yet another dock, the same
position she'd held since arriving in St. Marys ninety
minutes ago.

Eight o'clock and she still hadn't found *the* dock. That
feeling of someone close by clung to her edgy psyche,
poking at her that someone was tailing her.

Storm couldn't have gotten here yet. Not this soon.
Could he?

No. If he had, he'd have shown his face if for no other
reason than to finish letting her know how much she'd
pissed him off. She'd sent him texts all afternoon, touching base as if she'd still been in Atlanta when she'd been
driving southeast instead. He'd answered, his last text
saying he'd found the Langaus in Atlanta and Tzader's

team had managed to capture one, which the healers were using to create an antidote.

And that he was on his way to meet her outside her apartment. In Atlanta, where she was supposed to be. The phone call to tell him that she wasn't there had been worse than she'd expected, which was saying something.

She'd seen Storm furious before, but he'd hit rage level when he'd found out she had a four-hour head start on him. She wasn't even sure he'd heard her "I'm sorry," right before she'd crushed her mobile phone to prevent anyone tracking her electronically.

He would never forgive her, but he'd be alive.

Balmy night air swirled softly. *Please let this be the right public dock.* She had to get on one of the private boats ferrying nonhumans to Cumberland Island.

The other boat docks had been too public for transporting beasts, and even though she could pass for a human visitor, she wouldn't trust Sen not to have someone watching for her at the public ferry.

A high-end private tour bus pulled into the empty parking area between her and the water. Two figures emerged. Hard to tell much about them from a hundred feet away, but one walked as if he or she wore ankle cuffs. That pair moved toward the dock but stayed in the shadows.

The docks on each side of the boat ramp were barely visible beneath single lights on tall poles. The figure in ankle cuffs shuffled up under the light and Evalle saw a tail dragging on the ground behind him.

She let out a pent-up breath.

This had to be the place.

Headlights shone over the parking lot as a fairly new white convertible BMW 650i spun in to park and a late-model silver Dodge pickup truck parked several car lengths away.

A woman with long white hair and a shining gold mask emerged from the sports car.

Imogenia had arrived. She tugged a chain, dragging along her Alterant, Bernie, like an unwanted child. No sack covered his head.

Doors snapped open and shut on the parked truck. One of the people who climbed out had to stand seven feet tall, appeared to be male and wore a collar that glowed neon red.

If that giant was an Alterant, how big would he be once he shifted?

Imogenia called over to the guy who had to be the giant's sponsor. "Alterant?"

"Yes."

Bernie whimpered, twisting a knot in Evalle's stomach. "Where's the boat?" Imogenia asked everyone in general.

Before anyone could answer, a troll emerged from the water, walking up the boat launch ramp. Water ran from his horned head and down his ten-foot-tall body that was covered in mud-matted hair.

No one said a word as he thumped over to the light pole and lifted a hand with claws to wave between the light and the water. He did it twice, paused, then twice more.

A boat motor rumbled as a sleek, thirty-foot-long speedboat approached from the darkness beyond the launch ramps. The craft stayed only long enough for the new arrivals to board, then it slid away, disappearing into the night.

She had to get on the next boat, but as she started to take a step toward the parking lot a twig snapped behind her. Calling up her dagger from her boot to her hand as she turned, Evalle whipped around ready for the attack.

Nothing there.

"What are you waiting for?" Evalle challenged. "A better opportunity to attack me isn't going to happen."

Nothing. No movement, no sound, just the sense that she was right. She didn't have time to bother with someone playing games.

The island was maybe a half hour away, but she had no idea how long it would take to find her way to the beast championship once she got off the boat.

That ping of being watched kept bumping her.

She opened her empathic senses and reached out toward the area of the last noise.

Fear hit her first, then desperation.

Could it just be a curious creature? But what kind?

Backing out of the coverage, Evalle warned, "I won't harm you if you don't give me reason to." Just as she started to swing around, her gaze caught on her SUV where the rear hatch was open. Hadn't she locked that?

She sent a gentle kinetic push and closed it, then locked the truck with her key fob and swung around.

Heading for the dock, she'd made it halfway across the parking lot when the *whomp, whomp, whomp* of an arriving helicopter filled the air. It was coming in fast.

Guess even wealthy sponsors had to travel to the island by the designated ferry, too.

Wind blustered about as the helicopter landed, then a man leaped out and headed her way with a stride that was both fluid and powerful.

Her mouth gaped open. "How did you . . ."

The brunt of Storm's fury reached her first. He headed for her with his head down like a pissed-off bull.

This was going to get ugly. She lifted the dagger, pointing the business end at him. "You can just go right back—"

He stopped with a couple of feet left between them, heaving deep breaths, when she knew he wasn't winded. "You really thought I'd let you go there alone?"

"*Let* me? It's not your choice."

"You want to do this, then I'm fighting. Not you. Besides, you need me to go in."

Pointing to her arm, she said, "I don't need you. I can get in with the armband and not fight." She hoped.

"You don't understand how these fights work, particularly this one, since it's all about Alterants. You *might* know if you hadn't lied to me and waited for us to drive here together."

She flinched at the "lied to me" but stood her ground. "I tried to tell you I didn't want you here."

"And that makes coming here alone okay when you knew I wouldn't stand by and do nothing?"

Her gaze drifted to where the helicopter sat with its blades turning slowly. "I'm sorry you did whatever you did to get here, and I know you're angry—"

"Angry? You think that's what this is all about?" He came straight for her until she had to whip her dagger out of the way or stab him.

He yanked her into his arms so fast that she barely caught a breath before he kissed her. Not a sweet kiss, but one born of raging emotions. Desire. Hunger.

More than all of it, she felt Storm's need. Nothing else would have gotten through to her as quickly as that. She needed him, too, but not to fight. She shook, fighting the bone's influence. She'd been calm on the whole trip here. *Just have to hold on a little longer.*

Using kinetics, she let the blade slide down to her boot, then wrapped her arms around his neck. She loved kissing this man. Had missed him every minute they'd been apart today. But this time, she wouldn't let the Volonté take over her emotions.

She wanted Storm to know *this time* it was her kissing him.

His strong arms banded her back, holding her tight against him for the long moments it took to ease the energy flowing between them.

He finally broke the kiss and murmured, "I wasn't angry. I chartered a jet helicopter because I was terrified that you'd get inside the ABC before I could find you."

He did all that in the last few hours? Who was this

man that he could command a helicopter at the snap of his fingers?

That didn't change her mind. "I won't take you in as my fighter."

When she leaned back, Storm lifted his hands to hold her face between them. He kissed her softly on the lips, then said, "This is how it works. If you enter as an Alterant with a sponsor, you have to fight. If you enter as an unsponsored Alterant, you *still* have to fight. The only way you can get inside there without declaring yourself an Alterant—and shifting to fight in beast form—is by being *my* sponsor."

That was not going to happen. "What if I want to use the bone to go in as an attendee just to watch?"

"Those are usually by invitation only and sell out quickly."

But that didn't mean they were all gone or that the host wouldn't be willing to trade for a Volonte, especially a finger bone. "You can be my sponsor."

"No. Even if I would agree, which isn't possible, I'd have to be willing to make a trade with the Medb *if* you survived all three matches. Think I'm going to do that? And if you go in solo and fight, then *you* would have to deal with the Medb."

"I can refuse to accept their offer." When he started to speak, she cut him off. "Can't I refuse their offer?"

He grumbled out some strange language she was pretty sure was a curse by its toxic sound. "Yes. You can, but you're not fighting."

"Then I'll get in another way."

"There is no other way. And you know I'd be in pain if I wasn't telling the truth. We might as well get moving and do this, because I'm not leaving here without you."

Time was spinning out of her grasp. "Maybe I could—"

He put a finger on her lips. "It's on. When we walk over to that dock, we're back to sponsor and fighter. Playing our parts in the Achilles Beast Championship means far more than it did at the Beast Club in the mountains. This place has immunity and is hosted by someone powerful. One of us makes a wrong move and raises the host's suspicions, no one will ever find our bodies."

How could she agree to this when she couldn't elude Storm?

He hugged her to him and whispered, "You can't call in Tzader and Quinn. You don't want to leave Tristan and all those Alterants in Medb hands. And the number one reason we have to do this? You can't go back empty-handed to Macha. This is the only way. Trust me. I can handle the fights."

Her throat felt like she'd swallowed a fist. Squeezing enough air out to talk hurt. *I will not lose you.* She made up her mind to do the only thing she could and deceive him one more time.

She had a plan, but it would take playing along with Storm as if she agreed with him until the last moment. "I hate this."

His face relaxed with a look of victory. "Welcome to my world."

She had to get going. "Okay. A troll—"

"—calls in the boats. I had a team scouting all the docks while I was getting here."

Storm had found her in a jungle in South America when no one else could, and he'd managed that in record time by private jet. Then showing up in this helicopter tonight. She didn't know as much as she thought she did about him, but she knew what mattered.

She could trust Storm with her heart and her body.

But he might not ever trust her again after tonight.

Pulling away, he said, "I've got something to give you first."

On the way back to the helicopter, Storm gave a hand signal to the pilot, who cut the motor. By the time she reached the aircraft right behind him, the props were barely moving. Storm leaned into the cockpit and pulled out a jacket covered in tiny glass prisms that reflected any bit of light they could grab.

He held the slinky covering up for her. "Put this on and take your hair out of the ponytail."

"Why?"

"This is a whole different beast game. Looking the part here carries as much weight as attitude."

That's when she took stock of Storm's lean black jeans and snakeskin boots with silver tips. Both jaguar eyes carved into his belt buckle had yellow stones again like the diamond he'd traded to get them into the Beast Club.

Edgy. Sexy. Hers.

Resigned to him being the expert here, she shrugged into the jacket that fit her perfectly. She pulled the elastic band off her ponytail, leaned forward to shake her hair, then stood up, letting it float back to her shoulders. "How's that?"

"Smokin'."

Only Storm could make her smile right now.

He reached inside the helicopter and withdrew a square velvet box the size of his two hands together. "Hold this."

Keeping her voice down, she said, "If I'm the sponsor, shouldn't *I* be giving the orders?"

His lips twitched. "Just being efficient. We're running close on time." He lifted a stunning emerald stone the size of his thumb that had been cut in a half-round pear shape with a flat back. "Hold still."

When she narrowed her eyes at him, he added, "Please."

He placed the stone where it would naturally lie against her chest *if* the gem dangled on a chain. As Storm held it in place, he started softly chanting words that could be Navajo, Ashaninka or some other language.

She felt heat from the stone, but not an uncomfortable feeling. What was he doing?

Storm lifted his fingers away and the stone remained on her chest. "Did you glue that to me?"

"No. It's held there by majik."

"It's pretty, but I'm not really dressed to wear jewels," she muttered to herself when Storm twisted around to tell the pilot he'd call when he needed the helicopter again.

With that handled, he led her away before the props started winding up. As they walked toward the dock, the whooshing noise behind them shielded his words from anyone but her. "The stone binds you to my majik so that I can find you quickly if we get separated."

She tried to pluck the jewel off her chest. "You *glued* a tracking device on me?"

He ground out a tired sigh. "It's more than a tracking device and I didn't glue it. I can remove it when this is over, but I don't trust the Medb."

"Or me?" She stopped walking, forcing him to face her. "Is that why you put this on me?"

His vexation was right up front in his gaze. "I trust you to do whatever it takes to save everyone but yourself. But when it comes to your neck, you stick it out there no matter how many hatchets are swinging for it." He ran his hand over her hair, lifting a strand to rub between his finger and thumb. "Someone's got to watch out for you."

His words reached inside her and gently caressed her heart. She was sticking two necks out this time and wanted him to leave with his intact, too. "I need your promise that once we get there, you will not argue with me over whatever I have to do to get to Tristan and the other Alterants on my own."

"I'm your fighter to do with as you wish."

No, you're not. "I don't want to own anyone." She noticed the troll standing near the light again and hurried this along. She wanted to be sure Storm would not get himself killed when he found himself not entering the fight. "What I mean is, you promise not to attack someone who acts aggressively toward me. This place will be overflowing with testosterone. I can handle myself, so let me deal with any conflict."

Glaring at her, he shook his head. Before she could argue, he said, "I will not interfere unless I think you're in mortal danger. That's the best I can give you."

She'd take what she could get.

He added, "And you can't interfere either. No one can use majik, kinetics or any means to help their fighter."

Not a problem, since he was going to be nowhere near a battle.

But she kept the conversation on track to gain more information. "What happens if someone is caught aiding a fighter?"

"The fighter is forfeited to the host, who can make a trade to the Medb, and the sponsor is ejected as a *minimum*."

In other words, much worse could happen to the sponsor.

He put his hand at her back. "Let's get this over with." When he reached the dock, he flipped the troll a gold coin that was stained with age.

The troll grinned and stepped close to the light, waving his hand across it to signal the boat again.

Evalle breathed through her mouth, glad the trolls back in Atlanta didn't smell like rotten fish.

Storm asked the troll, "This the only pickup point?"

"Nuh-uh. Two more runnin' ta-night."

This time the boat that floated up to the dock was a twenty-five-foot Sea Ray.

Storm cupped Evalle's arm as she stepped down. She

suffered quietly through being treated like some delicate little doll.

Just as he dropped down onto the boat deck, he swung his head around sharply, looking at the dock where the troll stood.

"What is it?" Evalle asked softly to avoid drawing attention.

"I thought I sensed someone else."

"I did, too, earlier, right before you arrived. I picked up a strong sense of fear, so I don't think it's a threat. Might be someone from here who's curious."

"Maybe. I don't smell anything." Putting his hand to the small of her back, he moved her toward the bench seat across the back and called up to the captain that they were ready.

She hoped so. No going back now.

TWENTY-ONE

Once the boat dropped them on Cumberland Island, Storm kept his senses wide open as he led Evalle along a winding footpath through a forest of pines, sprawling oaks and palm trees. He didn't want her here in any capacity, not even as a sponsor.

She asked, "Do you know anything about this island?"

"A little." He'd gotten enough information from a local source and lined up a private boat to get them off the island if they had to make a run for it. "That big-ass house where the boat dropped us is Plum Orchard, built by the Carnegie family right before 1900. They were steel magnates."

A horse nickered nearby. Evalle muttered, "Wild horses, pigs, deer, armadillos . . . it's a freakin' wild kingdom here."

Storm chuckled at his city girl.

One day he'd take her camping and show her that the woods could be fun. The day this was all behind them. "We don't have to worry about the wild animals. They have enough sense to avoid the preternatural." Based on the directions the boat captain had given Storm, they'd reach the ABC pretty soon.

He wanted to know what to expect from Evalle. "How do you plan to get to Tristan?"

"If he's the Medb representative, as Imogenia claims, I'm hoping he'll be easy to find. Once I see him, I'll figure a way to get close enough to talk, and if he agrees to leave, Nicole gave me a potion that will turn him invisible for an hour. There's enough for at least five or six Alterants to drink."

Then Tristan would get her trapped somehow. "What if he won't leave with you?"

She walked along so quietly that she had to be thinking. "I can only save someone who is willing to save himself. If I can't convince him that he, his sister and any other Alterants with him aren't better off with Macha, then I'll have to accept that he's marking himself as the enemy."

He squeezed her hand. "Good. There comes a time when a person has to be responsible for himself."

"But I have to be convinced that he's really signed on with the Medb."

Her loyalty was one of the things that made Evalle who she was, but Storm feared one day that same loyalty might get her killed for someone who couldn't possibly appreciate her sacrifice.

She pushed a branch out of the way and ducked past it. "You said the host was powerful. Did you find out who's hosting this?"

"Yes. A centaur by the name of D'Alimonte."

"Deek?"

"No. Kol D'Alimonte. Who's Deek?"

"A centaur who owns The Iron Casket nightclub in Atlanta."

"Probably a brother then."

"If he's anything like Deek, he's very old and dangerous."

Trees thinned out as they approached a wide-open tract of land. He released her hand, fighting the urge to toss her over his shoulder and drag her back to Atlanta.

The entire way here, his gut had churned with a deep fear for her. He'd thought for sure it meant she'd already gone inside the event. Relief had turned his knees to Jell-O when he'd seen her emerging from the woods at the boat dock.

Holding her close should have reassured him she was fine, and entering as her fighter would keep her safe, but that sick sensation wouldn't leave.

"Where is the event?" Evalle asked in a hushed voice as they left the woods and entered an open field.

Two guards wearing Spartan outfits over bodies that bulged with muscles stood two arm lengths apart.

As though they were protecting the open space behind them.

A shimmering silver cloth twelve feet tall appeared between the guards.

Storm answered her, "The ABC is hidden behind that curtain."

"You're kidding."

"No. D'Alimonte has cloaked the entire event, which means there's only one way in or out and you're looking at it." He couldn't risk not having access to his majik here. Lowering his voice for her ears only, he said, "This is when you start calling the shots. Tell them you're entering a Skinwalker. Showtime."

She surprised him by not arguing but instead saying, "Okay."

This would work out after all.

Evalle squared her shoulders and angled her chin up, then took a couple of long strides toward the guards. Before she could speak, the guard on the left held his hand out and a pale blue holographic image of a woman's head took form. Eyes moving to take in Evalle, she said, "I am Dame Lynn, the Domjon. What do you want?"

Evalle pushed the slinky jacket sleeve and shirtsleeve up to show the armband. "I want to buy in for admittance only."

"What?" Storm snapped. He should have known that Evalle was going along too easily. "No. *I'm* your fighter."

Evalle turned on him, her mouth as hard-lined as her attitude. "No, you're not."

The Domjon turned her head to face Storm. "What are you?"

"Shifter. Jaguar."

"Are you the black jaguar fighter from the Beast Club in Georgia?"

"Yes."

Dame Lynn announced, "Request to fight denied."

"Why?" Storm doubted she could know who he was from South America, but even so he'd never been refused entrance as a fighter.

"You have been accused of fighting under fraudulent

terms by claiming you were a shifter," Dame Lynn replied in a flat tone of finality.

"I told you. I shift into jaguar form."

"That wasn't the issue. Imogenia of the Carretta Coven filed a complaint that you misrepresented yourself as a were-shifter. Her fighter also claimed you used majik that had not been declared. Until that's cleared up with the injured party, you're barred from fighting in the Achilles Beast Championship. Or, you can request to be subjected to a truth test to prove Imogenia wrong. If she is found guilty of lying, she and her fighter will be ejected . . . after facing a sanction. However, if you lie during this test, you die."

That pain-in-the-ass Imogenia.

Storm couldn't prove he was a were-shifter, since he wasn't, and he *had* lied by omission.

Dame Lynn added, "And there are no observation-only tickets left."

Evalle swung around to Dame Lynn. "Not even for a Volonte *finger* bone?"

"No."

Evalle looked over at Storm, determination so strong in her gaze that he had to bite down to keep from shouting no at her, knowing she had only one other move. *Don't do this.*

Evalle told Dame Lynn, "Then I want to enter an Alterant."

"No, Evalle." When she ignored him, Storm growled a low warning.

Dame Lynn's head leaned from side to side on the guard's hand. "I don't see an Alterant."

Evalle reached up and lowered her glasses enough for her green eyes to glow bright in the darkness. "Now you do."

"Accepted. Admittance is granted to you." Dame Lynn emphasized the *you*. These fights had a no-tolerance policy when it came to anyone trying to trick them to gain access.

Storm's nightmare unfolded before his eyes.

If Evalle walked in there as an Alterant, she'd have to fight. He told Evalle, "I'm going in with you."

Dame Lynn clarified, "At this point, *you* can't enter as a sponsor, since you did not represent yourself as such up front."

He put his hand on Evalle's arm. She turned to him, saying, "I have to do this."

"I won't let you go without me."

Evalle held his gaze for two heartbeats, long enough to realize he would back his words and die fighting his way inside if she tried to enter without him.

Pushing her glasses back into place, Evalle addressed Dame Lynn. "Alterants can enter for free, right?"

"Correct."

"Would the host be willing to trade this Volonte to allow me to bring a *guest* in with me?"

Storm hadn't considered that, and Evalle still had to get that damn bone off her arm.

"No."

Storm buckled his temper only for Evalle's benefit. "What about a healer?"

The Domjon allowed, "With a Volonte, she can bring in one healer."

Storm asked, "What's the specific ruling on using majik inside?"

"No one can aid his or her fighter *during* a match in any way. You can use majik only to heal a fighter between matches. Any infraction of the rules results in sanction, then ejection."

That sanction part could be worse than death in a place like this.

The Domjon continued, "Additionally, the fighter is forfeited to the host, who can keep said fighter or trade it to the financial backer for this event, the Medb. However, a sponsor or healer can help someone *else's* fighter as long as their own fighter is still alive and in a match."

"Why would anyone help someone else's fighter?" Evalle murmured.

Storm would never risk losing Evalle by using his majik where he'd be caught, and the rule *should* prevent others from helping a fighter that might eventually hurt their own entry, but his gut feeling was that no one in this place could be trusted. Not when one sponsor might cut a deal to help another sponsor if it was beneficial. Anything was possible in these battles.

Evalle asked, "When will the Medb representative face the truth test?"

Dame Lynn blinked up at Evalle. "That was an hour ago, and the Medb priestess passed the test. She stated the terms for negotiating trades with Medb representatives. Any Alterant surviving an Elite match will be offered the chance to become a warrior who can conquer death."

Storm asked, "How are winners decided?"

"Alterants fight two matches against non-Alterants. If they survive, their third and final match is against another Alterant. A match ends either in death or relief, with the exception of an Elite round, where the Medb priestess can declare a winner and a loser if she chooses."

"What do you mean by relief?" Evalle asked.

"The losing fighter begs to quit, and *if* the opponent agrees, the loser is handed over to the Medb with no trade for the sponsor."

Evalle shifted her gaze to Storm, her eyes begging him again not to go inside with her.

He stated, "I'm her healer." And he hoped like hell he wouldn't be needed for that.

Dame Lynn told Evalle, "Give the Volonte to the other guard."

Turning to the Spartan not holding a hologram of a head, Evalle told him, "You must tell me that you want this Volonte. Do you?"

"Yes, I want it," he boomed and extended his arm.

Evalle lifted her arm and whispered the words Imogenia had used, then followed the same steps that ended with snapping the band on the guard's arm.

Her entire body relaxed as if she'd been wrapped in barbed wire all this time and the binding had suddenly snapped. She let out a long breath of air, glad to be rid of that evil bone.

With that done, Dame Lynn issued final instructions.

"Fighters can use whatever powers they possess and can bring one weapon of choice into the theater."

Evalle hesitated.

Before Storm could tell her she couldn't sneak anything past this group, the Domjon said, "If you keep the dagger, the blades in your boot soles won't work in here. If you want the boot blades, then your dagger will disappear as soon as you enter."

"I'll keep the dagger."

"What name do you fight under?"

When Evalle cut her eyes at him, Storm said, "Moonlight Warrior."

"Welcome to the Achilles Beast Championship," Dame Lynn said before her head vanished.

In a place that was very likely wall-to-wall witches in some form, he didn't want her to use her real name even if somebody might recognize her face. He put his hand at her back, so damned glad that bone was gone.

Each guard reached for the center of the curtain and drew back his half, revealing lights blazing over a towering room that held a thousand if it held one.

Raucous voices pelted the air with excitement.

Storm indicated for her to enter ahead of him, giving her a two-step lead.

She missed a step and turned around, frowning. "Did you bump me?"

"No." Storm sniffed the air, catching a smell similar to one he'd barely picked up around the troll's potent stench. He knew that scent. One sniff would smell human, then the next would smell like some creature he couldn't identify. Now wasn't the time to discuss it, when he couldn't think past the idea of Evalle fighting beasts. He nodded at her to keep moving.

With the armband off, she could shift into her beast form, but would she?

And if she didn't, how was he going to keep her from being killed?

TWENTY-TWO

L
anna followed Evalle and Storm through the silver
curtain and paused inside the noisy arena.

Her head throbbed from the strain of holding her cloaking in place and constantly camouflaging her scent. Her muscles ached from being in so many difficult positions while trying to be quiet, too. Riding in Evalle's SUV had been simple, but shielding herself from view between the car and boat ride had taken much work.

Her cloaking would fail soon.

Lanna scurried through crowds moving around this place that smelled of many different beings. Where would be a good place to hide?

Storm had sniffed in Lanna's direction when he and Evalle had come inside, scaring Lanna that she had been found out. She was sure the spell she used to mix Nicole and Feenix's scents had been right. It should mask her scent from anyone but shifters.

She had not expected Storm to drop from the sky like an avenging angel. Angry angel. He knew her scent and had startled her when he'd noticed her presence as she'd snuck onto the boat.

Her heart had tried to climb out of her chest.

Squeezing between people, Lanna pushed through to keep up with Storm and Evalle. Looked like a small city in here. Tents scattered around. People sat in seats built like stairs. The crowd moved around two large fight rings with sparkling lights like invisible domes made of flickering stars.

How could Storm let Evalle fight in this place?

Lanna had already seen two mages and enough witches to fill several covens. These witches practiced dark arts, not like Nicole, whose aura shined with light.

Nicole would discover that Lanna had escaped once she checked the bed in her guest room. Maybe even by now. Lanna had left the covers pulled over a body shape that lifted and fell like normal breathing. To have stayed would have put Evalle's friend and Feenix at risk.

Evalle had been careful on the drive to Nicole's, watching for threats, but Lanna feared the wizard would find her even if she did not make another powerful draw on the elements. Doing that was like sending up a signal flare.

Grendal was in Atlanta.

Lanna's idea had been such a simple plan.

Leave with Evalle and hope Grendal would believe Lanna had left Atlanta for good, but who knew Evalle would drive almost seven hours? And where was this Cumberland Island place? Lanna had to stay with Evalle now to get back to Cousin Quinn.

Her hand started taking form.

She carefully pushed power down her arms to turn her hand invisible again, but her body trembled from the strain. She could only hold cloaking this long because she had been able to rest in the Expedition on the way here. She hid in a very small area at the rear of the SUV and did not have to cloak while Evalle drove.

Her fingertips showed again.

She shoved them in the pockets of her jeans. *Stay calm.* Getting upset would disturb her focus, and cloaking would fail for sure.

Evalle and Storm paused up ahead, observing something Lanna couldn't see.

She looked everywhere for a place to hide. Not an easy trick, since this place was like an outdoor tournament. She smelled food vendors, then took another look at the stair-step seating. Could there be space beneath the tall seats?

Maybe. She had to get through the crowd without drawing attention.

Bumping the legs of humans startled them.

Bumping the legs of someone with power was much more dangerous.

Women wore fancy clothes, like those at Cousin Quinn's hotel. Fighters had studded chokers, belts and leg restraints that all smelled of majik.

Much money passed hands at this event.

Something else dawned on her. She had seen no one her age. Pulling her hand out to check for cloaking, she moaned at the pink flesh coming into view.

The crowd parted in front of her, finally offering a fast path.

She looked up as a man ahead of her stopped and slowly turned, his face intent as though searching for someone. He was tall, several inches over six feet, and he had short, thick hair the color of a ripe lemon. The long black robe only made his skin look more sickly, but that wizard was not ill.

Evil had turned Grendal's skin that color.

Lanna froze. Her mind screamed at her to run, but her knees became jelly as her cloaking gave way.

TWENTY-THREE

"How much power does it take to hide this much area at one time?" Evalle muttered. "I thought Sen was the only one capable of this much, but I have a new appreciation for centaurs."

Storm strolled casually alongside Evalle, but his gaze moved constantly, taking in everything. "This isn't just a shield warding. One way in and one way out. This D'Alimonte has some help, maybe multiple wizards or mages, keeping the entire area secure, even against teleporting in or out without permission."

Which meant Tristan wouldn't be able to teleport out. She couldn't decide if that was a plus or not. "This looks like an inflated tent, if tents came with hundred-foot ceilings. Has to be that high up there. I see two fighting arenas . . . *theaters*," she corrected herself, calculating the stadium seating around the two battle areas to accommodate an easy thousand. "And that wide building connecting the theaters must be what? Locker rooms?"

"Individual waiting areas to keep the fighters separated and allow them a place to be healed out of view."

Nothing had happened the way she'd intended, starting with Storm showing up. At least he wouldn't be fighting, but how could she battle an Alterant if she didn't shift into beast form?

Macha had allowed Evalle to make her own decisions, free of repercussion, as long as Evalle didn't put Macha's pantheon in conflict with VIPER and acted in the best interest of the Beladors.

Entering the ABC put Evalle clearly in conflict with VIPER, based on what Sen had said. But if Evalle was successful in preventing Alterants from signing on with the Medb and handed VIPER evidence of Noirre majik being traded, she had bargaining power with the Tribunal.

If Macha backed Evalle at that point. Big *if*.

Changing into her beast form would screw all that, since VIPER rules forbade Evalle's changing into anything more than the Belador battle form. That amount of change strengthened a Belador's body and amped up power, but nothing like the strength of her beast form. But it also took a toll on her energy, so she'd have to absolutely need it to use it. She might get away with fighting if she could win without shifting and walk out of here with Alterants who would testify that Noirre majik was traded, which she knew had to happen tonight.

But if she put Macha's pantheon in conflict with VIPER, then Evalle couldn't claim working in the Beladors' best interest, now, could she?

Thanks for nothing, Macha.

"What's wrong?" Storm asked, his gaze taking in everyone and everything, right down to the sunken level of the battle theater they passed. His mood hadn't improved a bit since he'd shown up in the helicopter.

"Just thinking through my options." She'd thought

he'd settled down after kissing her, but that had been only a momentary break from the anger surging off of him.

Storm walked along, then made a sound of utter frustration. "That's not a straight answer. Just like the text messages you sent me, stepping around the truth is lying, Evalle. What's bothering you?"

She could cut through stone with the edge in his voice. "You." When someone jostled her in passing, Storm's glare slid from her to the clueless woman digging through her oversize purse.

Storm tilted his head to indicate they should move out of the flow of traffic circling the battle rings. Once they were far enough off to the side to provide some privacy, he resumed his cool reserve, crossing his arms as if his glare had failed to communicate his aggravation with her.

Her jaw muscles locked and unlocked. "Would you just get over that I left Atlanta without you? I couldn't face putting you at this kind of risk again."

"*I'm* not the one at risk. You are."

"Comes with the territory of the job I do."

His mouth tightened and his eyes turned almost black. "Not this. You'll have to fight some unknown creatures, and *if* you win those matches, you still have to face another Alterant who will shift into beast form when you won't. And if that isn't enough . . ." He rubbed the back of his neck, all of a sudden looking . . . guilty?

"What, Storm?" When he didn't answer her, Evalle echoed, "Lying by omission is still lying."

"That damned witch doctor I've been hunting for. I'm concerned about her getting close to you."

That last sentence gave her mental whiplash. "The licorice-smelling one?"

"Yes." He washed a hand over his face and shook his head at a silent thought. His jaw muscles moved, then he faced her again. "She should be trying to kill me, but my gut tells me she could be a threat to you, and I don't know why."

Like that made her feel better? "What's her interest in me?"

"I don't know. I would have told you sooner, but I really thought I'd had that vision because she'd learned we were partners at VIPER and that she'd figured if she found you she'd find me. When you disappeared on me today, I—" He shook his head, and this time when he looked at her his eyes were haunted. "I thought she had you. She could have taken you somewhere I might not find you."

That explained the core of his anger. Evalle had scared Storm. Nothing frightened this man.

To know that he cared that much for her struck so deep she experienced a moment of happiness that had never been in her life before him. She would not let the witch doctor harm Storm. "The minute I get out of here, we're going after her."

"And that's exactly why I never told you much about her. I may have stumbled on her up on the mountain today, but now I think she can find me if she wants to, so you going after her would probably play into her plans, whatever they are."

Evalle wanted to get her hands on that crazy witch, but that wouldn't happen if she didn't walk out of here alive. Taking a deep breath, determined to say this with conviction, she told him, "You have to leave. Now. You obviously have resources. Get out of here."

Storm lifted his hand to her face, but didn't touch her when his glance around reminded her they had roles to play. He lowered his hand. "There's nothing you can say to convince me to leave you."

And that was why she wanted a chance to be with him.

He moved with the grace of a dangerous jungle cat, put Adonis to shame with his warrior body and wore honor with the same ease other men wore their favorite jeans. But he had come for her every time she'd been sure she had no one to turn to, and he would stand by her against impossible odds.

Her palms were damp. She didn't know what to say to a man who gave so much and asked for so little in return. "I . . . you . . ."

"I know," he said gently, a warm smile tipping the corners of his lips. "Let's just get through this with you alive. I want to find a place to watch the matches where you can see me. I can't use majik, but I can still coach you."

Dame Lynn's voice filled the room, projected from some invisible spot. "*First round opponents Varkal and Ixxkter have entered the holding areas. Our first match starts in two minutes.*"

A roar of cheers and boos went up, shaking the air.

Since Storm was more familiar with these venues than Evalle, she let him take the lead. They'd just moved through a clump of people when he took a step and leaned down, looking between bodies.

Evalle followed his moves and whispered, "What is it?"

Storm muttered a curse. "Lanna."

"Not possible!"

He shot forward into an opening and Evalle followed as he swung in front of Lanna, who looked ghost white. "How'd you get in here?"

Lanna stared straight through him. Her voice trembled. "He's here."

Evalle turned to see what had terrified Lanna. She caught a glimpse of short yellow hair and sallow skin she'd seen at the Oakey Mountain Beast Club before the crowd had swallowed the creepy guy. Had he frightened Lanna? In spite of wanting to strangle the girl, Evalle leaned down in front of her. "Who's here?"

"Grendal."

Storm's words floated down to them. "We need to move."

Thankfully, the crowd was engulfing them now. Evalle told Lanna, "Cloak yourself and follow us."

Lanna's glazed look finally cleared. "Not possible yet. I must rest."

Evalle stood up, asking Storm, "Can you do something?"

"Yes, but I need to limit using my powers, since I might need them to heal you." He told Lanna, "We're going to go over to the stands and find a place to put you. Walk between me and Evalle. Don't look at anyone or say anything."

"I understand."

At his nod, Evalle led the way through the crowd, sure that Storm kept Lanna sandwiched between them. To draw attention away from Lanna, Evalle lifted her hands from time to time, which did two things. Her sleeves caught the light, practically blinding some people, and others took a step away each time, suspicious of anyone with powers moving their hands around.

When they reached a wide opening between stadium seats, a pair of cookie-cutter young men with short silver hair, wearing identical baggy orange pants and yellow jackets with no shirt beneath, offered action for those wanting to place wagers on the first fight.

A cylindrical scoreboard hung over one of the battle zones with a glowing sign that indicated Battle Theater One. Odds flashed on the board for each opponent in the first five matches.

Evalle scooted around the patrons negotiating bets in everything from jewels to spells. She found an opening where the back of the stands met the ground. When she reached it, she found a dark cubbyhole six feet tall and four feet wide. Large enough to comfortably hold Lanna.

"How deep is it?" Storm asked from close behind.

Evalle leaned down to look. The space ran about twenty feet deep until it stopped at a solid wall.

Not ideal with only one exit, but she had to get Lanna out of sight or they'd all get ejected the minute someone realized Lanna had crashed the party.

Actually, Lanna and Storm would face punishment and ejection. Then Kol D'Alimonte would take possession of Evalle, which would end with bloodshed.

Hers and Storm's, since he wouldn't go quietly.

She straightened up as Lanna rushed over to the space. Evalle told Storm, "I need a minute."

"I'll shield you." He swung around, and Evalle trusted him to do his majik thing to protect them.

Dame Lynn's voice shouted, "*In Battle Theater One, Varkal, a shape-shifting rhino, entering from Gate One, and Ixxkter the Alterant entering at Gate Two. Second round opponents who will fight in Battle Theater Two are . . .*"

Stomping and shouts shook the stadium at the announcement of Ixxkter. Evalle stepped close to Lanna to be heard. "We can't take you with us, and you can't be seen here. You may be eighteen, but you look younger and you have no buy-in. You're shielded from anyone seeing you as long as you stay here."

Grunting came from Battle Theater One, probably the rhino having shifted, then a deep-chested roar of challenge followed. Had to be the Alterant shifting.

Evalle waited until the noise settled down to a rumble to continue. "What were you thinking, Lanna?"

The girl faced her, eyes bulging with regret. "I am sorry, Evalle. I did not mean to cause you trouble."

"No, that doesn't work. You did this with full knowledge that you had no idea where you were going, *and* you lied to me when you agreed to stay at Nicole's."

Evalle felt eyes on her and turned to see Storm lifting

an eyebrow at her that asked how it felt to be given the slip. How had he heard that over the crowd? She *had* lied to Storm about waiting at her apartment for him, but she'd been given the responsibility of keeping Lanna safe.

Grumbling under her breath about annoying men, Evalle ignored him and got back to dealing with Lanna. "Why did you leave Nicole's?"

"Grendal could have found me there."

Evalle forced her hands to remain at her sides and not grab Lanna, or she'd shake the breath out of her. "Brilliant. So instead of staying somewhere he *might* be, you go to where he is and let him see you. We can't leave to take you home."

"Storm could, but he would not leave you. Too much honor."

Lanna was pulling out all the stops to win points, but she wasn't making headway with Evalle, who ran her hand through her hair. She'd forgotten until now that she'd left it down and would have to pull it back before she fought.

The thud of fists or a club hitting a body echoed over the crowd noise. Something howled in pain.

Right now Evalle and Storm should be watching to see what she might be up against, but with everyone focused on the matches, this was the time to hide Lanna.

Evalle motioned to Storm to come over. When he was close, she asked, "Can you cast a spell to keep even a wizard from finding Lanna here?"

"Yes, if she doesn't tamper with it."

Lanna perked up. "That is good. I need time for my powers to return."

"You'll have plenty," Evalle assured her.

Storm told Lanna, "You'll be safe as long as you don't try to do something like leave this ten-foot-square area."

Horror crossed Lanna's gaze. "I must be able to move."

"No, you don't. I expect you to be right here when I come back."

A shriek split the air, then gained power until a sharp snap ended the sound.

Dame Lynn announced, "*Ixxkter wins his first round in record time. Place your bets while the cleanup team finds all the rhino parts. Ozawa Windago versus Moonlight Warrior will be the next Battle Theater One event. Opponents have five minutes to move to respective holding areas.*"

Evalle had an idea what Ozawa Windago was if his name was a hint, and from the tension shooting off of Storm, he did, too.

TWENTY-FOUR

"Lanna will be safe there, right?" Evalle asked Storm as they headed toward the holding area. She had to get her mind ready to fight.

If Ozawa Windago was actually a play on the term *wendigo*, that meant Evalle's first opponent was in fact already dead.

Killing one seemed like an oxymoron.

"I shielded Lanna's form and her scent," Storm said, directing Evalle through the crowd with subtle touches. "If she doesn't do anything to draw attention to herself, no one should find her. But I'll pick a spot on this side where I can keep an eye on her while I watch you."

Evalle felt the raw power Storm emitted that parted the crowd. The opposite of pheromones? Had to be something feral rolling off him, because this was not a crowd to be easily intimidated.

At the entrance to the holding area for Battle Theater One, a Spartan guard waited until Dame Lynn appeared in his hand and said to Evalle, "You're in holding area one, room seven. If you don't find what you need, let someone know. The lockers are keyed to your touch."

Evalle took the lead. When she reached area one, she stepped inside a pristine room, where beige marble walls and floor dominated the space. Over to one side stood an oyster-shell-white table ten feet long and four feet wide with an overhead light that had her thinking operating room. An alcove had been created with a pale yellow sofa and chair, positioned as if they expected fighters to sit and chat.

Hey, what's your strategy?

Don't be the one looking for body parts when it's over?

Upon further inspection, Evalle found another area with a short wall of yellow lockers. She'd need sunglasses for this place even if she didn't have sensitive eyes. Two fully stocked vanities held personal grooming products and medical provisions. An oversize shower in one corner would accommodate her beast size.

She picked a locker to hold her jacket. After pulling her hair into a ponytail, she walked out to the central area where Storm waited.

His brown eyes reached across the distance and held hers. "You'll have to shift if you want to win."

She started to tell him she would if she had to, just to take that worry from his gaze, but that would be a lie. Even if she could, she wouldn't lie to him any more tonight. "I can't."

"You won't."

"Macha—"

"Isn't here to help."

She had no arguments left. "I'll do what I have to do. That's the best I can say."

His chest moved with a slow breath, eyes simmering

hot as embers threatening to blaze at any moment. Acceptance settled in his tone. "You fight to the death."

"Unless someone asks for relief."

"To the *death*, Evalle," Storm instructed her with the emotion of an icicle. "If the other opponents, especially the Alterants, see you show mercy, they'll know you have a weakness they can exploit. And don't trust *any* fighter to give *you* relief."

A tap at the door preceded a guard pushing it open. "One minute until your fighter moves to Gate Two entrance."

"She'll be there," Storm replied in the same chilly voice, his eyes not moving from her.

The door shut quietly.

She didn't want to part like this, not when she had no idea what she would face or if she'd see Storm again, but going back empty-handed was out of the question.

There was never enough time to do what she wanted.

Fishing out the potion, she asked, "Would you hold on to Nicole's potion for me?"

He nodded yes.

She handed it to him, intending to leave without making this any worse, but his hand on her shoulder stopped her.

She didn't move, unwilling to face more disappointment or anger. His fingers tightened gently. His emotions were so conflicted that even with her limited empathic ability she knew he barely restrained himself, when he wanted to pound a wall and shout at her not to walk out that door.

When he spoke, his tight voice came out on warm breath that teased the hairs falling loose from her ponytail. "It's you or them. I don't care about them."

His lips brushed her neck, then he let her go.

If she turned around, she wouldn't make it out of the room without her control cracking.

She nodded.

The door opened again and Evalle exited, following the guard to where he stopped at the entrance to a corridor maybe fifty feet long. A gate of silver bars blocked the other end, where light glared from the theater.

At the entrance to the passageway, the guard blocked her way while he issued instructions. "You're fighting in a warded dome. Involuntary contact will toss you back into the theater. Anyone trying to actually pass through the ward from either side instantly combusts into a fireball."

Please tell me Storm knows this. He might be pissed off at her, but he'd gone through a plate-glass window once already to pull her from the jaws of a Svart troll.

The guard stepped aside.

She trudged forward until she reached the last barrier to the theater, where she peered between the silver bars to the empty battle zone. She dug around in her mind to pull up what she'd studied on different creatures. Wendigos were Algonquin creatures who . . . *crud* . . . no details surfaced.

She was pretty sure they were huge, dead monsters.

What else?

Tiny lights sparked across the dome-shaped area that rose to fifty feet above her head, defining the ward boundaries.

She had plenty of room to move. Two basketball teams could play a regulation game in this much space.

Dame Lynn announced, "*Ozawa Windago enters from Gate One and Moonlight Warrior the Alterant enters from Gate Two.*" Shouting from the stands rocked the dome.

Gate Two vanished. Evalle stepped into the arena, her boots crunching over the hard, packed-dirt floor. The silver bars reappeared behind her. No way out until someone won.

Gate One had disappeared as well.

Her opponent ducked his head even though the gate area had ten feet of clearance. The crowd noise died down to a tense murmur when the gate behind the wendigo—yes, that's what she had to fight—blocked his exit, too.

Anticipation mounted as Ozawa struck a pose, head raised, back arched, massive chest pushed out.

Emaciated and muscular at the same time. Lavender-gray skin pulled taut over that cadaverous body looked as cold as the air had become in his presence. He had a narrow waist, canine-shaped legs with thick thighs, and paws as long as her forearm, tipped with curled claws. Two huge arms hung down to the ground with long, pointed fingers with joints that reminded her of spider legs.

At least, she *thought* he was male.

A three-foot-long shock of gray hair grew out of his chest and hung down between his knees. That hair probably hid genitals. Orange-red orbs glowed inside the deep-set black holes for eyes on each side of his narrow face, and another mass of the feathery gray hair sprouted off his bony head and fell past his shoulders like a headdress.

He reached over his back, pulled out a sword as long as her leg and raised it above his head.

The bloodthirsty crowd screamed with delight.

She had no intention of spilling any of hers to entertain them, but between Ozawa's reach and the length of that sword, she might not have a say.

Her sixteen-inch dagger had a spelled blade that killed demons, but pulling that out right now would only get her laughed out of the place.

Ozawa emitted a low, grunting noise sounding like a crazed boar. His mouth hung open. A brick-red tongue snaked out, then back in. He drooled red saliva.

No, that was blood sliding off his jaw. Now she remembered. Wendigos were insatiable cannibals.

He didn't just want to win.

He wanted to eat her.

Ozawa rushed her, swinging the blade with the ease of a demonic Highlander.

Watching his eyes change from red to glowing yellow centers, Evalle dove away from the gate as the blade whistled past her shoulder. He would have sliced her in half. She could use a kinetic shield to hold him off. She hoped.

Quick on his feet, Ozawa spun around and pursued, flipping the sword from hand to hand. His eyes boiled red again.

She waited for him to get close, then bent her knees. Calling forth a short burst of kinetic power, she leaped to go over his head.

But he jumped just as high. Higher.

And swung the sword across his body at the same time.

She whipped her hands forward, pushing a blast of energy in front of her.

His blade slammed against the wall of energy, and the blow knocked her sideways. Felt like a bus had hit her. She flew through the air, hit the packed-dirt floor rolling and lunged to her feet, hands up, ready.

That's when she noticed something useful. His eyes brightened to yellow once more, and when they did, his sword sizzled along the edge.

Avoid him during yellow eyes.

She dodged his next strike, then started racing around the dome with him turning and chasing.

The crowd booed her.

Screw 'em.

Ozawa's blade caught her across the back of her hand. She hissed at the pain but didn't slow down. When he missed her the next time, he swung his sword to cut her leg.

She backed out of range and should have been clear.

But he released the sword this time, letting it slice across her thigh.

The blade cut her skin as clean as a scalpel through a firm tomato.

Her momentum threw her forward and down. She tumbled over and over, landing against the dome wall that sparked with the contact. That mild shock was nothing compared to feeling the skin on her hand and leg burning, literally.

She could smell smoldering flesh.

Ozawa raised his sword, taking his time to cross the dome to her. He waved his weapon in the air, stirring the crowd.

A show-off cannibal.

Lying on her back, one arm tucked at her side and the other flung away from her body, she took deep, ragged pants.

Letting her head loll to the side, she caught sight of Storm plowing through people.

When his gaze met hers, she gave a tiny shake of her head, mouthing the words *Trust me.*

He hesitated, then kept coming, his eyes on her whole time.

Ozawa moved toward her on huge canine hind legs, stopping close enough for the wide paws he stood on to gag her with the smell of rotted skin. He grasped the sword hilt with two hands and raised it slowly for a dramatic kill.

As the blade came down, she heard Storm's roar from outside the dome.

She drove all her kinetic energy into a shield between her and the sword, parallel with the ground.

The sword crashed down on her protective field, driving her hard against the ground. Her arm gave, bending at the elbow, but she shoved back with all her power.

My turn.

Yanking her other hand away from her body, she whispered to the blade on the dagger in her hand, telling it to stop at nothing. She sliced horizontally above the ankles, cutting through both of the wendigo's legs.

Ozawa's fierce gaze lost its yellow glow. Confusion filled his red eyes. Stunned, he teetered, then fell backward, bouncing hard when he hit the ground.

Evalle released her shield of energy and flipped her hold on the dagger. She shoved to her feet and leaped over Ozawa's prone body, deftly landing inches from his head.

She drove her dagger into his eye socket.

He reached up with sharp claws that he dragged down her arm.

She tightened her grip, fighting a scream at the pain, and twisted the dagger. His body rocked back and forth. Taut skin stretched over his torso cracked and peeled away from muscle that shriveled. His jaw dropped open. Howling black spirits shot out in all directions, flashing into fireballs when they hit the dome wall.

When his body stopped jerking, Evalle ripped out her dagger and wiped the gray liquid on his headdress hair. She forced herself to stand and gritted her teeth at the searing burn in her wounds.

She headed for Gate Two, catching a glimpse of

Storm in her peripheral vision before he disappeared in the direction of the entrance to the holding area.

Just as she reached the hallway, an explosion shook the ground beneath her. She sidestepped, but kept moving. If the place was blowing up, she hoped Storm would get to Lanna.

The guard waiting at the other end of the hall appeared too calm for any crisis, so the explosion must have been something that happened in the other theater. Before Evalle could ask, the guard told her, "You have a minimum of sixty minutes before another match. If you fail to be ready at any time after that, you forfeit your match and become the property of the host."

Belong to Deek's brother?

Not happening as long as she could breathe. She nodded her understanding.

Storm stepped into view.

As the guard moved away, Storm reached out to touch her.

Anyone could be watching.

She shook her head.

His dark gaze turned black. He said nothing as he walked beside her while she limped to holding area one, room seven.

She hissed out, "How's Lanna?"

"She's still hidden and unhappy, but she's safe. No one's paying her any mind."

Evalle hobbled to one of the chairs next to the operating table and avoided looking at her throbbing hand. At least he hadn't caught her dominant hand.

Storm closed the door, taking his time to reach her.

Might as well get this over with. "What?"

He didn't yell, which would have been better than hearing his disappointment. "You can't survive these battles if you don't at least shift into Belador battle form."

"I'm trying to save that." She feared not being able to stop shifting all the way into an Alterant if she got caught up in the battle.

"You can't make the next round unless you survive the current one. You've been trained to kill in defense or to protect someone. These fighters kill, period. They don't care if you look like their mother, if they even have one."

He had a point, but she didn't have to admit it. "You need to get busy healing," he growled. "If you can't do it, I can."

Guess our little strategy discussion is over. "No, let's keep your majik in case I need it. I want a shower and I'd like some clean clothes."

"I'll get some." With that, he walked out.

As bad as her wounds felt, her heart hurt worse.

He was disappointed, because he thought she wasn't trying hard enough. She could use some encouragement right now, but she'd feel the same way if he refused to shift into his jaguar form to battle a dangerous being. Limping to the shower, she stripped down and turned the hot water on full blast, washing a pool of watery blood down the drain. The liquid soap reminded her of a fresh rain, and the shampoo smelled like peppermint.

Of course, if Kol was anything like Deek, he'd have nothing less than the best.

Feeling clean, she slid down to the granite floor and let the hot water beat down on her as she shut her mind down to all but healing herself. Her Alterant beast stirred, ready to break free, but Tristan had taught her how to control her beast so she could draw on that more powerful side when she needed to heal.

As she focused on each injury, her hand healed quickly, proving the wound was not that bad, then she focused on the deep ache in her thigh. Once she felt strong enough to move around without pain, she turned off the jets and stepped out. A thick bath sheet sat on the bench next to a stack of clothes.

No sign of Storm.

She dressed, pulling her wet hair back from her face. By the time she walked out to where he paced the front room, her wounds were no worse than dull aches. "How much time do I have left?"

"Forty minutes. Let's go."

She didn't want to do anything with him this angry. "Where?"

"To watch the other Alterants fight if you plan to reach the last round."

She should be glad he wasn't fawning all over her, right? So why did she feel hurt? "If you're going to spend every minute mad at me, then just go away."

"You think I'm pissed?" His voice shook with quiet power.

"Sounds that way. If not, what's bothering you?"

That might have been the wrong question, because Storm drew in a breath and unloaded. "I'll tell you what's wrong. I want to beat Tristan to a pulp for not coming in to meet with Macha the first time. And Macha's no better in my book for putting you in this position where neither Tzader nor VIPER can back you up." He strode over to her, shoulders bunching beneath his shirt when he leaned in. "But the thing that pushes me right over the edge is how little value you place on your life."

"I value myself."

"No, you *don't*, because, with the exception of a small group of friends, you've been treated like a bastard child. Macha didn't do you a favor when she blackmailed you to do her wet work in trade for freedom, and now you're trying to save an entire race of Alterants who aren't even helping you. On top of all that, I can't do a thing to protect you that doesn't put you at greater risk. *Pissed* doesn't even come close to what I'm feeling."

When he put it that way she had a hard time denying he made valid points, but he was wrong on one thing. She did value herself. Closing the space between them, she put her hand on his chest, where his heartbeat pounded at a dangerous pace.

Muscles in his throat flexed, taut with strain.

She wanted to meet him halfway but didn't know where that was. "I do want to survive this, and *you* are the reason why. But if I don't make it out of here, I want you to know . . . I regret having wasted what time together we've had."

He released a long breath that came out in a groan of pain, then he reached for her.

Thrilled to feel his body next to hers, she folded into his arms, her heart bursting at being close to him again. His kiss fed the longing in her chest. Pleasure raced over her skin and down through her core.

She wrapped her fingers around his neck, hanging on tight to the one person she didn't think she could live without.

He cupped her head and held her gently, but his mouth was hungry and demanding.

Why couldn't they be back at his house, lounging in front of his fire?

She licked his lips and kissed him, wanting to feel all of him, skin to skin. And this was all her, no armband driving her insane to have him. He grabbed her butt and scooped her up against him. She hooked her legs around his waist, shuddering with the desire that rocked her.

He slid a hand beneath the tail of her T-shirt and crawled his fingers up until he flipped the front clasp of her bra. His thumb brushed over her nipple and she jerked up with a hiss.

His touch drove her crazy. She kissed him harder, demanding what she needed from him. He kept up the gentle assault until her skin felt alive everywhere.

She pulled her mouth from his. "We could . . . maybe here . . ."

He went still, his body tense, his chest heaving with ragged breaths. "No, we can't." His forehead dropped to hers. "This is not the place for you to experience making love the first time. Not when guards can walk in whenever they want. Damn, I should know better than to let this get out of hand, but I lose my mind around you."

She smiled at his grumbled admission.

When he lifted his head back to find her smiling, he tweaked her breast lightly.

She lost her grin. "That's torture."

"Uh-huh. Nothing like what you've been putting me through for weeks."

"I'm kicking the butt of anyone who stops me from leaving here with you."

Moving his hand from her breast, he lifted her so she could drop her legs to the floor. She'd never discussed what happened to her as a teen, but she felt the need to be honest right now. "You should know, Storm, that when we do . . . come together it won't be my first time. I may be inexperienced, but I'm . . . I'm no virgin."

Storm placed his hand on her cheek, his words tender. "There's a difference between the clinical definition of having sex and making love, but you didn't experience either one, did you?"

She dropped her chin, unable to face him. "Let's just say I know how the parts work."

Pulling her to him, he held her for a while, then asked gently, "What happened?"

She didn't want to recall that night alone in the basement, locked in with a man she'd come to think of as her only friend. Even though she was ready to be intimate with Storm, she still had her doubts about shifting involuntarily if she felt trapped and the nightmare took over her mind.

Storm deserved to know the truth.

Drawing a shaky breath from the feelings still racing through her body, she told him quickly before she changed her mind. "My aunt raised me after my dad abandoned me, or *sold* me. She said her brother paid her a salary and had no interest in ever seeing me again, since I was a freak that had to be kept out of the sun. A bastard embarrassment."

His fingers paused, then continued massaging her muscles.

"My mother died in childbirth, so I don't know her side of the story. My aunt kept me locked in the basement she'd finished out to be a small apartment. She left during the day to work at some hospital as a nurse."

"Where's your aunt?"

That would have been a simple question if it hadn't come out with a load of threat beneath Storm's words.

"Dead. When I reached my teens, I started having muscle pains and cramps, so she convinced a young doctor to make house calls. At least, I thought he was a doctor. He was curious more than anything about someone who couldn't go out in the sun. He was nice and gave me medicine that eased my cramps, but he kept stopping by during the next month until one day he said he had to examine me. A gynecological exam."

The warm hand stroking along her back stilled. Storm was tense but calm when he said, "Go on."

"That was . . . difficult, but the *doctor* said everything

was fine and left. Then he came by one night to tell me my aunt was staying at the hospital overnight to help out because they were shorthanded. I told him I was fine alone, but he got this strange look in his eyes. I knew he wasn't listening. First he tried to convince me he wanted to examine me again. When I said no, he forced me down and started tearing my clothes off. I screamed, but nobody heard me. I fought him. He was bigger than me. Ripped my clothes off. He . . ."

She shook, seeing his crazed face and feeling his hands on her again. He'd slapped her, then balled his fist and hit her over and over, yelling at her to stop acting like a child while he shoved inside her, ripping her. Her heart had beaten so loudly she'd heard each *thump* in her ears. She'd screamed until she was hoarse, then her arms started changing, skin breaking with cartilage pushing through.

Her jaw had stretched . . . then he'd stopped hitting her.

His face had turned white with fear.

Storm's voice finally cut through Evalle's horror. "Shhh, take it easy, sweetheart. I'm here." He held her tight. "Calm down."

Her arms were bulging with muscle *now* and her jaw felt out of shape. Her Alterant was coming to the surface.

She had to stop shifting.

Storm kept talking softly, telling her she was safe with him. Slowly, her arms and body eased back into her human form. She moved her jaw and ran her tongue over her teeth. Natural teeth.

Hugging him, she swallowed against the sick plunge her stomach took. Storm kissed her hair and her forehead.

She feared facing his pity or disgust, but when she met his eyes all she found was rage.

He held her face in his warm hands. "I want a name."

"He's dead."

Storm nodded, assuming she'd killed him.

Well, she had in a way. "I started shifting for the first time, which scared me. I didn't manage to shift all the way, but I terrified him. He ran out, locked the steel door, and I heard his tires squealing when he left." She closed her eyes, wishing she could erase it all forever. "My aunt came home twelve hours later all upset, yelling at me that here she'd found an orderly willing to take me off her hands and I'd ruined it. Crashed his car and lived long enough to say he'd seen a monster."

"Son of a bitch. Your *aunt* sent a grown man who wasn't even a doctor to you, knowing what could happen—" Storm couldn't finish his words.

She'd never told anyone about the rape.

Sharing that with Storm hadn't left her feeling ugly inside, as she'd always feared, but at ease. "It's in the past, but now you know why I'm concerned about losing control around you."

He kissed her forehead and smoothed his hand over her hair. "I'm not concerned. We *will* have our time, and when we do you'll be fine."

She would trust him when the time came.

If she lived to see it.

Dame Lynn's muffled words came through from outside the door, announcing Chi Dalvin versus the Alterant Boomer.

Storm sighed wistfully and kissed her one more lingering time. "Time to scout out the competition."

"I don't know what I'm fighting next."

"Doesn't matter. We need to observe the Alterants."

She took his looking toward the final matches as a positive sign that he believed she'd win her next one. Flexing her hand that was sore, but usable, she headed to the door. "What have you found out so far?"

"Saw a female Alterant called Black Satin who isn't any larger than you when she shifts, but her skin is covered in a mottled brownish-gray hide that looks tough to pierce, and she's got some wicked fangs."

"What'd she fight?"

"A Thracian giant."

"Don't know what that is."

"Huge bastard that outweighed her by a couple hundred pounds even after she'd shifted. He wore one hand covered in steel spikes a foot long and looked like he could defeat an army single-handed, but Black Satin took him down. She wasn't quick about it, but she won." Storm slowed when they reached the area where Lanna sat with her legs pulled to her chest and head down on her knees.

He asked, "Want to talk to her a minute?"

Evalle considered it, then shook her head. "Not until we come back. That way I only catch grief once." She watched as people passed until she was convinced Lanna was still out of sight.

Moving on, Evalle drew attention from the crowd.

Too many admiring glances for Storm's peace of mind.

He hooked his arm around her shoulders in a blatant show of possession. "How did Black Satin kill the Thracian? She have a weapon?"

He kept his words low for her ears only. "That part bothers me. She didn't have a visible weapon, but I think she used a spell, maybe even Noirre majik, to enrage him. She stayed just out of reach, teasing him like a matador playing with a bull until the giant charged her."

"He didn't gut her with his spiked fist?"

"Nope. Her hands turned into two snake heads that had flat fangs as sharp as blades. And she's fast. She gouged him a couple of times, which didn't look too bad until he started convulsing and running around crazy, then just dove headfirst into a wall and—"

"Exploded into fire," Evalle finished, now realizing that had been the loud *kaboom* she'd heard. You could get knocked into the wall, but if you ran head-on into one intentionally you were toast.

"Then there's Trojan," Storm said.

"What is a Trojan? Is that his name or his sponsor?" She snapped her fingers, trying to lighten Storm's mood. "I've got it. He fights naked to scare his opponents with his big weapon." She snorted. "From what I've heard from the women working the streets at night, the men who brag generally don't measure up. Literally."

Storm tried to smile, but his worry would not relinquish its hold on the tight muscles in his face. "Think more along the lines of a Trojan horse with hidden surprises. Nasty ones."

"Oh." She twisted her neck to catch a second look at a man who ducked and disappeared into the crowd. That couldn't have been Horace Keefer. Tzader wouldn't send in Beladors, especially when he suspected Evalle was here, plus Horace was retired. Tzader would never send him to something like this.

Had to be a mistake.

"That's all you have to say about Trojan?" Storm asked.

She turned back to him. "Is he anything like a purple cannibalistic zombie with a bad hair day?"

"Not even close."

TWENTY-FIVE

"How ya doin'?" Evalle asked as she walked up to Lanna twenty minutes later. The teen couldn't look more miserable if she tried.

"I have headache." Lanna sat back against the base of the stadium seating.

Storm had his back to them, keeping Evalle and Lanna shielded. He glanced around at Lanna. "Stop trying to cross the spellbound area and you won't have a headache."

Ignoring him, she argued, "I am rested. I can cloak myself. Let me out and I'll help you."

"No." Evalle had all she could handle keeping Storm from interfering. Lanna's middle name was Meddler. "Just sit tight. I've been called to my second round. As soon as I finish the third round, we'll go."

"If you win," Lanna started saying, then quickly amended her words. "*When* you win, they will offer you immortality. I have heard this. You will not accept?"

"From the Medb? No, of course not."

Dame Lynn's voice interrupted, announcing, "*Moonlight Warrior takes on Sandspur in five minutes. Place your bets.*"

"What is Sandspur?" Lanna asked.

Evalle considered the match she'd just seen and answered, "Have no idea, but with any luck it won't be twelve feet tall with an arm span just as wide."

Storm said over his shoulder, "People are noticing that you're over here."

"I'm coming." Evalle told Lanna, "I'll be back soon. Okay?"

Lanna pulled her knees up tight and sent Evalle a teenage glower for an answer.

What made Quinn think I had a clue about how to deal with Lanna? Evalle returned to her holding room just as the guard came for her. Storm gave her arm a squeeze and left.

Her wounds had healed. She was as ready as she could be and reached Gate One as Dame Lynn announced, "*Moonlight Warrior the Alterant versus Sandspur.*" But this time when both gates vanished then reappeared, no opponent stood on the other side.

Evalle stepped into the battle dome, surprised when her boots sank into sand as fine as sugar. She searched the stands on her right for Storm and found him close enough to see the lines in his frown.

Maybe she was getting a pass or . . .

Energy entered the dome.

Evalle spun her attention back to the far side where a knee-high lump pushed up from underground at the mouth of Gate Two.

Displaced sand bulged as a fat, cylindrical creature five feet long burrowed forward.

Evalle didn't move as her opponent continued to

worm its way to the center of the theater. Shouting quieted to a low rumble of murmurs. Excitement mounted as everyone waited to see Sandspur.

When the critter finally burst out of the sand, Evalle had her dagger in hand, ready.

Sandspur pushed its head up first, two horns bouncing, as if rubbery. Lifting half its body upright, Sandspur was a caterpillar version of the Michelin Man, but this overgrown bug didn't have the little legs wiggling along the underside. Tigerlike black stripes reached around the aqua-colored body with the wide bands narrowing as the tips almost touched on its belly. Sandspur's head resembled a daisy, with three white petals fanning out and huge pink eyes with blue centers.

Cute, in an odd way.

Feenix would love that for a playmate.

How was she going to hurt, much less kill, something that didn't even have legs? How did fighters come into these rings—theaters—and attack something that had never threatened them?

She could see how boxing was a major sport, but beast battles weren't sport.

This crowd demanded dismemberment and death.

Smiling at the cute little devil would send the wrong message. She'd try to scare Sandspur into begging for relief. Storm wouldn't be happy with her, but he'd just have to get over it. Flipping the dagger end over end and catching the grip, she moved into a crouch attack position.

Sandspur opened a maw of finger-length sharp teeth

and let out a yell that might be impressive for a caterpillar, but was too thin and high-pitched to be anything scary. Laughter bucked through the crowd.

Evalle had to bite her lip to keep from smiling. Poor thing. Hopefully, this wouldn't take long. She didn't want to see Sandspur humiliated.

"Come on, buddy," she called over quietly, her words shielded by the roar of laughter. "Let's rock and get you out of here."

Sandspur's eyes went from pink to hot blue flames. Six black tiger stripes wrapping its body unleashed, stretching ten feet out on each side. Along the edge of each stripe, tentacles spiked up like shark teeth and sharp pincers clicked at the tips.

Crap.

Sandspur moved forward as if on a supersonic railway.

One tentacle whipped at her.

Evalle pushed off the ground with kinetic force and landed on the opposite side of the dome.

Sandspur spun in place like a whirligig, tentacles flying in all directions.

So that's where it got the name.

Getting close enough to stab the fat body would be tough.

Sandspur spun toward her with amazing speed. Its pincers clicked close to her face as she dove away once again. A row of teeth along the tentacle caught her left shoulder, ripping open skin and tearing muscle.

Fighting harder only pumped the blood faster.

No choice.

With a quick roll away from the flying tentacles, Evalle shoved to her feet. She called forth her Belador battle form that she could use without sanction. Her arms bulged with muscle. Cartilage broke through the skin, then her shirt. Her neck thickened and her legs split the jeans.

Her Alterant beast wanted to surface, but she kept her control locked down tight.

Cartwheeling away from another attack, Evalle landed with her feet planted, facing the overgrown worm. "That all you got?"

Sandspur paused, its flowery head tilting to one side, then the thing actually laughed.

I'll show you funny, you miserable . . .

Big mistake. The fat little turd's action had been meant to distract her. And it worked.

A tentacle lashed out fast as a whip.

This one stretched way longer than the other five and sliced her calf, jerking her off balance. She bent around and slashed the tentacle with her dagger.

The three-foot piece of appendage whimpered as it crawled off, its pincer snapping at air.

Another tentacle shot out from Sandspur's body the same length, but this one went for her face.

She dropped her blade to use both hands to catch the black arm just below the pincer. Rubbery skin over rigid cartilage or bone inside. Jagged one-inch spikes along the edge cut into her palms. Her shoulder was losing strength. She struggled to keep the slashing pincer away from her face.

Could Sandspur stretch only one tentacle this far at a time? Looked that way, but now it was using her hold for leverage to inch its fat little body across the sand with the other four arms reaching for her.

Not as fast when a tentacle was caught?

Blood oozed through her fingers.

Two spikes pierced all the way through her palm and stuck out the back of her hand. Pain wrenched her mind in different directions from her hand to her shoulder and leg, but she would not lose to a freakin' worm.

Dizziness washed over her. Bile rushed up her throat.

Could those spikes on Sandspur's tentacles be fangs that injected some kind of venom?

Gritting her teeth, she clenched harder on the tentacle, tightening to cut off any blood flow, if blood ran through this thing.

Sandspur trembled, then emitted a crunching and growling sound. It started whipping sand into a cloud.

If Evalle lost her glasses in this bright arena or that much sand hit her in the face, she'd be blinded. But she couldn't release a hand to grab her dagger, or the pincer would take a piece of her skull.

With the sand tornado circling its body, Sandspur drew its remaining tentacles back around itself and started growing larger.

But it stalled out and wobbled.

Pressure eased from the tentacle Evalle wrestled. She risked a look to glare at Storm, warning him to stop helping her. He gave her a *What?* look in return.

Ignoring him, she arm-wrestled the tentacle toward

the ground. The pincer bent back on itself and bit at her wrist, cutting a gouge.

She rallied everything she had and pressed down with her forearm. That freed one hand to snatch up her dagger. She stabbed the tentacle, pinning it to the ground.

Sandspur screeched and jerked.

Didn't like that one bit, huh?

The little bastard spun harder to reach her.

Evalle shoved up her hand, palm out, and blinked to clear her vision. Sandspur crashed into a kinetic wall of energy.

Whispering to her dagger to stay where it was, Evalle pushed up to stand. She staggered but kept shoving the kinetic barrier at Sandspur. Forced backward, Sandspur keened as it stretched the stabbed tentacle.

When Evalle held the creature trapped against the ground, Sandspur had the audacity to laugh at her.

Nice try.

Evalle wouldn't make the same mistake twice.

Extending her trembling, bloody hand toward the lopped-off tentacle still making angry clicks as it crawled around, she called the appendage to her with kinetics. It flew to her hand. Gritting her teeth, Evalle gripped the angry pincer that snapped viciously at her face and swung it around to face down.

Sandspur stopped laughing.

With one last burst of energy, Evalle released the kinetic wall for a second and stabbed the pincer right below Sandspur's three-petal head.

Its toothy maw opened and squealed.

The pincer had no loyalty beyond ripping at whatever it touched. Murky red flowed from the ripped wound. Sandspur's hot blue eyes turned pink, then changed to a dried-up brown as its head fell away from the body.

Evalle left the pincer stuck there and turned around. The tentacle her dagger held in place had begun to shrivel.

Swaying toward the Gate Two exit, she called the dagger back to her hand, catching it as she stumbled down the hall.

She exited the hallway limping badly and lurching from side to side. Storm was running toward her.

When he reached her and made a move for her legs, she gave a wobbly shake of her head. "Don't even think about picking me up."

Cursing, he opened the door to her holding area.

The minute Evalle stumbled into the room, Storm kicked the door shut and lifted her in his arms, heading toward the shower area. "Don't start with me."

She didn't have it in her to complain. She moaned at the movement and didn't want to look at her hand, which throbbed as if it had swollen to the size of a baseball catcher's mitt.

She wanted to calm Storm down. "I'm not dying."

"Really?" Icy sarcasm dripped from his one-word question, but she heard fear beneath all of it. He was afraid for her. "You left a trail of blood that looks like a carotid artery's been slashed, and you're dragging your leg." He lowered her to a bench outside the showers and slipped her boots off, then her socks, lifting one that dripped red, then tossing it aside. The coppery smell of fresh blood soaked the air.

He ripped her jeans apart with his bare hands, removing the denim in pieces.

She fumbled with the ragged shirt, trying to drag it over her head before the blood dried to her back. Storm took over, lifting it gently even though he was so tense that lightning should be popping all around them. He tossed the bloody shirt over with her socks. That left her in panties and a bra.

She had to get up and shower on her own. "I've got it from here."

When he didn't move, she said, "Please."

Storm stood up and backed away, arms crossed and frustration pouring off him.

She could do this and would, just as soon as the room leveled itself out. Pushing up, she felt a moment of arrogant pride that she could stand on both legs. Then she took a step, and her gashed leg buckled.

Cursing, Storm caught her under the arms. "Your skin's turning green. Probably a poison in your bloodstream."

"Bathroom." She barely got the word out before he swung her around and into the bathroom stall, where she unloaded her sour stomach.

Her head spun. She sat back against the wall.

Storm handed her a cup of water she used to rinse her mouth. Anything sent south would come right back up.

With that done, he helped her up until he could put

his arm around her and walk her to the shower stall, where the water jets already gushed water.

Cold as ice.

She jerked at the shock to her hot skin.

"Easy." Storm started speaking in the strange language she'd heard him use before.

Heat swirled inside her chest just above her breasts. She looked down at the emerald, a blurry green shape. The stone glowed a little, then got brighter the longer he chanted.

She could feel the venom receding.

Pausing briefly, he told her to use her Alterant beast to start healing herself, then kept chanting as he held her under the cold water. She managed it again, but this time took longer. Not an encouraging sign when she had to face off with an Alterant next.

Strength slowly returned to her arms and legs. Her shoulder stopped aching and her vision cleared. "Think I'm good now."

"I'm not." He turned her around and held her against him. He reached out and shut off the water, then his hand pressed her head to his chest. "*Watching* you fight is torture."

She'd feel the same way if he had fought instead of her. "I understand and I appreciate what you did, but you can't do that again."

He eased her away, staring down at her. "What're you talking about?"

She pulled free and stepped out of the stall, where

she found a thick bath sheet to wrap around her. "When Sandspur was stuck." She wiped her face and started drying her body. "You did something to hold him in place and weaken his tentacle."

"No, I didn't."

Lowering the towel, she asked, "Who else would have . . ." Evalle figured it out at the same moment Storm said, "Lanna." Was the girl trying to get killed? "That means she's escaped her safe zone and is running around with her cloaking."

Storm frowned, pondering on something. "If she broke free of the spell I used and intervened with Sandspur, that means she's a hell of a lot more powerful than we realized. I should have realized that when she got past the Domjon."

"But she possesses untrained energy, which means she's still no match for that wizard Grendal. We have to find her before he does."

TWENTY-SIX

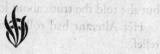

Lanna snuck around the edge of a crowd gathered to watch security capture a witch who had given aid to her Alterant during a beast fight.

Two scary men dressed in warrior clothes similar to those worn by the guards outside the entrance rushed to grab a young witch with long white hair.

Her gold mask hid all her face except her mouth and chin.

"Let go of me." The witch yanked her body back and forth.

Another guard walked up in front of her with his hand out.

Dame Lynn's translucent head appeared on his palm. "Imogenia of the Carretta Coven, you were observed aiding your fighter—"

"I didn't do anything," Imogenia cried out, struggling against the powerful guards, whose grips did not budge.

"—and will forfeit said fighter, plus face sanction for your transgression."

"How can you eject me when my fighter didn't even win?"

Lanna agreed with Imogenia, whose fighter had shifted from a skinny young man to an Alterant beast large enough to battle a were-bear, but then had run in fear. The witch lied about causing the were-bear to trip, but she told the truth about losing.

Her Alterant had rolled into a ball and begged for relief.

Imogenia's eyes narrowed to tiny slits inside the holes of her mask. "I demand to see Kol."

Dame Lynn merely said, "If you insist."

Fine hairs along Lanna's neck lifted at something unsaid in Dame Lynn's pleasant tone.

A centaur—part man and part horse—appeared next to the guard holding Dame Lynn's head. Dark hair fell past the centaur's neck. Strong face and attractive, but frightening, too. He had no shirt, just lots of muscles under olive skin covering the human upper body that grew where the neck and head of a horse should have been.

"I am Kol," he boomed to the crowd, muscled arms outstretched and front hooves prancing. He grinned his appreciation at greetings being shouted. His goatee gave him a wickedly sexy appeal. He dipped his head in a bow to Imogenia. "Your wish is granted. I am here. What can I do for you?"

The witch's lips curved with coy intentions. She breathed deeply, which pushed her bulging breasts even higher above her low-cut neckline. Lusty noises murmured through the crowd. On her exhale, Imogenia said, "I would appreciate a *private* moment to discuss my little mistake."

Kol had blue eyes the color of a deep sea that twinkled, but not in a nice way. "If only that I could grant this one small wish, but to do so would have more women vying for my affections than I have time for now."

Imogenia's smile faltered.

Kol's tone took a deadly turn. "And to be honest, I hold affection for no one. You have broken my laws. You will pay the price."

"No, please don't, I—" Imogenia arched her back as her arms jerked above her head, and her face muscles strained against some invisible assault. The black hooded cloak tied at her throat flew off and over the crowd, landing behind Lanna, who gathered it up quickly, then stood on her tiptoes again to see.

Veins beneath Imogenia's skin bulged, breaking her skin in blue and purple lines that fingered out like lines on a map. Blisters boiled on her chin and arms. She screamed when her hair ignited, burning down to the scalp. In the next second, she had a bald head covered in angry sores and welts.

Her dress poofed away in a cloud of gold dust that fell to the ground, leaving her naked for the world to see sagging skin and hideous, oozing blisters.

Finally, her arms dropped, free of whatever had held her in place. She looked down at herself, eyes rocked with horror. "Noooo, oh, nooo . . ." Tears streamed down her face, then her mask disappeared. It had hidden a purplish-red birthmark that covered her right cheek.

Kol shouted, "I have granted you another favor. The flaw you've kept hidden now draws no attention."

Imogenia moaned, weaving where she stood until her knees started to fold.

Kol shouted, "No! You will walk out of here."

"Pleeease," she begged, but her legs locked straight and started walking stiffly toward the exit. The crowd parted, drawing back to avoid touching her. She twisted around, her upper body fighting against her legs. "Please, Kol, I'll do anything you want."

"You already have, my sweet. You're preventing anyone else from testing my rules again, because—" He paused, taking in the crowd. "Let it be known that the next one to cross me will not get off with such a light punishment."

Imogenia's sobbing could be heard all the way to the exit.

Lanna shuddered at the idea of getting caught.

She backed away from the crowd on shaky legs. Had anyone seen *her* help Evalle? Hands damp, she kept moving until she found another space beneath the towering steps and rushed inside it, sitting down hard when her legs gave out. She could not get upset and lose control or she would draw Grendal's attention.

But neither could she stay here.

First, calm down and think. Imogenia had been caught immediately. Evalle had fought over an hour ago. If anyone had noticed Lanna's help, they would have shouted foul then, right? She started breathing easier, but she still had to get moving.

She looked at Imogenia's cloak still in her hands.

Crawling forward, she peeked out to make sure no one was standing nearby and scooped up a fist of gray-brown dirt. She sat back and dropped the wadded-up cloak on the ground between her bent knees. Sprinkling the dirt over the cloak, she gently called upon the earth, asking to dull the color of the cloak.

A color no eyes strayed to.

Finished, she lifted the material now the color of dirt and stood, wrapping the covering around her shoulders. Lucky for her that Imogenia was short, too.

Pulling the hood over her head, Lanna took a tentative step away from her hiding place. She should return to the place where Storm and Evalle had left her, but she did not want to be locked up again in his spell. Breaking out had hurt, and she might not escape next time.

Storm and Evalle did not understand that she could not sit in one place and risk being caught by Grendal.

He had eyes everywhere.

Dame Lynn's voice announced, *"Elite matches will begin in ten minutes. Eligible Alterants are to be in their respective holding areas at the times designated."*

Lanna listened for Evalle's battle as Dame Lynn called out matchups. Evalle's was one of the last fights, same battle dome as her first two matches. With Storm and Evalle free to move around the event until Evalle had to fight, Lanna had to own the scent on Imogenia's cloak or Storm would find her. Weaving slowly through the crowd, she kept her head down, searching for a place to watch Evalle's fight.

She did not want to face Kol, but she could not let Evalle die.

Dame Lynn announced, *"Moonlight Warrior the Alterant versus Boomer the Alterant in ten minutes."*

Spotting a vendor setup that faced where Evalle would battle, Lanna considered the table draped with a cloth and displaying silver jewelry. Not an ideal spot to hide, because the vendor might lift the drape to look under the table for inventory.

It would have to do. Lanna waited until enough customers surrounded the table to shield her slipping underneath at one end. She could not waste energy cloaking when she would need it later to leave undetected, or she would put Evalle and Storm in danger.

But what if Evalle needed her help again?

Lanna had not been seen helping Evalle.

She could do it again.

TWENTY-SEVEN

Evalle still ached from her last wounds, which should have healed all the way by now. She paced her holding room, pretending to be burning off anxiety when in truth she was trying to stretch out the tight muscle in her calf that complained with each step.

To avoid talking about her injury, she pointed out, "I haven't seen Tristan since we got here. Or Kizira."

"How bad is it?" Storm asked, totally disregarding her words.

"I'm talking about Tristan."

"No, you're avoiding telling me how bad your wound is." He leaned against the table, arms crossed.

Guess she hadn't hidden her lingering pain as well as she'd thought. "Not bad."

Storm merely lifted an eyebrow, claiming that to be a lie.

"Not as bad as it could be," she amended. "Maybe I'll end up with Bernie, if he survived." She could offer him relief *if* she could win the match against a shifted Alterant.

"He's still alive, but Imogenia hasn't fared so well."

"What happened?"

"She used majik to help Bernie and got caught. I heard bits and pieces on the way to meet you. Kol took the Alterant and disfigured Imogenia to make a statement, then booted her."

Poor Bernie. Kol would probably trade him to the Medb.

Storm scratched his chin, thinking. "Sandspur's venom must have interfered with your ability to heal completely."

As long as Storm knew what was going on, Evalle decided to try again. She stood very still and called up her beast power to heal herself. Her muscles rippled with an impending change to her beast. She stopped abruptly before that happened. "I'm trying to heal, but it's not working. My body wants to shift all the way. I can't control the power so I can stop at the point of healing like the other times."

"Maybe when you're this drained it won't work unless you do shift all the way." He held up a hand. "I'm not trying to convince you to shift, just thinking out loud."

The ominous tap at the door sounded right before the guard stuck his head inside. "One minute."

When the door closed, she looked at Storm, constantly wondering if any moment would be the last time she saw him.

He pushed off the table and walked to her, wrapping his arms around her. She hugged him back, drawing strength from just holding him. When she lifted her head, he kissed her so tenderly that she felt her eyes well up.

Breaking the kiss, he laid his palm on her face. "I won't lose you. Do whatever it takes to win, because if you can't walk out of there under your own power, I'll destroy this place and everyone in it . . . except Lanna."

No pressure there. "You heard what happened to Imogenia."

"I don't care."

Her heart warmed at his declaration. If not for the fear that there was enough supernatural power in this place to blow a chunk out of the planet, she'd feel cheered at the idea of someone taking vengeance on her behalf.

He kissed her forehead and released her. "And if Tristan doesn't come willingly . . ."

"I'll leave without him." But Tristan had been captured trying to save her. Why wouldn't he leave if he had a chance to escape?

The guard opened the door again. Evalle gave Storm one last kiss, then left, not turning around again for fear of being unable to walk away from him.

Don't let it end this way between us. Not when she'd found a man who understood her better than she understood herself.

His words tumbled through her mind. *I won't lose you.*

She should have told him how much he meant to her. Why hadn't she? *Because I'm a fool.*

Next thing she knew, the silver bars of Gate Two were vanishing as Dame Lynn announced, "*The final Elite battle match pits Moonlight Warrior entering from Gate One against Boomer entering from Gate Two.*"

Evalle stepped forward, hands loose at her sides.

Sweeping a look over to find Storm, her gaze snagged

on a face that disappeared in the crowd when she blinked. She would have sworn it *was* Horace Keefer this time. Was he actually here?

Or was Sandspur's venom playing with her mind?

Locating Storm next, she looked back to where she thought she'd seen Horace, but he was gone.

Storm had told her about the Langau being caught, but until she received the all clear from Tzader, she couldn't use telepathy to reach anyone. Otherwise, she'd call out to Horace and ask where he was at the moment.

She had to be mistaken.

Shouting erupted on all sides of her dome, snapping Evalle back around as the bars disappeared and her opponent entered from Gate Two.

She stepped in to find the ground hard-packed again.

At six and a half feet tall, Boomer had a cocky stride and carried a five-foot-long, two-inch-thick metal pole. His shoulders looked as wide as her sofa, and all he wore was a pair of red shorts. That's all. No doubt that he would shift, but right now he was just showing off his bodybuilder physique.

Green eyes blazed from a Samoan-shaped face.

If he thought that would intimidate her, he'd never seen a demonic Svart troll.

She'd won that fight.

Big money bet on Boomer drove the shouting louder for him to finish her off quickly. Even more demanded blood.

Evalle had caught announcements of Elite matches to

this point. Two Alterants had died, five more had folded, pleading for relief.

Sounding bored and ready to get this moving, Boomer called over, "You first, Hollywood."

He expected her to shift.

She shook her head, gaining a shrug in return.

Then Boomer hunched his arms forward, clenching his fists and bunching his muscles in a bodybuilding pose. But he started shifting, bones popping and muscles doubling in size. His head changed shape twice as it kept expanding with a jutting forehead, bulbous nose and thin slits for eyes. Half of his head was ear-to-ear mouth that had two rows of sharp teeth a barracuda would envy.

Power shook through her body, trying to force her to shift, and not just to battle form. Her Alterant beast fought to break free. Was she reacting to Boomer's change?

She locked down the urge and stuck her hand out, calling her dagger up from her boot. The hilt hit her palm just as Boomer finished turning into a Samoan Hulk.

Words came out of his mouth garbled, but she understood "On yar neez, bitch. Beg."

She angled her head and stared at a hairy groin where genitals protruded. "Do condoms come in teacup size?"

"Goonna enjo killin' you." Lifting the pole, he started spinning it around one finger as if the thing weighed nothing.

She prepared to leap or dive away, anticipating when he'd release the pole.

He ordered the pole, "Attack Alt'rant," right before he let it fly straight up in the air, where it floated overhead.

How would the pole distinguish between the two of them?

Maybe it just picked the one who hadn't spoken the order.

Watching Boomer and the pole divided her attention until the weapon zeroed in on her and flew straight for its target. She dodged back and forth, leaping and spinning to get away from the thing tracking her with the diligence of a heat-seeking missile.

Slashing a side-handed swat of kinetic energy at it, she knocked the pole off course, thinking she'd sent the pole to the ground.

Boomer yelled and barreled at her, forcing Evalle to jump in the same direction she'd knocked the pole, just as the pole bounced off the warded wall of the dome. It flew back, catching her ankle in passing and snapping a bone.

She crashed to the ground.

A broken bone in this match meant death.

Boomer veered off, going after his pole.

She called up her warrior form and struggled to her feet, shaking with pain. That's when she saw Horace Keefer, and he wasn't trying to hide his presence.

Something lifted her off her feet.

Boomer was using his kinetics on her. She shoved a

blast of energy back at him, but it glanced off his much more powerful Alterant beast energy.

Then he gripped her with his kinetics and slammed her down to the ground. She hit on her side and felt a bone fracture in her left arm.

When she looked past Boomer, she saw Storm moving through the crowd, getting closer to the dome.

He knew what Kol had done to Imogenia.

Reality hit Evalle between the eyes. With Horace here, what did she have to lose at this point? Sen had probably sent him, which raised a ton of questions Evalle had no time to consider. Bottom line?

She was screwed no matter what she did.

Macha had given her autonomy. In Evalle's thinking, shifting would be in the best interests of the Beladors if Macha wanted the Alterants kept out of Medb hands.

Evalle couldn't do that unless she survived. Heading toward her, Boomer swung his pole back and forth with a major-league cut to his swing.

She launched a blast of kinetic energy at Boomer to buy herself a moment.

Her beast wanted out so badly that all she had to do was relinquish control. The Alterant change burst through her body, ripping her clothes. Her boots burst with the expansion of her feet and her dagger fell away, but she could call it to her when she needed it. Her head doubled in size and her face stretched, jaw aching as it grew wider for a double row of jagged teeth. Bones popped and muscles exploded into a massive body just as hideous as Boomer's, though not quite as big. She sent healing energy first to her arm then her ankle and used kinetic strength to lurch to her feet.

Boomer bumped back from the kinetic wall and stopped, his green gaze assessing this new change.

Her arm improved immediately, but the complex bone structure of her ankle would take longer to mend. Hobbling to her left, she let Boomer think she still couldn't move. When he spun up the pole and sent it at her again, instead of evading she stuck her hand out and caught it.

The thing struggled against her hold.

Sentient?

She started toward Boomer, gripping the pole with two hands. This thing definitely broke Alterant beast bones. Boomer made a move toward her and fell over his own feet.

She stole a quick glance to the stands and found that Storm had stopped at ground level.

She hated changing into a beast in front of him, but his eyes were filled with admiration and something wonderful she'd like to call love. Having just seen Boomer stumble, Storm lifted his shoulders and mouthed *Lanna*.

If that girl survived this event, Evalle would help Quinn deliver her to VIPER headquarters, because she was safe nowhere else.

Boomer lunged up and attacked before Evalle reached him. Fists the size of small boulders swung at her face and chest. She ducked, but he caught her in the ribs, cracking several. Gasping for air, she whipped the pole across his leg.

Bone gave way and he went down on a knee.

She hit his shoulder, crushing more bones, then whipped an uppercut that shattered his jaw.

Jumping back and forth as she attacked, Evalle landed off to one side after her last hit. Adrenaline had overshadowed her mending ankle, which chose now to give way, but she managed to stay upright, if leaning a bit. She'd rather not kill Boomer, since she needed to recruit as many Alterants as she could.

If she could convince them the Medb offer for immortality was a trick.

Winning this battle without killing him would go a long way toward talking him into leaving with her.

Boomer twisted his neck and shoulders, bones cracking and popping back into place.

He regenerated faster than anything else she'd ever seen. Talk about a smug look on a beast face. He stood up and held his hand out, trying to lift her with kinetics again.

She pushed a hand up, using her energy to hold herself down, then swung the pole with her free hand. Time to gamble. She forced her jaws to work and gave the pole an order loud enough to be heard. "Break Al-ter-ant." Swinging across, shoulder high, she smacked Boomer's neck.

A loud *crack* sounded from his spine.

Boomer's head lolled to the side. He fell backward,

arms and legs limp when he hit the ground. At the same time, the kinetic power pushing at her subsided. She walked over, using the pole to prod at his body.

Broken neck. Crap. Not as if she'd had a choice.

She turned to claim her victory, but hesitated when she heard a grunt of pain.

Before she could turn around, the pole was snatched from her hands and a hit of power shoved her sixty feet across the domed area. She smashed against the warded boundary.

Electricity sizzled across her skin.

Boomer had to be a nickname for Boomerang, as in *he bounced back*. That would be his strength, but arrogance was his weakness. Killing him might be impossible at the rate he healed, but cutting the head off anything usually worked, and she'd just changed her mind about his usefulness.

Growling, she powered up her kinetics and shoved off the warded boundary, spinning around as Boomer came at her. She called up her dagger that flew to her hand. She pointed it at his groin, then pulled back to throw.

Boomer skidded to a stop, dropped the pole and covered his genitals with one hand, then shoved a kinetic hit at her with the other. A one-handed blast was easier to dodge.

In the same second, she launched herself up in the air and forward, then whispered to the blade, "Stay put," as she drove the blade into Boomer's throat with deadly accuracy on her way past him.

The blade buried to the hilt, sticking out both sides.

She hit hard on her bad ankle.

He grasped the handle, gurgling and staggering as he fought to pull it out. Blood gushed from around the wound and out of the corner of his mouth. He wheezed for air. His face swelled and turned as red as a thumb smashed with a hammer. When he stumbled around toward her, hands reaching for her throat, Evalle dragged herself backward.

Boomer went to his knees, then fell on his side, making gurgling noises. His eyes closed.

He shifted into his human form.

She snatched her dagger out and straightened up to shouts, jeers and cheers.

Because she'd won or because she stood with her back to them, buck naked?

A guard walked out with two robes. He handed one to her, then dropped the other robe on Boomer and left.

She pulled on the thick burgundy robe and turned around to find Storm with his arms crossed, waiting as they'd agreed. He would give her time to talk to the other Alterants. She'd told him she'd touch the emerald on her chest if anything odd happened and she needed to let him know she was fine.

For a man who had shown limitless patience with her, she could tell just by looking at him that he practically vibrated with the need to come inside the dome.

She touched the emerald.

His eyes moved, following her action, then the stone

warmed against her skin, sending a soothing balm through her. He smiled and winked.

Had he really pushed his majik through this stone?

Dame Lynn declared, "*Moonlight Warrior wins her Elite round and the option to negotiate with the Medb. A deal has been struck for the loser Boomer. All fighting will cease in Battle Theater One.*"

Searching the stands, Evalle's gaze landed on Tristan and Kizira. And Petrina, Tristan's sister, was there.

Evalle met Tristan's gaze.

He nodded slightly and Kizira scowled, her gaze locked on Boomer.

Evalle poked the big Alterant with the tip of her boot, pushing him onto his back.

Boomer's eyes opened. He coughed and rolled to his knees, clutching his neck that was already healing. Hate glared at her.

Definitely not a recruit, but neither had she wanted him traded to the Medb. "The fight is over."

More glare. Not so mouthy after losing.

She called upon her beast power and forced her ankle to finish healing. She could feel it mending more quickly now that she'd burned the rest of the venom from her body.

Or because Storm had sent her a dose of healing through the emerald.

Dame Lynn announced, "*All surviving Alterants not already claimed by the Medb are directed to Battle Theater One to wait as the Medb representative completes negotiations for trades.*"

That gave Evalle no chance to speak with Storm first. She waved a hand, telling him she'd be over in a minute to talk.

He nodded, though clearly not happy to wait.

Now would be her only chance to find out if Tristan was really on the Medb team or not.

TWENTY-EIGHT

Alterants filed into Evalle's battle dome from both Gate One and Gate Two. Adding Tristan and his sister to the other Alterants, Evalle would have eight to convince to leave, nine if Boomer could be swayed.

Alterants eyed each other with wariness, all ready to attack at the first provocation. Silence fell across the dome as if someone had sucked the air from the room.

Evalle walked over to where Storm stood on the other side of the warded dome. "Can you hear me?"

Reading her lips, Storm shook his head.

She could use this soundproofing to her advantage. Lifting a finger to ask for a minute, she walked back to the others mingling around and keeping their distance from each other.

Since Tristan had been in captivity for the past week, he shouldn't have the infection going around in Atlanta. Evalle reached out to him telepathically.

The call echoed back at her as if someone had back-handed it.

She couldn't waste what little time she had before Kizira appeared. She walked into the middle of the Alterants and started her pitch. "The Medb offer is a trick."

Several turned to her. Boomer coughed again. He

might heal quickly, but his throat had to still be raw. "You got a better offer than immortality?"

"Not exactly."

"Then shut up."

She'd have to fight Boomer again, but with words this time, not her weapon of choice. "Sorry I had to stab you, but I was trying to not kill you."

"*You* couldn't kill me."

"Wrong. If I hadn't pulled out my dagger, it would have stayed until you bled out. But let's talk about options. The Medb will use you to do their dirty work. Once that's done, you'll be of no use to them."

Boomer came back with, "What's a little dirty work if we're immortal?"

"There's a catch to that offer. Has to be." She looked around, gratified to find everyone listening. Bernie had moved close. Evalle had heard about Imogenia getting caught. If Bernie was here, Kol had traded him to the Medb. And Bernie had a girlfriend.

Evalle believed he'd be her first recruit. "The goddess Macha has offered protection inside her pantheon for Alterants. She's submitted a charter that will give us status as an accepted race." Just as soon as Evalle showed up with Tristan's information on the origins of Alterants and five Alterants willing to claim loyalty to Macha. No point in cluttering her speech with a lot of detail right now.

"But no immortality?"

Boomer would not let that go. "No, and you're a

fool to believe you'll get that from the Medb. Whatever they do, they'll turn you into their slaves. Wouldn't you rather be free?"

"I'm practically invincible," Boomer bragged. "Give me immortality and no one will dare try to enslave me."

She gave up on Boomer and turned to Bernie. "Doesn't that sound good to you?"

Bernie had his arms wrapped around his chest, shoulders hunched. "But we've been traded to the Medb."

Black Satin piped up. "He's right. I haven't seen an Alterant sponsor who isn't a dark witch, mage or wizard. They're all cutting deals to hand us over for Noirre majik right now."

"You're sure?" Evalle asked.

Black Satin's head bobbed up and down. "Heard them."

Evalle had another card to play, but it was a gamble. "If *you* will testify at a Tribunal meeting that you were traded for Noirre majik, and"—Evalle looked around the room—"if the rest of you'll agree to go with me, I have a way to get us out of here safely regardless of any deal." She doubted she had enough of the potion for all of them, but Evalle would risk contacting Tzader.

If he'd answer a telepathic call, she could depend on him to send in Beladors to bust the other Alterants out of here.

Bernie asked, "Will someone help me get my girlfriend away from Imogenia?"

Evalle told him, "If you leave with me, I'll personally help you."

As more Alterants asked similar questions, Evalle gave more assurances, telling them all they'd have the full force of the Beladors to support them if they joined Macha's pantheon.

"Why should we believe you?" Boomer asked. "The Medb passed a test to prove they weren't lying."

Energy sparked and Tristan appeared in the battle dome, which meant he had use of his teleporting ability inside here. He ordered the room, "Everyone line up between the gates."

The others immediately shuffled into a wobbly line.

Evalle crossed over to Tristan and kept her voice soft. "I've been trying to find a way into TÅµr Medb to help you, your sister and your two Rías friends escape. This was the only way I could—"

"Get in line, Evalle."

"Listen to me, Tristan. One of the Alterants has evidence of the Noirre majik deals. I can call in the Beladors if you'll help me get these Alterants out. If you're worried about your sister being safe, I have a potion that will turn her invisible. Storm's here and he's keeping it for me. We'll go after your two friends, too."

Tristan let her finish. "The only place I can go from here is TÅµr Medb. Get in line."

"Have you really swapped sides?"

He caught her by the throat and lifted her.

She grabbed his arm, squeezing to break bone.

Clenching his teeth, he brought her to his face and whispered, "I'm compelled, dammit. I can't do anything to help you or any other Alterant. Kizira will be here soon.

If I show you any leeway, she'll kill me and my sister. She only brought Petrina here to dangle her life in front of me if I show any sign of not being under her power."

Evalle caught on quickly that he was covering their chance to talk by manhandling her, but Storm would be livid.

Tristan's grip loosened, but he kept a deadly glare pasted on his face. She struggled against his hold to make their confrontation look believable and whispered, "I don't want to leave here without you and your sister."

"You're not leaving and neither will any of the others. Kizira won't allow it. You want to help us, come to TÂμr Medb."

"I can't. VIPER and the Beladors will think I've gone rogue."

"Sen's waiting outside for you."

"What?"

Tristan murmured, "Kizira's coming," and shoved Evalle away. "Get. In. Line. Now."

She got up, dusted her pants and stepped over to the end of the line . . . next to Boomer.

Storm watched it all from outside the dome. Evalle gave a small shake of her head, telling him not to try anything. His jaw was set with determination that worried her about just what he might do.

Purple haze swirled, spinning a moment, then ending with Kizira, priestess of the Medb, in skintight black pants and a snug top. "Congratulations on surviving your fights and to those of you who won your Elite matches in the Achilles Beast Championship."

Kizira continued, "Negotiations have been completed. You now belong to the Medb."

"I don't have a sponsor, so I speak for myself," Evalle said. "I don't believe you can make good on your offer."

Kizira turned on her. "Oh? Then why did you enter the beast championship?"

Evalle had been expecting that. "To tell these Alterants that they have another option."

"If they didn't belong to me, that might be true," Kizira countered, then addressed everyone. "But why would any of you turn down the opportunity we've offered that would allow you to protect yourself and those you care about?"

Rumblings of approval rolled through the group.

Boomer leaned over and told Evalle, "I'll be a free man as soon as I become immortal, and when I do, you're the first one I'm going to kill. The next one's going to be your pretty healer." Then he shouted at Kizira, "Take me first."

Several more made noises of agreement. Even Bernie wouldn't meet Evalle's gaze. This was a dismal failure. Evalle told Kizira, "They may not know better, but I do."

"You mean you'd rather leave and have your healer face Kol to answer for helping during your match with Sandspur?"

Evalle looked at Storm then back at Kizira. "He didn't."

"He'll have to prove it, because a wizard by the name of Grendal claims you were helped and that he *can* prove it."

Evalle couldn't give up Lanna.

Neither could she let Storm face Kol.

With no comeback from Evalle, Kizira kept selling her program to the entire group. "You are all offered a chance to become warriors who can defeat death, but I do not want any who are not willing to prove themselves worthy. Step forward if you wish to join us in TÅµr Medb, where as warriors you will be treated well and trained fully. If you do not step forward, you become the property of Kol D'Alimonte." Kizira's gaze landed on Evalle when she added, "And as I understand it, VIPER has a contingency of agents waiting to apprehend any Alterant caught leaving here."

This was the reason Sen had been so accommodating when she'd asked for the warded SUV. Just a piece of cheese for his trap, because he'd assumed she would come for the chance at immortality. It wouldn't matter that she'd come for the right reasons, she was still going to be facing a Tribunal if he took her in.

Evalle watched every Alterant in the dome take a step forward. All but her.

None of this bunch would give up the opportunity Kizira outlined.

Leaving this beast championship after being seen by plenty of people who would sell Evalle out in a minute would end with her facing the Tribunal. Macha would not come to her defense once she found out no Alterants returned with Evalle.

If Evalle refused Kizira, Storm would be at Kol's mercy. If she accepted the Medb offer, she'd have to walk away from the Beladors, and Storm, forever.

TWENTY-NINE

Evalle's eyes met Storm's. He hadn't moved from watching the battle dome activity, but he couldn't hear what was going on either.

Her heart hadn't beaten this hard when she was fighting Boomer. She lifted a finger and touched the emerald, mouthing the words *My choice*.

Then she stepped forward to complete the line of Alterants accepting Kizira's Medb deal.

Storm's mouth dropped open. He started shaking his head and yelled a string of words she didn't need her hearing to know were curses. Then he took off to his left.

Toward the access hall for the holding area and this battle dome.

Would the guards let him come in?

Give her one chance to say good-bye?

Shouting echoed down the long walkway beyond Gate One, but the disturbance came no closer.

Moments later, a guard entered the battle dome carrying Dame Lynn's head. The Domjon addressed Kizira. "Our commitment has been satisfied."

Kizira sent an appraising look over her group of Alterants. "Agreed."

"We've had an issue that requires locking down the premises until it's handled."

"In that case, we shall vacate the premises immediately."

What had happened for Kol to lock down the event site?

The room lost shape in the next instant, swirling with a blur of colors, and the air whistled around her. Evalle's stomach went into spin cycle.

That was the last she saw of the Achilles Beast Championship.

Maybe the last time she'd see Storm. And Lanna. She trusted him to take care of Lanna and get the girl home safely.

Someone clutched Evalle's legs.

If it was Bernie, he'd be sorry as soon as they landed. She wouldn't make it far without throwing up.

When the spinning ended, Evalle stumbled to her right and ran into a wall. Her stomach wasn't happy, but no volcanic eruption so far. She blinked at the dark room, dizzy and straining to see where she'd landed.

Even in pitch black, she had sharp night vision.

Gradually, very low light filled the room.

Evalle removed her glasses. She'd been dumped in a bedroom with a tall king-size bed covered in a gold-, black- and ruby-colored comforter with piles of pillows to match. Cushy contemporary sofa and chair in gold against one wall, with a Tiffany-style lamp on a glass table where the furniture met at a right angle. Strange mix of old and new.

Kizira appeared.

Evalle shoved the sunglasses back in place and crossed

her arms. She leaned against the wall to appear at ease, but in truth it was to keep from losing her balance. "Where am I?"

"TÂµr Medb. Wasn't that your goal in entering the beast games?"

No, her goal had been to free Tristan, not get captured, too. "I'm not going to work for the Medb."

"Your stay here will be short, and it can be pleasant if you so choose. It can also be painfully unpleasant."

"So you play good cop, bad cop all by yourself?" Evalle taunted.

"Careful. You're not the only one who will suffer if you fail to comply."

What was she talking about? Evalle had no one. She'd vanished in front of Storm without a word, and the Beladors would disown her immediately.

Evalle shrugged, as if she didn't care about anyone. "What else can you do to Tristan? He's already a zombie slave." The best way she could help Tristan, and maybe herself, was by pretending she believed he'd drunk the Kool-Aid.

"I wasn't talking about Tristan." Kizira floated across the room and spoke very softly, as if they were conspiring on something. "You may think your friend shows bad judgment to associate with a Medb, but I would challenge that he shows far worse judgment by trusting you with his family. I suggest you rest and eat. You'll need your strength for the next forty-eight hours once we start tomorrow."

"Who're you talking about?"

"If you're as bright as you've been touted, you'll figure it out. Just make sure no one leaves this room but you. I changed the sofa to a sleeper, which should accommodate your needs."

With that, Kizira vanished.

Evalle studied on her words. *You may think your friend shows bad judgment to associate with a Medb, but I would challenge that he shows far worse judgment by trusting you with his family.* She eyed the sofa bed.

Had Kizira been talking about Quinn and referencing Evalle's poor job of taking care of Lanna?

If that was the case, then when Kizira said Evalle wouldn't be the only one to suffer, she meant . . .

"Show your face, Lanna."

Quinn's cousin took solid form beside the bed.

Evalle hadn't thought this could get any worse, but Lanna had just proved her wrong. "What are you doing here?"

"I am sorry. Grendal saw me again! I got away before he could touch me, but . . ." Her eyes shifted down with guilt.

"All you had to do was stay put and leave with Storm."

"I could not go to Storm," Lanna said meekly, raising pitiful eyes to her.

Evalle felt a chill ride across her skin at the fear in Lanna's voice. "What happened?"

"I wait near holding area for you, and Storm came running up. Then guards surround Storm."

"Why?"

"Grendal said Storm snuck spy inside beast fights. That Storm was reason VIPER waited outside. Grendal described me. Said I was spy and I would tell VIPER about Noirre majik trades."

Evalle grabbed her head, feeling it might explode at any minute. "Unfreakinbelievable."

"That is why I follow guard with Dame Lynn head to where Alterants held. Only place Grendal could not enter. I thought if no one find me, then no one can prove Storm did anything wrong."

For a teenager, she had good survival skills. Evalle had to give her credit in the logic department, too. Lanna was right. Kol might be a lunatic demigod, but punishing someone without proof would undermine his next event.

Please tell me Storm got away without harm.

But if VIPER waited outside the event, what had happened then?

Evalle didn't know. She could only hope that maybe Storm used the potion, even though she doubted he would, then shifted into his jaguar form so he could disappear into the night.

Cumberland had miles and miles of undisturbed forest.

And Storm had resources. He had the invisibility potion and would have had a plan in place to get her off the island. But now she had Lanna to contend with and keep safe. "You can't leave this room, Lanna."

"Ever?"

"I have a good and bad feeling that this is a short visit based on what Kizira said, but she knows you're with me and I don't have any idea what the Medb have planned."

"I heard what she said. Why does she let me stay?"

Evalle debated on how much to tell Lanna, but the truth might be her best choice considering where they were and what Lanna could hear before leaving. "Quinn has known Kizira a long time. I don't think Kizira wants to harm anyone related to Quinn."

Lanna frowned, thinking hard, then glared at Evalle. "You would accuse my cousin of befriending the enemy?"

"I'm not accusing Quinn of anything, but he does know her. You can ask him about it when you see him again, but please don't repeat that to anyone here or back home." Evalle hoped that she and Lanna would see Quinn sooner rather than later. "In the meantime, don't make this any more difficult than it already is. If they come for me, cloak yourself until I'm gone and do *not* leave this room, no matter what."

"I understand."

"Yeah, well, that whole 'I understand' won't work. Quinn believes you're good for your word, so I want you to say you will not leave this room unless I tell you."

Some teens might pout, but not Lanna. Her jaw was rigid with annoyance. She didn't like being outmaneuvered. "I give my word. I will not leave this room unless you tell me."

"Thank you."

"But you will lose our best chance for information if

you do not use me. I can stay cloaked for half hour now and I am working on *other* abilities."

For a fleeting moment, Evalle considered allowing Lanna to move around invisible for intel, but she just as quickly dismissed the idea as stupid. "Do your practicing in here and keep it quiet when you do."

"You should help me."

Do I look like a majik trainer? "I doubt any of your tricks can help us here. We're in Medb central, the hub of dark majik like nothing you've ever seen. Even Grendal couldn't get us out of here."

"That is because Grendal cannot do something that I can."

Evalle walked over and dropped to the sofa, sinking deep in the soft cushions. Her body had healed, but she was beat. On a drawn-out sigh, she asked, "What are you practicing that a powerful wizard can't do?"

"Teleporting."

THIRTY

Lanna's claim of teleporting had sounded much more promising last night.

When Evalle heard a *thunk*, then "Ouch" for the fiftieth time, she rolled over on her back on the king-size bed and pushed up on her elbows.

Lanna stood next to the door to a bathroom just as large as this bedroom suite. She rubbed her shoulder.

Evalle admired Lanna's determination, but she doubted the girl's body would survive this training. "You're going to be black-and-blue when Quinn sees you again. He doesn't need another reason to kill me besides letting you end up in TÅμr Medb."

"I am not thinking something right, but this would be easier outside in open area."

"I don't think they have an outside like at home. This is another realm. I heard that Queen Flaevynn can't leave the tower because of some curse. If the TÅμr Medb realm included land like Treoir does, we'd probably be able to see it through the windows. We'd *have* windows."

Lanna got that not-ready-to-quit look on her face and vanished, reappearing in the middle of the room.

Evalle clapped. "There you go."

"That is simple," the girl muttered. "We need to

travel much farther to escape. I must go from one room to another before I can go distances." She walked to the corner farthest from the bathroom and vanished again.

Then *thunked* the same door.

Evalle winced when Lanna appeared, rubbing her head this time. "Take a break, okay. And don't try to go anywhere outside these two rooms."

"I gave my word."

"Didn't mean to insult you. Just don't want you tele-porting into Flaevynn."

"Evalle?" a brusque male voice called from outside the room.

Lanna dove into the bathroom, pulling the door almost closed and flipping off the lights.

Surprised to get any notice before someone popped into her new holding cell, Evalle answered in her surly I-haven't-had-coffee-yet voice, "What?"

"The queen wants to see you. Get dressed."

"Why? Nudity bother her?" Not that Evalle was leaving here without clothes on.

"No, because I'm opening this door in sixty seconds."

The chuckle at the end of that belonged to Tristan, who would call her bluff.

Crap. Evalle scrambled out of the bed in nothing but her panties. Kizira must have supplied the clothes that Evalle and Lanna had found in a wardrobe, in both their sizes. When Evalle couldn't locate a bra, she yanked on a gray T-shirt and jeans and was zipping up her boots when Tristan opened the door.

Evalle shoved back a mass of hair that had yet to see a brush and stood.

Tristan, on the other hand, looked as if he'd just showered before putting on a long-sleeved powder-blue knit top and black jeans. Dressed for success at Medb Inc? He stepped inside, closing the door, then gave her a decidedly male once-over.

Where was her dagger when she needed it?

Kizira had relieved her of it during teleporting last night. "Look at me like that before I've had coffee and I'll hand you your gonads in a jar."

"Damn, you're evil in the morning."

"You have no idea." Especially after a night of dreaming about Storm, who might have had to fight his way to freedom, *if* he hadn't decided to make good on his promise to destroy the place. She hoped not. She wanted him safe and missed him so much she felt physically ill. "What does the queen bitch want, Tristan?"

"That's not the right attitude if you want to survive being here."

"I don't *want* to be here to begin with."

"Then you shouldn't have shown up last night," Tristan snapped back at her, but that wasn't anger behind his words. She heard concern and guilt when he added, "I wish you hadn't."

Evalle walked over to him, keeping her voice down. "Work with me and we'll get out of here."

"I'm trying to find a way to get you and Petrina out, but you can't depend on me. Flaevynn has Kizira compelling all of us. I can only talk about something

I haven't been forbidden to discuss, and I can't do anything to help you escape."

"What does Flaevynn want with Alterants?"

"To kill Brina and take over Treoir."

"How?"

He opened his mouth, then closed it, shaking his head.

Evalle growled, "How is that helping me?"

"You don't understand. I can't physically say the words. Just like when I was in the ABC last night, I couldn't have walked out of there if I'd had an armed escort. Being compelled by the Medb is absolute, but only with regard to what you are specifically compelled to do. So remember that."

Drawing back, Evalle said, "You think they're going to compel me?"

"I know she is. Don't fight it. Every time you do, they realize they need to narrow down their orders to you. Go with whatever they say, then figure out how to get around what you can. Just like me talking to you last night at the games."

"Kizira said something about resting because the next forty-eight hours would be physically demanding."

"She's right and now it's less than that."

"What's going to happen?"

He rolled his eyes and gritted out, "Compelled. Got it?"

She let go of her anger and finally paid attention. Tristan was enlightening her on what she had to look forward to and how to prepare. "Sorry. Kizira indicated

I wouldn't be staying long. Can you say if that means I'm leaving soon or we all are?"

"All."

"Then we have to get the others to join our resistance so we can escape when we leave."

Tristan answered with grim disappointment. "No one is getting out of here until we head to Treoir." His gaze traveled over her face. "Might want to brush your hair."

"Why?"

"I'm here to escort you. Kizira said Flaevynn and Cathbad are ready to decide if you're worth keeping alive."

"Cathbad?" Evalle thought back on her studying. "Wasn't he a druid a long time ago?"

"There was an original Cathbad the Druid who lived during the original Queen Maeve's rule. The Cathbad here is a descendant. Every six hundred and sixty-six years the torch is passed on, so to speak, to a new Cathbad the Druid and Queen Medb, but Flaevynn isn't interested in anyone else being queen if she can't live forever. I've gotten parts of the story out of Kizira. Tell you more when I can."

"You can start by telling me what you know about the origins of Alterants for the next time I get a chance to talk to Macha."

"About that. I was wrong and found out—" Tristan paused, staring past Evalle's head for a few seconds, then his gaze returned to hers. "Kizira said to bring you now."

"You have telepathy with her?"

"Yes, and you will, too, once . . ."

"Once what?"

Tristan shook his head, indicating he couldn't answer that question. He grabbed her arm and the room spun. Teleporting. Couldn't they walk through this tower?

THIRTY-ONE

Cathbad stood beside Flaevynn in front of her jeweled waterfall that functioned as the queen's scrying wall. Now they would see Evalle fulfill her part of the prophecy, or curse as Flaevynn constantly corrected him. "'Tis time for Evalle ta accept her destiny."

On a sound of disgust, Flaevynn lifted her hands and moved them across each other. A two-story wall of water cascaded over precious gemstones. Diamonds, rubies and more, many as large as his head. When she lowered her arms, a wide-screen image revealed a picture of Evalle standing alone in a pit deep inside the tower that was known as the arena.

Titanium bars covered the only exit for walking out.

Evalle stood in the middle of the room, looking up, down and around. "Helloooo. Thought queenie was looking for me."

Flaevynn's waist-length black hair separated into a pile of thick tendrils that raised and twisted, hissing.

"Calm down, Flaevynn. Evalle wants ta get a rise from ya so you'll come face her."

"You're *sure* we need her?"

He smiled at the edge in her voice. Flaevynn would not get her way with this. "If ya kill her ya might as well start celebratin' your last birthday now."

"Yo, mama," Evalle yelled. "Listen up. I'm no one's bitch and I don't give a rat's ass about your test. You screw with me, you'll bleed."

Flaevynn's hair twisted into a knot of squirming locks. Cathbad groaned under his breath. Flaevynn was reaching the limit of what little patience she possessed.

He'd best be keeping her busy. Cathbad told Flaevynn, "Conjure the image of Tristan's sister the way I told ya so that Evalle can no see her, but anyone else can."

A battered image of Petrina appeared on the floor not a foot from Evalle. Blood pooled around the body from multiple stabs.

He asked, "Does Tristan know about his sister yet?"

"He's being told as we speak. You're sure Evalle can't communicate telepathically with Tristan?"

"No until she's linked ta Kizira. 'Tis why I said to wait until all the Alterants become gryphons for Kizira ta bond with the new ones."

"Are you sure Evalle will evolve into a gryphon if she kills another gryphon?"

"Yesss, Flaevynn."

"If she's so important, maybe we should have her kill a wyvern like Tristan did."

"No. I have no told ya wrong yet. I had Tristan kill a wyvern just ta show you how this works, but Evalle is far more powerful. We can no make a mistake now. Give Evalle the sword, bloody the end of the blade and open the gate. 'Tis time she embraces her destiny."

In the next moment, Evalle held a beautiful Medb

sword that dripped fresh blood. She lifted the sword, studying it.

As the bars vanished, a roar echoed, gaining strength as it neared. Heavy feet pounded toward the arena, then Evalle's opponent rushed into the room. Now in gryphon form, Tristan took one look at his sister's body that Evalle couldn't see and howled in pain, wings stretching wide.

Green eyes glowed with wrath from his eagle-shaped head.

Translucent scales covered skin the color of a thundercloud. Wings stretched away from his lion-shaped body when he reared up.

Evalle backed away a step, lifting the four-foot-long sword with surprising ease in her human form. She called out, "You get your kicks watching people die, Flaevynn? Because that's what's going to happen to your pretty pet."

Tristan opened his jaws and released a cry of agony, then shot a stream of fire at Evalle.

She jumped backward, kinetic power allowing her to flip in the air before she landed on her feet. Her face and the front of her arms had been singed red from the blast.

She freed a hand from the sword and swung a hit of kinetic power at the gryphon, which only rocked the two-ton creature back a step.

He lunged at her.

She jumped high in the air.

Swinging her sword as she twisted, she sliced into a wing.

That sent the gryphon off balance. He hit as hard as a duck with bad landing gear.

Cathbad could see why Evalle was touted as not being one to squander an opening in a fight. She spun and leaped on the gryphon's back, then shoved her sword down between his shoulder blades, straight to his heart.

He arched up and bucked her once, but finally flopped on the floor.

She pulled out the blade and stepped off the dead beast. Turning in a circle, she yelled, "Get your rocks off watching some poor thing get killed for no reason? You disgust me."

Flaevynn snarled at Cathbad, "She didn't evolve!"

"Wait a moment. Would be easier for her if she had already shifted into her Alterant beast form, but she will evolve."

Evalle's arms shook so hard that she dropped the sword. Her back hunched and she started growing. She screamed as if ripped in half. Her clothes shredded as the aqua-blue body of a lion took shape with a golden eagle's head. Black outlined the predator green eyes and a blend of blue and green feathers covered wings that grew and extended from her back.

She stretched her neck, looking at her body and pulling a wing into view.

"She's perfect," Cathbad purred. "And that, Flaevynn, is the golden head each of the five chosen gryphons will have."

A snarl vibrated through the arena.

Moving her gryphon form around awkwardly, Evalle

froze when Tristan shook his head and wobbled to his feet.

Flaevynn murmured, "He isn't dead."

Realization climbed into Tristan's gaze once he took in the Petrina vision and the Evalle gryphon. Wings back, claws extended on his paws, he was ready to kill.

Leaning forward, Flaevynn warned Cathbad, "Evalle's not ready to fight. We can't let them—"

Tristan opened his vicious beak wide and lunged at Evalle.

She raised a lion's paw in defense.

Tristan hit an invisible wall and bounced backward.

Cathbad smiled. "She adapts faster than we could have hoped for. Took two days ta get Tristan ready ta fight, an' he's strong. Evalle will kill Brina an' take Treoir for us."

"She's not going to be as easy to break as Tristan. We hold his sister's life in our hands."

"We do no need ta break Evalle, only compel her."

THIRTY-TWO

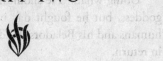

Tzader stood on the walkway leading up to the castle entrance on Treoir Island, ready to break the doors down.

He was tempted to dive through that warding and test it, anything to get to Brina. She couldn't be serious about marrying that guard. Was Macha pressuring Brina to do this?

How could Macha do this while knowing Brina had been his since they were teens? Maybe Brina had agreed to be engaged to buy her and Tzader more time to figure a way to be together. He wanted the truth from Brina herself. Sen had teleported Tzader so he wouldn't have to ask Macha or Brina to bring him. He couldn't cross the castle threshold, thanks to his and Brina's fathers, but they could speak face-to-face at the castle entrance.

Guilt plagued him every time he got angry with his dead father, but what the hell?

A fucking ward on the castle separated him from the only woman he'd ever want.

Macha appeared next to him. "What can I do for you, Tzader?"

Since when did the Celtic goddess over all the Beladors act as a receptionist? "Where's Brina?"

"Busy."

"Doing what?" He shouldn't take that tone with the goddess, but he fought day in and day out to protect humans and his Beladors. He'd never asked for anything in return.

That was changing. "I want to talk to her."

"I told you she's engaged. She has plans to make." A granite bench with a white velvet cushion appeared and Macha sat down gracefully, her sea-green gown moving until satisfied with each fold and ripple. "What else do you want to discuss?"

Push the issue and get slingshotted back to Atlanta, or suck it up and once more deal with his duty?

He snorted at himself, a mean sound.

Like he would ever shirk a duty? "I think Evalle got captured by the Medb."

The goddess turned statue still at that. "Why would you say that?"

"Because we have a report that she entered the Achilles Beast Championship and fought as an Alterant." He wasn't sharing anything that Macha wouldn't find out and might even already know, especially when Sen had been the one to inform Tzader.

"She *fought*?" Macha said with a bite. "What happened to the other Alterants?"

"The Medb took them . . . and Evalle."

"Evalle was supposed to bring them back, not *join* the enemy."

"I'm sure she didn't—"

"Oh? The way I understood the Medb deal was that they would take Alterants who *accepted* their offer of immortality." Macha rose to her feet now, power glowing all around her.

Tzader stuck to his main concern. "Regardless of what the Medb offered, Evalle got caught and we have to get her back. I can't do that if you don't help me."

Macha's voice turned as cold as an Arctic night. "Evalle swore to me she did not want immortality. If she left with the Medb, she has broken her vow as a Belador and is now the enemy. You will capture her and bring her to me."

This hadn't turned out the way Tzader had expected. He stood, too. "Are you telling me she went there without talking to you about it, because that just doesn't fit. Not Evalle, who is constantly trying to win your favor and find her place in our tribe."

Yes, he was angry, but he'd had enough of Macha's cryptic games with Evalle. And, if he was really honest, he was pissed that Macha hadn't tried to help him and Brina get together.

Macha's narrowed gaze warned him. "Evalle had a clear understanding of our conversation."

Just one time, he'd like to get a straight answer out of the goddess. "But *I* don't have a clear understanding of your conversation, which would help."

Once again, Macha sidestepped Tzader's request. "Bring me proof that she did not accept the offer of immortality and I'll consider that."

Tzader would not condemn Evalle without hearing her side. He believed in her commitment to the Beladors.

The castle door opened and Brina appeared just inside. "Tzader?"

His chest squeezed with pain at not being able to touch her. He searched for the right words, something he could say with Macha present, but another figure came into view behind Brina.

Allyn, Brina's personal security . . . and fiancé.

The same man Tzader had witnessed standing too close to Brina and acting possessive the last time Tzader had entered the castle in holographic form.

Macha beamed a maternal smile Tzader quietly scoffed at. "Hello, Allyn."

The guard bowed. "Greetings, Goddess."

Turning to Tzader, Macha said, "Was there anything else?"

He sure as hell couldn't say what he wanted with an audience present. Glancing at Brina, he could swear he saw longing in her eyes . . . and sadness.

"I'm sorry," Brina said, backing away. "I didn't mean to interrupt."

"You're not interrupting," Macha cooed. "How are the wedding plans coming?"

Wedding? This was more than a phony engagement.

Macha rattled on as if every word didn't shove a knife deeper in his heart. "Ask Allyn's mother to help. What mother of the groom wouldn't want to play a role in his wedding?"

Tzader's mouth dried up. He couldn't look at Allyn without lunging through the ward to kill him, and he couldn't look at Brina without admitting he'd never stop loving her.

Mumbling that he had to talk with Quinn and the other Beladors guarding the island, Tzader stepped away, careful not to fall when his vision blurred.

Brina gripped the door frame so tightly that her fingers were white. She had to hold on to something to keep from running down Treoir's steps after Tzader. All the fury she'd bottled up for weeks while she'd waited patiently for Tzader to fight for her she now turned on Macha. "How could you do that to him?"

"About the wedding? He knows."

Brina had intended to tell Tzader, at the right time, as part of her plan to outmaneuver Macha so that she could be with Tzader, the only man she'd ever love. But Macha had interfered, as usual. What exactly had she told Tzader? Brina shoved a furious gaze at the goddess. "You might have consulted me first before *announcin'* my engagement."

Macha lost all lightheartedness. "What are you waiting on? It's not as though you have other suitors besides Allyn coming to the door, now, is it?"

"We had an agreement. I am upholdin' my part. There was no reason to be forcin' my hand, as I still have time." Brina had foolishly thought Macha would help her and Tzader find a way to be together in spite of the warding, but the conversation had backfired when Macha had accused Brina of not allowing Tzader to move on.

Macha thought Tzader would turn his back on the love he and Brina had shared since their teens, but Brina believed in him. In her heart, she was sure Tzader would never give her up without a fight, even with their impossible situation with the ward on the castle.

Shrugging off any concern over Brina's anger, Macha said, "You might as well plan your wedding, since I don't see Tzader interfering."

Under no circumstances could Brina step outside the castle and risk dying, but Macha had allowed a loophole in her agreement with Brina. The only way to take advantage of that loophole had been to devise a strategy that was a high-stakes gamble, but Brina would risk all for a chance to be with Tzader.

She'd convinced Allyn to act as her new romantic interest to push Tzader along more quickly since she'd been forbidden from telling Tzader about her agreement with Macha. The Goddess contended that Tzader had too much honor to tell Brina the truth if he wanted to break off the doomed relationship. He would never hurt her that way.

Much as it had pained Brina, she *had* admitted that he deserved a fair chance to make that decision. That's when Macha had twisted the situation around on Brina, gaining an agreement that had cut her heart into pieces only Tzader could put back together. What a tangled situation that had gotten out of hand.

Brina had put all her hopes on Tzader not being able to walk away. But he just had. He'd said nothing at hearing she would wed another man.

No reaction of anger or hurt. Could Macha be right after all?

For the first time since agreeing to do her part in the breakup, Brina felt true fear of losing Tzader. He was her life.

How would she breathe without him?

THIRTY-THREE

The woman he loved more than life was going to marry someone else.

Tzader stood off to the side, waiting as Quinn gave directions to three patrols. Treoir Castle loomed a quarter mile away. Until now, this had been the land of his childhood. A place he'd expected to call home at some point only if Brina had to live here.

He didn't want a damn castle.

He wanted Brina.

"Who kicked you in the proverbial jewels?" Quinn asked in his clipped British accent.

"Life." Rather than answer the curiosity in his friend's question, Tzader moved on to yet another problem. He was ruining everyone's day. "Evalle's missing."

"What happened to her?"

Tzader caught Quinn up on the beast championship. "Macha's ready to declare Evalle the enemy, but I know she didn't willfully join the Medb."

Quinn was quiet, staring off at the horizon. The man who defined style on casual days looked out of place in a long-sleeved dark-green pullover and jungle camouflage pants. He'd climbed out of a Russian gutter to become a financial genius and powerful Belador with mind locking ability like no other.

Releasing a stream of air, Quinn raked his hair. "How are we going to get her back?"

"I don't know, but there's another problem. Lanna."

"What's the brat done now? Destroyed Evalle's apartment?" Before Tzader could reply, Quinn lifted a hand. "Tell Evalle to put her in VIPER lockdown. I told Lanna I would put her there if she caused any more problems. She'll be safe until I can get to her."

"I don't know what she did, but she's missing."

Quinn's face warped into that of a dangerous warrior. "Bloody hell, that wizard has her."

"What wizard?"

When Quinn told him about Grendal, Tzader speculated, "Grendal may not have her. Evalle took Lanna and Feenix to her friend Nicole's to watch while Evalle was gone."

"Does Nicole know where Evalle is?"

"No. Nicole contacted me when she couldn't find Lanna. She thinks Lanna cloaked herself and slipped out with Evalle."

"Sounds like the brat," Quinn ground out.

"So Lanna is either hiding somewhere—"

"Or with Evalle," Quinn finished.

Tzader nodded. "Storm was with Evalle at the beast championship."

"What'd he tell you?"

"Nothing yet. Haven't been able to find him." Taking a last look at the castle, Tzader said, "I know you're worried about Lanna, but I need you here. I'll hunt for her and Evalle, and let you know what I find out."

The urge to leave and go hunt for his teenage cousin was written all over Quinn's face, but he was a warrior and Belador first. Plus, he shared a bond with Evalle and Tzader, and knew he could trust Tzader to do as much as Quinn could. "I'll stay."

Tzader squeezed Quinn's shoulder, thanking him for his trust. "I'll turn loose everything I have at my disposal to find them."

But he had to do so quietly. If Macha realized he would not declare Evalle the enemy, she'd remove him as Maistir and send in someone who would do her bidding.

THIRTY-FOUR

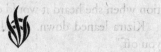

Why did dying have to be so painful?

Evalle couldn't raise her arm. Breathing took more effort than blinking her eyes. The five gashes ripped across her chest bled down her pretty new aqua skin.

Storm would never see her as a gryphon.

Boomer laughed at her, his claws dripping her blood. He'd morphed into a gryphon with black and gold scales. Cardinal-red feathers speckled with black covered his wings.

In her head she heard him say, *Not such a badass after all, are you?*

She really wanted to cut his golden head off and see if that would kill him even as a gryphon.

He wouldn't have won this battle if not for the two swords he'd been given. And his elastic body that healed itself so quickly.

Kizira flashed into the arena, hands on her hips and scowl in place. "Get up. We don't have time for you to waste."

Evalle added Kizira's head to her death list.

"Oh, come on," Kizira complained. "Heal and get moving."

After watching others like Tristan die and then regain

life, Evalle thought she'd be ready for this transformation when she heard it would only make her stronger.

Kizira leaned down. "Heal or I'll let Boomer finish you off."

Boomer made a happy growling sound.

Evalle decided right then to live, if for no other reason than to kick his miserable hide. Drawing on her beast energy, she sent it rushing through her to the five wounds on her chest, her broken hind leg and the ripped wing.

She'd never healed that fast even in Alterant beast form.

One flap of her wings and she reached her feet, towering over Kizira.

Evalle asked, *How many more times do I have to die?*

Kizira answered her telepathically this time, *That's it for now. You can only die three times and come back to life. After that, you won't survive another mortal wound. We want you to go through this once just to be stronger.*

Three times? That's it? That's limited immortality.

Kizira admitted, *I know. It's just a temporary regeneration of life.*

That would mean you lied at the beast games.

Kizira glanced over at Boomer, who waited with arms crossed.

Evalle assumed his nonreaction meant he couldn't hear her conversation with Kizira. *How'd you get past the lie detector at the beast championship?*

The Medb never claimed to offer immortality. Like any secondhand information, things are embellished or modified once they become hearsay. We told Kol the Medb would offer the Alterants a chance to become warriors who could conquer death. And at this moment, you have conquered death, fulfilling our offer, but only for two more times.

Kizira swept around to face Boomer. "You're done here."

Boomer hung his head, clearly disappointed not to kill something else.

"We've got two more to turn into gryphons." With a wave of her hand, Kizira brought Bernie on scene. He took one look at both Evalle and Boomer, then passed out.

Evalle told Kizira, *Let me stay and coach him. He has a big beast form.*

He can't communicate with you telepathically until he takes gryphon form and I bond him to the group.

Evalle hadn't been in human form since she'd battled Tristan, and she wondered how hard it would be to change back. Tristan had done so once he'd calmed down enough to realize he'd been tricked into believing Evalle had murdered his sister.

Reaching inside herself, Evalle called the change, and with a few painful twists and snaps, she shrank into her human body.

Naked.

A bulge started developing under Boomer's lower feathers.

Evalle snapped at Kizira. "Clothes!"

Gray sweatpants and a matching jersey top covered Evalle in the next instant. Her face felt just as naked without sunglasses, but she hadn't really needed them since shifting into a gryphon.

Did that mean she could go out in daylight?

And watch a sunrise or a sunset?

Yearning to do that with Storm hit her hard. She clutched her stomach and forced her mind back on track.

With a look up at Boomer, who still sported a rod under those feathers, she warned, "Don't give me a reason to test my new strength."

Kizira rounded on Evalle and Boomer. "Listen up, you two. None of the gryphons are to be killed more than one time. Break that rule and you'll face Flaevynn. Trust me, you don't want to annoy the queen."

Boomer spread his wings and made a half bow in reply.

Kizira ordered him, "Go train until I come for you." She made a sweeping gesture with her hand and Boomer disappeared. Then she told Evalle, "Coach Bernie later. Tristan's waiting to brief you."

"On what?" The room around Evalle disappeared and another location took shape. This one had wood paneling, a thick Persian rug and a polished wood desk with a sleek office chair that Tristan sat in.

He stood up. "Looks like you survived the hardest test."

"I don't want to go through that again anytime soon." She hadn't decided how she felt about being a gryphon, other than enjoying a more attractive beast form than she had as only an Alterant. "Have you died more than once?"

"No. The Medb are adamant about one time per gryphon."

"Why?"

"They have future plans for us and don't want to use up our other two get-out-of-death-free cards right now." He walked around the end of the desk and leaned back against the front.

Evalle took one of the two cushioned chairs facing him. "You're supposed to be briefing me. What about?"

"Attacking Treoir."

"I won't do it."

"Yes, you will. You haven't been compelled yet. Once you are, you'll cut off your own arm if they tell you to."

Evalle scoffed at him. "You would kill your sister if they told you?"

"I did. That's how she went through her first power change."

That shocked Evalle. "Did you know you were fighting Petrina, or did they trick you like they tricked you into believing I'd killed her?"

His eyes hooded with shame. "Yes, I knew I was attacking Petrina. That was the point. To let me know just how much power they have over me."

Her heart broke for Tristan. He'd gone through battles and horrors to protect Petrina. "I will fight them if they compel me."

"I know you want to, but fighting isn't the way around the compulsion."

Evalle glanced at the walls and ceiling, then back at Tristan. "Aren't you worried about them hearing you?"

"I figured out the strange ward Kizira placed around this space. The walls actually glow when anyone approaches or if Flaevynn tries to watch us through her scrying wall. Once Kizira bonded me to her, I could see the same changes in the room that she saw when someone wanted to eavesdrop or visit. She allows me to visit with my sister here even though we're supposed to be kept apart."

"What a considerate hostess."

"In spite of all that I've been through with Kizira, I've come to realize since being here that she's Flaevynn's puppet, just like I'm now Kizira's."

"There has to be a way to get you out of here."

"No, I'm screwed. I won't be allowed to travel with you to Treoir, but I'm trying to convince Kizira to send Petrina with the rest of you. If she does, I'm hoping you pull one of those maniacal stunts out of your ass and save her."

Not flattering, but a compliment coming from him. Evalle would not attack Treoir or leave Tristan here. "What's the attack plan?"

"I can't tell you that." He opened his hands in apology. "Part of the compulsion spell."

"Then what are you supposed to be telling me?"

"How the attack is going to function. First, the gryphons will follow the one person who is the strongest."

Evalle interjected, "Like the alpha in a wolf pack."

"Right. Kizira is that person as she's the one who holds power over the bond. Five of you will have specific targets, since you're more powerful than the other gryphons."

Reaching up to her head, Evalle stopped before stroking over her hair as if she still had feathers. "The golden heads? I saw four others." She looked at Tristan, recalling that his wasn't, which he must have read in her gaze.

"Nope. I'm not one of the"—he lifted his fingers to make air quotes—"chosen five."

"You can teleport. Why wouldn't they want a gryphon with that power?"

He shrugged. "Who knows? Anyhow, once you all arrive on Treoir, two will sweep a one-mile-wide perimeter around the castle, torching everything to tighten the fighting zone. Two more will be inside that zone using kinetics and streams of fire to mow down Beladors who won't be able to link. A gryphon can easily kill one Belador, which would destroy everyone linked."

"You're sure?"

"Our kinetic strength alone is far more powerful than a Belador's."

Envisioning the potential massacre made her sick. If she couldn't stop the attack from happening, she had to find a way to warn her tribe. "I know you hate the Beladors, but they don't deserve this."

"I don't hate them. Not anymore. After talking to Kizira, I've come to realize I was wrong about our origins as Alterants."

Forgetting everything else, she zeroed in on the question that had plagued her life as a half-breed. "What's the other half of our blood?"

When he didn't answer, she shoved to her feet, fingers curled into fists. "No more stonewalling me, Tristan. What are we other than Belador?"

"We all have Belador blood and that of an ancient warrior called Cú Chulainn. In battle he would turn berserker and change into a beast. That's where we get the beast traits. He was a celebrated warrior during the time of the original Cathbad the Druid and Queen Maeve."

"Maeve, as in the first Medb?" When he nodded, she raised her hands in the air in a frustrated motion. "That was like . . . forever ago."

"Right. She and the original Cathbad created a prophecy, to take down the Beladors. They set into motion a perpetual changing of the guard where a female blood descendant of Maeve became queen and mated with a druid descendant of Cathbad, of which there were different lineages. Those two always produce a female child, who becomes the next Medb queen six hundred and sixty-six years later, upon her mother's death. This has gone on for generation after generation, but Flaevynn refuses to play by the rules."

Evalle tapped her finger on her lip, thinking. "What's supposed to happen *now* that hasn't happened before or won't in the future?"

"That's the one question no one has been able to answer."

"Or won't tell you," Evalle pointed out.

"No, I think they really haven't figured it out, because the curse is written as a riddle. Flaevynn doesn't care. She's determined to be the last queen standing even though the prophecy doesn't actually designate her as such. Word is that Flaevynn's rushing the time line and risking everyone's life to beat the prophecy, which she calls a curse, so this may blow up in everyone's faces."

"Do you believe she can do this?"

"Unfortunately, yes. And you have no idea what creatures she and Cathbad have accumulated here in six hundred plus years. If she destroys the Belador power base, she'll be able to unleash things worse than demons on the mortal world."

"But how can she beat the curse if the other queens didn't before they died as scheduled?"

"By becoming immortal. Once Brina is dead and a Medb—Kizira—has control of Treoir, Flaevynn and Cathbad believe that either the cycle of the curse that imprisons them in TÅµr Medb will be broken or Kizira will bring back water from the river beneath Treoir that will turn them immortal. Either way, they expect to be able to leave here at that point."

"I will die before helping turn those two immortal," Evalle declared under her breath, then ran back over something he'd said a moment ago. "If we all have the same blood, what makes five of us different?"

Tristan seemed reluctant to answer, but he said, "Your father was in the military, right?"

"Yes."

"So were mine and Petrina's. We're not blood brother and sister. We were both captured by a troll when we were teens and stuck in cages. Together, we figured out how to escape."

Evalle nodded. "I can see why you're close."

"Before I was captured, *again*, by the Beladors and stuck in a spellbound prison, I was searching for other Alterants. I found out about three more, all with fathers in the military. I'll bet your mother got pregnant after your father was stationed in one of a handful of places."

"Don't know. I told you she died at my birth and my father's never spoken to me."

"Right. I *had* thought the Beladors had found men with Belador blood and cast a spell on their offspring while we were in the womb. That was before the Medb brought me here. Now I've finally put it all together. The Medb figured since Beladors are born warriors, they would gravitate to the military. The women who didn't were alphas and attracted to alphas, thus they were drawn to the military environment."

"Reasonable guess, since we have a lot of Beladors in militaries in allied countries."

Tristan chuckled softly, a sarcastic sound. "They didn't guess. Their depth of planning over many centuries and amount of resources would scare you."

"Why would they let you know any of this?"

"I've worked hard to convince Kizira that I'm on board with her plans as long as my sister is safe. I've been on the outs with the Beladors for a long time, so convincing Flaevynn and Cathbad of my loyalty wasn't that hard."

Evalle hoped he really was only acting loyal. "You

were saying about the Medb knowing where to find Beladors in the military," she said, prompting him to continue.

"Alpha males are drawn to strong women. Kizira said the sperm of male descendants of Cú Chulainn and a Medb witch had been held in a spelled cask for all these years. Thirty years ago, a druid with Medb warlock blood traveled to fertility clinics located near military locations where Beladors were known to reside. As a Celtic druid, he could identify Belador descendants, even those who were not warriors."

"Let me guess. This happened around the time we were conceived."

"Right."

She waved him on.

"The druid used majik and compulsion to guarantee only Belador descendants were impregnated, plus he placed a spell over the non-Belador husbands of Belador females so that those humans could not impregnate the women. Kizira said the Medb speculated that not all inseminations had taken, only those destined to become Alterants."

Evalle was sickened. "So using the sperm of descendants of Cú Chulainn and a Medb witch, unsuspecting Belador women were inseminated without their knowledge."

"That's the way I understand it."

Had Evalle's mother gone to a clinic without her father's knowledge? Evalle had once read in a magazine where a woman desperate to get pregnant had gone to be inseminated without telling her husband because he'd refused to consider the problem was his and go for testing.

She'd never known her father, but he'd abandoned her, so she had no problem thinking that might have been what happened to her mother.

If that was true, Evalle's mother had been wrongly accused of infidelity. Only guilty of wanting a baby.

Tristan kept explaining. "Kizira has the ability of precognition. She saw that five children, or Alterants, would be more powerful than the others."

"What makes the five of us with golden heads so special?"

Regret darkened his gaze. "The five mothers who would bear powerful Belàdors were inseminated with sperm from the only descendant of Cú Chulainn and Maeve, the original Medb queen." In the sad voice of someone delivering news of a death, he said, "You're one half Belador, but you're also a direct descendant of the most powerful Medb queen ever, and that blood rules you."

Evalle couldn't form a thought past the idea that she was Medb.

THIRTY-FIVE

"Evalle can't be trusted!"

The walls shook with Flaevynn's outburst. Kizira didn't flinch, having endured much worse ones in the past. To be honest, she'd initiated this conversation and raised the doubt in Flaevynn's mind about Evalle.

Kizira glanced at Cathbad, thinking her da could step in any time and help. No such luck. "If the proph . . . curse calls for those five to lead the charge, then you need all five."

"You just said Evalle is already trying to fight the simple compulsion spell," Flaevynn argued. "She'll find a way to screw up our plans."

"Not once she's fully under our control. Tristan has followed orders without a problem."

"Conlan was compelled, too, but he proved to be a disappointment."

Kizira could not argue that point. She'd compelled Conlan to aid her in trapping Tristan, which had gone well. In fact, Conlan had been coming along just fine until Flaevynn had pushed him to service her sexually and he'd balked.

She'd sent him to the dungeon for that.

Flaevynn moved around her private domain, float-ing a foot above the ground, back and forth in a frenzied motion. With so much energy swirling around the room, lightning sparked from above her waterfall where the water connected with the electricity in the air.

Kizira hoped her timing was right. "That is why we must test Evalle's loyalty."

If Flaevynn refused and Kizira argued, Flaevynn would become suspicious and not support Kizira's plan. Or throw her back in the dungeon.

Still waiting on you to jump in, Da. She pinned him with a testy look.

Cathbad held his hands out to each side. "What test can we do with so little time left?"

Flaevynn paused in whipping around the room and appeared in front of Kizira and Cathbad, addressing him first. "You said we needed *her*"—she pointed a wicked finger at Kizira—"to bond with these beasts. She's the one fully in control of them. This makes it Kizira's problem to bring me proof of Evalle's loyalty, or I'll turn them over to Tristan."

That could not happen. Thankfully, Kizira's unbound hair hid the sweat that trickled down the back of her neck. She hadn't told Cathbad her plan, and wouldn't. He'd probably send her to the dungeon himself if he knew what she was going to attempt.

Flaevynn shifted the full force of her glare to Kizira, who decided now was the time to gain Flaevynn's confidence. "I will bring you proof and I will lead the gryphons, who will deliver the victory you expect."

"Then what are you doing still standing here?"

Glad to leave, Kizira vanished from Flaevynn's sight

and teleported to the small chamber where she'd sent Evalle to meet with Tristan.

Tristan merely blinked at her arrival, but Evalle turned a glare bursting with hatred toward her. Kizira asked Tristan, "What's going on?"

"I just informed Evalle of her *dual* heritage."

"How was that pertinent to the attack?"

"The sooner Evalle realizes whose team she's playing for, the sooner she'll get with the game plan."

Kizira gave him a silent kudo for possibly helping her cause. She told Evalle, "Queen Flaevynn has requested proof of your loyalty."

Evalle snickered. "Tell her not to hold her breath, unless she can die of suffocation. Then, by all means, go for it."

"Leave us, Tristan."

He vacated the space immediately. When Evalle turned to Kizira, the Belador warrior sent the Medb priestess a glare that dared anyone to push her another inch right now.

Kizira might sympathize with her if she had the time to spend on ridiculous emotions. Evalle hadn't spent her entire life being ground under a Medb thumb. "As for your DNA, none of us gets a choice in whose genes we carry."

"Telling me I'm part Medb will not make me one."

"True, but saying that to Flaevynn is not wise."

"Tell that bitch to—"

"Shut. Up."

Evalle paused. "That works."

"I meant you. We're running out of time too quickly to waste it on your smart mouth. You know where you came from. Deal with it and get over it."

"You seem to think I actually care about *your* schedule."

"You will," Kizira assured her.

"Right. Tristan told me how once you turn me into a Medb zombie slave and compel me, I'll dance on your puppet strings. Go for it, but know that I'm taking everyone down with me if you try to make me kill Beladors."

Jaw tight, Kizira muttered, "Your stubborn attitude may kill more than the Medb."

Evalle pulled back at that, confused.

Kizira kept an eye on the walls that would lighten in color when anyone touched this space with majik, be it teleporting in or Flaevynn snooping with her scrying wall.

Crossing the area between her and Evalle, Kizira ignored the aggression building around Evalle. "Have you not realized that some of the times you and the Beladors have defeated . . . your enemy . . . you had a bit of luck on your side?"

"Enemy? Would that be the Medb?" Evalle asked, as if speaking to an imbecile.

What qualities did Quinn see in this woman that made him care about her?

Kizira held her temper. She had no time for angry rants and could not risk Flaevynn's tossing her into the dungeon again. "A man once wanted to ask me questions I could not answer due to my being compelled, so he created a game of words."

Watching Evalle for a reaction, Kizira lost hope in her lack of immediate enthusiasm. Did Evalle not realize she was being offered a chance to do what Kizira could not—save Quinn?

How had Macha not killed this one yet?

Evalle dialed back her urge to retaliate against all things Medb and considered what Kizira was saying. The priestess hadn't outed Lanna and had answered Evalle's questions, even allowing her to talk to Tristan in this warded room.

What was Kizira trying to tell her now? How to get around a compulsion spell to gain information? Was that how Quinn had dug up information during the Svart troll attacks on Atlanta last week?

Evalle had suspected Quinn's intel had come from Kizira. Now it made sense.

She didn't want to feel anything akin to respect for Kizira, but the woman had to face worse than being sent to a dungeon if Flaevynn ever found out that Kizira was aiding her enemy. "So you're saying you'll be straight with me?"

Kizira's eyes brightened with hope. "Take care to ask the right questions."

"Okay, I understand. No asking direct questions you're compelled against answering." Evalle chewed lightly on her thumb, thinking, then dropped her hand. She didn't know yet how she would get word to the Beladors, but she needed a better time frame than what was left of this forty-eight-hour window. Probably a day at the most in the mortal world.

Evalle started with, "When would be an optimum time for someone to start a war?"

Kizira shook her head.

"Crap. How can a Belador survive an attack on Treoir?"

Huffing out a breath in irritation, Kizira shook her head again.

Maybe she shouldn't have used the name Treoir. "What would prevent gryphons from reaching a mystical island?"

Kizira grabbed her head. "You are *terrible* at games."

"Maybe because I. Don't. Play. *Games!* You freakin' tell me what I need to know."

"I can't tell you what I'm compelled to keep secret."

Evalle growled and leaned toward her, out of patience. "Then tell me something you're *not* compelled to hide, blast it."

Tension fired through the room until Kizira gasped. "Wait. That's it." She gripped her hands together, excited. "You gave me an idea. First, we have to come up with a way to prove your loyalty to Flaevynn."

"Back to that, huh?" Evalle said, disgusted.

"You have the patience of a gnat. Answers to your questions will do you no good if you remain here in TÅµr Medb."

The lightbulb practically electrocuted Evalle's brain when it dawned on her that she had a chance to go back to Atlanta. A chance to get word to the Beladors *and* see Storm. She'd figure out how to play chess if that ended in a ticket home. "Hey, I'm in. Give me another chance. What do I have to do to prove my loyalty to Flaevynn?"

Calm swept over Kizira. She nodded, determination firing in her words. "If you brought back something valuable belonging to one of the Beladors you're close to, Flaevynn might accept that breach of trust as a sign of loyalty."

"Why? Wouldn't she think I just asked for whatever I get?"

"Not if you're compelled in front of her to steal the item and leave clear evidence that you committed the theft. Maybe something from a hotel room." Kizira raised her eyebrows, encouraging Evalle to grasp her meaning.

Hotel room. That would have to be Quinn's, which would mean she'd have to steal . . . "A warded Triquetra? Are you nuts?"

"So you admit failure before trying."

"No, I'm admitting nothing, just thinking out loud." And coming to grips with the idea of leaving evidence of betraying Quinn. His Triquetras were custom-made in a secret location, especially the warded one he used for personal security. "How would I get inside his room?"

"I can get you in there."

Evalle walked off a moment, arms hugged around herself as she tried to hold off a chill that had nothing to do with temperature. It was one thing to be thought a traitor and another to be proven one. She hoped he'd give her a chance to explain if she survived . . . if the Beladors didn't kill her in the attack on Treoir.

What was she thinking? Everything would change after this battle.

Regardless of whether the Medb won or lost, how could Evalle ever go home if the gryphons attacked Treoir? Anyone with a brain would quickly figure out the Medb had turned Alterants into gryphons. That meant she couldn't waste this one chance to return to Atlanta.

She had to explain to Storm so he wouldn't hate her. Worse, he'd be hurt. She couldn't live the rest of her life with that on her conscience. "I'll go, I'll bring back the Triquetra and I'll convince Flaevynn I'm on her team."

"About time."

"Speaking of that, I'm not going unless you give me some extra time there."

"How long?"

"Six hours."

"I can't give you that much. The attack is—" Kizira grabbed her throat and coughed, struggling to breathe.

So that's what happened when you tried to go against being compelled? "Oops."

Icicles should be hanging off Kizira's chilling glare. She rubbed her throat. "I can give you four hours."

That would have to suffice, but Evalle now had a time frame for the attack. She had to get going. "Okay. Now, what idea did I give you a minute ago?"

"You said to tell you something I wasn't forbidden to say. First, understand that you will be compelled to not speak to anyone about your time here or the attack. You'll be compelled to tell no one about Alterants changing into gryphons or that you have evolved into one. You just saw what happened when I almost made that mistake."

"I need to know what I *can* say."

Kizira pinched the bridge of her nose, then lowered her hand. "Pay attention and curb your sarcasm. I will *not* compel you to share your deepest wishes."

What did that mean? "What deepest wishes?"

Kizira's shoulders eased with relief. "For example, I will not compel you to tell someone *not* aligned with the coalition that it would make you happy if your two closest friends were to spend the next twelve hours watching over Atlanta instead of traveling to faraway places."

Evalle sorted through Kizira's cryptic suggestions and realized the Medb priestess wanted her to warn Quinn and Tzader away from Treoir. "You think I would intentionally undermine Belador defenses?"

Kizira lost her fleeting look of hope and snarled, "Can't you figure out the simplest puzzle? Do you even care about anything besides how this affects you?" Calming herself, she pleaded, "Think, Evalle. This is a game where we both stand to lose people we care about."

That backed Evalle up a step mentally. She replayed their conversation. This was about protecting Quinn more than anything. "You really care about—"

"*Him*," Kizira said quickly, her eyes glancing around as if in fear.

"Thought this place was secure."

"It is, but I never risk his name."

Evalle couldn't pin down how she felt about seeing this side of Kizira. "What's the deal between you two?"

"I don't wish to discuss this further, especially if you aren't going to do your part."

"Oh, I'll play the game now that I understand how to manipulate the words."

"Not that I'm hearing." Looking away, Kizira whispered with desperation, "He has no one to protect him."

A guilty weight had pressed on Evalle's chest for weeks about Quinn. If Flaevynn did not know about Quinn, then it seemed logical that Kizira could solve an internal conflict Evalle was tired of wrestling with. "Tell me something. Speaking of *him*, did he or did he not tell you how to find me when I was with Tristan in the Maze of Death a couple of weeks back?"

That startled Kizira, drawing her gaze back. "Yes, but involuntarily. I withdrew the information from him while he was incoherent. You want to know if he's still your friend. He's done nothing to betray you. Anything you've heard, especially the day Tristan took you to the house in the country, is a twisted tale to turn you against him."

Evalle believed Kizira. The weight lifted a little, allowing her heart to thump with peace again. And, if what Kizira said was true, Tristan had been tricked as well. He'd taken Evalle to meet an old Belador so pitiful he'd needed an oxygen tank to breathe.

Had that old guy been the traitor instead of Conlan O'Meary, who was still on the run? "Speaking of that day with Tristan, where's the old Belador who told me those twisted tales?"

"He was not an old man but Conlan O'Meary wearing a glamour."

"So Conlan *is* the Belador traitor after all."

Kizira shook her head. "No. When he offered to join up with us, we suspected a trick."

"You didn't help him escape the prison beneath VIPER's southeastern headquarters?"

"Why would we risk our people when we didn't need him?"

Well, duh. "If Conlan's not the traitor, then who is?"

"That I can't tell you."

Evalle wondered, "Do you think Qu-. . . our mutual friend helped Conlan escape?"

Kizira bared her teeth. "How can you think that? He is too honorable to do such a thing. What kind of friend are you?"

Maybe not a good one if a Medb had to stand up for Quinn. Evalle held up her hand. "I didn't say I believed he did. Where's Conlan?"

"When he failed to prove *his* loyalty to Flaevynn, she threw him in the dungeon. Cathbad claims you are significant in Flaevynn's plans, but trust me when I say that *can* change and you'll end up in the dungeon if you don't prove to her you can be trusted to execute the attack."

"Aren't you concerned about the Beladors stopping the gryphons?"

"No, and if you're digging for a weakness, save your breath. Nothing can prevent the gryphons from succeeding. Once they leave here as a unit, they'll follow my every command. *All* of you will."

What happened to us being allies? "I thought—"

"Don't misunderstand me, Evalle. The attack will happen, and not just because I have no choice in the matter. *I* need it to succeed. It's up to you to protect those you love, just as it is up to me to do the same."

That killed the tiny warm and fuzzy feeling Evalle had been suffering. But changing her tune now would alert Kizira that Evalle had made a mistake in seeing Kizira as an ally. "I want my four hours to start in Atlanta, but I need a few minutes in my room, alone, before I leave."

"No, you don't. Lanna is content to practice her teleporting."

"Just send her back with me."

"No. I'd be a fool to let you walk out of here with nothing to lose. Lanna is insurance that you will steal the Triquetra, deliver the message and return in four hours. I'll give you two minutes with Lanna, then it's up to you to convince Flaevynn you are under my control." Kizira lifted her hands.

THIRTY-SIX

Evalle deserved an Academy Award for acting sub-servient in front of Flaevynn to prove that Kizira's compulsion spell had Evalle under control. The minute the queen agreed to the trust test, Kizira teleported Evalle to the mortal world.

When the spinning ended, Quinn's luxurious hotel suite in downtown Atlanta came into focus. Evalle didn't fall down or throw up. Maybe teleporting was like being seasick. If you did it often enough, you got used to the vertigo.

She glanced over to catch Kizira looking longingly at Quinn's bedroom. "You know Macha will toast him if she ever finds out about you two."

Kizira stiffened and turned around. "Your four hours are ticking."

Good point. With one tiny window of time, Evalle was not wasting it here. "His Triquetra's not on the door. Guess he only needs it to keep out *uninvited* Medb."

"He hides it on top of the cabinet next to the door, something only someone *close* to him would know," Kizira tossed right back with smug arrogance.

Crossing the room, Evalle reached up and felt a piece of flat metal that sizzled with energy. She was almost disappointed that Kizira had been right.

Evalle couldn't pick it up, just as Lanna had explained, until she said a Gaelic phrase. Then the flat blade came to her hand. "Good thing we checked with Lanna," Evalle pointed out, reminding Kizira she hadn't known everything.

She pulled the triangular-shaped Belador throwing blade down and reached again to find the leather case for carrying it sitting on top of the cabinet. Tucking the blade in the case and both in her jacket pocket, Evalle turned to Kizira. "Where do you want to meet?"

"When it's time, I'll find you wherever you are, now that you're bonded to me."

Right now Evalle had to find Storm, and she needed Kizira's help if she wanted to get rolling.

Heat warming her chest drew her eyes down to where the emerald glowed. The gem hadn't changed at all in Medb Land.

Would Storm know she was back?

All she wanted was to finish here and go to him.

She wouldn't have this opportunity if not for Kizira.

It galled her to thank the priestess for anything, but Kizira *had* given Evalle a new set of clothes and her custom sunglasses even though the light didn't bother her now. Evalle hadn't shared that new ability with anyone yet, which was why Kizira had brought her here while it was still dark out.

Monday night. Would the invasion happen tomorrow?

That was the impression Evalle had gotten from Kizira's short word game.

Evalle felt every second tick against her. "I appreciate the clothes. Think you could conjure me up a motorcycle downstairs?"

"Teleporting would be more efficient."

For Storm, Evalle would teleport across the world. "I like the way you're thinking."

"Remember, Evalle, that being compelled is not a joke. You might harm someone you're with just as much as yourself."

She'd gotten that part loud and clear when Flaevynn had said one misspoken word would take the life of those Evalle loved.

Watching Kizira almost choke had made her a believer.

Kizira reminded her, "Make sure you face the security camera when you leave, and hold up the Triquetra so Quinn will know what happened to his warded blade. As soon as you do that, I'll teleport you."

Evalle gave the priestess a thumbs-up. "Got it."

Kizira disappeared in a swoosh of colors, and Evalle exited through the door to the hallway. She found the camera and made sure she faced it and pulled the Triquetra out of its sleeve long enough to be filmed. In the next two steps, she walked on a sidewalk in Storm's neighborhood.

Nerves hit her all at once.

Would Storm forgive her? She had less than four hours, maybe the last hours she'd ever get to spend with him.

She touched her hair that fell past her shoulders.

Kizira could have sent her here in warm-ups with dirty hair, but Evalle was freshly showered and outfitted in clean jeans, an aqua knit sweater, boots sans the fighting blades and a short leather jacket.

When she reached the walkway to his front door, fear gripped her chest.

What if he wasn't here?

Or if he just shut the door in her face?

As much as needing him to warn the Beladors, she craved his touch. To feel him one more time. Swallowing past her thick throat, she pushed herself down the walk, up the steps and onto the porch.

When she reached out to knock, the door flew open and Storm stood there.

Tension vibrated the air until she couldn't breathe.

All the things she'd thought about saying fled her mind.

"I'm sorry . . ." She lunged forward and he caught her. Powerful arms pulled her to safety, crushing her to him.

Her heart started beating again.

His mouth crushed hers. His hands were everywhere as if unsure she was really here.

She reached up and shoved her arms around his neck, holding on with everything she had.

Holding tight to everything she'd ever wanted.

Cupping her bottom, he lifted her up and spun her around. She hooked her legs around his waist. The door slammed shut. Her sunglasses went flying, but everything was dark inside and she didn't need them anyhow.

He backed her against the cold wood surface of the door. His hot body stoked the furnace building within her.

She grabbed his hair, dragging him closer, aching. Wanting to feel him everywhere.

His tongue plunged into her mouth, tangling with hers. She could kiss him for days without stopping. Her heart beat as loud as war drums in her ears.

Long fingers swept under her sweater, unclipped the front clasp on her bra and . . . oh, dear goddess.

His thumb brushed over her nipples that were tight and hurting for his touch. She arched up against him, feeling the long, hard ridge pulsing inside his jeans.

He growled and nipped at her neck, panting with labored breaths. "Can't believe you're here."

"I can't believe you're stopping."

A savage emotion lit his eyes.

She rubbed up against him and kissed his neck, then his ear, not sure if that was the right move. He growled a sound that came out closer to jaguar than man. She eased back and lifted her gaze to his, making one thing clear. "This is me. Not the armband."

He pulled her to him in a shuddering hug and kissed her hair, his voice raw when he whispered, "I thought you were dead . . . or worse."

There were many things worse than death in the supernatural world.

"I know." She ran her lips over his eyes and cheeks, then his mouth, sharing her hunger and giving him all the feelings she'd held back too long.

The feelings she'd been too scared to share.

She was tired of being a coward with Storm.

He wrapped his arms around her and turned, moving through the house to his bedroom, where it was darker than midnight. She didn't care where he went as long as he took her with him.

His mouth touched hers again and she drifted into a fantasy world of nothing but Storm's touch. Firm lips kissed her, then caressed her cheek and her neck.

Her jacket came off with a sweep.

The man had the hands of a magician.

She felt herself falling back, cradled in his arms. He followed her down, nuzzling her neck as he lowered her to his huge bed. When he covered all of her with his body, he slowed his kisses to tender touches all over her face and neck, his mouth burning a path. He slowed the tempo in spite of breathing harder than Evalle could ever recall.

His fingers brushed her hair, then inched down over her chest. He moved with ruthless control, holding back instead of unleashing that powerful body.

She should have been terrified by the hot desire staring down at her, but she wasn't and trembled with her own need. Reaching up, she clamped her hands on each side of his face, forcing his gaze to hers.

Storm still couldn't believe he held Evalle. He was out of his mind with joy over having her in his arms. Knowing she was alive and safe. He was the danger right now, wanting to feel himself inside her. Sex terrified Evalle, and he was acting wilder than his jaguar.

Had he rushed her? "I'm scaring you."

"No, you're not."

"I'll slow down . . . or stop." For her, he'd take all the time she needed, even if it killed him, and stopping might.

"No, you won't."

He searched her face and saw that she meant what she said. "Tell me what you want, sweetheart."

The tip of her pink tongue made a swipe along her lips. "You. Only you."

She had no idea what those words did to him. How deeply she touched him in a place no one else ever had. "I'm all yours and you're mine."

Bold possession gleamed in her eyes. "Touch me. Make me yours."

"Oh, yeah. I'll touch you everywhere, but we'll take it easy."

"Don't baby me in this, Storm. I'm fine. I've . . . got my beast under control."

"Your beast won't be a problem because you know you're safe with me." He touched his forehead to hers. "I need you more than my next breath. I will never hurt you."

"I need you, too. I trust you."

He lifted his head to see her feelings unshielded and honest. "Thought I'd never hear that."

No one had ever looked at him the way she did right now, as if he was her world. She whispered, "Thought I'd never trust a man the way I do you. Never feel what I do for you."

Caring this much was dangerous for someone like him, but it was too late to worry about that.

She was his.

He wasn't giving her up.

Easing up off of her, he pulled his knees alongside her hips for support and eased his hands beneath her sweater, sliding up to lift her bra out of the way and push her top up until he could take one of her nipples in his mouth and brush his tongue over the tip.

She sucked in a sharp breath.

Slow. Easy. "Put your arms above your head, sweetheart." When she did, he worked the sweater up her arms, stopping when it was halfway off and leaning down to suckle the other breast.

She cried out, trembling. Her reaction washed over his skin and sent blood rushing to his cock.

"Open your eyes, sweetheart."

When she did, he held her brilliant green gaze with his.

The smooth green emerald glowed on her chest. He'd thought about removing it, but he'd changed his mind. Not until he knew she was safe from the Medb and the witch doctor.

"You're beautiful, you know that?" he said, talking calmly to her as he pulled off his long-sleeved T-shirt. Her eyes widened, watching him, no doubt expecting the jeans to go next.

He brushed his thumbs over each of her beaded nipples at the same time.

She moaned and arched hard, her body shaking.

Damn, what passion had been buried all this time.

The only time she'd been touched intimately had been by the bastard who'd attacked her. She might as well be a virgin and this her first time. This first time would be all hers. The next time, and there would be many more, he wanted to drive deep inside her and feel the passion thrumming through her when she crested.

Soon.

Running his hands up her arms, sliding the sweater to her hands, where he lifted it off, then held her hands with his. Not an imprisoned grip, but an affectionate one. He kissed her slowly, taking his time to drive her to the point of begging.

He wanted her so overwhelmed she could think only about what she needed. Only then could he take his jeans off.

Smoothing his fingers down her arms, he started kissing her at her neck, then her shoulders. He moved to her breasts, using his tongue to tease her nipple until she trembled.

While he had her focused on that, he unzipped her jeans and eased them down, kissing his way to her belly button, then sitting back on his knees and moving until he pulled her jeans off.

She wore a thin pair of black-and-red lace panties.

Sweet mother of . . .

His throat was too dry for words.

Her hips lifted and he dipped his head, tugging the panties down with his teeth, then pulling them off. What a view. She surpassed his fantasies, and his were pretty damned hot fantasies.

Running his hands along the insides of her thighs, he inched up until he touched her heat. Her legs quivered.

She arched her back, then, amazing woman that she was, Evalle shoved away from the headboard, sitting up. She grabbed him and kissed him. Attacked his mouth.

She never did anything halfway.

He'd suspected she'd be a powerhouse in bed, and she wasn't disappointing him. He cupped her breasts and brushed his thumbs over nipples crying for attention.

Evalle broke the kiss. "You're still dressed."

She was wet, but was she ready for him, all of him? He stepped off the bed and unzipped his pants, shucking out of them and groaning at the feel of springing free.

He climbed back on the bed, kneeling in front of her. "Okay?"

"No." She shook her head, but the smile on her lips gave away the tease. "I'd call that spectacular."

"Wild woman." He kissed her all the way back down to the bed, loving the feel of her under him.

She reached between them, curling her fingers around him.

Muscles tightened across his shoulders with the effort of fighting the urge to thrust. He didn't have to ask if she was good with this. He'd know the minute anything changed, and right now he could feel desire wrapping both of them.

"I trust you, Storm. Don't hold back."

He didn't.

Kissing her again, he unleashed the hunger he'd

fought since the first time he'd touched her. She released him and gripped his shoulders with the strength of a warrior.

But she rubbed up against him, and hot blood roared through him. He swept a hand down to slide into the slick, hot moisture between her legs. The second he pushed a finger inside her she arched up, gripping him hard.

She was ready.

He suckled her breast at the same moment his fingers stroked in and out of her. His thumb moved across the nub at the center of her heat, and he could feel her coiling toward climax.

Her nails dug into his back. "Storm . . . yes . . . I . . ."

He stroked her again and grazed his teeth over her nipple. At the moment he pushed her over the edge, he lifted up to watch her first orgasm. Green eyes glowed with passion. She arched up against his hand and shrieked, chest heaving.

"Oh, my . . ." She couldn't speak.

When her shudders slowed, he wrapped her up and rolled over with her draped over him. He ran his hand up and down her back, calming her.

She rubbed against him, not calming him in the least.

He gritted his teeth. "Careful, sweetheart. Been a while for me."

Pushing up on his chest, hair wild all around her face, Evalle laughed. Laughed. The hellion. "That's not like all . . . is it?"

The hellion.

She crawled up his chest and deliberately rubbed her damp opening against him.

He grabbed her hips. "Wait or I'll forget to put on a condom."

"Then get it."

Damn, he did love that cocky side of her. He stretched over to his nightstand, pulled out a condom and sheathed himself. But one look at Evalle and he knew she was shaky on this part.

He brushed hair off her face. "Afraid?"

"A little, but I want this."

"Kiss me, sweetheart."

She smiled at the gentle order, drew a breath of confidence and proceeded to rock his world with her kiss. As she did, he reached down and used his fingers to bring her back to the place she'd been a moment ago.

So wet his fingers were drenched.

Moving her sweet lips across his cheek to his ear, she whispered, "I want you now."

"Then take me," he told her, turning her words back on her. "Take all of me."

He watched her face for any fear as she lifted her hips and lowered herself down on him. No fear. Not his Evalle.

She clutched his shoulders as she pushed down onto him.

Nothing could ever feel as incredible as being inside her. When he was all the way in, he gripped her hips and started a rhythm as natural as life itself.

The look of ecstasy on her face was one he'd hold in his heart forever. She met his thrusts, every stroke urging him to explode. He drew on all the control he owned to keep from reaching his climax.

When he could feel her clenching him, he reached down and took her over the edge once again. She had her hands on his chest, arching back and calling out to him when she stepped off that cliff again. He took over, stroking harder and faster, lost in the feel of her, until he tensed and exploded, rocking into her again and again.

She was his joy.

His life.

His woman.

THIRTY-SEVEN

Evalle shook off the urge to sleep.

She couldn't waste what time she had left with Storm. She should tell him she was leaving.

Not yet. She'd had so little in her life to celebrate that she didn't want to give up this amazing moment with him until she had to. She'd faced her fears and walked away with more than she'd ever expected.

Her face lay against Storm's warm chest. His muscles flexed smoothly when he moved his arm to stroke his fingers lightly across her back.

When she played with the smooth skin around his nipple, his chest muscles tightened. He touched her breast, probably expecting her to call time after what they'd done for the last three and a half hours.

She nipped his skin instead.

He groaned, a husky male sound. "You're exhausted, sweetheart. I want to hear what happened when you left, but get some rest for now." He kissed her hair. "We have all night."

No, they didn't. Might as well get this over with. "I have to leave soon."

His fingers stilled. "Why?"

"I wouldn't have made it back now at all if I hadn't

negotiated a deal with Kizira. She needed me to do something and I wanted to see you. She gave me four hours." Evalle pushed up and turned to face him.

The last time she'd seen that look on Storm, he'd destroyed two Svart trolls who'd almost killed her. He spoke with the confidence of a man who backed down from nothing. "I'm not letting you go."

"I don't have a choice, Storm, but I do have a plan."

"No. You're not going back to the Medb."

"Kizira has the power to find me anywhere right now and to teleport me away without a word."

The curse he let loose should have turned the air bloody. "I'll take you to VIPER lockdown. She can't get in there."

Bringing VIPER into this would be a mistake. Evalle shook her head. "That wouldn't work either."

"She can take me with you."

"Then I wouldn't be able to escape when the time came because you'd end up in the Medb dungeon where I couldn't get to you. And I wouldn't leave you." Evalle kissed his chest. "I trust you. Now you need to trust me that I know what I'm doing."

He ran a hand roughly over his head. "You make me crazy."

"You've told me that before." She smiled, hoping to lighten his mood, then remembered something. "How did you get away from the beast fight on Cumberland?"

"Used my majik and a sip of your potion. Walked right past the guards and Sen. I still have it. You can use it."

"No, I can't and I can't explain why, but I need you to do something for me."

"What?"

"It's not easy to explain, because I've been compelled from divulging certain things."

"Dammit." With the liquid movements of the jaguar inside him, he shot up and loomed over her. "What did they do to you?"

"I can't really talk about being there, because of the spell. But I can share some things if I'm careful about the words I choose. That's why I need your help. There are people who need this information, and I can't talk to them at all. People who you know will help me when the time comes."

"Tell me."

Feeling lost and staring into his tight gaze, she started talking before her brain engaged. "I need you to tell—"

Her throat tightened. She wheezed, gasping for air.

"What's wrong?" His every movement said he wanted to hurt something for touching her.

"It's okay," she croaked out, massaging her throat. She'd almost said Tzader's name. "I didn't realize I couldn't say a name."

"Would it be easier for you to write it down?"

"Yes. That might be a better idea. That way I could check for a slipup before I handed it to you. The spell doesn't attack me until the point I actually share information I shouldn't." She yawned, wishing she could just lie down with him and sleep for days.

He hooked his arm around her waist and pulled her

to him with possessive strength. He kissed her with more than passion. Something deeper. As if leaving a mark.

His whispered love words wrapped around her, sliding past her senses, but one word slipped inside her and grabbed her heart. *Mine.* Had she heard that . . . or felt it?

The world around her might still be spinning along on course, but hers stood still at that moment.

Had he just done something to bind her to him?

Did she care?

Yes. It made her happy.

She gripped his biceps, holding on to the one person who had been her anchor since the day she'd met him. His fingers touched her breasts, barely grazing the sensitive skin, then leaving too soon. After hours of making love, she shouldn't be up for another bout, but when his fingers slipped between her legs she was on fire all over again.

Guess she wasn't as tired as she'd thought. But time was disappearing for her. "Storm, I want—"

He lifted his eyes to hers, then cupped her face in his hands. "What? Say the word and it's yours."

You are all I want. Instead, she said, "Time, which is something neither of us can control."

She stretched and squinted at the glowing clock on his nightstand. With twenty minutes left, she didn't want to have Kizira appear in the middle of them tangled up again.

And Evalle wanted a chance to say good-bye this time, to tell Storm she would do everything in her power to return.

He asked, "How long?"

Sometimes she could swear he read minds. "Twenty minutes. I want a quick shower."

A sigh filled with regret spilled out, then he sat up, pulling her with him. As comfortable naked as he was wearing the sleek coat of a jaguar, he got out of bed and turned around, picking her up.

"I can walk," she said with dry sarcasm.

"I know." He deposited her in a glass shower large enough for two that had to be part of a remodeling, since this house had been built during the time of small tubs and shower curtains. "I'll make coffee and find you something to write on."

After thoroughly kissing her one more time, he walked out, beautifully naked. She could spend hours watching him do mundane tasks with no clothes on.

That wouldn't happen unless she left a message that Tzader and the Beladors could figure out.

Or if she failed to survive the attack on Treoir.

When Evalle finished showering, she walked through a cloud of steam while she dried her hair. The heat had turned what was left of her muscles into noodles.

The sound of coffee brewing gurgled in the kitchen way down the hallway. Maybe Storm was making break-fast.

Warmth tingled on her chest.

The emerald was glowing. She had to ask him about that.

She tightened the towel wrapped around her breasts

and started to head to the kitchen until she saw a pen and paper on the bed.

She should write the note now.

The minute she got within two steps of Storm, she'd forget anything except touching him.

Getting a message to the Beladors was the other reason she'd traded for the four hours here. Kizira could sit on her broom and spin if she thought Evalle intended to tell Tzader and Quinn to not protect Treoir.

No way would Tzader stay away with Brina under threat, and he needed Quinn's powerful mind, especially to stop the gryphons.

Evalle might possess Medb blood, but she had a Belador heart.

She sat down, dropping the towel on the bed, and hurried to write the note. She wrote two sentences, scratched them out and started over. When she finished, she hoped Storm could explain the rest of what she couldn't. Otherwise, this would sound stupid.

Storm—

Give this note to the person I trust as much as I trust you, and explain that all I can do is give a hypothetical tale because I've been compelled.

If a person had pets who didn't need ears to hear words and couldn't die, that person might teach her pets how to steal a special home in a faraway place. But she would have to travel with her pets, because of being the only one who could control them with silent commands.

If her pets proved to be successful, she would rule not just her new home but homes everywhere.

But for every strength there is a weakness and hers is in her heart.

And considering any of these pets friendly could be royally dangerous.

Evalle read it over quickly, trying to think of what else she could tell Tzader. She hoped Storm would not take out that last line, where she basically was saying she was just as dangerous to Brina as all the other Alterants. Another look at the clock gave her eleven minutes. She gripped the pen, determined to leave one last message for Storm to have when she left.

Also, Storm, this is for you only. Thank you for being everything I could ever want in a man. You live in my heart every minute that I breathe. Trust me that I will find a way to come back to you. Please don't make me face you in battle. I won't be able to protect you. In fact, I'm now the greatest threat to those I love.

I love you,
Evalle

Laying the note on the nightstand, she put on Storm's shirt, which she intended to take with her, then glanced over and realized she'd left the note facedown. *Turn it over so he sees the message.*

Before she could reach over to touch the paper, the air in the room stirred with energy.

Kizira stood on the other side of the bed.

Evalle hissed at her, "You're early. I have ten minutes."

"Unavoidable. Flaevynn's on a warpath looking for you."

Crap. "Let me go tell—"

The room spun out of focus.

Evalle yelled, "Storrrmmm," but she knew she'd already left the room behind.

THIRTY-EIGHT

Kizira had better come prepared for a fight.

Storm pulled two mugs from his kitchen cabinet. Evalle should be finished showering. His jaguar stirred, wanting more.

He wanted more, too.

Just thinking about Evalle made his jeans too snug for comfort. More than that, he struggled against the urge to shift into his animal and kill anyone who tried to take Evalle from him. He wanted to pack her away somewhere dark and safe.

The human part of him was barely restrained.

He tried to convince himself it was nothing more than the protectiveness he'd felt since first meeting her. But that was a lie. All he had to do was breathe her scent and she became a part of him.

Mine. He'd mated with her. It had happened fast, an unconscious action that came of the innate knowledge that he'd met the only woman for him.

That didn't excuse his lack of control. She should have been given a choice. Should have been told that he had no soul. It was done, and he'd die to protect her, but he still should have told her before he made love to her.

And he'd planned to, until he'd opened the door to

find her standing there. Every thought had fled his mind except touching her.

But he still had to get his soul back, and his father's, which he would just as soon as he killed the witch doctor.

Not wanting to give up even a couple of minutes with Evalle, Storm turned away from the counter with intentions of heading back to his shower in case she hadn't finished.

A rush of smoky licorice engulfed his senses.

The witch doctor stood between him and Evalle. The witch doctor couldn't teleport, or hadn't been able to the last time he'd seen her, but she had some strong majik to pull off getting past his security. She cooed, "I've certainly missed . . ." Her eyes drifted down his half-clothed body, pausing at his groin. "You."

Sick bitch. She was just trying to throw him off track.

Her yellow eyes twinkled with sinister delight. As if in answer to his unspoken questions, she boasted, "My powers have gotten stronger since we last met, yes? Do you like how fast I can move *and* mask my scent? But I actually gained access because you were too distracted when you first came home to notice a herd of elephants crashing through here."

She'd been here since he'd arrived an hour before Evalle had shown up? She'd hidden her presence and scent from him.

But she hadn't tried to take control of him. She still feared him, and should.

Just when he thought he couldn't feel any more contempt for this female vermin, Nadina surprised him. He might as well think her name if she'd found him and breached his security.

This wasn't the time to fight with her, but he was ready and hoped Evalle stayed in the shower.

His fingers curled, wanting to choke the life out of her, just not yet. Not until he reclaimed all he'd lost. "Give me back my soul—and my father's—I'll let you leave alive."

"I'm up for a trade when you're ready."

"No trades. You owe me two souls you stole."

"You won't even trade for Evalle?"

Power rushed through him, driving his jaguar to break free. Storm drew fast breaths, fighting the change, because she was trying to push him to shift.

Anything Nadina wanted, he didn't.

If she touched Evalle, he'd make Nadina's death slow and excruciating. "You can't have Evalle, and she would destroy you anyhow."

"Don't put your money on the wrong one so quickly. I'm not the same witch doctor you knew back in South America."

"Egotistical, reality-challenged sociopath. I don't see any change."

She smiled with confidence, so much that a ripple of concern ran up Storm's back when she bragged, "Oh, I've changed quite a bit now that I'm aligned with Hanhau."

Hanhau? That explained her new and improved powers. Storm hid his shock with a scoff. "Only a fool would make a pact with him."

"Fool?" Her eyes narrowed in warning. "Careful how you speak of someone favored by the ruler of all demons and Mitnal," she said, referencing the land of the dead.

"Of demons in South America, not here," Storm countered. "Speaking of Mitnal, why aren't you there now?"

"I'm not one of his demons."

"Pity. You missed your calling."

"I'd love to chat, but not right now. I'm pressed for time. This is your one warning. Come to me soon, Storm, and willingly, or I'll take what you most desire. Evalle."

Kai's words echoed in his brain. His guardian spirit had warned him that if he did not kill Nadina, she would take what Storm most desired. He'd thought Kai meant his soul, but he now knew it was Evalle.

He was ready to fight, but not when Evalle believed she would disappear soon. "You can die *trying* to take her."

"You don't even know she's gone, do you?"

"Liar."

"Am I?"

It hadn't been twenty minutes, so Evalle still had time, but Nadina had spoken the truth. Storm started toward his bedroom and Nadina swirled into a blur, moving out of his way. She claimed not to be the same witch doctor he'd known before, but she was wise enough to realize she didn't know how he'd changed either.

He raced into the bathroom, then back to the bedroom, yelling, "*Evalle!*"

"She's gone." Nadina appeared in the doorway and sniffed. "Smells like Medb in here."

He ignored the burned citrus odor. He looked around for Evalle's note and saw a blank piece of paper on the nightstand.

Nadina taunted, "You don't know the best of all this. *If* Evalle does find her way free of the Medb and you have not come voluntarily to me, I will call her to me instead."

"How do you figure that?"

"Remember the Volonte bone?"

His scalp tingled with warning. "What about it?"

"Did you think that ended up on Evalle's arm by accident?"

No. "She's not wearing it anymore."

"I know. That was all part of my brilliant plan. Just like Imogenia, I can call Evalle to me anytime and anywhere. I cast a spell on the bone that created a leash between me and those who wore it next."

His mouth dried out. Storm's fingers curled into claws with his impending change.

Nadina took a step back. "I can see you're still not ready to discuss this. Guess I'll have to take *her* if you won't come to me voluntarily."

Fury crashed over him so fast that he started shifting, his hands changing shape into paws. Sharp claws curled. Fur covered his shoulders and chest where hair never grew due to his ancestry. But he wouldn't be able to talk and deal with Nadina in animal form, so he tightened down on his control and forced his animal to retreat.

She moved in a blur, disappearing.

He rushed into the kitchen, where she'd stopped near his closed front door. Not teleporting. Speed from black majik, because he never lost her scent.

She smiled with predatory happiness. "Just a tiny demonstration to spare us any posturing. My timing isn't by accident. I know you mated. You have until she returns."

The door opened on its own and Nadina strolled out.

When Kai had searched Storm's future, she'd warned Storm that he would lose Evalle before he won her.

The time had come to end this. He snatched open a drawer, grabbed out a pen and paper and scribbled a note he hoped Evalle would find if . . . *when* she came back.

Sweetheart—

I've gone to deal with the witch doctor and end this so we can be together. Then I'm coming for you no matter where you are.

Storm

He rushed out, hot on Nadina's trail. He could follow her as long as she didn't teleport. Once he found her, they'd both find out just who had become the most powerful since they last fought.

THIRTY-NINE

"Y̶ou bitch!" Evalle shouted even before the spinning from teleporting stopped. The minute her feet hit the carpet of the private study in TÅµr Medb, she dove for Kizira, who disappeared.

"Are you crazy?" Kizira yelled from behind her.

Crazy didn't begin to cover the homicidal rush surging through Evalle. She flipped around to face Kizira. "One minute was all I needed. You owed me *ten*."

"I would have given them to you if I could. I bought you as much time as possible. We're leaving here in one hour. Angering Flaevynn right now will not serve either of us."

One hour? That cut through the red haze of anger blinding Evalle. "I *am* going with you."

"Not if you don't get moving and calm down while you're at it."

"Take me to the queen bitch."

"Get the Triquetra."

Evalle took in her jeans, the leather jacket and blue sweater. What had happened to Storm's shirt? She panicked. "Where's the long-sleeved T-shirt I had on?"

Kizira made a grinding noise deep in her throat. "I sent it to the bed in your room with Lanna, for crying out loud. It smells of him. Wearing that around Flaevynn would cause her to question what you were doing in Atlanta when you were supposed to only be there to retrieve the Triquetra."

Got it.

Evalle would draw blood if anything happened to that shirt. Reaching into her jacket, she pulled out the soft case shielding the Triquetra. "Let's go."

Evalle's location changed so quickly that she didn't have time to blink. She was back in Flaevynn's personal chamber, where the witch sat on a golden throne. Pompous bitch had it carved to look like a dragon.

The dragon's head moved until its eyes narrowed at Evalle.

Ohh-kay.

Kizira's demeanor changed in a flash to stiff and professional. "Evalle was successful in completing her task."

Flaevynn pointed a long black fingernail sparkling with diamonds at Kizira, whose face turned red. The priestess clawed at her throat, making gagging noises as tears spilled from her eyes.

Evalle caught on quickly. "She's not lying. I have it." She withdrew the Triquetra from the case, then played up her role, snarling, "I hope you're happy. I *stole* a Belador warded Triquetra."

Flaevynn's acidic eyes, heavily lined and sprouting lashes an inch long, whipped at Evalle. "How do I know someone didn't give it to you?"

Didn't I make that same point to Kizira? "Because I was forbidden from even *speaking* to a Belador or VIPER agent when Kizira compelled me," Evalle spat. "She was so thorough I couldn't have accepted this even if someone handed it to me on the street. And this belongs to Vladimir Quinn of the Beladors, who is . . . *was* one of my best friends."

The strangling noises stopped.

Evalle glanced over at Kizira, whose throat now sported claw marks. The priestess leaned over, a hand on her knee as she fought for a breath.

"Is this true, Kizira?" Flaevynn asked.

Standing upright again and coughing first, Kizira nodded. "Yes. And the hotel security tapes will show Evalle leaving his room with the Triquetra in her hand."

If Tzader and Quinn didn't figure out how to stop Kizira and the gryphons from the cryptic note Evalle left with Storm, then Evalle hoped they'd at least realize the one thing she tried to make very clear—that Evalle was a threat to Brina, and thus the Beladors. If they had any doubt that she'd joined the Medb, that hotel security tape would probably cinch the deal. She couldn't stand to consider how low Quinn and Tzader would think of her, but if they survived the attack on Treoir, that would have to be enough.

She only regretted not having a chance to tell Storm in person that she loved him and to ask him to please forgive anything he heard about her after tomorrow, which evidently was today. She'd lost all track of time zipping between realms.

Drawing herself up with regal poise, Flaevynn said, "I compel you to tell the truth or bite off your own tongue, Evalle. Now, tell me why I should trust you."

"You shouldn't—"

Kizira made a small noise.

Evalle pasted contempt on her face as she looked at Kizira, then back at Flaevynn, and continued, "I was saying you shouldn't trust me if I wasn't compelled. I would do all in my power to help the Beladors if I could, but I can't, and the minute I show up as a gryphon they'll have every reason to kill me. Self-preservation alone will force me to defend myself, and Kizira's control over my actions will force me to carry out your plan." Evalle made sure she loaded plenty of bitterness on her words. Not hard to do when it flowed in her veins, because she'd spoken the truth.

Flaevynn lifted a hand as if calling someone.

Cathbad appeared next to her throne. He observed Kizira for an unguarded moment but washed his face of emotion so quickly that Evalle wasn't sure she'd actually seen concern.

Addressing Cathbad, Flaevynn said, "As you can see, they're back. I am convinced of Evalle's loyalty. I want all the attack plans laid out here, where I can observe."

He cast a furtive glance at Kizira, who ignored him when he said, "I have spoken to our contact who will be on Treoir."

That blasted Belador traitor who was costing her everything. She'd cut that throat in a heartbeat.

Cathbad went on. "Our contact tells me the coast of the island is heavily guarded, but he will open an area one hundred yards wide for Kizira and our army of gryphons to enter."

Evalle held herself still, purposely showing no reaction to news that the traitor was actually on the island. At least she'd been able to leave Tzader and Quinn a message.

Hands clasped behind his back and walking around the room, Cathbad continued speaking with the confidence of a general headed into battle with superior forces. "Once our army arrives on the island, our warlocks will engage the enemy, occupying them while the gryphons enter."

"Only the five," Flaevynn interjected.

"Yes."

Evalle's heart sank. How could she get Tristan out of here if he couldn't fly with them?

Kizira said, "I want to take all ten."

Cathbad paused in pacing. "Why?"

"You gleaned the additional information about the destiny of the five powerful gryphons from old bards' tales. That once they invaded Treoir, gryphons would roam the island forever. If that's the case, why not use *all* of them and ensure victory?"

Evalle wanted to cheer at a chance to get Tristan and his sister out of here, and at the same time, groan at the idea of an even greater force of gryphons attacking Treoir.

Cathbad grinned. "'Tis not a bad thought, Flaevynn."

"Fine. Take them all." The queen gave a dismissive wave of her hand, then sent a pointed look at Cathbad. "Did you tell her?"

Kizira turned to Cathbad. "Tell me what?"

Watching this scene play out between the three Medb gave Evalle an insight into Kizira's life all these years in the Medb Coven. For the first time, Evalle actually pitied Kizira.

When Cathbad stepped up to Kizira, his eyes flashed with compassion, then turned ruthless. "The minute Brina is dead, you are compelled to stand upon the steps of the castle and wait for Flaevynn to arrive."

Cathbad's position blocked Kizira's face from Flaevynn's view, but Evalle caught the flicker of disbelief . . . or hurt in Kizira's face.

But that didn't stop Cathbad. "If you do not walk out on those steps within one minute after Brina's death, or if you touch the immortal river before Flaevynn does, your skin will begin to peel from your body."

"I thought I was bringing the water *to* Flaevynn." Horror spread across Kizira's face. "Why would you—"

"Once Brina is dead and you control the castle, Flaevynn and I will be free to leave this tower." Cathbad spoke as though no emotion flowed through his veins, but Evalle saw regret tinge his eyes when he added softly, "'Tis the only way I could convince Flaevynn you would do as told."

Evalle had opened her empathic senses, and she got swamped by the rage and regret pulsing off of Cathbad.

Silence built into a living thing between Kizira and Cathbad until the queen added her bit. "I'll be watching from here, Kizira. Do not fail me."

Struggling to pull herself together, Kizira blinked away moisture building in her eyes and stared with hatred at Cathbad. "When do I leave?"

Cathbad answered, "The six hundred and sixty-sixth anniversary of Flaevynn's birth will arrive in three hours. Our contact on Treoir is expecting you and the gryphons to arrive one hour before that."

FORTY

Tzader shoved a kinetic blast at the front door of Storm's house. At least he hoped it was Storm's house. This was where Nicole had sent him.

He made short work of searching the house, where a full carafe of coffee was still warm.

No mugs. No dishes.

What was that smoky smell? Licorice?

Native American incense?

Tzader lifted a piece of paper that had fallen on the kitchen floor. A note from Storm to *Sweetheart*. Evalle?

So Storm expected Evalle to come here?

Hunting further, Tzader found the bedroom and immediately identified the smell of sex lingering on the rumpled bedsheets. Had Evalle been here? Even the towel on the floor was damp. Quinn kept telling Tzader not to smother Evalle with being overprotective, that Storm cared about her.

Evalle wouldn't have opened herself up like this unless she trusted Storm with her life.

Where could Storm and Evalle have gone?

But she wasn't with Storm if he'd left a note for her.

Tzader scratched his neck, circling the bedroom once more before he spied another piece of paper on the nightstand. Blank. Out of habit of being thorough, he snatched it up and flipped it over, where he found Evalle's handwriting. Why had these two written each other notes? He started reading, confused until he slowed down to read the words a second time.

Ah, hell.

What had the Medb done to Evalle? What kind of *pet*? A dangerous one.

The paper shook in his trembling hand. How was he going to explain this to Quinn?

His belly hurt, as if he'd taken a sword to the gut. First he had to inform Macha and Brina about this.

Then he had to prepare Quinn, and himself, to kill Evalle.

FORTY-ONE

"You should join the Beladors," Evalle suggested. "They might not like you, but they wouldn't torture you the way the Medb do."

Kizira had taken Evalle to the private study with the warded walls. The priestess hadn't zipped away as usual. Head down, she seemed to need a moment to regroup. She raised eyes so dark with desperation that Evalle knew she had to be in pain. "You can believe me or not, but I have worked very hard to see the end of the war between the Medb and the Beladors."

"Why?"

"Because I love . . ."

"Him," Evalle finished, since Kizira refused to speak his name here, and from everything she'd seen, that was probably for Quinn's benefit.

"Yes. I had planned to enlist your help once we got to the island. I thought . . ." Kizira spoke haltingly, and tears threatened at the corners of her eyes. "If I could get inside the castle and to the river, I could stop the battle before it reached the castle. I didn't want immortality so I could live forever, but so that I could stop Flaevynn from surviving past her birth hour."

"Have any of you thought about the fact that the castle is warded against any immortal crossing the threshold?"

"Cathbad claims that anyone who becomes immortal *inside* the castle should be able to break the ward."

Would that help Tzader? No, he'd still have to cross the threshold first to reach the river, so he'd die before he got there. Evalle brushed off Tzader's love-life problems in favor of taking advantage of this turn of events. Kizira loved Quinn. If Evalle could convince Kizira to help her, they might be able to save Brina and Treoir.

If that happened, Macha might not torch Kizira, Evalle and all the gryphons.

As long as I'm having wild fantasies, I might as well wish for freedom from Sen and a life with Storm. Getting back on track, Evalle said, "What happens if you lose the battle?"

"Flaevynn dies, then I die. She won't pass her crown to me. A day later, Cathbad dies."

"Wait, are you related to those two?"

"Biological parents."

And I thought I had it bad. Before now, Kizira's dying would have been on the top of Evalle's wish list, but now that she knew where Kizira stood, Evalle couldn't throw her out with the rest of the Medb. Evalle knew what it felt like to be of no value to family. "If you live past Flaevynn's death, would all the Medb Coven follow you?"

"Technically, yes."

"What happens if Flaevynn leaves TÅµr Medb before her time here is up or before the curse is broken?"

"She'd burn like an asteroid diving into the Earth's atmosphere, but Cathbad has figured out something he had not shared until today. He thinks that once Brina is no longer in control of the castle, he and Flaevynn can leave this tower. I held out hope that he was in my corner, but I was wrong. He's watching out for himself."

"What happens to you if Flaevynn dies by stepping outside this tower?"

Kizira cocked her head, thinking. "I was told I would automatically become the reigning queen, but that was never possible because—"

"She would never leave TÅµr Medb." This would probably get Evalle torched, but she technically had two lives left if Cathbad was right about the gryphons having three. "Would you vow to uphold peace between the Medb and Beladors forever if you were queen?"

"Of course. That's what I told you I've wanted ever since—" Kizira cut off her words.

"Then make that vow to me and I'll help you."

"How?"

"Change how you compel me once we get inside Treoir so that I can talk to Tzader and Quinn. We'll *stage* the takeover of Treoir and Brina's death so you can call in Flaevynn."

Where Kizira had looked like a woman facing her death moments ago, she now was energized. "That would work, but it would take everyone's cooperation."

"Cathbad would probably follow Flaevynn out of here," Evalle reminded her.

"After the way he just compelled me, I would not spit on him if he were on fire."

No family baggage left there. "I want something else. I want to talk to Conlan. He may have information that could help us."

"How am I supposed to get him out of the dungeon?"

"Tell Flaevynn you suspect he was sent in as a spy for the Beladors and you want to show them they can't fool her. Tell her we can use him to confuse the Beladors, since he's your puppet. They'll take him to Brina since they're on the island, and when they do he can tell you where she is in the castle."

Kizira cocked her head in thought. "That might actually appeal to her ego."

Evalle just hoped she wasn't setting things in motion that she would regret later, but she trusted Tzader to keep Brina safe. Tzader would not want Conlan left behind in this place. That reminded her of two more people she had to save. The list just kept growing. "Tristan won't agree to leave his two Rías friends who were captured with him and his sister."

"You expect me to get *them* out of here, too? Flaevynn won't go for that. She'll be suspicious the minute I bring it up."

"Rías are enough like Alterants that someone would have to be close to them when they shift to see that their eyes aren't green. Convince Flaevynn that they'll be a sacrificial diversion." Evalle snapped her fingers. "No! Have *Tristan* go to her and demand that they stay here. He can tell her the deal wasn't to use them in this attack and they'll never survive. If she thinks they're of any use right now, she'll have to use them."

Kizira arched an eyebrow. "I like the way you think, but we're leaving here with or without them."

"Understood." Evalle would save as many as she could.

"I'll send you to your room with Lanna," Kizira said. "If I don't see you again, it means I ended up in the dungeon, too."

That would screw up the plans. "Tell Tristan and his sister what's going on, too."

"Done." Kizira waved her hand.

Evalle didn't even stumble this time when she landed in her Medb bedroom. "Lanna?"

The girl appeared next to the bathroom door, then ran to Evalle. "Where have you been?"

Evalle had never been much for touching in the past, but Storm had changed that. She opened her arms to Lanna, hugging the girl and actually enjoying the moment. "I've been busy trying to get us out of here."

Lanna stepped back, eyes brimming with excitement. "We're leaving?"

"Very soon. You're going to cloak yourself and ride on my back."

"I am confused."

"Oh, I forgot to tell you that—" Evalle paused, not sure if the compulsion spell meant she could or couldn't tell Lanna. "Look, I've been compelled not to share some things, so you're going to have to trust me and, for once, do exactly what I say."

"I will not make mistake. I will do everything you say."

The poor girl was terrified, and with good reason. Evalle tried to help her understand. "You know I can change into other forms, so just be prepared for something that surprises you, okay?"

Lanna nodded.

She was bright and resourceful. Evalle had no doubt the girl would do her part and follow Evalle's lead. She explained as much as she could without going against her compulsion spell, telling Lanna what she had to do when they landed on the island.

No mentioning Treoir by name, but Lanna was quick. She asked two questions, and after that, she didn't ask any more when Evalle shook her head.

Energy whistled through the room, then Kizira appeared with a pitiful-looking guy who sagged next to her.

Evalle gently pushed Lanna aside and stepped over to Kizira. "How'd it go?"

"Flaevynn is addressing her witches and warlocks about the attack, so I found Cathbad instead and told him he owed me. I reminded him he should know better than Flaevynn just how capable I am of sidestepping their plans, and that if he wanted to see me on those steps calling them in, he had to do something for me."

"Nice."

"I've got to get with Tristan next." Kizira wrinkled her nose at Conlan. "Also, even with Flaevynn busy, it may not be safe to talk here, where she can drop in."

Lanna spoke up. "I can shield their words, but you must compel Evalle to allow a teenage girl to listen."

Kizira appeared impressed and gave a shrug. "Fine. Be ready when I come back." She compelled Evalle, but Evalle held up her hand to stall Kizira's exit.

Evalle stepped around Conlan, who stood hunched over as if he'd been in that position for a while. He smelled worse than week-old restaurant garbage. Dried blood covered more of him than not, and his back had been split open over and over—it looked like it had been beaten with a cat-o'-nine-tails. One arm hung at the wrong angle.

Pointing at him, Evalle said, "How about healing his wounds and cleaning him up?"

Sighing as if she'd been asked to do the laundry, Kizira swept a hand past Conlan.

The stink dissipated, replaced by a fresh-scrubbed smell. He wore a clean gray sweatshirt and new jeans. When he finally stood upright and lifted his head, he no longer had a thick beard. He was attractive, and edgy as an animal waiting to see if he had to maul something to get away.

But nothing would remove the haunted look deep in his eyes. His voice was rough and dry. "All this time I thought nothing could sway you from your Belador oath."

Evalle flinched as if struck, but Conlan didn't know what was going on, and last she'd heard, he was still considered a traitor.

Kizira said to Evalle, "Get your mini-me to do anything else you need," and vanished.

Lanna stepped up. "You must stay in one spot. I am not as good as Storm."

Just hearing his name poked at the ache in Evalle's chest. She told Conlan, "Even though I was told you're suspected of being a traitor, I've learned more and am willing to hear what you have to say. You should want to hear what I have to say, since I got you out of that dungeon."

His eyebrows dropped over repentant gray eyes. "Okay."

"Let's sit down and make this easy for Lanna. She's Quinn's cousin."

Conlan's sharp gaze went to Lanna. "Why would he let—"

"Not yet, Conlan," Evalle said, moving to the sofa.

Once they were seated, Lanna said, "I cannot talk to you while I do this or I may make mistake and cause thunderstorm."

Guess mini-me had a few bugs to work out in her spell casting.

Evalle waited until Lanna nodded at her, then Evalle turned to Conlan and told him how she—and Lanna— came to be at TÅµr Medb. Then she laid out what she knew about the impending attack on Treoir. "So, right now, I'm the one suspicious of *you*, since you escaped VIPER headquarters and you came to the Medb voluntarily, right?"

"I did."

When Evalle pulled back, Conlan lifted a hand. "Let me explain. Quinn did see the vision of me offering to join the Medb in the part of my mind that projects the future, but that isn't always reliable, because the future can be changed."

"But it *didn't* change."

"That was intentional."

Evalle didn't want to believe it of Quinn, but someone had freed Conlan from VIPER lockdown, and Quinn had refused to accept that Conlan was a traitor. But Kizira didn't believe Quinn had committed that crime.

Evalle didn't either. "Who helped you escape?"

Conlan said nothing for several seconds. He finally drew a long breath and, on the exhale, said, "Guess it won't matter if we don't save Treoir. Tzader got me out."

Tzader? Stunned didn't quite cover what she was feeling. Try nauseous, disappointed and hurt. But should she believe this about Tzader any more than about Quinn? "Why?"

"He knew I'd never get out until someone delivered the traitor to Macha, but we'd had no breaks on finding the traitor for several years. He told me he'd free me if I was willing to take on a secret duty, because if I didn't he thought I'd be safer staying in VIPER lockdown. He wanted me to use what we learned from my vision to infiltrate the Medb."

Why hadn't Tzader told her? "Did Quinn know?"

"No one knew but the two of us. Tzader wouldn't put anyone else at risk, especially you or Quinn."

Poor Tzader had shouldered this on his own with no support from her and Quinn. "Have you found out who the traitor is?"

"No, but I do know he has a scar of two *X*s entwined with a snake. It's high on his right forearm. I heard Flaevynn marked him so there would be no doubt who her people should trust." Conlan scratched his short hair. "Speaking of trust, why should I trust you and Kizira?"

"Because we have a plan to save Treoir, and if it doesn't happen, the Medb will hold the power to turn the world into their playground. Are you in or not?"

FORTY-TWO

Not looking forward to what he had to tell Quinn, Tzader waited as Quinn separated from the last division of warriors heading out to fill in spots along the coast of Treoir.

"Any word on Evalle or Lanna?" Quinn's shoulders dipped with the weight of worry.

"Sort of." Tzader explained about finding the notes in Storm's house, then showed Evalle's to Quinn. "Evalle must have gotten a chance to return to Atlanta for some reason and used that to get a message to us. I have no idea what Storm meant about a witch doctor, but I think Evalle is telling us a bunch of Alterants are coming here, but they've changed—or something is different—"

"Like they can't die," Quinn finished on a grim note.

"Yep. Sounds like they *did* become immortal as the Medb promised." Another strike against Evalle. Tzader pushed his emotions aside and focused on defenses. "Macha will turn *all* her power toward maintaining the ten-mile-wide ward around the castle to stop the Alterants, but if enough of them attack it with immortal power, she might not be able to hold them."

"What's our plan?"

"Who do you think will be controlling the Alterants?"

Quinn didn't hesitate. "Kizira."

"Can you mind lock and interfere with her control?"

Quinn rubbed his forehead. "If all of them are tied to her, it might be like trying to break through one Belador mind when a group is linked. That's damn hard to interrupt, but I'll try."

If anyone could do that, Quinn could. Tzader hadn't shared his secret weapon yet. The Belador healers wanted twenty more hours without a reported infection before clearing anyone to use telepathy, and Macha had agreed. Tzader could use telepathy with only one person who believed himself immune to the infection. Quinn. "The note indicates this group will have telepathic communication. I'm guessing that's their Belador blood allowing that, which means *we* should be able to contact the Alterants."

"You think to intercept their thoughts?"

"No, I plan to cause major interference in their entire internal systems, from thought to navigation to coordination. Are you sure you're immune to the infection?"

"Ah, I see. Yes, I'm immune. How are we going to infect them?"

This was the part that turned Tzader's stomach. "We brought a healer and one of our warriors from quarantine who is still infected."

"Might not work unless he's a powerful telepath."

"That's why we have Trey McCree here. The healers say the stronger the telepath, the faster the infection has traveled. Trey's willing to be infected, then to reach out . . . to Evalle."

Quinn's face sagged with disappointment.

Tzader swallowed past the knot in his throat. "Read the last line she wrote for us. Evalle was telling us not to allow her to reach Brina. But this is my decision. If we can take her alive, that's my goal. If not, I'll make that call. I just need you to deal with Kizira."

FORTY-THREE

Gryphons in all shades of green, blue, black, red and purple gathered in a hall two hundred feet in diameter inside TÅµr Medb.

Evalle and four other gryphons had golden heads.

Bernie was one of them.

Evalle smiled over that irony, then lost her amusement as she paid attention. She had to keep Conlan hidden inside her wings until it was time to call Lanna over. Kizira had shielded the girl from view nearby, but Lanna would have to cloak herself to leave that shield. Evalle was holding off as long as she could so Lanna would have maximum time to stay in Kizira's shield.

Two thousand warlocks and witches stood on the marble floor of the hall. Flaevynn and Cathbad would teleport their bloodthirsty Medb army only ten minutes after gryphon departure.

Flaevynn and Cathbad stood high above them on a dais. Flaevynn raised her hand, and rumbling murmurs quieted. "This is the day we take back the island that has been in the hands of the enemy for too long. After today, the Medb will rule Treoir and the mortal world. Every one of you who returns from this victory will be given a section of the world to call your own."

Deafening cheers roared.

"Make me proud."

Floating ten feet above the marble, Kizira approached the gryphons at eye level and well below the queen of TÅµr Medb. Kizira spoke to them as a unit. "You all know your roles. I will be in telepathic communication once we are airborne and the entire time we're in Treoir. You are compelled to follow my every command."

Boomer and two other golden heads snarled, ready to go.

Evalle thought about rolling her eyes. She spoke to Conlan telepathically. *I'm lifting the tip of my wing at Lanna, then she'll come over to cloak you so you can both get on my back.*

A minute later, she felt the weight of Lanna and Conlan. Lanna tugged on Evalle's feathers. *Make her stop that, Conlan.*

I've got her.

Evalle stretched her neck to see if everyone was in place.

As agreed, Kizira stepped onto Tristan's back, placing her feet between his two Rías friends who sat there in human form, shivering. Tristan said he'd told them to appear afraid, but that looked like real terror on their faces. Tristan had been outfitted with a gold-and-red harness with a leash that Kizira lifted as she stood on his back. She could teleport the entire group, but the gryphons needed a chance to fly as a unit before entering enemy airspace.

Kizira gave the signal to go airborne.

A wall vanished on one side of TÅµr Medb, revealing an empty black sky.

Evalle flapped her wings and pushed off, sailing through the opening behind Tristan and Kizira. She'd never even been in an airplane and couldn't believe the exhilaration of flying on her own. She wanted to share this with Storm.

Once the gryphons were all airborne, Kizira's voice came into Evalle's mind just as it would in the minds of the other nine. *Be ready to teleport. The minute we come out, you'll be flying low over the Irish Sea. We'll enter an opening between two mountains. Once there, you know what to do.*

Accustomed now to the swirling shift, Evalle relaxed as soon as the teleporting took over. She glided during the change. It lasted longer than usual, which might be due to Kizira having to teleport so many at one time.

Evalle knew the minute she entered the airspace above the Irish Sea.

Winds buffeted her sideways. She yelled at Conlan to hold on and felt someone grip her neck. Flapping hard, she fought to right herself. Boomer cartwheeled past her, and she was glad to see she wasn't the only one struggling.

Maybe Flaevynn should have built in more flight training than the short time they had on the way here.

Bucking waves pounded twenty feet below her.

Salt air stung her eyes, but . . . she was flying in day-light without sunglasses. She'd never seen the world during the day. Her heart leaped at the joy.

Why couldn't she share this moment with Storm?

No, she was glad he was safe in Atlanta. Tzader would never bring an outsider to Treoir purposely, especially now.

A mountain range with an obvious break between two of the peaks came into view.

Kizira stood with her soft-booted feet slightly apart, holding the leash in one hand and directing with the other. She called to the gryphons, *Enter through there, then divide up and start the attack.*

As soon as Evalle sailed through the dip in the mountains, the air calmed to Treoir's normally peaceful state. She looked around, hoping to see the traitor, but with this spot in the security breached he was probably heading to the castle to be there when Kizira arrived.

Boomer led a group of gryphons to start burning a band of ground between the sea and the castle, separating the defenses. Another bunch broke off, heading toward strategic points where warlocks and witches would be teleported in.

Evalle warned Conlan, *Get ready to bank left.*

The hold on her neck tightened just before she leaned left and soared over mountains, then valleys, wondering if a jet fighter pilot felt this way. As soon as she located a spot inside the area that had been designated as the burn perimeter, Evalle landed a mile from the castle in the only opening she could find amid the trees.

Conlan and Lanna jumped off. He yelled, "I'll get Lanna to the castle and keep her safe."

Lanna added, "And I will sneak him inside."

Evalle answered Conlan silently. *Thank you. Tell Lanna I'm really proud of her and to please be careful. And tell Quinn I'm sorry she ended up at TÅur Medb.*

Will do.

With a quick couple of flaps, Evalle lifted off. She hadn't gone far when she heard Trey come into her mind. *Evalle, where are you?*

He sounded tired. Could she tell him, or would the compulsion spell kick in? *I don't think I can tell you, but if you look up, you'll see me. I'm aqua with a golden head.*

What . . . are you a dragon . . .

A gryphon.

She laughed, then her eyes blurred and vertigo sent her spinning. Her stomach turned into a washing machine with rusted gears. She lost altitude, waffling as she headed straight down.

Her wings moved but not in unison. She started flipping over and over. Trees. Sky. Mountains. Sky. A blur of green and brown. She curled into herself and prepared to crash.

Kizira yelled, *Boomer needs help. He's on the ground and they're killing him.*

FORTY-FOUR

Quinn listened to the radio reports coming through to the mic in his ear. He couldn't believe what he was hearing about dragons, then Trey's voice came into Quinn's mind, overriding everything. *I reached Evalle and . . . passed on the infection. I powered up the telepathy. She's a . . . gryphon. Golden head. Flying overhead, but sick now. Falling.*

I'll pass that on. Go to the healer before you lose consciousness.

When Trey withdrew, Quinn picked up a radio call that a female witch was riding a gryphon. Kizira?

He put the radio away and closed his mind to everything except calling out, *Kizira, where are you?*

Quinn? You shouldn't be here. Evalle was supposed to warn you. Where are you?

Evalle hadn't warned him away, but then Evalle would know that Quinn and Tzader would never avoid a battle necessary to protect their warrior queen and Treoir.

He mustered a weak voice and replied, *I need you.*

Sad to use that ploy to call her to him, he waited as she followed the connection to where he sat on a log in a highly visible spot.

In the next moment, a giant gray-blue creature landed and Kizira jumped off its back. Now that he could see it better, Quinn recognized the lionesque body and eagle-shaped head.

A gryphon.

But not a golden head like the one Trey had mentioned.

Kizira said something to the gryphon, then the creature dipped its head and took to the air again. She hurried over, but stopped fifteen feet from Quinn, suspicion in her frown. "You don't look hurt. What's wrong?"

"I'm sorry." He pushed to enter her mind and got shoved back.

"What . . . what are you doing?"

Powering up, he surged again, blasting his way past her defenses.

She grabbed her head. "Stop it, Quinn. I'm not here to hurt you."

He was relentless, reaching deeper, banging into the other voices booming in her mind, probably the gryphons'. She started screaming in her head.

At that moment a massive golden-headed gryphon barreled down at him from the sky.

Quinn twisted around and threw his hands up, forcing a kinetic blast at the gryphon.

The beast stuttered in flight as if buffeted by the wind, then rolled away and kept coming. Quinn watched in shock as the gryphon landed in a skid, jaws open, roaring.

Using his kinetics had weakened Quinn's hold on Kizira.

The gryphon's forward momentum threw the beast

at Quinn, who couldn't release Kizira in order to use his mind lock on the gryphon.

She vanished and reappeared in front of Quinn as a massive claw swiped at him.

It ripped her middle open.

Quinn released her mind, shouting as he dove into the gryphon's mind, then funneled his kinetics inside to explode the beast's head.

The headless beast flopped backward, its wings quivering.

A whimpering sounded wrenched Quinn's eyes to Kizira. "No, no!" He dropped and lifted her into his arms. The claw had gouged a wide canal from beneath her breasts to above her hips. He begged, "Heal yourself, Kizira."

Blood ran from her lips. "I . . . can't. Flaevynn took that . . . away right before she sent me here. I need . . . to tell you . . ."

Quinn cried, tears streaming down his face. "Please don't die." He'd never said the words that fisted his heart, but they poured out now with panic that he was losing her. "I love you."

"I love you, too, Quinn. I tried . . . for peace."

He bawled, pleading with every god in the universe to save her.

She moved her hand to his wrist. "The bracelet I made of your hair . . . don't lose it."

"I want you, not a bloody bracelet. I'm so sorry. I should have believed . . ."

"Quinn, please listen." She jerked and coughed.

"Anything, my love." He covered the gaping hole, trying to hold on to her life force.

When her lips moved again, he leaned his ear to her face. "Don't let . . . the Medb get her."

"What do you mean?" *Evalle?*

Her eyes started to roll back.

He clutched her to his chest, pleading, "Please don't leave me."

She clenched with pain and said, "Promise me . . ."

"Anything." He brushed his lips over hers, savoring the feel.

"Find Phoedra. Keep her safe."

"Who's Phoedra?"

"Our daughter." She gasped and the light went out of her.

Quinn's howl of pain shook the trees and ground.

FORTY-FIVE

Still tucked into a falling ball, Evalle hit trees. Limbs snapped. Sharp edges stabbed and scraped her body. She bounced down a hillside, finally landing at the bottom, where she sprawled her wings open.

Every bone felt broken or cracked.

Vertigo still swamped her. Bile raced up her throat. This had to be the infection.

Trey had intentionally infected her.

Didn't Tzader understand her message? Evalle had really thought that between Tzader and Quinn, they'd realize all they had to do was have Quinn take control of Kizira's mind.

Pain throbbed, cutting off everything but her desire to stop the hurt. She reached inside herself and drew upon her beast. Healing energy flooded through her. Bones shifted, mending. Nerves around raw places and deep wounds stopped screaming. Her vision cleared.

She sucked in one deep breath after another, feeling amazingly better in just seconds.

With no infection.

With a grunt, she folded her wings and rolled over, pushing to rise on her hind legs. Stretching, she tested her wings. *Wow, that was fast.*

But where was the buzz of energy? That connection to Kizira? Evalle called to her. *Kizira? Are you okay?*

No answer.

She didn't want to risk calling any other gryphon in case they'd been infected. Trey was so powerful that he could push into any mind receptive to telepathy.

Evalle stopped, hit by a bad feeling. What if something had happened to Kizira? She didn't want to consider that, but if Kizira wasn't answering, she was no longer in control of the gryphons.

Leading the group would fall to the next most powerful gryphon.

Boomer had died twice, the second time only moments ago when Kizira had called out that he was down and being attacked.

A niggle of suspicion climbed Evalle's neck. Would Boomer intentionally go through his third death to reach his highest level of power?

Of course he would.

Where was he?

With a push, Evalle took to the air, flying high enough that she couldn't be attacked from the ground. Below her, a string of Gryphons spaced out like quarter marks on a clock were burning the outer circle as instructed. There had to be five thousand Beladors defending the island, but with the other nine gryphons backed up by two thousand warlocks and witches, the Medb would gain the upper hand.

Flying faster, Evalle searched closer to the castle.

She found the gryphon she searched for. Hard to miss Boomer's size. He fought off Beladors attacking him, but he was staggering. She watched as he fell.

While facing an enemy that would certainly kill at least one warrior, Beladors wouldn't link and risk ending all lives bound together by that link. Even if Boomer was infected, he should be able to fight off that small group . . .

Unless he was trying to die a third time on purpose. But Kizira wouldn't allow that *if* he was still under her control.

He knew the Medb goal was to bring Flaevynn to the river. With Boomer no longer under anyone's control, he'd go for that river himself.

That's why he was willing to use up his third death and revival.

Everything was falling apart.

Kizira had sworn she'd compel Tristan to find a place to hide Petrina and stay there with his sister until Evalle called to him. She hoped he hadn't figured out that he was no longer under Kizira's orders and tried to leave on his own.

Banking hard to her right, Evalle headed for the castle. Had Lanna and Conlan made it there?

Two golden-headed gryphons landed in the open field in front of the castle, looking like strange airplanes touching down in an area as large as Hartsfield-Jackson airport back in Atlanta.

An army of Beladors surged to block them from getting near the castle.

Evalle swooped low, heading for the castle doors that

were behind that line of warriors but barred by fifty more Beladors.

Tzader stood at the front.

She hated to do this, but she raised her front paws and sent a series of short kinetic blasts, swatting warriors aside like bowling pins. Even Tzader. They might be banged up and knocked out for a bit due to getting hit with kinetics like they'd never felt before, but none would die.

Tzader, however, would never forgive her for taking him out when he was standing between the enemy and Brina. She would lose a friend, but she'd save the Beladors.

Pulling up at the last minute, Evalle's momentum sent her plowing into the tall wooden doors that burst into the castle. Black iron hinges ripped from the walls. Chunks of wood flew like shrapnel.

The pressure of her explosive entrance and flying debris knocked out the guards inside the massive three-story hall.

From the top of the stairs, Brina raced down, a sword sizzling with power in hand.

Evalle called to her. *Go back! Hide!*

At the bottom landing, Brina paused. *Evalle?*

Yes. Get out of here.

Taking a look around at bodies sprawled everywhere, Brina looked up in shock. *Is that aqua thing you?*

Yes. I'm a gryphon. Where's Macha?

She's using all her power to hold a ward against . . . you and the others.

How had Evalle gotten past? What kind of ward? *Nothing even slowed me down.*

We heard you were immortal. But you aren't. That's why you didn't die crossing the threshold.

The stupid beast championship rumors.

Why, Evalle? Brina asked in a heartbroken voice. *These are your people.*

I didn't kill them. They're just knocked out. Evalle didn't have time to explain further. Boomer would be coming, and she had only one hope of stopping him. First she had to force Brina to help her. Evalle said, *I'm not here to kill you, Brina, but to protect you. I need your help. I've trusted you, now you trust me. A gryphon is coming that no warrior in human form can stop.*

Brina hesitated only a minute, then she raised her sword, every bit the Belador warrior queen. *What do you need?*

You have to kill me.

Are you crazy?

I don't have time to explain. Just do it and trust me.

I can't!

You must. We have no time! Do it. Trust me.

Tears streaming, Brina gripped the sword and drove it into Evalle's chest.

Evalle gritted her teeth against the pain and leaned down as Brina drove the sword into her heart once, twice, three times. *Okay, enough. That should do it.* Evalle folded a wing so that she'd keel over to the side and not crush Brina.

Brina stumbled back, a tear streaming down her

cheek, and stared at the blood-drenched sword she held. "Evalle?"

Evalle hissed at the pain, breathing hard. She had to ease Brina's horror. *I'll live. Give me a minute.* The world receded as Evalle's life bled out until her thoughts shrank into a black void with only a pinpoint of light pulsing.

What if she didn't regenerate?

Then the light brightened, and with it came the incredible pain of regenerating. In her mind, Evalle cried out, but in the TÅµr Medb battles she'd heard the other gryphons' high-pitched wailing, so she knew she was making an ungodly sound about now.

Bolts of energy streaked through her chest, shocking her heart back to pumping and healing the damaged tissue.

Rolling to her side once more, she leveraged herself up and shook her head, drunk from healing again in so short a time.

An earth-shaking roar approached from a distance.

Boomer.

Evalle called upon her beast powers to flood her body, and the explosion of energy lifted her off the ground. She settled on her hindquarters. If she felt this good after a second death, what would Boomer be experiencing after three?

Brina stood shell-shocked as Evalle rose to her full height.

Conlan's voice entered Evalle's mind. *We're inside and Lanna has us cloaked, or Brina will probably kill me.*

Evalle took a look over her shoulder to check on

Boomer, who was not in view yet, then turned back to Brina. Evalle had to give her yet another shock. *Lanna and Conlan are inside the castle, too.*

When Brina raised her sword out of instinct, Evalle quickly added, *Conlan is not the traitor. Tzader will tell you this when he talks to you, so don't hurt Conlan. He's with Lanna. Tell them to show themselves, then please get out of here so I can fight without worrying about you. That incoming gryphon is heading for the immortality river beneath the castle.*

Brina lifted her voice. "Conlan O'Meary, show yourself."

A Belador could not refuse that order. Lanna and Conlan came into view, with Conlan standing in front of Lanna, shielding her.

Conlan said to Brina, "Give me a sword, tell the others not to kill me, and I'll join the battle!"

With one look at Evalle then back at Conlan, Brina nodded, and a Belador sword appeared in front of Conlan.

Evalle told Conlan and Brina, *Move these knocked-out warriors out of here or they might burn to death with two gryphons battling.*

Brina and Conlan used their kinetics, stacking the ten warriors and moving them up the stairs, where Horace Keefer came hurrying down with a sword in hand.

Evalle lost all patience and yelled telepathically, *Get everyone out of here now! Conlan, you go out and protect the warriors I had to knock out. Do not engage any gry-*

phon. Brina, will you please do something with Lanna and Horace?

Conlan grabbed the sword and dashed out the door.

Brina shot her a glare, but the Belador warrior queen understood that staying would jeopardize Evalle's chance to survive, as well as her own. And Brina was the sole living Treoir descendant. She had to remain alive to protect the Belador power base.

The sound of flapping wings approached as Brina herded Horace and Lanna out of the room.

Evalle stepped around to face Boomer.

He slid into the room, his green eyes as bright as two electric balls. His jaws opened and he spewed a torrent of fire at Evalle, who blocked with a kinetic blast that sent flames licking the walls. She pushed forward on her hind legs, forcing the surge of fire back at Boomer, who realized he'd torch himself if he didn't close his mouth.

When his jaws snapped shut, Evalle dropped her protective shield and lunged at Boomer.

Her jaws opened wide to clamp his throat.

He swung a paw at her before she reached him, sinking his claws into her throat.

They went down in a snarling twist of gouging beaks, wings beating and claws ripping open bloody gashes.

FORTY-SIX

Lanna would not leave Evalle. She turned to go back and help.

Someone grabbed her shirt, yanking back. "No, you don't."

She twisted to face Brina. "You do not understand."

For a pretty woman, Brina could make a fierce face. "You're not understandin'. Much as I'm wantin' to fight beside Evalle, we all have duties. Mine is to protect the Belador power. Yours is to do as I say, and Horace's is to protect our backs."

Digging in her heels when Brina started pulling on her again, Lanna said, "Boomer is more powerful than Evalle. He will kill her."

"Take it from me. She'll come back."

"No. Only three times."

Brina paused from dragging Lanna. "Three times? Explain yourself."

Since Lanna had not been compelled, she spilled everything about the gryphons.

Brina whispered, "That's why they're not really immortal?"

"Yes." Lanna nodded, in a hurry to get Brina to understand. "Boomer has died twice. He gets stronger each time."

"Evalle said he was tryin' to reach our river of immortality."

Lanna felt the blood leave her face. "That means he has died three times. Evalle cannot stop him."

"She just died a second time. I killed her."

Yanking away, Lanna shouted, "You killed her. Do you not know what she has gone through for her Beladors?"

Brina scowled at her. "Do not push me right now. Evalle wanted me to do it so she would be stronger."

Horace had been watching their backs with his sword raised, though Lanna thought the old man would fall over in a strong breeze. He swung around, ordering, "Get moving if you don't want Evalle's effort to be wasted."

Outnumbered, Lanna continued toward a room that reminded her of an old-fashioned solar, with unusual plants in handcrafted pots and unique furniture carved of strange wood and covered in plush cushions.

A solar except that the room was entirely stone with no windows. A safe room.

Lanna plopped down on a sofa, squeezing the cushion on each side of her legs as stress relief until she heard Brina making strangling noises. Jerking her head up, Lanna saw the old guy standing behind Brina, tossing sparkling dust on Brina.

Rotten lime smell stung Lanna's nose.

Noirre majik. She knew it.

Thin green and purple threads began to wind around Brina. She struggled and tried to shout, but the threads wrapped her mouth. Why did she not call guards telepathically?

Lanna leaped up.

He paused in chanting and said, "You knew a troll killed my wife and child while I fought with the Beladors. Macha knew, too. But she wouldn't bring them back. Now she'll know what it is to lose what she can't replace."

Lanna raced over and threw all her weight at Horace.

He shoved up a hand.

A pair of double *X* scars marked his forearm.

The traitor.

Lanna hit an invisible wall. Kinetics. A force tossed her against Brina. Dust hit Lanna in the face. Threads started wrapping her up against Brina's body. Lanna fought against the binding, reaching a hand until she found Brina's and gripped it.

She told Brina, "Stay calm. I will teleport."

Brina whispered, "No. I will . . . hologram."

Whatever Brina meant was not working.

Lanna's air squeezed from her chest. They would both die. She held her breath, hoping she didn't send them into a wall.

Could she even do this with Horace placing a Noirre spell on them? She closed her eyes, whispered a few words and teleported.

FORTY-SEVEN

Fangs chewed on her shoulder. Evalle slashed her claws at Boomer, who showed no sign of weakening.

Unlike her.

But she couldn't split her focus from fighting Boomer to call on her beast form to heal her wounds, or he'd have the opening he needed to rip her head off.

Drawing her energy into her wings, she flapped, lifting them off the floor with Boomer clutched to her chest and ripping chunks out of her shoulder.

She flew toward a wall, slamming his head. His gold head bounced and shoved his jaws deeper into her shoulder.

She winced.

Wings still flapping, she swung around and flew at another wall, ramming his head again. Stone broke and chunks fell to the floor. Her shoulder was taking just as much of a beating.

Then his jaws released her shoulder and his head wobbled.

This was her only chance to get him in a vulnerable position. Get him outside where she could fly to Beladors who would finish him off.

She flapped around, wobbling as she lost energy.

Her wings couldn't hold both of them any longer.

They hit the castle floor with a loud *bang*, but at least Boomer was beneath her.

She struggled to lift her head and chest. The space where the castle doors had stood was only a few feet away, but she'd have to heal first, and Boomer was rousing.

Someone raced toward them from outside, yelling, "*Brinnnaaaa!*"

Evalle shouted telepathically, *I'm Evalle. Cut off the head on the floor.*

Lightning exploded around the entrance when the warrior broke the threshold. The warrior screamed in agony.

Boomer's eyes glowed with power.

A sword blade slashed down across Boomer's neck, killing the power in his eyes.

Evalle shuddered with relief and took a breath, ready to heal when her vision cleared.

Tzader collapsed on the ground next to Boomer, gasping. Dying. Tzader was immortal, and the ward on this castle killed any immortals who were not Brina or Macha.

Evalle cried into his mind, *Tzader, nooo!*

He said, *Protect . . . Brina.*

That's your job. Evalle opened the link between them, but Tzader was too weak to connect. Or refused to open his link. Gryphons were more powerful. She just kept telling herself that and drove harder to open the link between them.

Tzader's thin voice said, *Don't. You'll die with me. Brina. Tell her . . . I love her.*

Refusing to quit, Evalle pushed more power into the link and the connection formed.

She could immediately feel her life essence flooding out, fast and hard. Not like the other two times. Maybe she was too damaged to regenerate, especially connected to another dying body.

She called on her beast and felt nothing, not even the link to Tzader that had gone cold and quiet. *No! Don't die, Z!*

The void swallowed her. No pinpoint of light.

She'd die with a clear conscience that she'd upheld her Belador oath to the end.

It's not your time, a female voice whispered in her mind.

Not you again. Evalle hoped this voice didn't follow her into the afterlife.

A feminine chuckle bubbled across her senses. Tired, hurt, disappointed and alone, Evalle snapped, *What do you want from me?*

Maybe I want to give you something.

So now you're my Secret Santa? Where were you for the past twenty-three years?

Evalle sensed sadness in the silence and felt bad for berating someone who had annoyed her and given her unwanted advice but had never caused her harm.

The voice said, *I'm sorry you never had birthdays or celebrated holidays, but you can have that with Storm.*

How do you know Storm?

Through you. He is your other half.

Great. Now a voice was making her depressed, as if dying with Tzader wasn't enough. Feeling guilty, Evalle said, *Didn't mean to take my bad mood out on you. Side effect of dying, I guess.*

The chuckle was back. *You must return to the living.*

I don't know that I have to, but I'd like to go back.

No, you must, because Storm needs you. Sending you back is my gift to you.

Storm needed her? Evalle's heart thumped with worry. But how could her heart thump if she was dead? A tiny light beamed in her mind's eye and started to glow brighter.

Pain—feeling—crawled through her body, stinging and burning as energy surged into her legs, wings and arms. Her heartbeat picked up speed, stomping against her chest. Power burst from her core, raging across her senses.

She opened her eyes and stared at twenty sword points.

Panicked, she yelled at every Belador present, *I'm Evalle. Don't touch me or you'll kill Tzader! We're linked!*

All eyes shifted to Tzader, who didn't move. Not even a breath. *Come on, Z.* Nothing. She refused to let him go.

She closed her eyes, searching for the link. She found it. Cold. Quiet. Careful with her energy, she forced a slow stream of healing power into the link, waiting for a sign.

He twitched.

She opened her eyes and kept sending him the constant flow of life energy.

He groaned. No sweeter sound had she ever heard. He drew a breath. Another.

Tears pooled in her eyes when he slid his palms forward and pushed up, shaking his head.

He twisted, his gaze searching hers. *Evalle?*

Yes. The tears fell, running free.

I heard you in my mind. How did you save me?

Long story that I'll tell you soon, but call off the guards first.

That's when Tzader looked up. He must have sent a telepathic message, because every sword pulled back and the guards stood down.

Evalle relaxed, tired of fighting. Tired of being a gryphon right this moment. Her body started changing before she realized the shift had come over her.

Tzader glanced down, did a double take, then ordered, "Everyone face away. Now."

Then he whipped off his T-shirt and handed it to her as she stood. She shrugged it on, thankful it was long enough to cover the important parts. Looking around, she asked, "Where's Brina? I can't believe she actually did as I asked and found somewhere safe to hide."

Tzader snapped alert. "Which way did she go?"

A warrior answered, "Down the back hallway."

He called for a sword. One of his men tossed him the weapon, and Tzader took off running. Evalle followed with a herd of boot heels pounding right behind her.

When Tzader skidded to a stop and turned into a room, Evalle smelled Noirre majik heavy in the air.

Horace stood with his back to the door, chanting and tossing dust at Lanna and Brina.

Tzader shoved his sword into Horace. The old guy screamed and dropped a bag that smelled of rotten limes.

Evalle raced over just as Lanna and Brina disappeared, leaving a holographic image of Brina.

Evalle reached toward it, then pulled back.

Tzader was next to her in an instant, his voice hollow when he whispered, "Where'd they go?"

"I don't know."

FORTY-EIGHT

With no idea what to do for Brina and Lanna, Evalle finally shook herself loose from the numb feeling of too many shocks at one time. Someone had to deal with the battle still raging on Treoir.

With Boomer can't-come-back dead and Evalle having regenerated three times, she'd become the most powerful gryphon.

She ordered the gryphons to stand down from any fight and fly to where they could circle the castle.

Seven answered her, which meant they had another dead gryphon besides Boomer.

Who had managed that? The only way one of the gryphons would not have gone through three cycles was if the head had been cut off.

Evalle told Tzader, "All the gryphons are under my control. I've called them in to circle the castle, and I need you to tell the Beladors to stop attacking. Once you do, I can turn the gryphons on the witches and warlocks."

Tzader looked at her with unfocused eyes, still paralyzed by terror at seeing Brina's lifeless hologram wrapped in a Noirre spell.

Evalle said as gently as she could, "Z, we need you."

The warrior in him shuddered back into place. He

nodded, his eyes fixed on a distant spot for a moment, then he said, "It's done. I've told our warriors the gryphons now belong to us and to fight beside them."

Evalle sent the gryphons orders to drive the Medb from the island, confident that the five thousand Beladors and seven gryphons outside would be successful.

Green power ripped across the room and Macha appeared, not looking as fresh as usual.

Holding the ward must have really zapped her.

Macha stared at the hologram with a sinking look of horror. "Where's Brina?"

Tzader told her what he'd found right before Brina and Lanna had disappeared. His voice came out gutshot. "I failed her, and I failed you."

Macha gave Tzader a thorough look. "How are you standing here inside this castle alive?"

He sighed and explained how he'd rushed in with no thought for his life, needing only to protect Brina.

Evalle could practically hear his heart shattering. Evalle said, "We'll find her, Z. Lanna was caught with her. She's Quinn's cousin and pretty powerful. Quinn may have family who can track Lanna. When I get back to Atlanta, I'll get Storm. He has other gifts and may be able to tell us more once we bring him here. If not for him, you wouldn't have gotten my note to know what was coming."

"He didn't give us the note," Tzader said.

"What do you mean? How'd you get it if he didn't?"

"I went looking for you." Tzader cut his eyes over at Macha to find her glaring at him. "You made me Maistir because you trust me to watch over all the Beladors and to know who I can trust and who I can't. I have never doubted Evalle and you shouldn't either, especially when she's the reason you still hold Treoir."

"We don't have Brina."

"That's not Evalle's fault, and she'll help us find her."

Evalle still wanted to know about the note. "What about Storm?"

Tzader said, "When I got to his house, no one was there. Your note was sitting on the nightstand."

"Was it a whole piece of paper or . . ."

"All of it. The part you wrote to Storm was still attached."

"Where was he?" She hadn't intended for that to come out panicked, but some emotions couldn't be controlled.

"I found a note he left you in the kitchen. The room smelled like licorice incense." Tzader pulled it out of his pocket and handed it to her. "You know what the note means?"

Evalle nodded, eyes blurring. Why had Storm gone after the witch doctor without waiting for her?

She wasn't sure she could restart her heart anymore today, but it was pounding in the danger zone.

Had the witch doctor tricked Storm?

FORTY-NINE

Cathbad stared in horror at the scrying wall, then turned on Flaevynn. "How could ya send our daughter out there with no way ta heal herself?"

Flaevynn's lips trembled. "She failed. They all failed."

"Ya whore. Ya killed your own child, and now ya will die."

Trembling, she turned to Cathbad, voice jumping. "Fix this. You . . . you know the curse. Make it . . . do something."

"Die, ya miserable waste of life."

Flaevynn railed at him. "This is all your fault!" She tried to strike him with her black fingernail, but she staggered back.

All at once, her body began warping and shriveling, then spinning until she turned into a human tornado of sparkling purple dust.

Cathbad stepped back, not too sure about this. He'd thought the old witch would just dry up and poof away like the others before her.

When the dust settled, Flaevynn was definitely gone, but another woman, a far more beautiful creature, stood in her place. Hair as black as sin fell around her shoulders, and eyes as green as a new leaf studied what should have been Flaevynn's body. She seemed as surprised as

Cathbad was to see her slender arms and fine shape in a purple gown fit for a queen.

Cathbad scratched his head. That had not happened in recorded history. "I do no understand."

The gorgeous female laughed, a full, throaty sound. "That's because the prophecy has been fulfilled. I have returned."

"Who are ya?"

"Maeve, the first and only true Medb queen."

"How can ya be here? The prophecy—"

She nodded, her eyes twinkling with mirth. "—said birth before death and death before birth. The Alterants were born, then died, then were reborn as gryphons."

Cathbad still battled to understand. "But the immortal queen . . . ?"

"That would be me."

"How?"

She sighed. "You don't have time for all of this, so I shall be quick. The female gryphon had to evolve by rising a third time, which she must have, because she fulfilled the prophecy and brought me back to life."

Cathbad processed everything at blinding speed. Now he understood what he had not seen coming. The curse had not been about gaining immortality for the reigning queen. It had been about reincarnating the original one.

But wrapping his head around that meant . . . "If 'tis so, then . . ." His body twisted and warped, going through the same gyrations. He yelled, but his voice sucked away with his life.

"I told you that you didn't have much time." Maeve

waved at him, laughing over the prophecy actually coming true. She had certainly hoped so when she and her greedy partner had come up with this plan.

When the druid's form stopped spinning, a breathtaking man with searing brown eyes gave her an admiring once-over. "Hello, Maeve."

"Good to see you again, Cathbad. It's been too long." She grinned at her own joke. "Can you believe that fool managed to figure it all out but never realized the whole point was for the two of us to be reincarnated?"

Returning her grin with a dazzling one, the original Cathbad the Druid said, "Now we'll show this world what a real queen and powerful druid can do."

FIFTY

Evalle couldn't take another heartbreak, or so she thought until she walked outside to find Quinn carrying Kizira's body toward the castle.

Behind him, gryphons were coming in to land across the open field. The warlocks and witches had been driven out of Treoir.

Evalle called to Tristan telepathically. *I'll meet with you before I leave, but I need you to keep the gryphons back where you are until I can come and talk to them.*

I'll do that, Tristan answered. *As long as Macha doesn't try to screw with us.*

Technically, the gryphons had to follow Evalle's orders regardless, but she understood Tristan's concerns. *Macha isn't going to bother you because she needs you right now.*

How do you see that?

Brina is missing, but her hologram is still inside the castle, which is affecting the Beladors. She'd finally gotten Tzader to walk away from Brina's hologram that hovered in the solar like a grand effigy. He had a sick, kicked-in-the-nuts look, but Tzader still commanded a force of Belador warriors whose powers were now in question.

Do the warriors have any powers? Tristan asked.

Some have limited use of their powers, but they can't link, and telepathy is spotty. Not having a Treoir descendant physically in the castle doesn't seem to be affecting our gryphon powers.

Tristan chuckled, but not in a nice way.

Evalle ignored it. *The gryphons will become a new security force—*

What?

Will you work with me for once, Tristan? I got you out of TÁur Medb, with your sister and your two Rías buddies. Alive, I might add.

After a grumbling noise, Tristan said, *Macha better feed us well.*

Evalle smiled. *She will. Just bunch up everyone and I'll come see you after I talk to her.*

Quinn reached Evalle. His legs moved as if he trudged through quicksand. Eyes swollen and red. His mouth sagged.

Evalle walked down the steps to meet him. "I'm sorry, Quinn. We had a plan that was going to save Brina and Treoir, plus get Kizira out of the Medb."

Tears trickled down his face. "She did a better job of protecting me than I did of protecting her."

There was nothing Evalle could say that would make anything he was feeling go away. She swallowed, and it hurt. She couldn't bring herself to tell him that Lanna was missing. Not yet.

Tzader stepped down beside her, silent and staring at Quinn before he finally said, "I'll convince Macha to let you take her body back to bury."

Quinn nodded his thanks. His Adam's apple moved hard against his throat.

Tzader angled his head at Evalle. "Macha wants to see you."

Walking over to Quinn, Evalle gave him a hug and held him a minute, fighting back tears that wouldn't help Kizira. She bent and kissed Kizira on the forehead. "Thank you for wanting peace and for loving Quinn."

She turned and climbed the steps, then waded through the destruction and a cluster of warriors to find Macha still standing in the solar, staring at Brina's hologram.

Macha didn't acknowledge Evalle's presence.

Evalle was in no mood to waste time. "The gryphons will remain to protect the island. There are two Rías, but they have control of their beast and will do whatever Tristan tells them."

Turning to her, the goddess said, "Why would we trust these gryphons?"

Evalle had used up her allotment of patience. "Because they have to follow the orders of their leader, the most powerful gryphon."

"Who is that?"

"Me."

"Very well, they can stay."

That wasn't enough for Evalle. Not after what every one of them had done to save Treoir. "And they are to be treated like the guardian protectors they are, not like outsiders. Every gryphon out there has Belador blood coursing through his or her veins and just fought next to our warriors to run the Medb witches and warlocks off of Treoir."

Macha lifted her chin with an astonished look, but when the goddess didn't threaten to turn Evalle into ashes, Evalle added in a nicer tone, "I'll explain their duties to them before I leave."

"Very well. And your duty is simple. You do nothing but hunt for Brina. That takes top priority."

"Actually, I'm going after the one person I know who can help me find her."

"Who?"

"Storm."

"I heard Tzader mention finding your note in Storm's house, on his nightstand. You've lain with him without permission." The goddess dropped that with plenty of accusation.

"That's *my* business."

"I will not approve of you mating with him."

"Again, *my* business, and this conversation is not helping to find Brina."

Macha studied Evalle for a moment. "Where is this Skinwalker?"

"To tell you the truth, I don't know everything yet, but I think he's hunting a witch doctor."

It took a lot to shock Macha, but that evidently did it. "A *witch doctor*? If he's tangled up with her, he's lost to everyone."

Evalle answered with force. "Not. To. Me. I'm going to find him."

"No, I forbid you to waste your time on that."

After all Evalle had risked, her next words were not that much of a gamble. "I'm not asking for your permission. Just letting you know that I won't be back until I find him."

"You dare to disobey me?"

"I dare to piss off the entire fucking universe if that's what it takes to get him back. Strike me down if you want, Macha, but know that if you do, you'll destroy the best chance you have of finding Brina *and* bringing her back alive. And while I'm hunting for him, you need to keep VIPER and Sen off my ass. Every delay for me is a delay for you."

Evalle turned and walked away.

After all Lyalle had asked, her next words were not that much of a gamble. "I'm not asking for your permission. Just letting you know that I won't be back until I find him."

"You dare to disobey me?"

"I dare to piss off the entire fucking universe if that's what it takes to get him back. Strike me down if you want, Vlacha, but know that if you do, you'll destroy the best chance you have of fulfilling Strijn and bringing her back alive. And while I'm hunting for him, you need to keep VIPER and Sco off my ass. Every delay for me is a delay for you."

Ivnlla turned and walked away.

Coming soon from Pocket Books

BOOK 5 OF THE BELADOR SERIES

DEMON STORM

With Treoir Island in shambles after a Medb attack that left the survival of the missing Belador warrior queen in question and Belador powers compromised, the Beladors have one hope for their queen's return and their own future: Evalle Kincaid, whose recent transformation has turned her into an even more formidable warrior. First Evalle has to locate Storm, the Skinwalker she's bonded with who she believes can find the Belador queen, but Storm stalks the witch doctor threatening Evalle's life. The hunter becomes the hunted, and Evalle must face her greatest nightmare to save Storm and the Beladors—or watch the future of mankind fall to deadly preternatural predators. . . .